Hunter stepped forward. "One night. No history. No interruptions. Just me and you."

"A date?" Her question was a whisper.

His hand reached up, gently grasping one of her curls. "What do you say, Jo?" His eyes met hers, blazing, electric, the pull almost physical. He released the curl, placing his big hands on either side of her head.

She blew out a shaky breath, unable to hide the effect he was having on her. His mouth was so close, his breath caressing her skin. His gaze explored her face, slow and intense. She tilted her head toward him, an unmistakable invitation. Her heart kicked into overdrive as he leaned forward. She closed her eyes, waiting, ready, willing, bursting.

His forehead rested against hers.

"I'm not going to kiss you until you say yes," he rasped.

Her eyes popped open. "Yes," she answered quickly, too quickly. Not that there was any point in denying what was happening. They both felt it; they both wanted it.

He smiled and stepped away from her. "I'll pick you up at seven o'clock."

A Cowboy's Wish

Sasha Summers & Amanda Renee

Previously published as *A Cowboy's Christmas Reunion*
and *The Lawman's Rebel Bride*

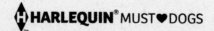

ISBN-13: 978-1-335-04184-5

A Cowboy's Wish

Copyright © 2019 by Harlequin Books S.A.

A Cowboy's Christmas Reunion
First published in 2015.
This edition published in 2019.
Copyright © 2015 by Sasha Best

The Lawman's Rebel Bride
First published in 2017. This edition published in 2019.
Copyright © 2017 by Amanda Renee

Recycling programs
for this product may
not exist in your area.

Printed in U.S.A.

www.Harlequin.com

CONTENTS

Sasha Summers grew up surrounded by books. Her passions are storytelling, romance and travel—passions she's used to write more than twenty romance novels and novellas. Now a bestselling and award-winning author, Sasha lives in the suburbs of Texas Hill Country with her amazing family and her beloved grumpy cat, Gerard, The Feline Overlord. She looks forward to hearing from fans and hopes you'll visit her online: on Facebook at Sasha Summers Author, on Twitter, @sashawrites, or email her at sashasummersauthor@gmail.com.

Books by Sasha Summers

Harlequin Western Romance

The Boones of Texas

A Cowboy's Christmas Reunion
Twins for the Rebel Cowboy
Courted by the Cowboy
A Cowboy to Call Daddy
A Son for the Cowboy
Cowboy Lullaby
Her Cowboy's Triplets

Harlequin Blaze

Seducing the Best Man
Christmas in His Bed

Visit the Author Profile page
at Harlequin.com for more titles.

A COWBOY'S CHRISTMAS REUNION

Sasha Summers

To the women who cheer me on and keep me
writing: Allison Collins, Joni Hahn, Jolene Navarro,
Storm Navarro and Marilyn Tucker.

Pamela Hopkins, thank you for being
the best agent a gal could wish for.
Your belief in me means the world.

To my generous and funny editor,
Johanna Raisanen. I'm so very proud to be
a Harlequin author. Thank you for making this
experience a dream come true!

And to my amazing family—
you make every day special.

Chapter 1

She'd know that butt anywhere. Hunter Boone.

Damn it.

In eleven years, his derriere hadn't changed much. Lean hips and a tight butt hugged by work-faded Wrangler blue jeans. And, apparently, the view still managed to take her breath away. Which was unfortunate because she'd come home believing he couldn't affect her anymore—not even a little bit. She had been 110 percent confident that Hunter was out of her system. She was so wrong.

Her hands tightened on the tray she held and her lungs emptied as a memory of the way that rear felt under her hands…

She sighed, completely trapped.

This was not the reaction she'd expected after so

long. Or the way she wanted to see him again. It…
it pissed her off.

This isn't fair.

"Need some help with that, Josie?" Her father's
voice made her wince.

She was hiding, clutching a tray of her dad's famous German breakfast kolaches and Danish, and
crouching behind the display counter. Why was
she—a rational, professional woman—ducking behind a bakery counter? Because *he'd* walked in and
thrown her confidence in her face—a face whose
forehead was currently streaked with flour and sugar
and who knew what else.

There was no doubt her father's amused question
had made all eyes in Pop's Bakery turn toward her.
All eyes, even the very dazzling blue-green ones
she was trying so desperately to avoid. There wasn't
much to do about it now.

She shot her father a look as she said, "Nope,
thanks, Dad. I've got it."

Her father winked, looking downright giddy. He'd
known exactly what he was doing, and, knowing
him, he could hardly wait to see what happened next.

Taking a deep breath, she stood slowly and slid
the tray of breakfast goods into the display cabinet
with intentional care. She refused to look at anything
except the pastries. Or the stuffed deer head over the
front door. That always made her smile—not that
she was a fan of taxidermy. But her father insisted
on decorating it for the seasons. It wore a red Santa
hat. Ornaments dangled off its antlers, which were

finished off with some tinsel and blinking twinkly Christmas lights. *Only in Stonewall Crossing, Texas.*

"I couldn't tell," her father continued. "You were all bent over, trying to balance that tray."

Josie's cheeks felt warm, but she wasn't about to admit she'd been hiding. "All good."

"Josie? Josie Stephens?" a high-pitched voice asked. "Oh, my God, look at you. Why, you haven't changed since high school."

Josie glanced over the display case at the woman speaking. Josie couldn't place her, so she smiled and said, "Thanks. You, too."

That's when her gaze wandered to Hunter. He was waiting. And, from the look on his face, he *knew* Josie had no idea who the woman was. Which irritated her. Him, standing there, looking like *that*, irritated her.

This morning gets better and better.

First one of the ovens died, then she'd argued with her dad over which pills he was supposed to take, her dad's dog, Sprinkles, had buried one of her shoes somewhere in the backyard and now this. Hunter Boone, gorgeous and tall and manly and still too-perfect, looking at her. *The front view is just as good*—bad—*as the back.*

He smiled—bright blue-green eyes sparkling, damn dimple peaking in full force. She swallowed the huge lump in her throat. Not that she could have said anything if she'd wanted to.

"So it's true?" the woman continued. "Your dad said you were coming to help him, but I couldn't imagine you back *here*. We *all* know how much you hated Stonewall Crossing." Her speech pattern, the snide condescension, the narrowed eyes. Josie remembered her then. Winnie. Winnie Michaels. "What did you call it, redneck hell—right?"

Josie watched Hunter frown at Winnie's question, the slight shake of his head. It was all so familiar, unsettling, confusing. She blinked, turning her attention to the deer head and its flashing holiday cheer.

"Guess hell froze over." Winnie kept going, teasing—but with a definite edge.

"Kind of hard to say no when your dad needs you," Josie answered, forcing herself not to snap. Instead, she smiled. "I'm here."

"She wasn't about to let her old man try to run this place on his own." Her father jumped to her defense. "No matter how busy her life might be."

Busy didn't come close to describing her mess of a life, but her dad didn't need more stress right now.

Her father dropped his arm around her shoulders and squeezed. "She's always been a daddy's girl."

She arched an eyebrow and shot him a look. "Are you complaining?"

Her father laughed. "Nope."

"I didn't think so." She kissed his cheek. "Now go *sit* down."

He shouldn't be up, but she knew better than to think he'd stay in his chair or use a walker. That was why she'd flown home from Washington, to take care of him. And because she needed someplace quiet to think things over.

"You know that's not going to happen, Jo." Same

voice, same smile, same butt, same irritating nickname that only he used.

"*That's* why I'm here." Josie was thrilled she sounded completely cool, calm and collected. Her heart, on the other hand, was beating like crazy.

"It's kinda weird to see the two of you standing here." Winnie glanced back and forth between Josie and Hunter. "I mean, without having your tongues down each other's throats and all."

"Well—" Josie stared at the woman, then Hunter. He wasn't smiling anymore. His jaw was rigid, the muscles knotted. *Interesting.* "It's kind of hard with the display case in the way," she teased.

Hunter was quick. "I could jump over."

Josie shrugged, but her heart was on the verge of exploding. It was all too easy imagining him sliding across the glass-top counter, pulling her into his strong arms and— *Not going there.* "Nah. You don't want to break Dad's case."

"I don't mind," her father murmured, for her ears only, as he retreated to his chair.

Hunter shook his head. "I think we'll have to wait for now." He cocked his head, eyes still pinned on Josie. "I've gotta get these kolaches to the boys."

Josie saw him take the huge box by the register. A swift kick of disappointment prompted her to blurt out, "Too bad, Hunter. If I remember it correctly, you knew how to kiss a girl."

He smiled again, shaking his head. "If you remember? Ouch. Guess I've had some competition the last few years." His eyes swept her face, lingering on her lips just long enough to make her cheeks feel hot.

She knew better but didn't say a word.

Hunter inclined his head ever so slightly. "Thanks, Carl. I'll see you later on. Have fun while you're back in hell, Jo. I'll see you around."

That would be a bad idea.

Josie watched him leave. His back—and butt—disappeared as he climbed into the driver's side of a huge dark blue one-ton extended cab truck. She saw him wink at her then and shook her head, a familiar ache pressing in on her. *Time doesn't heal all wounds.* How many hours had she spent wishing she hadn't pushed him away? That she hadn't set him up for failure, because she had… No point in rehashing it again.

She turned back to the display counter to arrange the pastries she'd made at four-thirty this morning. Dad's fall had shaken them both. He was the last stable thing she had left. He needed her—that was the only reason she'd come home. The last thing she wanted was to be back exactly where she'd been eleven years ago, working in her father's bakery in a town she couldn't wait to escape. Yes, she'd hoped coming back would dispel some of her fantasies about Hunter Boone. And, if she was really lucky, she could finally get her heart back. After seeing Hunter again, one thing was certain. As soon as her dad didn't need her, she was gone.

Hunter put the truck in Reverse and blew out a slow breath as he craned his head to check his blind spot.

"Was that her?" Eli asked, his voice and eyes cold.

Hunter glanced at his son but wasn't up for an argument. "That's Jo."

"She's not that pretty," Eli grumbled.

"No? I think she is." His voice was neutral. Pretty didn't come close to describing Jo Stephens. Silver-gray eyes, wild curly hair, with curves to drive a man to drink. She was beautiful. There wasn't a man alive who wouldn't admit that. Except his son. "And she's funny. Really funny."

"Huh." Eli wasn't impressed.

Hunter knew Eli's blue-green eyes—eyes his boy got from him—were watching him. He could feel Eli's anger—over Jo. But there wasn't much to say.

Amy, Eli's mom, had done too good a job of trashing Jo. And as much as he'd like Eli to believe that Jo had nothing to do with the bitter end of his marriage to Amy, he knew better. Jo Stephens had held his heart since he was sixteen. And he didn't mind too much. Seeing her this morning was like downing a pot of coffee—

"Did you get enough for everyone?" Eli interrupted.

Hunter smiled at his son. "I don't know. But I got a lot."

Eli grinned. "We're growing boys, Dad."

"I know, kid." Hunter looked at Eli, taking in the slight sharpening of his features. His son was growing up. There were still traces of roundness on his ten-year-old body. In no time, his son would be all arms and legs, big feet and teenage awkwardness.

He was a good-looking boy. And in the years ahead, Eli Boone was going to be a good-looking man. More important, he was smart and kind and had solid common sense. Hunter was proud of that.

He'd done the best he could by his son. The two of them took care of each other with little complaining. Balancing his son, the ranch and teaching at the university veterinary hospital was hard work, but it was worth it. No matter what, he made sure Eli *suffered* through every school trip to the opera, the museums or anywhere else that broadened his son's horizons. He knew there was a big world out there, and he wanted Eli to know it, too. He wouldn't have his mistakes cause his son to miss out on anything.

"Uncle Fisher gonna make it to this one?" Eli asked.

"He said he'd be there." Hunter nodded. And his brothers always kept their word.

Eli nodded, too, then said, "Dara thinks she's gonna get a one."

"She can dream, can't she?" he teased gently.

Dara Greer had joined the local Future Farmers of America club this year. Her family had moved from the city and her folks wanted her to "fit in." Problem was she was nervous around animals and uncomfortable in the show ring.

"I know." Eli grew thoughtful. "But she's sweet. And she's trying really hard. You know?"

Hunter looked at his son with a new sense of understanding. "Oh?"

Eli nodded, red streaking up his neck and coloring his face. "Y-yeah." He pushed his dad on the shoulder, laughing.

Hunter turned back to driving. He knew. Boy, did he know.

Jo had been a lot like Dara when she'd moved to town. She was this guarded, thoughtful type whose gaze seemed to search his soul. Every attempt he made to get her attention had earned him an eye roll or a shake of her curly-haired head. She'd hated his "boot-wearing, deer-shooting ass." He'd teased her for her Hunting is Murder T-shirts. And her light-ning-fast comebacks had driven him crazy. They'd fought, long and loud, refusing to admit the other might have a point or a right to their own perspective.

But when he'd grabbed her in the high school ag-riculture barn, her kiss had set his blood on fire. He was done for even if she was still hesitant. He didn't know then that Jo didn't believe in love, romance or commitment. Mostly because she'd never seen it. Her mom had changed husbands more often than most women had their hair done. Moving in with her dad, to Stonewall Crossing, was a way to get away from the drama and uncertainty she'd grown to hate.

It had taken him a long time to get her to trust him, for her to believe he was hers. Sure, they'd still argued, all the time, but they'd been just as quick to make up.

Some things were just too big to forgive.

When she'd left, when she'd had to leave, half of his heart had gone with her. The other half had gone to Eli.

Josie ran to the phone, slipping once on the water her hair was sprinkling all over the tile floor. Only her dad would still have one house phone, with a cord no less, placed in the middle of the hallway. Sprinkles sat, staring at the phone, barking and howling.

"Hush, Sprinkles." She answered the phone. "Hello?"

"Jo?" Of course he would call her while she was in the shower.

Sprinkles kept yapping. "Shh." She took a deep breath. "Um, hi, Hunter."

"You okay? You sound kinda out of breath?"

"I'm in— I was in the shower." She laughed airily. "I'm making a puddle on Dad's floor as we speak." Why was she sharing that information with him?

He chuckled. "Want me to call you back?"

Sprinkles jumped up.

"I'm out now." The dog howled. "Sprinkles!" Sprinkles sat, staring at her. She ignored Hunter's laugh. "What's up?" Not that she wanted to know why he'd called…

"I was wondering how long you were going to be here." He sounded hesitant.

"At least through Christmas… Then see how Dad is. Why?"

"Well, the FFA chapter here always builds a Christmas float and some of the parents thought it might be nice to build one around your books."

"Oh." She didn't know what to say.

"I'm in my truck right now—" He paused. "And I'm about to go by your place. Can I come in and show you what they came up with?"

"Oh, um…" *I'm just wrapped in a towel and dripping wet.* "Well…"

"Okay. See you in a sec." And he hung up.

"Damn it." She glared at the handset. "Damn it, damn it."

Sprinkles barked.

"Joselyn Marie Stephens," her father chastised her from the living room.

"Really, Dad?" She peered around the corner to find her father sitting in his recliner. "You're right there and you couldn't get the phone? And I'm almost thirty. I can say damn it. I could even say—"

There was a knock on the door. Sprinkles started barking like mad.

"Someone stopping by?" he asked.

"Shit," she squealed, then almost tripped over Sprinkles and ran back into the bathroom.

"Come in," she heard her dad call out. *Or go home.* She pulled her thick robe on and picked through her brown curls quickly. She rolled her eyes at her reflection. *Chill. Relax.* She straightened her shoulders and opened the door.

There was no help for it. She'd have to walk past the living room to get to her bedroom. Which meant Hunter would be treated to a view of her wrapped in her fluffy black-and-blue bathrobe. She could almost hear her mother scolding her. *A single woman must always look her best when keeping company with a handsome man.* Josie sighed, grabbed an extra towel and started drying up her watery path from the bathroom to the hall.

"Oh, hey." Hunter laughed. "You really were in the shower."

She turned, one eyebrow arched, all sarcasm.

"What makes you say that?" A boy peered around Hunter then. And Josie felt her irritation slip.

This was him… Hunter's son. She felt pain. Pain she thought she'd worked through years ago. She stared at the boy.

The boy stared back. He had Hunter's intense gaze and startling eyes.

She held up a finger. "Let me get dressed."

"We're not going to stay long." Hunter's voice was soft.

She pulled her gaze from the boy, her toes curling into the area rug beneath her feet. "Well, you're going to have to give me a second because I refuse to have a conversation with someone while I'm wearing a robe. Okay?" And she needed a minute to get a grip. She half ran to her room, almost tripped over Sprinkles again and closed the door without a sound. "Shit," she murmured with feeling.

Dad needs me. That's why I'm here. I don't have to do this float or spend time with Hunter…or his beautiful son. But I do have to take care of Dad.

She pulled on her underwear and dug through the suitcase, then the piles of clothes all over her room. She sighed, pulling on a pair of jeans and a thermal shirt. A quick search unearthed her fuzzy pink bunny slippers, which she slipped on while she headed back to the waiting crew.

"It's the best I could do in two minutes," she muttered when she saw her father's disapproving glance. "I'll put on my hoopskirt and pearls next time, okay?"

The boy smiled briefly, while Hunter laughed.

"Nice to meet you." She stuck her hand out to the boy. She couldn't ignore him—she didn't want to. He looked like a Boone, which was a good thing. If he'd looked like Amy... She swallowed. "I'm—"

"Joselyn," her dad offered.

"Or Jo," Hunter added.

"Or Josie, even." She rolled her eyes.

"Eli," he said, shaking her hand quickly. He nodded and then sat by her father on the couch.

The door opened and Josie felt a moment's panic as she spun around. If it was Amy—

"Well, if it isn't Miss Joselyn Stephens." Two hands picked her up, holding her eye to eye with a large wall of a man.

"Fisher?" She couldn't believe this...this person was Hunter's little brother. "What happened to you?"

He smiled. "I drank milk." He pulled her into a bear hug.

"By the truckload?" She hugged him back. "You look great."

"I do." He nodded.

She giggled, stepping away from him as he put her on the ground. "At least your sense of humor hasn't changed."

"Not that I mind you all stopping by, but can we start over so I know what's going on?" her dad interrupted. He was a stickler for his routine. The bakery opened at six, so he was in bed by nine each and every evening. She glanced at the clock. It was ten after nine.

Hunter spoke first. "Christmas float time. FFA met tonight and came up with a few ideas. One of them was to build something around Josie's story characters."

Josie didn't know where to look. If she looked at Hunter, she felt…all sorts of conflicting and over-whelming *things*. If she looked at Eli, she felt empty. And if she looked at her dad, she felt rumpled and unattractive. Fisher was her only option. He winked at her when she glanced his way. It helped.

"You don't have to tell *me* it's Christmastime. Christmas parade kicks off the Gingerbread Festival." Her father winked at her. "Which means Josie and I will be up to our elbows in the stuff for the next week."

"Can't wait." Josie smiled. "Bonding while baking is a family tradition." She made the terrible mistake of looking Hunter's way. Hunter, who was watching her. His crooked grin and cocked eyebrow stirred up a series of memories. A flash of him smiling at her while they floated down the river. Another of them lying on a blanket under the stars. Him teaching her to drive stick shift. Making love for the first time. *Not thoughts I need to have right now.* Her heart lodged itself in her throat.

"Family traditions are good." Fisher grinned. "Even better if it puts food on the table, right? A man's got to eat."

"Which characters?" her father asked, turning to Eli.

Eli shrugged. "Thirty-four, probably. Since some of us have calves."

"Thirty-four?" She tore her gaze from Hunter.

"It was Dad's calf, right?" Eli asked.

Josie nodded, rattled. "Yes, his state champion calf." Her gaze settled on Eli. He looked a lot like Hunter when they'd first met. Her heart hurt. "What can I do to help?"

"Well, we're gonna build the float. But they—we—were wondering…" Eli was clearly uncomfortable. "Would you ride on it?"

She shook her head. "Um, I hate the spotlight, Eli."

"It's just a parade." Eli's eyes were scornful. "In Stonewall Crossing."

"Come on, Josie," her father said. "You wrote books about this place, the town and people."

Fisher elbowed her. "You are a celebrity here, kind of."

"And it's for the kids," her dad added.

She held her hands up. "Really, Dad? You're going to play the for-the-kids card?"

Hunter laughed, sending a wave of awareness along her neck. "Nothing to add, H-Hunter?" She stumbled over his name. It was stupid. Not like she could call him Mr. Boone. *It's a name, for crying out loud.* Saying it shouldn't affect her, or send the slightest shiver down her spine.

His gaze traveled over her face before peering into her eyes. "You might make some good memories before you go back. Something for a new book."

She couldn't look away. And she really needed to look away. He might not be grappling with memories, with need and want, but she sure as hell was.

"Come on, Josie. Live a little," Fisher added.

She should say no, but Hunter had found her

weakness. A new book… Wouldn't that be something? Not that anyone knew she was in the midst of the longest creative drought of her career. That's why she was considering the teaching position in New Mexico. She wanted to feel inspired again.

Maybe working on the float could help. At this point, it couldn't hurt. Her career, anyway.

"So?" Eli's question ended her tortured introspection.

"Yes." She smiled at Eli as she spoke. "Thanks, Eli. I mean, it's nice to feel special for my stories." *Don't ask. Don't ask.* But she did. "Did you ever read them?" Thinking about Amy reading her stories to Eli made her stomach twist.

Eli looked at his dad. "Dad used to read me *34* and *Floppy Feet* all the time."

Fisher snorted. "Hey, hey, now. I've read the cow one—"

"It's called *34*," Hunter answered.

"Right, *34*." Fisher nodded at his brother. "A time or two, Eli."

Eli grinned at his uncle.

Josie risked another glance at Hunter, but he was staring into the fire with a small smile on his face.

"That reminds me, Josie, Annabeth called from the elementary school earlier. She wants you to do a story time there." Her father spoke up.

"I'd love that." She smiled. Other than her father, Annabeth was the only one in Stonewall Crossing she'd kept in touch with after she'd left.

Hunter looked at her, his voice soft as he said, "The kids would, too, Jo."

Jo. For an instant she wanted him to grab her and kiss her, just as he used to. When he'd kissed her, nothing else mattered. She nodded, staring into his eyes wordlessly.

"We should go, Dad. I've got a math test Monday morning." Eli stood up. "Thanks for helping us out… Miss Stephens."

She turned away from Hunter and beamed at the boy. "You really can call me Josie, Eli, please. I don't like feeling old."

"Yes, ma'am." He barely glanced at her, his answering smile forced. "Thanks for the breakfast this morning, Mr. Stephens."

"How'd you do?" her father asked.

"Eli got a one at the stock show." Hunter smiled at his son, placing a hand on the boy's shoulder. "He's been working real hard with Bob, his steer. And the judges could tell."

It was clear Hunter was a devoted father, just as she'd always known he'd be. Something hard settled in the pit of her stomach, a hollow, empty ache.

"I wasn't the only one." Eli's cheeks were red. "Now there's nothing big until after Christmas."

"Time to get ready for the next one." Her father winked at the boy. "You should be proud, Eli."

"Thank you, sir." Eli nodded and headed for the door.

"Don't get up," Josie said to her dad.

"Now, Josie—" her father started to argue.

"Dad." She held her hand up.

"We know the way out. Don't get Jo all worked

up." Hunter shook her father's hand. "Have a good evening, Carl. Thanks for having us over."

Her dad winked. "You're welcome anytime, Hunter. You know that. You, too, Fisher."

She knew her father cared for Hunter—he always had. After all, Hunter had been almost family. Her gut twisted. She led Hunter to the door, needing him to go—now.

"I know you're a big-time author now, but I expect to see you some before you go." Fisher hugged her again before following Eli out and into the truck.

Hunter lingered in the doorway. His gaze wandered over her face. "You and Carl want to come out to the ranch tomorrow? Have dinner with us? I've made a lot of changes."

Josie stared at him, surprised. Did she want to go? No, she really didn't. It would be awkward and painful. *Us.* She didn't think she could handle seeing his family unit together, in a place she'd truly loved. Where Amy now lived. "I don't—"

But her father interrupted her, loudly. "Sounds good."

No, it doesn't. It sounds like a nightmare. She mumbled, "Are you sure that's okay?"

Hunter smiled that crooked smile. "It's my home. Of course it's okay. See you about six?"

She stood there, searching for some sort of excuse, while he climbed into his truck and drove away.

Chapter 2

Hunter didn't say much on the drive back to the ranch. Fisher, who was never at a loss for words, kept Eli talking all things steers and Future Farmers of America. And Hunter was thankful for it. Spending time with Jo was harder than he'd expected. Leaving her was worse. If he could get her alone, if he could talk to her... What would he say? He was eleven years too late to apologize.

Fisher said good-night and headed to his place, leaving Eli to his homework and Hunter to his paperwork.

"I guess she is kinda pretty." Eli sounded thoughtful.

"Who?" Hunter looked at his son over his laptop.

"Josie." Eli gazed at the homework spread out

on the table all around him. He tapped his pencil on the table, then added, "I guess I sorta get it. But Mom's prettier."

Hunter looked at his son. "Your mom is beautiful, Eli." Amy had always been pretty—to look at. But her beauty was skin-deep. Underneath was something else entirely.

No point being negative. Chances are she'd be coming through town for the holidays. Sometimes it went well, sometimes it didn't. But he wanted his son to have a relationship with his mom, no matter how he felt about his ex-wife.

"So are you going to date her?"

Hunter looked at his son again. "What?"

"Are you going to date Josie?" Eli's bright eyes challenged his father unflinchingly.

"No." No matter how much he wanted to. "She'll be heading back after the holidays, anyway." He kept his voice neutral.

"If she wasn't leaving, would you?" Eli's gaze continued to burn into his.

Hunter studied his son for a long time. "Yes," he answered truthfully. "But I don't know if she'd want to date me, kid. It's not that easy, you know?"

"Why?" His son's eyes narrowed a little.

He hedged. "It's just not. Women are…complicated."

Eli sighed and looked back at his homework. "I know."

Hunter stared at the top of his son's head. "What does that mean?"

"Woman *are* complicated." Eli was bright red

when he looked at his father. "I asked Dara if she'd have lunch with us…at the county show."

Hunter bit back his smile. "Did she say no?"

Eli shook his head, then shrugged. "She didn't say anything."

"You should ask her again. You might have surprised her. What did you say?"

"I don't know." He paused, thinking. "Something like, 'Have lunch with me at the next show.'"

Hunter nodded, fighting the urge to laugh.

"She just stood there, staring at me." Eli looked at his paper.

"Did you ask her or tell her?"

Eli tapped his pencil again. "I think I asked her."

"Ask her again."

Eli frowned at his paper, the pencil tapping faster. "It's no big deal. I gotta get this done."

"Need help?"

Eli shook his head.

Hunter sat, trying to stare at his computer. His son had his first crush and he didn't know what to tell him. He thought Dara was a nice enough girl, but they were both so young. And shy. Eli had probably scared the shit out of her, at the very least surprised her. But Hunter knew better than to push. If Eli was done talking about it, then they were done talking about it. Eli had homework and so did he.

He had a good group of fourth-year vet students, partly because he was so hard on them. The semester might be winding down, but clinical rotations weren't. Not like the patients disappeared because it was winter break. If his students didn't like it, they could take a look at the long waiting list of eager candidates waiting for any open spot to remind them of how lucky they were to be there, working through the holidays.

He leaned back in his chair, propped his feet up and logged on to the University of East Texas website, then the College of Veterinary Medicine intranet to access his files. He had two classes of finals to grade and his caseload of patient files to review. His fourth-year students were doing most of the patient charting, but he had to check each and every note.

Most were spays and neuters. A couple of dogs with parvovirus. He glanced over their charts. Poor dogs had to be isolated and hooked up to an IV to keep hydrated. It was expensive to cure and messy to treat. All it took was one easy vaccination to prevent the whole thing.

He clicked ahead, skimming the fourth years' notes. No errors so far. He closed those files, then opened Mars's file. They were all getting attached to the sweet yellow Labrador. She'd been with them for two weeks now. Her owners had carried her in, bleeding and limp, after she'd been hit by a car. He hoped her paralysis was temporary, but the dog wasn't improving the way he'd expected. They'd have to perform a cesarean soon. He didn't have much hope for the three puppies she carried, but he prayed Mars survived. He added a note to schedule the surgery for next week and closed the file.

"Dad," Eli said. "Did Uncle Fisher get the four-wheelers back?"

"Yes." He glanced at his son. "But you're not driving them."

"Uncle Fisher would let me." Eli frowned. "And Uncle Archer and Uncle Ryder would let me, too."

"They might. But they're not your father." He nodded. "You'd best not bother them about it too much, or you'll end up working this weekend."

Eli smiled. "They wouldn't make me do that. I'm their favorite nephew."

"You're their only nephew." He chuckled.

"Harsh, Dad." He laughed, too, then turned back to his homework.

"You'll always be their favorite." He worried about teasing his son sometimes.

"I know." Eli arched an eyebrow, grinning.

Hunter shook his head, but he smiled. God, he loved his boy.

He was lucky—he knew it. He had a job he loved. The research he and his brothers had been doing on the ranch had led to a partnership with the state agricultural agency. Their hard work and dedication had made Boone Ranch one of the biggest conservation and rehabilitation sites in this part of the country. They'd had a plan, a good plan. And once Hunter had a plan, he stayed with it until the end.

Losing Jo hadn't been part of the plan. And nothing had ever hurt like that.

Jo.

He fisted his hands, wishing he could stop wanting her, needing her. She was here, so close, yet still out of his reach. Seeing her now reminded him of everything he'd had and lost. Thinking about her wouldn't bring her back, wouldn't change what he'd done—

"Do you still love her, Dad?" Eli was looking at him.

He hadn't realized that he wasn't looking at his computer anymore. His gaze had wandered, and he'd been blindly staring out the window.

"I'm supposed to go to Tommy's house tomorrow night. Remember?" Eli asked. "Don't want to leave you alone if it'll be…weird," Eli finished.

Fisher had already told them he wouldn't be coming, but he hadn't offered up an explanation.

Hunter glanced at his son. "Guess it's a good thing her dad's coming for dinner, too."

"Why?" Eli asked.

"Because when Jo and I are alone, we tend to fight."

Josie was tired. And stressed. And tired of being stressed. And now she was getting a headache. Probably because she was heading to dinner with the love of her life and the only person she'd ever hated. Not hated…just actively disliked. That was why she'd made her father and Annabeth promise not to bring up anything to do with Amy. Or Hunter. She didn't like who she was, how she felt, where Amy was concerned.

"Holy crap," Josie breathed as she pulled through the huge stone entranceway, the intricate wrought-iron gate open wide. This was nothing like the Boone ranch she remembered. This was something else. She drove slowly, following the twisting limestone drive until she reached three outbuildings.

One was obviously a ranger station. It was elevated, with a two-story ladder the only way up. A small building sat next to it, a long ranch house of sorts with two large trucks parked beside it. Then there was the main building, several stories tall, all wood and native stone and rather impressive.

Almost as impressive as the man sitting on the porch. She sighed. Hunter sat, a laptop on his knees. He looked gorgeous—and a little bit dangerous to what remained of her heart.

She put the car in Park, trying not to stare as he smiled at her. He closed the laptop and walked down the steps to greet her.

The throbbing in her head was matched by the pounding of her heart. Whether it was from nerves or exhaustion, she didn't know. But watching him walk to her car did little to calm her nerves. It was going to be a long night.

She rolled down the passenger window as he leaned forward to say, "Hi."

"Hi." She forced a smile. "Dad bailed at the last minute." Which had led to a thirty-minute argument. At least Eli would be there as a buffer.

A strange look crossed Hunter's face and then he smiled. "His hip giving him trouble?"

"Yes." That's what her father had told her, though she suspected he was trying to play matchmaker. Why her father was trying to fix her up with a married man was a mystery. After the hell her mother's indiscretions had put him through, she'd expected him to place a little more value on the whole faithful vow thing. He'd always been on the eccentric side, but this was ridiculous. Hunter was off-limits, no if, ands or buts about it.

"Can you give me a ride?" he asked. "Or we can take some horses."

"How much farther is the main house?" She let her eyes travel over the buildings again. "And why don't I recognize any of this?"

His eyes traveled over her face. "Did you think you'd recognize it?"

"Of course." She rolled her eyes. "I mean, I figured you'd made some changes, and you obviously have, but…"

"I didn't own this when we… In high school this wasn't part of the family ranch. We bought this about six years ago." He paused.

"That makes sense. So, if I remember correctly, this must be the guest lodge?" She took it all in, impressed. "Am I right?" She waited for him to nod. "Well, wow, congratulations. Looks like your big plans are coming together."

"Most of them." He nodded, his eyes boring into hers. "So horses or driving?"

She looked down at her skirt. "Driving. Didn't know horses were part of the evening."

He opened the passenger door and climbed in. "Just stay on the drive to the left. It's a ways down yet."

She drove on, and her small red four-door rental seemed to shrink as the silence stretched on.

It was too quiet. The pounding in her head seemed

to echo. "Too bad you didn't have paved roads when you taught me to drive. Maybe I wouldn't have totaled that truck."

"You didn't. That thing was like a tank." He looked at her. "It wasn't for a lack of trying, though."

"I guess I should blame my teacher." She flashed him a grin.

He chuckled. "Sure. If that makes you feel better about wrecking my granddad's truck, you just go on telling yourself that."

"God, I felt terrible." She shook her head. "I still do."

"Don't. Still drive it back and forth around here when I need to run errands or deliver something. Imagine I'll teach Eli to drive in it." Hunter rested his head against the headrest.

As they crested the next hill, Josie saw the ranch house. It had always been a special place, where her most treasured memories took place. She was hit with a case of nerves so intense she almost turned the car around. Instead, she did what she always did when she was nervous. She talked.

"You've made a lot of improvements to the house. I knew you'd never tear it down, since your grandmother was born here." She paused, but he didn't say anything. "I guess it's nice to have some privacy for you and your family. I mean, you haven't said anything about the way the ranch works now, but I remember the way you said you wanted it to work. Population studies. Rehabilitation center. Animal preserve. Did you ever get the white-tail deer breeding program started?" Her head felt as if it had a band tightening around it. "Guess you're keeping cattle, too, since Eli is raising a calf?" She stopped as the car pulled up in front of the house. Crippling anxiety gripped her, the throbbing pulse around her skull excruciating.

Any second Amy was going to walk out that front door. Any second Hunter was going to put his arm around Amy, his wife, and they were all going inside to have a meal together. Why had she come? She felt very nauseous.

"You okay?" he asked.

She looked at him, watching the traces of amusement turn into concern. "I'm not sure. I'm feeling a little...off."

His forehead creased as he stared at her face. "You're really pale." His hand touched her cheeks and forehead. His touch felt so good. "But you feel cool. Let's get you something to drink."

He climbed out of the car and walked around to her side. He opened the door, but she was paralyzed with fear.

"Maybe I should go home. I feel weird about leaving Dad home alone." Which was partly true.

"Okay," he said slowly. "You can leave. Once there's some color in your cheeks and you don't look like you're gonna pass out. Don't think this car would take a beating the way Granddad's truck did."

She glared up at him. She pinched her cheeks, then smiled thinly. "There. Color in my cheeks."

He laughed. "Don't make me pick you up, Jo."

She slipped from the car, grasping the roof for support.

They stood there, regarding each other in the warm rays of the setting sun. No one came out to greet them. Other than the faint coo of a dove, the moo of a distant cow and the slightly rhythmic whump of the windmill's blades, it was quiet.

"Drink?" he asked. He held out his hand awkwardly.

She stared at it and pushed off her car, not taking it. "I think I can manage to walk to the door, Hunter. I'll have my drink and hit the road and you can have a peaceful evening with the family."

"Eli's out." He sounded amused. "Fish, Archer and Ryder all have places of their own. But Renata still lives with Dad so she can take care of him. She always was a daddy's girl."

Josie felt bile in her throat. He wanted her to sit through dinner with him and Amy? She felt angry suddenly.

"Don't you think it might be a little awkward?" She turned toward him. "Okay, a *lot* awkward."

"Why?" He looked genuinely surprised. "Why would being alone with me be awkward?"

Josie was distracted by the shift of emotions on his face. The tone of his voice was soft but coaxing. He seemed to take a step toward her, rattling her from her silence.

"Alone?" A full-fledged pounding began at the base of her skull. Shooting pain focused right behind her left eye.

He nodded. "Let's get you inside. You can lie down, have your drink, and once you're better, you can leave, if that's what you want to do."

"I should go now," she argued. "Pretty sure it's a migraine and once it gets started—"

"You'll be down for the count." He nodded, slipping his arm around her for support. "You're not driving, Jo. It wouldn't be right or gentlemanly."

"You could be a gentleman and drive me home now." She didn't have the energy to argue, but she refused to lean into him.

"In a bit." He swung her up into his arms.

"Hunter—" His name escaped on a startled breath, right before she was bombarded with his scent. Everything about him was familiar. The earthy spice of him, the strength of his arms, the warmth he exuded, the feel of his breath against her forehead. It was sweet torture. "I can walk," she bit out, sitting rigidly in his arms. She would not relax. She would not melt in his arms and press herself to him. She would not kiss his neck or run her hands through his thick, dark blond hair. She would not think of doing those things, either.

He carried her into the house, ratcheting up her nerves. This was how she was going to see Amy? In his arms? Her whisper was urgent. "Please put me down."

And he did. On the couch. "Sit," he murmured before leaving the room.

"Bark bark," she muttered childishly. Her gaze bounced around the room, searching, waiting.

He laughed. "You still do that?"

"You still order people around?" she snapped.

He left and then walked back with a glass of water and a bottle of pain pills. He sat on the coffee table opposite the couch, offering them to her.

She stared at him, deciding whether to take the offered answer to her pain or suffer through out of sheer stubbornness. She took the bottle and the water.

"Still get migraines?" he asked.

She shrugged, pouring a couple of pain relievers into her hand before putting the lid back on the bottle. "Sometimes." She glanced at him. "Still have sneezing fits?"

"Sometimes." He smiled. "Still painting? I mean, other than your illustrations."

"Yes." It was ironic that, even though she'd been desperate to leave the state of Texas and everything about it, Texas landscapes were one of her favorite things to paint. "Still write poetry?"

"No." He stared down at her. "You wanna lie down? Eli's room is a mess, but you can rest in mine if you want."

Rest in his room? *Amy's room?*

She shook her head. "No, thank you. If I lie here for a minute, will you let me leave?"

He stood over her, still smiling. "I'm not kidnapping you, Jo. You can go whenever you want to go. As long as you can make it all the way back into town with no problems."

She sat up and felt instantly nauseous.

"Yeah." He sighed. "Stop being so stubborn and lie down."

"I'm stubborn?" she snapped as she lay back on the cushions of the couch.

"Relax for a few. Dinner's almost ready." He winked at her. "The protein'll do you some good."

She pulled her gaze from him, shaking her head.

"Where is everyone again?" Being alone with him wasn't good for her. She didn't like feeling so vulnerable, so needy. As a matter a fact, she was feeling way too much right now. Even with her pounding head, she was preoccupied with thoughts of being wrapped in his arms.

"Eli's spending the night with a friend. My brothers have their own places. They're probably off doing what grown men do." Hunter shrugged.

"That sounds…dangerous," she muttered, waiting for the rest. But Hunter didn't say a thing about Amy. She narrowed her eyes. He was going to make her ask, wasn't he? She started to, but couldn't. It had taken her a long time not to wince just thinking Amy's name. She sure as hell wasn't going to say it, out loud, here.

She'd turn up sooner or later—she always did.

"No interruptions. You rest. I'll work. You can eat later and I'll drive you home."

She continued to glare at him, even as she lay back on the couch cushions. Her head was pounding, making her ears ring. She closed her eyes, trying to relax. But she couldn't.

She was alone with Hunter. Just the two of them. She opened her eyes, looking for him.

The place had changed, but it still felt the same. The inside had obviously been gutted and redone. The walls were painted a warm cream with knotty wood trim. The ceiling was dark, with heavy exposed beams. The cast-iron wagon-wheel chandelier was the same. So was the wood-burning stove in the far corner.

But the room felt bigger—was bigger. The dining room was now part of this room—separated by a long brown leather sofa. On the far wall, beneath a huge picture window, was Hunter's old-fashioned drafting table. Her mouth went dry at the memories that table stirred up.

They'd spent most of that morning bringing in the round hay bales in the tractor. Once they'd been left alone, she'd dragged him inside with obvious intentions. Her lips had fastened on his neck, tasting the salt of his sweat. When her lips suckled and nipped at his earlobe, he'd tugged her jeans off, tossing them hurriedly over his shoulder before grasping her hips and setting her onto the table. With his jeans around his ankles, he'd loved her hard and fast. How could she remember the feel of him, as though he was with her now?

They'd been young, too young… But they'd loved each other, really loved each other. And then life— Amy—had gotten in the way.

She swallowed. Her head was spinning. She needed to get the hell out of here. She needed to put as much space between them as possible. The only way to do that was to get rid of her headache.

She took a slow, steady breath and forced herself to relax against the pillows.

Hunter set the table as quietly as he could.

She'd been asleep for almost an hour. But he knew the longer she slept, the better she'd feel.

He moved to the couch and stared down at her.

The years hadn't touched her. She'd never been

a fan of makeup, so her skin was still smooth and silky. She had some faint lines bracketing her mouth and eyes, where she crinkled when she laughed. And when she laughed, she looked so damn beautiful.

He ran a hand over his face, shaking his head. If he could go back in time, follow her, he would.

No, he wouldn't. Because then he wouldn't have Eli. And as much as he regretted losing Jo, he loved his son.

Jo stirred, her movements capturing his attention. Her mouth parted, then smiled slightly as she turned onto her side. There was a flutter of movement under her eyelids, and she sighed.

He spread the blanket from the back of the couch over her before heading into the kitchen. He turned down the stove and put the salad back in the refrigerator. Dinner would keep—she needed sleep.

Once he'd turned off all the lights, he went to his desk and opened his laptop. He glanced at her, then at the desk. He'd had to patch the lid after Amy had ripped it off at the hinges. She couldn't stand the *H.B. + J.S.* that he'd carved into the wood. Even though he'd been the one to replace the lid, he still looked for the carving whenever he opened the desk for supplies.

Did Jo have someone special? As much as he wanted her, he wanted her happiness more. He wondered if she'd made any other men as happy as she'd made him. She probably had. Eleven years was a long time to go without. And Jo was a passionate woman. He remembered that about her with great fondness.

Everything about her was like a living, breathing fire. From her sparkling eyes and lightning-fast humor to her equally fast temper and her instant and all-consuming desire. She'd been every young man's dream.

His gaze wandered back to her. She was still his dream.

A distant rumbling made him glance out the window. The sky was flashing. They needed the rain. There was a burn ban in effect and two fires had already claimed thousands of acres on surrounding properties. All it took was one asshole throwing his still burning cigarette butt out the window and, poof, a whole season's worth of work was up in smoke.

Maybe he should wake her. If it rained too hard too fast, the road would wash out and he wouldn't be able to get her back home. Not home, to Carl's, he reminded himself. She didn't live here anymore and Texas had never been her idea of home. He'd thought he might be able to change that once, but he knew he didn't have that kind of clout now.

He forced himself to work, reading over his students' notes on the dog they had in clinic at the moment. Vitals were good. The leg was healing. He flipped the page back, skimming the latest X-rays of the fracture. If they kept on track, they'd be able to send him home before Christmas, which meant Hunter might be patient-free for the holidays.

The windowpane rattled as thunder hit—closer now. A blinding flash of lightning flooded the room with white light.

"Hunter?" Jo's voice was soft.

"It's just a storm. Go back to sleep, Jo." He kept his voice low, watching her.

She rolled over, burrowing into the blanket. But the next clap of thunder had her on her feet. He saw her grab her head, leaning against the edge of the sofa.

"Still hurting?" He'd do just about anything to make her feel better. "Want me to take you home?"

She nodded, but then the sky seemed to open up. Sheets of rain dumped onto the tin roof, followed by a show of flashing lightning and roaring thunder. She looked out the window and shook her head.

He smiled. "Still afraid of storms? And you live in Washington?"

"Yes. Yes, I am." She tried to give him a look, one that showed him how capable and tough she was. But the thunder sent her from the couch to his side. "It doesn't storm like this there. It just rains…a lot."

He hesitated only briefly before slipping one hand around her waist. His heart picked up and he waited, but she was too focused on what was happening outside to notice his touch. She was warm—he could feel that through the thin fabric of her shirt. He tugged, pulling her into his lap gently, hungrily. When she sat, her body pressed against him, he couldn't stop the tremor that racked his body.

"I forgot how violent storms get here," she whispered.

He couldn't answer. She was in his arms, in his lap. She felt just the same, warm and soft in all the right places. He stared at her face, rediscovering the shape of her. He used to hold her like this for hours.

Sitting, talking, kissing and being happy. How could so much time have passed? She hadn't changed, and neither had his feelings.

"Is it… Are we safe?" she asked, glancing at him. And then she realized she was in his lap, his arms were around her. Her eyes went round. Surprised. Startled. Pleased? He couldn't tell.

He swallowed. "Inside we're safe. We should probably try to wait it out, though, instead of taking you back."

She nodded, her eyes never leaving his. He expected her to tense, to pull away from him. But she seemed just as wrapped up in him as he was in her. Her breath hitched, her gaze falling to his lips. He knew an invitation when he saw one.

He bent his head, moving close, slowly. She watched him, her breathing picking up. Did she know how she affected him? He didn't want to push her, to lose her. Everything he wanted was right here, in his arms.

And then she pulled away. "We can't do this, Hunter." Her voice was husky and not at all convincing.

"Sure we can."

"No, we can't." She pushed halfheartedly against his chest. But her fingers gripped his shirt.

He knew his need for her was there, on display, but he didn't care. He wanted her, he'd never stopped. To him, she was still his. "Why?" he asked.

Something about that question pushed Jo over the edge. She was out of his lap in no time, staring down at him with blazing eyes and an angry twist to her mouth. "Why?"

He looked up at her, confused. "You want me. At least, I think you do. And I know I want you."

She froze, her hands fisting at her sides. "You do?"

"Hell, yes." He stood as he spoke, his hands resting on her shoulders.

She shook her head, but she was staring at his mouth. "No. Hunter." He saw her indecision, her frustration. "What we *want* has nothing to do with what's *right*."

He heard "what we want" and pulled her against him. His hands cupped her face, his thumb brushing across her lower lip. He felt her shudder, saw her lips part, before she stiffened. Why was she fighting? He'd missed this, the feel of her in his arms, the wholeness he felt deep in his bones. How could he tell her, make her understand? His throat tightened as he stared at her, willing her to know what was in his heart.

Her chin quivered. "Hunter," she whispered, her voice hitching. "I can't do this to Eli. To Amy."

Hunter's chest grew cold. "Amy?"

She winced when he said the name. "Yes, A-Amy." She pushed away from him, wrapping her arms around her waist.

He didn't know what to say to that. He'd hoped that there might be some way for them to come to terms with what had happened, what he'd done. He'd never expected her to take him back, but he'd hoped she'd forgive him. She was here, but somehow Amy was still between them.

His phone rang, but neither of them moved. It could wait. "Jo—"

It rang again.

"Aren't you going to get that?" she murmured, her eyes cold.

"I'd rather talk to you."

"There's nothing to talk about." She shook her head, her anger building. "Nothing. I shouldn't be here. This—" she pointed frantically back and forth between the two of them "—is wrong."

Her words hurt. "Wrong?" He swallowed. "How can you—"

"How can I? You promised me, remember? I'm not going to let you break my heart again, Hunter. Do us both a favor and leave me the hell alone." She grabbed the phone. "Hold on," she said into the phone before tossing it to him.

He caught it, Fisher's voice reaching him. "Hunter? Hunter?"

"Yes?" he spoke into the phone, keeping his gaze locked with Jo.

"Fence is down in the far pens." Fisher laughed. "You're going to have to get Jo back into bed later on."

She crossed her arms over her chest, scowling at him. She looked so damn vulnerable, wounded somehow. But then she picked up her purse and headed to the door.

He stepped forward, blocking her path, fear rising. "Jo, hold on—"

Jo shook her head, pushing around him. "I don't want to hold on, Hunter. I don't want this. I don't want you. Not anymore." She ran out into the rain and climbed into her car.

"Hunter?" Fisher sounded stunned. "You there? You okay? Shit, I'm sorry—"

He cleared his throat, swallowing the lump to say, "On my way." He watched her car back up, then turn around, disappearing into the driving rain and darkness.

Chapter 3

Josie straightened the remaining pastries and sat in the little chair in the doorway between the kitchen and the bakery. Sprinkles lay on her back, her fuzzy white stomach bared as she slept soundly. Josie envied the dog—she could use a nap. She glanced at the clock. It was almost two, closing time.

But today she had to help with the gingerbread, mountains and mountains of it. Her dad's fall had put the gingerbread dough-making behind. Somehow, she had to make eighty gallon tubs of cookie dough in the next forty-eight hours. The Gingerbread Village was a huge part of the Stonewall Crossing's Christmas on the Square celebration. Most families made a gingerbread house to display. Some made them look like their own home, others followed the theme for the year. This year's theme, which Josie thought left a lot of room for interpretation, was Images of Christmas.

The phone rang and she answered it, pen and notepad at the ready.

"Pop's Bakery. This is Josie. How can I help you?"

"Hey, Miss… Jo… Josie. It's Eli Boone." He paused. "I have the plans for the float. Can I come by and show it to you?"

She smiled. "Sure, Eli. But I'll warn you. You might just end up elbow deep in gingerbread dough when you get here."

"O-okay." He sounded uncertain. "Can I bring someone with me?"

"Can they hold a mixer?" Josie added. "Just kidding. Bring as many as you like."

He didn't laugh. "Yes, ma'am. Be there soon."

"Sounds good." And she hung up the phone.

Eli was a good kid. He was just like his father. Or how he used to be, anyway.

She didn't linger over thoughts of Hunter. Whatever memories she had of him were tarnished somehow. She'd been so young—they both had. He'd loved her with an unwavering strength. He'd been hers and she'd been his. It had been right and good and real. Losing him was like losing a part of her, the pain of which had faded to a steady hollow ache she still couldn't erase.

But maybe the Hunter she remembered had never existed. Maybe he'd cheated on her with Amy as eagerly as he'd been willing to cheat on Amy.

It scared her, how tempted she'd been.

But saying Amy's name had snapped her out of it and pissed her off. She'd been just mad enough to drive herself home. By the time she was home, her head was throbbing in time to the beat of the rain. She'd crawled into her bed in her wet clothes, angry, needy and confused.

She'd spent the past two days not thinking about him. It wasn't really working…

And now she was going to spend some quality time with his son.

The phone rang again. "Pop's Bakery."

"Got your voice message. I talked to our librarian and she wants you to come read to the kids next Friday." The voice on the end of the line was soft, tired.

"Why, good morning, Annabeth. I'm fine, thanks for calling. How are you?" Josie teased.

"Work is crazy, girl. I'm sorry." Annabeth sighed. "How are you?"

"Not half as tired as you sound."

Annabeth Upton had been Josie's only real girlfriend in high school. She'd been there through everything, from Hunter's betrayal to her mom's endless string of weddings and divorces. Josie had tried to return the favor when Annabeth lost her husband to a sniper in Afghanistan. But she didn't know how to ease the pain of losing the man you loved while having to be a coherent, positive single parent to a rambunctious boy.

"I won't lie. I'm ready for the break."

"I can't imagine why. Being an elementary school principal is one of the easiest jobs in the world."

Annabeth laughed. "R-right."

"Are you going to get a break? Heading to Greg's family this year?"

"No, not this year. His parents offered to take Cody for New Year's so I could do something." She snorted. "What the hell am I going to do? Alone? In Stonewall Crossing?"

"Whatever you want," Josie said.

"That's the thing. I have no idea." She sighed. "So, how's it going? I know you're spread thin, with your dad and the bakery and the gingerbread craziness. And Hunter—"

"Dad's being ornery, but that's why I'm here." Josie was quick to interrupt her. Not thinking about Hunter. Not talking about Hunter. "We're heading to the doctor on Monday, so we'll see what the verdict is."

"Ready to get out of here?"

"Not really." Leaving meant going back to an empty apartment. This would be her first holiday without Wes. She didn't blame him for leaving, but she was lonely.

"You sound surprised." Annabeth paused. "And I did notice your attempt to dodge the whole Hunter topic. Not very subtly, either, I might add."

"Okay, let's talk about him."

"Let's. Over wine and dinner?" She added, "You can call Lola to come over and keep your dad company."

"Lola?"

"Josie, get your head out of the clouds and look around you. Lola, from the beauty shop two stores down the street. She's sweet on Carl."

Josie was surprised, in a good way. "And Dad?"

"I have no idea. Your dad rarely has a harsh word for anyone. So, call her so your dad can get a love life. Then we can have dinner and drinks and talk about our nonexistent love lives."

"Deal." She'd call Lola right away.

"Good. Oh, hold on." There was a pause. "Will next Friday's story time work?"

"Yes, ma'am, Mrs. Upton. I'll put it on my calendar."

"Thanks. Gotta go. Duty calls… Kindergarteners, noses and peas… Bye."

"Bye." Josie laughed, but the phone was already dead.

She stared out over the freshly mopped wooden floors, her gaze drifting around the bakery. Lola Worley was a blue-haired sweetie. And, come to think of it, Lola had enjoyed a cup of tea and a small bear claw every morning since Josie had arrived in Stonewall Crossing five days before.

She packed up a plate of pastries, patted the flour from her clothes and walked quickly down the sidewalk to the Lady's Parlor. It was cold out, surprisingly cold, but she'd been too preoccupied to think of grabbing her sweater. She pushed through the door, the smell of acetone and bleach stinging her nose. Four heads turned to look at her.

"Joselyn Stephens?" Lola stepped forward. "What a surprise."

"Afternoon, Miss Worley. I thought I'd bring by some pastries for your patrons."

"Don't that just beat all?" Lola took the pastries,

smiling. "What can I do for you, sugar? A haircut? Polish for your nails?"

Josie looked at her nonexistent nails before shoving her hands in her pockets. "I was wondering if you could help me."

Lola set the plate on the counter. "Sure thing, sugar. With what?"

"My dad. He's a little stubborn."

"Just a little." Lola Worley turned a very fetching shade of pink.

"Annabeth and I would like to go out this evening. Would you be willing to come over, take care of him? I won't be late."

Lola took in a deep breath. "I'd be happy to."

Josie could tell that was an understatement.

"Anything else?"

"Well—"

"Go on, sugar. You're among family here." Lola patted her arm.

Josie looked around the beauty parlor, where chatter and laughter filled the air. "I'm swimming in all the gingerbread. Dad won't sit so—"

"I've got a half-dozen grandsons I'll send down this evening."

"Lola, you're an angel." Josie nodded. "I'll return the favor, if ever I can."

"Aw, now, I don't know about that, sugar. I'll see you about six?" Lola asked.

"Yes. And thank you." She hugged the woman before dashing out of the parlor and back to the bakery. Eli was waiting outside with a red-haired girl.

"You can go in. I know its cold out here." She held the door open for them.

Eli nodded at her. "Hey."

"Hi, I'm Dara. Nice to meet you, Miss Stephens," Dara gushed.

"You, too, Dara." She beamed at the girl, then at Eli. Eli didn't smile back. "Can't wait to see the sketches." She waved them back behind the counter.

Eli stood between the two of them and spread open a large piece of drafting paper. A chair sat in the middle of the float, flanked by two supersize books.

"These will have the covers for *Floppy Ears* and *34*," Eli pointed out. "Mrs. Upton said she wants to get the little brothers and sisters of the Future Farmers of America kids to ride on the float with you. Make it like you're reading to them."

Josie nodded. "And these?" She pointed to two blob-like shapes.

"One will be a cow and one will be a rabbit," Dara said. "We're going to make them out of garland and wrap them with lights. You know, those topiary things?"

"It looks great." Josie was impressed. "And a lot of work."

"It was Eli's idea." Something in Dara's tone made Josie look at the girl.

"It's a great idea," Josie said. She saw Dara cast a timid glance Eli's way, saw Eli's red cheeks. Just when Eli looked at Dara, the girl looked back at the drawing.

The bell over the door rang.

"Hey, Josie-girl." Fisher was all smiles. "How's it going?"

"Gingerbread madness has begun." She grinned. "Nice of you to stop by to help."

"I'll help eat my fair share. It sure smells good." Fisher sniffed for emphasis.

"Tastes pretty good, too." Josie offered the three of them a gingerbread man.

"Damn good," Fisher agreed, eating the cookie in two bites. "You good with the plans?"

She nodded. "Since I'm not building it, yes. Looks great."

Dara's phone rang so she walked outside to take the call, and Eli followed.

"They're adorable," she said to Fisher.

"Eli's too young for a girlfriend," Fisher argued. "He's just a kid."

"I don't think they're talking marriage, Fisher." She offered him another cookie. "How've you been?"

"I'm good, real good. Nothing like living your dream while being seriously good-looking, you know?"

She giggled. "You're incredible."

"I've heard that before." He winked at her.

She kept laughing. "Behave."

"Not in my nature," he countered.

"Fisher," she wheezed. "You're going to make me have an asthma attack."

He chuckled. "Never done that to a woman before."

She shook her head. Fisher had always been funny. Once she was able to breathe and talk, she tried again. "I'm really impressed by the ranch. Looks like the family has been working hard."

"Mom and Dad set the bar pretty high. And Hunter. He's going to reach that bar, and then some. Archer's a genius, really taking the whole refuge thing to the next level. I mean, we're getting eleven abused horses—that's a lot. But he'll figure it out." He shook his head. "Now, Ryder's still more interested in cars and petite blondes than anything else, but he works hard when we need him."

"How's Renata?" Josie had always felt for Renata, Fisher's twin sister. She couldn't imagine having four brothers and Teddy Boone for a father.

"Renata's working for the chamber of commerce. Does their PR and events and stuff."

"Sounds like the Boones still own Stonewall Crossing."

"Can't help it if our people were competitive from the start. We don't own it, exactly."

"No? Just most of it?" She argued, "If I remember the little tour I took when I first moved in with dad, they said the town was named Stonewall Crossing because your great-grandfather put up stone walls to line his property."

"Great-great-grandfather. Man is a territorial animal, Josie. Those walls are a surefire way to let people know where not to trespass." Fisher shrugged.

"How is your father?" She'd missed him. Teddy Boone was a great barrel-chested man who let everyone know when he entered a room.

"Fine. He lives in the Lodge. He still misses Mom a lot. Think leading guests to check out the flowers when the hills are blooming, or hike, or bird-watch keeps him busy. In the hotter months, he's with the aunts in Montana. He's here now, so stop by and say hi. He'd love that."

She nodded. "He must be so proud of everything you have accomplished."

"Hunter started it, getting all successful. We couldn't let him show us up, you know?" He swiped another gingerbread cookie. "That Boone competitive streak. You know Hunter. Hell, I think you know Hunter best of all." His expression turned serious—as serious as Fisher ever got.

"No, not really."

"Aw, come on, Josie. That's not true—"

"Years ago, maybe." She put the sample plate behind the counter and began to wipe down the counter. "Why does everyone keep talking about the past?"

"What's got you so worked up?"

She shut the display case with a little more force than necessary. "Nothing."

"Right."

"Moving on." She shot him a look. "You dating anyone?"

He winked at her. "I'm flattered, but I don't think that would go over too well with my brother."

She hadn't meant to yell, but she did. "Why the hell would Hunter care if I dated anyone? He's married, remember?"

If she hadn't been yelling, she might have heard the bell over the door jingle. But she didn't. So Eli's angry words took her by complete surprise. "My mom divorced my dad when I was three."

Josie couldn't think. Or speak. Or breathe. The agony on Eli's face was unbearable. "I… I didn't know. I'm sorry, Eli," she finally managed.

"You should be," Eli bit out. "It's your fault she left."

"Eli," Fisher cut in.

Josie was reeling. "Eli, I…" She had no words. She knew nothing she said could make a difference.

Dara placed a hand on Eli's arm. "Walk me home?" Eli didn't look up as Dara led him from the bakery.

Her heart ached for him, truly ached for him. She knew how hard it was, growing up without a mother. If she'd been the cause of that… No, surely not. Hunter was a man of his word. He'd married Amy—he wouldn't have let it fall apart without a fight.

"What is all the yelling about?" Her father hobbled into the kitchen through the door that connected their home to the bakery. "I could hear you all the way in my room."

Josie watched Eli and Dara walk away. She saw the slump to Eli's shoulders, knew the anger and pain in his voice.

"How the hell did you not know he's single?" Fisher asked, stunned.

"What are we talking about?" her father asked.

"Hunter." Fisher reached around the counter for another gingerbread cookie.

"Oh." Her father sounded far too pleased, so she looked at him. "What?"

"What?" she echoed. "That's all you have to say?" *Hunter Boone is single.*

Her father's smile disappeared. "You told me if I ever mentioned him you'd never talk to me again. Guess I figured the more time the two of you spent together, you'd figure things out."

"Seriously, Josie?" Fisher shook his head, then ate another cookie.

"Every time I brought him up, you changed the subject. I got the point," her father continued.

"That was a long time ago." He hadn't mentioned Hunter or the rest of his family in years. Because she'd told him not to. Josie grabbed the plate and shoved it into a cabinet out of Fisher's reach. "I was young and hurt—"

"You're my baby girl. And I listened to you," her father interrupted. "I figured someday you'd find out that he was here, waiting for you."

Josie glared at her father. "Daddy, I know you love Hunter. But that's ancient history—"

"Maybe for you." Fisher's eyebrows went up.

Her father's voice was cautious. "Now, Fisher—"

Fisher leaned forward, staring into her eyes. "Ask me how many dates my brother's been on since Amy left."

She didn't want to know, did she? No. She didn't.

"Let's give her some time to get used to things, Fisher." Her father chuckled. "Her whole world just got flipped upside down."

She lied quickly, to herself and the two of them. "Nothing has changed. Nothing. I'm here to take

care of you, Dad, not relive some teenage romance."
She yanked the apron over her head and threw it on
the back counter.

"Josie," Fisher groaned. "Come on now."

She held up her hand. "Stop. *Please.*" She paused.
"I'm tired. I need a shower. I just hurt a boy that I'd
never in a million years want to hurt. So, please,
just stop."

Her father exchanged a quick look with Fisher before he sighed. "It's closing time, anyway."

"I'll lock up," Josie offered, looking pointedly at
Fisher.

Fisher took the hint. "Eli will be all right. You okay?"

She nodded but wouldn't look at him.

Fisher left and Josie locked the door behind him.
She took her father's arm, leading him back into
the house.

"Should I have told you, Josie?" her father asked.

"No, Dad." She patted his hand. There was no
way to go back. Thinking about what could have
been, what might have happened, was pointless. "It
doesn't matter. Now go sit, and I'll get you some
water. Maybe a snack?"

Her father nodded, moving slowly to his recliner
in the other room. She headed into the kitchen, grappling with too many emotions to understand. But a
part of her—a part deeply buried inside—felt relief.
He wasn't a cheater. He wasn't a liar. He had loved
her. Maybe he still—

"Josie, bring the car around," her father yelled.
"We gotta get Sprinkles to the hospital."

* * *

Hunter's cell screen lit up. *Amy.* He hadn't had enough coffee for this yet.

Tripod, the black three-legged cat that roamed the hospital, glared at the phone from his napping spot on the corner of Hunter's desk.

Hunter nodded in agreement. "I know the feeling."

Tripod yawned, stood and stretched, then curled back up in a ball on the desk. Hunter stroked the cat's silky side, letting the animal's reverberating purr calm him before answering the phone.

"How's the sexiest man in the world?" Amy's drawl was light, teasing. "Wearing your tight jeans and your jump-me doctor coat?"

He'd learned not to bite to her teasing. "How are you, Amy?" He clicked the end of his pen a few more times.

"All business this morning? Guess it's hard to talk dirty at the office." She sighed. "I'd be better if I was there with Eli. And you."

"You coming through town?" He kept clicking the pen.

"I'm trying. You know I want to be there." She sighed again. "I'd never miss Christmas with my baby if I could help it." She paused, but he kept quiet. "But I've got a chance to ride in Vegas through New Year's. Big show, you know?"

Amy spent more time with the cowboys on the rodeo circuit than riding in it, but all he said was, "I'll let you tell Eli."

She made that noise, that irritated, impatient

sound she made when she wasn't getting her way. He remembered that noise all too well.

"Don't use that tone with me, Hunter Boone. I don't need your approval or your permission."

"I know." He tossed his pen onto his desk and leaned back in his chair, staring up at the white insulation tiles of the ceiling.

"Good. You don't know how hard it is, to live without the perfect parents and buckets of money just sitting around their big ol' fancy house." Her voice was shaking. "A gal's gotta eat, Hunter."

There it was. "How much do you need?"

"I don't need a handout," she snapped.

"You're Eli's mom, his family. It's not a handout. It's family taking care of family."

The phone was silent for a long time. "You don't miss me at all? Us?"

He didn't say, "No, Amy. I don't. I won't. Stop messing with our son and grow up." He'd learned not to have any expectations when it came to Amy— then there was no disappointment. But Eli was a boy—a boy wanting to believe the very best about his mother. Even if a lot of it wasn't true. And now his mother was missing Christmas with him…again.

It tore his heart out to see his boy hurting. He was used to buying a present and putting Amy's name on it, but he resented having to cover for her. It shouldn't be his job to maintain a relationship between his ex-wife and his son.

"Dr. Boone." Jason, one of his students, came running into his office. "Larry ate Hanna's hair scrunchie again."

"Hold on a sec, Amy?" He covered his phone. "Is Larry breathing okay?"

"Yes, sir. But he's coughing a little."

Hunter sat back, ran a hand over his face. Why Larry the emu liked eating hair scrunchies was a mystery. But they could be dangerous to the animal if they got stuck in his trachea. "Please ask Hanna to set up the ultrasound machine. I'll expect her to assist in fifteen minutes." Since he'd told Hanna several times to remove her hair accessories before she went into the pen, she would help him scan the bad-tempered bird and, if necessary, remove it from the bird's long neck.

"Yes, sir." Jason left.

"Still there?" he asked.

"I'm here, waiting. But I've got people waiting, too. I'll call our son tonight." And she hung up.

He was about to throw his cell phone against the wall when a soft "Dr. Boone" was followed by a knock on his office door.

He repressed an irritated sigh as one of the school deans entered. He stood, extending his hand to the older man. "Dr. Lee," he said. "Nice to see you."

"You, as well." Dr. Lee nodded, shaking his hand. "I hear you have a procedure in fifteen minutes, so I won't keep you. But I need your help. We have received a substantial donation from the Harper-Mc-Gee family—an in memoriam for their deceased son Nate."

Hunter nodded. The Harper-McGees were one of the school's most devoted supporters. The past five generations of Harper-McGees had earned their doctor of veterinary medicine degrees from UET's College of Veterinary Medicine. Nate would have carried on that tradition if he hadn't been killed in a car accident midsemester last spring.

"Part of the donation is to be used for a mural in the waiting room. His parents have a drawing he did when he was young. They want something like it to cover the wall over the admissions desk."

Hunter looked at the drawing Dr. Lee offered him, then back at the older man. "I'm not sure—"

"Dr. Hardy told me you're very close with the local artist Joselyn Stephens. That she's visiting right now. Dr. and Mrs. Harper-McGee were delighted. They hoped you'd convince her to consider their commission."

Hunter blinked. "I don't know Miss Stephens all that well. But I do see her father now and then." He didn't know if he could see her again, to talk business or otherwise. Her angry words were a hot band around his heart.

"Perhaps you could ask her to contact me, then? Their donation is incredibly generous, Dr. Boone. I'd like to be as accommodating as possible, you understand?" Dr. Lee nodded at the drawing. "These are for Miss Stephens." He placed a sealed envelope on top of the sketch. "If she has any questions, I'm sure there's contact information inside."

Hunter stared at Joselyn's name on the envelope. "I'll get it to her."

"Thank you, Dr. Boone." Dr. Lee nodded. "Good luck with Larry."

Hunter smiled. "Good training opportunity."

The older man paused at the door. "How's the pharaoh hound?"

Hunter ran a hand over his head. "Bad-tempered. Stubborn. And spoiled." But the owners were willing to keep spending thousands of dollars on their rare breed, so until puppies were a guarantee, the damn dog was Hunter's problem.

"Any animal that needs help procreating has a right to be all of those things." Dr. Lee chuckled.

"Never thought about it that way," Hunter agreed. "We can only hope the procedure works this time."

Hunter thought letting Tut have some fun the old-fashioned way might sort out his quick temper. But the owners were determined, and footing the bill, so petri dishes, test tubes and no hanky-panky were all Tut had to look forward to.

"Poor Tut. We shall hope for the best. I do hope Larry behaves for you." Dr. Lee stopped at the door. "If I don't see you before the holiday, enjoy your break."

"Thank you. You, too." No sooner had Dr. Lee left than Hunter's office phone rang. He tried not to snap as he answered, "Dr. Boone."

"Dr. Boone, we're checking in Sprinkles, Mr. Stephens's rat terrier."

He could pass the dog off to another resident. Maybe he should. But Carl was recovering right now. And Jo— "On my way." It took him two minutes to leave the administration wing, pass the massive lecture halls and labs, and enter the teaching clinic.

The first thing Hunter saw was Josie, her arm around her father. Her hair had slipped free from

the clip on her head, falling down her back in thick
reddish-brown curls. Her shirt was covered in a fine
coating of flour; two more streaks ran across her
forehead and into her hairline. He smiled at the flour
handprint on her hip.

Her words rang in his ears, branding his heart.
But seeing her worried and disheveled only reminded
him that she was hurting, too. This time, right now,
he could make it better.

She saw him then, her gray eyes widening before everything about her relaxed. "He's here, Dad.
It'll be okay."

Damn, she looked beautiful. "Hi."

Carl was clutching a trembling Sprinkles to his
chest. "Hunter, I didn't know if you were working
the clinic today—"

"You think I'd let anyone else take care of Sprinkles?" Hunter patted the dog's head, looking into
the small canine's brown eyes. He glanced at the
desk clerk. "Call Dr. Archer in to assist with Larry.
Jason and Hanna should have him prepped and ready
to go."

"Yes, Dr. Boone. Room four is open," she added.

He nodded, assessing the situation. Yes, Sprinkles was sick, but Carl was clearly worn-out. "How
about I carry Sprinkles?" Hunter took the dog. "Follow me."

He placed his hand over the dog's chest, count-
ing the beats per minute. One thirty-six. Nothing ir-
regular. Breathing was a little labored, but Sprinkles
didn't like riding in the car, so that was just as likely
to cause her panting as anything. Once they were in

the exam room, he put Sprinkles on the metal exam table and looked at Carl. "What happened?"

"Dad, please sit." Jo pulled one of the chairs closer to the table.

"I don't know." Carl sat in the chair, resting his hand on the dog's head. "I just don't know. Sprinkles and I were watching a John Wayne flick, a good one. Then Josie and Fisher were yelling in the bakery, so I left to see what they were going on about. Sprinkles was in my chair. I came back and she's lying on the floor, acting like this." He pointed at Sprinkles for emphasis. The dog was definitely not her normal, bouncing, yapping self.

Hunter put the earpieces of his stethoscope in and listened to Sprinkles's stomach. "Did she eat anything?"

"Her food," Carl answered. "You give her anything, Josie?"

Hunter looked at Jo and froze. She was staring at him, intently. In the depths of her silver gaze he saw something that made him ache. What was going on inside that head of hers?

"Josie?" Carl repeated, making Jo jump and reminding Hunter he had a job to do.

"No, I didn't." Her hand rested on her father's shoulder. "You've told me a dozen times she's on a special diet."

Carl patted his daughter's hand.

Hunter focused on the dog. "Could she have gotten into something?"

"She gets into everything," Carl admitted.

"I've had to chase her out of my suitcase every morning." Jo smiled.

"She eat something bad? Josie, you have perfume or something that could make her sick?"

"No, Dad. Besides, if she'd drunk my perfume, she'd smell better." Jo's voice was teasing.

"That's not funny, Joselyn Marie."

Like hell it isn't. Hunter winked at Jo.

He saw the splash of color on her cheeks, the way she blinked and looked at her father. "Sorry, Dad." She bent, pressing a kiss to Carl's temple.

"I don't think we need to get too worried just yet," Hunter said as Sprinkles stood up. Her little stomach tensed and she vomited a glob of clear gelatinous fluid onto the metal exam table.

"Sprinkles," Carl groaned.

"Jo?" Hunter used a long exam swab to poke the goop. "You use any sort of face cream?"

"Yes. Anti-wrinkle gel."

Hunter stood back and grinned. "I'd check the container when you get home. Bet it's gone."

Carl glared up at Jo.

"Dad." Josie shook her head. "It was on the vanity counter, out of her reach."

"Sprinkles has always been a good jumper, if I remember," Hunter said. Sprinkles had belonged to old Mrs. Henry for three years before she'd decided a cat was less work for her. Hunter had offered to help find the dog a home. Carl and Sprinkles had taken one look at each other and clicked.

Carl nodded. "Guess I need to put on some of those baby locks to keep her out of things."

Sprinkles vomited again, shaking.

Hunter watched. "Might be best if we keep her here—"

"Nope." Carl shook his head. "I'll keep an eye on her."

Hunter glanced at Jo, who shrugged at him. "Dad—"

"No." Carl wasn't taking no for an answer. "She'll be happier at home. We can keep her in her kennel."

"You need to keep her hydrated," Hunter said.

"Anything else?" Carl asked.

"Don't feed her." Hunter glanced between the two of them. He couldn't help it if his attention lingered on Jo. "Not today, anyway. We'll see how she is tomorrow."

"Okay," she said, her gaze meeting his. "Maybe you could swing by and check on her later?"

Hunter stared at her then. He was more than willing to make a house call for Sprinkles. But he'd expected Carl to make the suggestion, not Jo, not after their exchange the other night. Did he dare smile at her? He wanted to.

"Hey, now, that's an idea." Carl nodded.

"If you're free?" She seemed uncertain, hesitant.

Now he really wanted to know what was going on in that beautiful, stubborn head of hers. "I'll stop by later." He'd leave work now if he thought it would mean more time with her. "And I'll install the baby locks, if you have them for me."

"Fine, but if we're putting you to work, we're feeding you." Carl stroked the dog's head. Sprinkles whimpered. "Come here." Carl pulled the little dog close.

"Carl," Hunter cautioned. "At least let me get you a towel. Things are gonna get messy real fast."

He saw Jo's nose wrinkle and laughed.

Carl rubbed Sprinkles's head. "See there, it's gonna be fine, little girl."

When Jo looked at him, her gray gaze was searching. She drew in an unsteady breath and mouthed, "Thank you." He couldn't stop staring at her then. He didn't want to.

The intercom buzzed. "Dr. Boone, you're needed in OR 1, please."

"On my way. Please ask Janette to bring in some diapers and a towel for the Stephenses."

"Yes, sir." The intercom went quiet.

"Thank you, Hunter." Carl shook his hand.

"Hunter, if…if you can't make it tonight—" Jo seemed nervous, flustered.

"I'll be there," he promised before leaving the room.

Chapter 4

"Something smells good," Carl called from his recliner.

"If you stay there, I might just bring you a taste," Josie yelled back. "You get up and you're having a peanut butter sandwich."

"I'm sitting, I'm sitting," her father grumbled.

"How's Sprinkles?" She finished basting the roast and slid it back into the oven.

"She's sleeping again," he answered her. "Poor little thing."

Josie shook her head. Better sleeping than needing another cleanup.

She dumped the homemade rolls into a basket and covered them with a fresh linen kitchen towel. Next she boiled some water and put in some tea bags to steep. Once Dad had lain down for his nap and Sprinkles was in a fresh diaper, she'd hurried to the small grocery store for food. She didn't know who was coming tonight. Dad, Lola and Hunter. Possibly Eli, or the whole Boone clan. A nice roast, complete with potatoes, carrots and fresh onions, had been simmering for the past couple of hours.

"You got the baby locks?" he called.

"Yes, Dad."

"You sure you have to go out tonight?" Her father kept up the semi-screamed conversation.

Yes, she was sure. What had she been thinking—inviting him over for dinner? She couldn't risk spending more time with Hunter. She wanted to, a lot, but there was no point. Hunter wasn't married—he could date anyone he wanted. *Except* her.

Eli hated her. As far as he was concerned, she was the cause of his parents' divorce. And there was no way to change that. If there was one thing life had taught her, it was that nothing should come between a parent and child. How many times had her mother missed her art exhibitions or play performances while dating or divorcing one of her husbands? Each and every time Josie was forgotten. It didn't matter that she'd eventually be drawn into her mother's new family, because that was temporary, too. Love and trust were the two things she didn't have a lot of experience with while growing up.

She wouldn't threaten the bond he and Hunter shared. In some pretty perfect world, she and Hunter might have been able to make it work. But that wasn't real life. Eli needed his father and Hunter needed his son. So, even though everything had changed, nothing had changed. Avoiding Hunter, trying to convince Eli she had no plans for his father, was all she could do until it was time to move to New Mexico—if she took the job. She'd been a vagabond for almost three years now, six months here, four months there. Signing on with the Art Institute in New Mexico would be a huge change.

She wasn't meant for love or marriage or relationships—she was too much like her mother.

Sprinkles croaked a bark, announcing their company's arrival.

"Come on in," her father called.

"Evening, Carl." She heard Hunter's voice and smiled. "What's cooking? My mouth is watering."

"Josie's been in there slaving away." She heard her father laugh. "Think she still feels guilty for poisoning Sprinkles."

"Dad!" She rubbed her hands on the front of her apron and walked into the living room.

Hunter, Eli and Dad were waiting. Her father and Hunter were grinning. Eli wasn't.

"He was funnin' you, Jo." Hunter shook his head, a bouquet of flowers in his hand.

"You brought flowers for Sprinkles?" her father asked. "Now, doesn't that beat all?" He winked at Josie. "Go get a vase, will you, Josie? We can put the flowers on the mantel there, so Sprinkles can see them."

She shot her father a look. Was he teasing? "Sure." She turned, heading back into the kitchen.

"I didn't know I was buying Sprinkles flowers." Hunter was behind her.

She spun around. "Oh?" He was so tall, so close, so mind-blowingly gorgeous. She stepped back, her hip bouncing against the corner of the kitchen counter.

"I'm a devoted vet and all, but you gotta draw the line somewhere." His eyes crinkled as he smiled.

"So the flowers were for Dad," she teased, filling up a cut-glass vase. She took the blooms, clipping the ends off.

"I don't make a habit of buying flowers for animals or old men."

She glanced at him, arranging the flowers. "Nice to know Dad's special, then. Makes sense to me."

They stared at each other for a long time. She wasn't sure what to say or do. He was just standing there. Taking up the air in the room. Staring at her, a crooked grin on his face.

"Sprinkles is awake," her dad announced, followed by the sound of the dog throwing up.

Hunter laughed. "How's it going?"

"A lot of that." She nodded in the direction of the living room. "Dad's been watching her like a hawk."

"Hello?" Lola's voice was singsongy. "How are both our patients?"

Josie relaxed.

"Evening, Miss Worley. Can I get that for you?" Eli entered the kitchen carrying a cake plate. Lola followed close behind. She gave everyone a quick hug.

"Mmm, something smells good." Lola peeked in

the stove. "You made fresh rolls, too? What a good little wife you'd make." She patted Josie's cheek. "You go on and have fun tonight. Me and the boys here will keep your dad in line."

Hunter looked at her. "You're going out?"

She nodded.

"A well-deserved night out." Lola smiled. "Just point me in the direction of the plates."

Josie showed Lola around the kitchen and handed off her apron before joining her father in the living room.

"Did you shave?" Josie asked her father. She realized he hadn't been wearing the plaid button-down shirt an hour ago. His hair had been a little less groomed, too. She leaned forward to kiss him on the cheek. "Aftershave, too."

Her father turned an adorable shade of red.

She stood, hands on hips. "Promise me you'll behave. No showing off for Miss Lola. Not tonight, anyway."

"Joselyn Marie." Her father scowled up at her.

"Don't Joselyn Marie me." She glanced behind her to see Hunter coming from the kitchen, no Eli or Lola in tow. "Thanks for stopping by, Hunter."

He nodded, his smile tight, eyes burning. Was he mad?

"Need my purse," she murmured, hurrying into her room. She ran her fingers through her hair, put on some lip gloss and earrings, and checked her reflection. She grabbed her purse and headed out, dropping another kiss on her father's head and calling out, "Thanks again, Lola."

She left through the bakery, catching the door before it slammed. She fumbled with her keys.

"You don't really have to lock up out here," Hunter said.

She spun around, dropping the keys. "Habit," she managed. "Did I get the right baby locks?"

He bent, picking up her keys. He nodded at the toolbox on the porch, then looked at her. The heat in his eyes, the hunger, stole the air from her lungs.

"You need anything? Supplies?" she murmured as his eyes slowly explored the details of her face.

He shook his head, stepping closer and offering her the keys.

She took them, the brush of his fingers against hers stirring a tantalizing awareness along her skin. It wasn't fair, that he affected her like that. One little touch and she shivered. "It's cold," she lied.

His eyebrow arched.

She scowled at him. "Night." She forced herself to take one step, then another, and another.

"Have a good time tonight, Jo." His voice was husky.

"Thanks." She didn't look back as she headed down the sidewalk to the pool hall on the far side of the square.

"So he's at your dad's house, cleaning up dog throw-up and putting up baby locks, and you're here with me?" Annabeth took a long swig of her bottle of beer. "What's wrong with this picture?"

Josie finished off her beer. "Absolutely nothing."

Annabeth groaned. "You have a warm-blooded

man waiting and willing and you're not tossing his butt into your bed?"

Josie shot Annabeth a look. "Because I'm getting drunk with you."

"Then let's go."

"I can't." Josie shook her head, peeling the label off the beer.

"You can, Josie." Annabeth took a deep breath. "I'm going to say something really harsh here, okay?"

Josie looked at her. "Um, no, thank you."

"Tough. You're being ridiculous." She shook her head, blinking back the tears in her eyes. "Don't you get it? I'd give anything to have someone to go home to. You're choosing to be alone when you have this amazing, loyal man—"

"Annabeth." She shook her head. "I'm sorry. I am."

Annabeth patted her hand. "What do you want? Do you know?"

"To get Dad on his feet again—"

Annabeth shook her head. "*You?* What do you *want*?"

"I'm not sure." She swallowed, then leaned forward. "I'm scared. Okay?"

"Please don't start with that I'm-my-mom crap, okay?"

"Eli hates me." And it killed her.

"But Hunter doesn't." Annabeth's eyebrows went up. "We went out once, did you know that? We talked about you the whole time. He's kept up with you, proud of you." She shook her head. "Whatever.

Enough about love and your need to throw it away. I want a man. Can you find me one?"

Josie laughed. "No. Don't have a lot of single men in my contacts list."

"Well, that gorgeous Ryder Boone is staring at us. I'm hoping he's checking me out and not you. That wouldn't be fair."

Josie glanced across the room. Sitting at the bar was a way-too-good-looking, smoldering-dark-and-dangerous type watching them.

"He looks annoyed." Josie tipped her beer back but realized it was empty. "So he's probably looking at me."

Annabeth rolled her eyes. "Oh, please. You don't annoy Hunter."

"You're right. *Annoy* isn't the right word."

"Arouse? Turn on?" Annabeth teased. "He just wants to jump your bones and make lots of babies with you."

"He does not," Josie argued, laughing. "Stop."

"What? What's wrong with intimacy? Seriously, Josie, you can't tell me you don't miss sex."

Josie leaned forward. "I didn't say I didn't, but—"

"So do it, have sex. Forget about the whole emotional baggage and focus on lots of good old wear-you-out, leave-you-smiling, rock-your-world, wake-your-neighbors sex."

"I'll drink to that." Ryder appeared, putting new beers on the table in front of them and making them both jump.

Josie stared at him. "God, Ryder, you're all grown-up—"

"And hot," Annabeth added. "I said that out loud, didn't I?"

Ryder looked at Annabeth, his heavy-lidded pale blue eyes smoldering. "I'll drink to that, too." He tipped his longneck, clinking it with Annabeth's.

"Please." Annabeth giggled, then rolled her eyes.

"Good to see you, Josie." Ryder was looking at her again. "Thought I'd get you ladies another round before heading out."

"Oh," Josie said. "Well, thanks for the beer."

"Thanks for the laugh." He smiled at her. "And have fun." He glanced at Annabeth. "You've got my number." He nodded at them both and made his way out of Shots.

Once he was gone, they both burst out laughing.

"I know I don't have the best field record at dating, but I think that was a not-so-subtle cue for you to call the bad-boy Boone."

Josie couldn't help but notice the very *thoughtful* way Annabeth watched Ryder Boone climb on his motorcycle.

Hunter sat on one of the rocking chairs on the front porch. He should go. Everything was done.

Sprinkles was doing better, but the diapers weren't ready to come off. The baby locks were installed and his tools packed away. While he'd worked on that, Eli and Lola had made a fridge full of gingerbread dough. Once Lola had retreated to a recliner to knit, he'd called Fisher to take Eli home. Lola dozed in the living room with Carl, so he managed to make a few more batches of gingerbread. Then cleaned up the kitchen.

When Lola walked out, she smiled down at him and patted his arm. "She's a good girl."

He didn't have a thing to say to that. He couldn't deny he was waiting around for Jo. He was.

"Walk an old lady home?" she asked.

He helped her into her coat and took her arm.

"Look at that moon." Lola pointed up at the low-hanging full moon. "Isn't it lovely?"

"Yes, ma'am." It was a gorgeous night. And there was nothing quite like seeing the town square and courthouse all lit up with Christmas lights. All the trees surrounding the courthouse were wrapped with thousands and thousands of lights. Even to his eye, it looked magical. "I love this time of year."

"Me, too, Hunter." She peered up at him. "What do you want for Christmas this year?"

He laughed, taking her keys and unlocking her door. "I'm too old for that, Miss Lola."

"Nonsense, Hunter. You're never too old for wishing. I've got one or two things on my list, but I'm not telling." She patted his arm again. "Thanks for the walk."

"Thanks for all your work."

"Josie needed a night out." Lola smiled. "Guess it's no secret I'm fond of that Carl Stephens." She waved, pulling her door shut.

Hunter set off back down the street to the bakery when he saw Josie. She lay on her back, sprawled out on the lawn of the courthouse. He didn't think—

he ran. When he reached her side, he dropped to his knees.

She looked surprised. "Hunter?"

"What the hell are you doing, Jo?" he asked, his panic quickly replaced by irritation.

"I'm looking at the lights. All the colors. It's like a giant Christmas kaleidoscope." She patted the grass beside her. "Lie down, you'll see what I mean."

He shook his head but couldn't deny the smile tugging at his lips. "Are you drunk?"

"Maybe. A little." She giggled.

"It's forty degrees. Too cold for relaxing outside," he argued. "Where's your coat?"

She sighed. "Are you going to lie down or not? You're blocking part of my view."

He stared down at her. Her cheeks were red, her breath coming in puffs from the crisp air. Beneath the thousands and thousands of lights, her hair seemed to glow a warm and inviting red. She seemed to glow, so alive, so soft. It took everything he had not to touch her.

Instead, he flopped down on his back at her side.

"It's cold," he said.

"Hush. Open your eyes and stare straight up." Her voice was soft, almost a whisper. "See how the colored strands on the street shops bleed in around the edges of your vision?"

He stared up.

"Can you see it?" she asked, her hand nudging his.

Her fingers were icy cold, so he took her hand in his. He didn't look at her or acknowledge that his heart was thumping. He held her hand and stared at the lights. And the colors seemed to bloom around the edges. "I see it."

Her hand squeezed his. "Isn't it amazing?"

"Yeah."

They were silent for a while. Nothing but the sound of the wind through the trees, the slight clicking of the bouncing strands of lights. He could think of nothing sweeter than staying right here, touching her. But each gust of cold made it harder and harder for him to ignore she wasn't wearing a jacket. And it was only getting colder.

"Jo?" he whispered.

"Hmm?"

He turned his head and smiled. Her eyes were shut. Long lashes rested against her smooth skin. Her mouth was parted slightly, releasing a regular cloud of breath into the chilly night. "You still looking at the lights?"

Her eyes popped open. She blinked, then turned to face him.

He reached up, smoothing a curl from her face. "It's late."

She nodded, her hand tightening on his.

"Can I walk you home?" he asked.

She nodded again.

He stood, keeping her hand in his to pull her up. She didn't sway into him and he didn't pull her into his arms, no matter how much he wanted to. Instead, he took one of her hands, rubbing it briskly between his. "Your hands are ice cubes."

She was staring at their hands, but he saw her shiver. "Let's get you home." He led her to the sidewalk.

"It's snowing." She grabbed his arm with her free hand, tugging. "Look."

He looked up, watching the white flakes falling. "I'll be."

"I'll be?" She laughed. "What does that mean?"

He grinned at her. "No idea."

She kept laughing. Her heavy curls hung around her shoulders, her navy blue pullover clung to her curves, and she was laughing. With him. In the snow. And the vision took his breath away. He cleared his throat, tore his gaze away and led her across the street to the bakery. He didn't want to let go of her hand, of the tender camaraderie they'd found.

"Thanks for checking in on Sprinkles," she said, opening the door and standing aside.

He followed her in. "She'll be feeling better soon. Not tomorrow, though." He smiled. "Have fun?"

She nodded, looking at him with a sudden intensity. "Annabeth likes to remind me to stop and have some fun now and then."

"Sounds like good advice."

"You think so?" she asked, still assessing him.

He nodded.

"Ryder thought so, too."

"Ryder was there?" He frowned.

"He bought me a beer."

"I bet he did." Women were drawn to Ryder like bees to honey. "Do I want to know what he considers fun?"

It had been a long time since he'd wanted to slug his brother, but the telltale blush that crept up Jo's neck said enough.

"He didn't really suggest anything. He just sort of agreed with Annabeth."

"What did she suggest?" He waited, beyond curious now.

She rubbed her hands together. "I think she worded it something like no-strings-attached, wake-your-neighbors sex."

He had no response for that. Part of him wanted to volunteer for the job. But the other part, his heart, knew there was no way he could ever have a no-strings-attached relationship with Jo. "And what do you think?"

"Well... I'm a little drunk." She grinned at him. "So it's probably something I should think about later. But it has potential, maybe."

He smiled. "Get some sleep, Jo." He opened the front door, glancing back at her.

"Sweet dreams, Hunter." Her sleepy-soft smile tempted him.

He swallowed, knowing damn well what his dreams would be. "You, too, Jo."

Chapter 5

"Pop's Bakery," Josie answered.

"Josie, it's Lola Worley."

Josie smiled. "Morning, Miss Lola. Staying warm?"

"You bet, sugar. Not liking the ice on the roads all that much, though." She paused. "I've got a favor. I know you're busy and all, but my grandson Tyler's in a fix."

Josie waved at the two older cowboys leaving the bakery. "What can I do?"

"Well, his uncle George was planning on coming in to talk to the kids about being a farrier for Career Night. But this ice has closed the roads and he can't get here."

"That's a shame."

"It is, it is. Especially since Tyler's getting extra

credit for bringing in a speaker. He's having real trouble with math this year, let me tell you. Would you be willing to stand in? As an author, not a farrier."

She laughed. "That's a relief. I don't even know what a farrier is. When is it?"

"Tomorrow night. I know it's short notice and all—"

"I don't mind at all." She paused, thinking of her dad. "Would you be free to keep Dad company?"

Lola laughed. "I was hoping you'd ask."

"Lola—" Josie hesitated. "Why don't you just tell my dad you're sweet on him?"

"Josie!" Lola was laughing harder now. "I'm not going to do everything for the old coot."

"When you put it that way," Josie conceded.

"It starts at six. I'll be over at five-thirty?"

"Okay."

"I'll see you tomorrow night. Don't you worry about feeding me, either. I make a chicken potpie your daddy just adores. Bye now."

Josie was still smiling when she hung up the phone.

"Any more gingerbread?" Josie looked up into the face of Teddy Boone. He had pale blue eyes framed by thick brown lashes. And when he smiled, as he was doing now, he had a wealth of fine lines to emphasize his good nature.

Josie was rooted to the spot.

"You better get over here and hug me, girl." Teddy waved her forward.

Josie ran around the counter and into the man's waiting arms. "Hi, Teddy."

"Hi, yourself." He held Josie back, inspecting her from head to toe. "You're a sight for sore eyes."

"And you look exactly the same."

He made a dismissive sound. "You look good, girl. Have time to sit and have a coffee? Or are you on the clock?"

Josie looked pointedly around the almost empty dining room and shrugged. "Coffee sounds good."

Teddy sat while Josie put a few sugar cookies and gingerbread men on a plate. She poured two cups of hot coffee, added some eggnog and carried the whole tray to the table.

"You look like you're getting the hang of things here," Teddy said once Josie sat.

"It wasn't that long ago I worked here, remember?" She grinned. "If Miss Worley and Eli hadn't made so many tubs of dough, I'd be in big trouble."

"Glad Eli was a help." Teddy sipped his coffee. "He's a good boy. But he has his moments."

"Doesn't everyone?"

"Reminds me a lot of his daddy." Teddy nodded. "How's your dad?"

"His checkup yesterday went really well. He can start walking and doing a little."

"A little, huh? Good thing you're here." He took another sip, his gaze meeting Josie's. "Planning on staying?"

Josie shook her head.

"You're missed around here."

Josie stared at the sugar cookies on the plate. "There's a lot I've missed about Stonewall Crossing."

"Oh?" Teddy took a gingerbread cookie. "Hunter said you're working with the kids on their Christmas float."

"I haven't done a thing except tell them how nice the float looks." She smiled. "And it does."

"What else have you been up to? You've been moving around a bunch."

She nodded. "I think being restless is part of the artist thing. But I've been offered a job teaching art at my alma mater in New Mexico."

"Good for you." Teddy looked impressed. "I always knew you'd do good things. Like your books. Eli's copy of *34* has a frayed spine and dog-eared pages, we read it so much. It helped him through some tough times. Hunter, too, I think."

She stared at the cookies. Before Eli hated her, he'd found comfort in her stories. And that was something. That he and Hunter shared them was all the better. The rush of heat in her cheeks assured her that, yes, she was blushing. Teddy's broad grin assured her that, yes, he'd noticed.

"Any more stories in the works?"

"Actually," Josie admitted, "Stonewall Crossing at Christmas deserves a story. Maybe." It had been a long time since she'd felt the pull of her sketch pad and writing journal, and she'd missed it. "But you're the first person I've told, so let's keep it a secret for now."

"Just me?" Teddy's brow furrowed. "No fella?"

"No. And that's okay." She shrugged. "I haven't found the right guy yet."

Teddy's smile was huge. "No?"

Josie couldn't help but smile back. "No."

"Well, I best be on my way. But I really do want to buy some gingerbread dough, please, ma'am. Something we can give our guests with hot chocolate. Been meaning to talk to your dad about letting me sell some out at the Lodge—good for business and all."

"Is that Teddy Boone?" her father called from the door that connected the house to the bakery.

"Hello, Carl." Teddy was all charm. "How's the hip, old man? Time to get you an electric scooter or is that walker working for you?"

"Kind of you to offer me yours, Teddy. But you can keep it for now. Come back in a month and I'll race ya, grandpa," her father shot back.

She wasn't sure if their back-and-forth jabs were adorable or pathetic, so she just stood there, hands on her hips, smiling.

"You're a lucky bastard, Carl. For not breaking your hip—" Teddy paused, smiling at Josie "—and for your sweet daughter."

"Don't I know it." Carl lifted two buckets of gingerbread onto the counter. "On the house. The least I can do after Hunter installed all those locks. According to Lola, he made a couple of batches, too."

"He did?" Josie asked, surprised. That's why he'd stayed late? After tending to a sick dog, a grumpy old man and household repairs—he'd stayed late to make gingerbread. And walked her home without kissing her good-night. She swallowed.

"You would have known that if you hadn't gone out partying with Annabeth." Carl sighed.

Teddy frowned. "Now, Josie, you need to be careful. You don't want to go 'round attracting the wrong sort of fella's attention."

Josie looked at each of them, then burst out laughing. "I know. Stonewall Crossing is full of shady sorts," she teased. At the look on their faces she added, "I'll be careful."

"Thanks for the gingerbread, Carl. I'll make sure Hunter knows it's from you." Teddy winked at her. "So good to see you, girl. Carl, I want you and Josie to come have dinner with us. Holiday dinners are always nicer when you're surrounded by friends and family."

Before she could argue, her dad said, "We couldn't impose on you, especially during the holidays, Teddy."

Thank you, Dad. No way she was up for a big Boone family dinner, during the holidays, with Eli reminding her of the wake of destruction she'd never meant to cause. No way, no how—

"I wasn't asking, I was telling." Teddy shook his head. "I'll see you both next Saturday, night before the parade and the Gingerbread Festival."

"Well, then, I'll bring some of my Portuguese sweet bread and some dessert."

"Perfect." Teddy picked up the two tubs of gingerbread. "This is gonna be the best holiday in a long time."

If that was true, then why was her stomach twisting in knots?

* * *

The heat was cranked up in the teachers' lounge, making Hunter shed his coat and hang it on one of the hooks on the far wall. He made a beeline to the coffeepot. Between Mars's deteriorating condition, the box of baby raccoons left outside the clinic doors and the explosive meltdown of one of his students, he needed a big cup of coffee to keep going. When he got home, he was going to have a couple of glasses of something stronger.

"Thanks for covering at the last minute," he heard Annabeth Upton saying to someone. "When Tyler told me he'd roped you into Career Night, I figured you couldn't say no. Not with your dad's love life in the balance."

He turned to see Annabeth and Jo, chatting just inside the teachers' lounge. He swallowed the last of his coffee and poured himself another. He didn't know how often he'd thought of her, eyes closed and lying in the snow, but the image warmed him from the inside every time.

"They're adorable," Jo said to Annabeth. "If I can just get my dad to man up and court her, I won't have to worry over him being alone."

"Says the woman who insists there's no good in relationships," Annabeth countered.

"I didn't say that." Jo sighed. "I said *I* was no good at relationships."

No good at relationships? His Jo? How could that be? They'd fit together naturally, mind and body. He'd never laughed as much or yelled as loud as he had when he'd been with Jo.

"Because you refuse to try." Annabeth shook her head, seeing him. "Which is a conversation for later. I'm going to make sure everyone's checked in."

Oh, to be a fly on the wall for that conversation. He crumpled the empty coffee cup and threw it in the trash.

"Sure." Jo watched Annabeth walk away before turning to look around the room. She looked a little lost, hesitant. And then she saw him and rolled her eyes. "I should have known you'd be here, Dr. Boone. All impressive in your white coat."

He glanced down at his white coat. "Jealous? I have an extra one in the truck."

She shook her head. "No, no, no. Wouldn't want anyone to think I could perform an emergency *something* on their…parakeet."

He nodded. "Emergency parakeet procedures are pretty damn tricky."

She laughed, surprising them both. "Good to know."

He tried not to stare at her eyes, her lips, the way she brushed the curls from her shoulder. He cleared his throat. "Here to inspire a future generation of authors?"

"Warn them, really." Jo smiled. "I was a last-minute addition."

"That was real nice of you, Jo." He hoped he wasn't imagining the flush on her cheeks.

"You two ready?" The high school principal, James Klein, asked. "We've got you both in the barn. Sorry, Miss Stephens, George Worley was a farrier, after all. Not the normal setup for an author, I guess. But it's a pretty impressive barn, you'll see."

Hunter tried not to smile at Jo's sigh. She knew all about the high school's barn. It was the place he'd kissed her until they were both dizzy. It had been a very good day. He glanced at her, unable to resist teasing her. "You ever been in the ag barn here, Miss Stephens?"

Her gray eyes went round, then narrowed. "Hmm, I don't think so. Nothing springs to mind."

He pretended to grab his chest. "Ouch."

She nudged him. He nudged her back.

"You started it," she murmured as they entered the barn. "You know that expression—if you can't stand the heat, get out of the kitchen."

"I like the heat, Jo." He winked at her. He missed the heat, her heat. He just didn't know if she'd want to know that. Or if she'd care.

"Dad." Eli sprinted up, his open smile and enthusiasm stamped out as he saw Jo. There was no denying the anger that tightened his jaw. "Miss Stephens," he all but snapped. Hunter didn't know whether his son needed a firm talking to or a long, strong hug.

Hunter watched Jo's startled blink, the effort it took to make her "Hi, Eli" somewhat cheery. It killed him. To see Eli fuming. To see Jo so hurt. He didn't know how to make it better, for either of them.

"Well—" Jo's voice wavered a bit, making him press his hands against his sides so he wouldn't reach out to her. "I guess I'll go see where I'm supposed to be." She stepped away from them.

"Follow me." Mr. Klein led her to the other side of the barn.

"What's she doing here?" Eli asked, his tone a little too sharp, too hostile.

"She's keeping Tyler Worley from failing algebra, Eli." He looked at the boy. "Watch your tone, son."

Eli frowned at his father, shoving his hands in his pockets.

"Eli." Hunter sighed.

"They set your table up over here." Eli walked away, kicking at bits of straw and dirt as he went.

"Hunter." Mr. Klein hurried up to him. "Would you mind sharing the space with Miss Stephens? There's a draft over there, something fierce."

"She's got a coat." Eli's grumble was too low for Mr. Klein to hear it, but Hunter did.

"I don't mind at all. Eli, go see if Miss Stephens needs help with anything." The look he gave his son left little room for misinterpretation. This might not be the time to discipline Eli, but the two of them were going to have a serious talk before the night was through. He wasn't about to let his son treat Jo with anything other than respect.

Eli's lips thinned, but he nodded. "Yes, sir."

Five minutes later, he and Jo were introduced to a group of twenty or so kids by the principal. Hunter sat on the edge of the table, letting her go first. It was the polite thing to do and he wanted a few more minutes to just look at her.

"Hi. As Mr. Klein said, I'm Joselyn Stephens. I'm an artist and an author. Art has always been an outlet for me." Jo's voice was soothing. "I used to finger-paint the walls in my parents' house. As you can imagine, that didn't go over well."

He smiled, envisioning a little Jo—all curls and smiles—joyfully smearing colors around the house.

"My parents hid the paint for a few years." The kids laughed. "Once I'd learned that walls weren't the best place to practice, my dad bought me my first art set. He was about to be deployed overseas. He told me to paint him pictures of home. So, instead of letters, I sent him pictures. He was the one who told me my pictures told stories. In time, other stories sort of popped up."

A girls hand shot up and Jo pointed at her.

"Are your stories really about here? Stonewall Crossing?"

Jo shrugged. "Yes." She glanced at Hunter then. "Some of the stories started right here, in this barn." She waved her hand at the empty arenas. "I wasn't very good at the whole animal-raising thing."

"I wouldn't say that." Hunter crossed his arms over his chest, shaking his head.

"Because you're a gentleman." She rolled her eyes and a few kids laughed. So did he. "Anyway, this was so foreign to me. I made notes and did so many sketches on everything that went into raising animals, exercising them, and the importance of stock shows. Once I was done with college, I'd learned how to put together a story. That's when I finished *34*. And, yes, it was based on Dr. Boone's state championship calf. The one that sold for *how* much at auction?"

Hunter waved her question away.

"Were you two *friends*?" a girl asked, the emphasis on *friends* unmistakable.

Hunter glanced out, his gaze wandering over the crowd. But then he saw Eli, standing by the show ring, scowling and frustrated. The way his son looked at Jo broke his heart.

Jo's voice wavered, drawing him back to the conversation. "Yes, we were friends."

"How do you start? Writing, I mean?" Hunter asked her, trying to redirect the conversation.

Jo looked at him, relieved. "The pictures. I have some author friends who don't write picture books and they start with a character. It's a pretty individual process."

"Is college really necessary?" another boy asked.

"I think it is," Jo argued. "I think college is a good move for anyone, no matter what they plan on doing with their life. Think of it as a way to expand your horizons." She paused. "I kind of stepped in here at the last minute. Does anyone have any questions?"

"Is this what you always wanted to do?" a girl asked.

He watched Jo, amazed at the smile that spread across her face. "It is. It makes me happy. I mean, it also makes me really unhappy, like when I get stuck on a story."

Jo stopped then, her smile fading. He followed her gaze to Eli. His son wore a look of pure disdain. Jo's voice distracted him. "But I guess all professions have ups and downs. Right, Dr. Boone?"

"Yes." He swallowed, hoping he didn't look as thrown as he felt. "Definitely."

"How did you get into veterinary medicine?" she asked, sitting on the edge of the table, deferring the floor to him.

"I grew up working with animals. My father and his father and his father before that. I wanted to heal animals early on. Everything from field mice to injured hawks." He pointed at the display board one of his teaching assistants had put together for him. "School was a challenge. I got accepted early, before I had my undergraduate degree. I won't kid you—school is tough and very competitive. But it's important to understand that some things take work to achieve. You have to want it. You have to do the work."

He talked for a while, trying to include Jo in the questions being asked, but she'd withdrawn. One look at his son spoke volumes. It would be hard to engage when someone was staring daggers at you. And there was no denying the resentment on his son's face.

Chapter 6

"I'm going to walk Lola home," her father announced.

"Now, Carl," Lola argued as she pulled on her thick coat.

He grinned, buttoning Lola's top button. "Hush now. Doc said it would do me some good. Didn't he, Josie?" Her father looked at her.

Josie managed to nod.

"See there?" Carl opened the doors. "Might take me a little longer, though—"

"I don't mind." Lola tucked her hand into his arm, winking at Josie. "Night, sugar."

"Night, Lola." She stared at the empty doorway long after they'd left. Her dad might just be catching a clue. *About time.*

"Jo?" Hunter's voice was soft, his knock on the screen door startling her.

"Hunter?" She braced herself. "Come in."

The past hour had been at once the best and worst time she'd had in a long time. She missed having that spark, that zippy back and forth that she had with Hunter. The way he smiled that crooked smile, arched his brow at her—she didn't know whether she wanted to kiss him or run far, far away.

And then there was Hunter's son. There was also the possibility that Eli's scowl might actually kill her. She'd been on the receiving end of quite a few stare-downs in her time, but she didn't know how to respond to Eli. If only there was something she could do or say to defuse some of his rage.

"Hey," she said, peeking around him, expecting Eli to join them. "How many future vets do you think you made tonight?"

"Maybe a few."

"It's the coat," she teased. "Something about its white splendor is so…so enticing."

"Is it?"

She rolled her eyes. "Why don't you ride on home before you freeze, cowboy?"

He laughed. "I'm going, I'm going, but I keep forgetting to give you this." He pulled a white envelope from his coat pocket. "I know you probably don't have time for this, but I promised I'd pass it along to you."

She stared at the UET Veterinary Medicine envelope. "Is it an order form for my own white coat?"

"You wish."

She chuckled.

Silence set in, long and awkward. She didn't have the nerve to look at him. Not now. Instead, she stared at the envelope in her hands. "Well, thanks for this." She tapped the corner of the envelope in her palm. "It's late—"

"Jo." His voice changed, from teasing to husky and a little too sexy in two minutes flat.

"Oh, am I supposed to open this now?" she asked, tearing the top of the envelope. She pulled out the papers, skimming over the letter. This was a commission? A very well-paid commission. For a mural for the waiting room at the teaching veterinary hospital.

"No." He sighed. "I was… I was wondering if you're free for dinner tomorrow night."

She stared at him, the commission forgotten. "But…" Did he not notice his son's reaction tonight? "Hunter—"

"Jo." His voice was a whisper. He moved forward, his eyes sweeping over her face.

Her entire body seemed to quiver, waiting for his touch. She stepped back but, somehow, he seemed even closer.

"Don't say no." His words were so low, gruff.

She couldn't say anything. Not now, when he was looking at her like that. Instead, she swallowed, searching for some sassy comeback to counter the dangerous warmth spreading through every single cell of her body. In two steps, her back was against the wall.

He stepped forward. "One night. No history. No interruptions. Just me and you."

"A date?" Her question was a whisper.

His hand reached up, gently grasping one of her curls. Something about the way he caressed her hair made her ache for his touch. "What do you say, Jo?" His eyes met hers. Blazing, electric, the pull almost physical. He released the curl, placing his big hands on either side of her head.

She blew out a shaky breath, unable to hide the effect he was having on her. His mouth was so close, his breath caressing her skin. His gaze explored her face, slow and intense. His nostrils flared and his jaw went tight. She sucked in a deep breath and tilted her head, an unmistakable invitation. Her heart kicked into overdrive as he leaned forward. She closed her eyes, waiting, ready, willing, bursting.

His forehead rested against hers.

"I'm not going to kiss you until you say yes," he rasped.

Her eyes popped open. "Yes," she answered quickly, too quickly. Not that there was any point in denying what was happening. They both felt it—they both wanted it.

His gaze searched her face, long and slow. Then he smiled and stepped away from her. He shoved his hands in his pockets and cleared his throat. "I'll pick you up at seven o'clock."

She stared at him, in complete shock. "But...but I didn't—"

"You said yes, Jo," he said softly.

"Hunter, that's not what I was saying yes to."

"What were you saying yes to, then?"

She swallowed. No way she was going to admit

she wanted him to kiss her, not with him standing there all cocky. "But my dad—"

"Tomorrow's bingo at the Senior Center. Think they're having a holiday party after that and I'm sure, what with Lola being there and all, he'll be going." He waited.

No arguing now. She stared at him, knowing he'd won. "Okay," she murmured.

"Wear something nice."

"Wear something nice?" she muttered.

His smile grew.

"Why are you smiling like that?" she bit out.

"I feel like smiling." He shrugged.

She tried to glare at him, she really did. But his smile was just too infectious. She liked him smiling. She liked that he could make her want to smile. Like now. In fact, there was no way she could stop the one spreading across her face.

The front door opened. "You two done? I'm getting a touch of frostbite out here." Her father walked in, rubbing his hands together.

"Dad." She wrapped an arm around her dad and led him into the living room. She tugged his recliner closer to the fireplace. "Sit and warm up. I'll make you some hot chocolate."

"Checking on Sprinkles, Hunter?" her dad asked as he sat. "Come on in and warm up. Josie can make you some hot chocolate, too, can't you, Josie?"

She glanced at Hunter. To her extreme aggravation, he laughed. "I'll have to take you up on that some other night. Eli stayed to help Mrs. Upton clean up, but I imagine he's ready for me to pick him up by now. You still playing bingo at the Senior Center tomorrow night?"

"Wouldn't miss it. Lola's asked a few of us over for a late dinner afterward." She heard the satisfaction in her father's voice.

"So you won't mind if I take Jo out for a bit?" Hunter asked.

She glared at Hunter. Was he asking her father permission? "Oh, please—"

Her father held up his hand. "I'll be honest, Hunter, I have a few concerns. Josie's lighter fluid and you *are* her match. You two left a lot of destruction last time around, for all those that love you."

She paused again, wrapping her arms around her waist. Her attention fixed on her father. He might be teasing, a little, but he was also making a point. She'd been so angry and hurt, she hadn't stopped to think about anyone but herself, not her father, the Boone family or Hunter. And she sincerely regretted the way she'd shut everyone out. "It was a long time ago, Dad." She tried to sound flippant but failed.

"It was," her father agreed. "But some wounds take a lot of time to heal—if they heal at all."

Hunter stiffened. Carl's words hung there, too big to ignore. He couldn't help but look at Jo then. The older man was right—some wounds took a long time to heal. He never wanted to open himself up to a hurt like the one he'd felt when Josie had left. It had broken him, clawed at his insides until he'd worried he'd split in two. But she hadn't left because of what had happened with Amy. She'd left him before Amy had been in the picture. She'd left because she'd wanted to.

Her gray eyes were looking everywhere but at him. He wondered about that. Did she know how alone he'd felt? That his love had felt insignificant when she'd tossed it aside so quickly.

Her college admissions letter had been her golden ticket out of Stonewall Crossing. Away from him. He knew the art program in New Mexico was the one she wanted most in the country. And he wanted only the best for her. He'd dropped hints about doing his undergrad work anywhere, but she'd never acknowledged them or asked him to come with her. She'd just left. He didn't blame her for leaving, for following her dreams. But it killed him to know that he hadn't been a part of them. To him, it had been their future. To her, it was about getting out and starting over.

That wound was one he still wasn't over.

What happened after that was all his fault. Jo had been gone for months, her calls getting further and further apart. He'd missed her, missed feeling loved and needed. Amy had been all too willing to ignore his drunken state and lead him home to bed.

Jo had been hurt—he'd hurt her. And he hated himself for what he'd done to her heart. If there was a way to apologize, to undo the heartbreak one tortured night caused so many people, he would. But Eli was the result of that one night, and his son was his life. Even if Jo was still the love of his life.

Hunter realized Jo was watching him, her forehead furrowed. "If you're against it—"

"I didn't say that." Carl waved his hand. "It'll be

good for you two to have some time, to work through whatever it is that's there. And enjoy some holiday cheer while you're at it."

Whatever it is that's there. His heart knew exactly what was between them. Jo's gaze met his then and his throat went dry.

"And Sprinkles is fine," Carl went on. "She's been trying to scratch her way through the linoleum for some…" But Hunter was watching the panic creep into Jo's eyes.

She was thinking, overthinking, letting her mind take over and fill in all the silent spaces with doubt. She'd always been real good at letting her head overrule her heart.

"…but she's eating fine," Carl finished.

"Good." Hunter nodded. "Glad to hear it."

Jo was scowling at him. And she looked mighty fine doing it. One look from her made it all too easy to forget any past hurts and move on to their next adventure. He knew the two of them would be better than ever, if she'd give them the chance.

His phone started vibrating. "Eli?" she asked.

He heard the catch in her voice as he checked his phone and glanced her way. "Yep."

She smiled. "It's awful cold, Hunter. Too cold to leave him waiting outside for long."

He shook his head. After the knives his son had been shooting at her all night, he was fine with letting his son suffer a few minutes of cold. "He's fine."

She scowled again. "Hunter—"

"I'm going." He patted Carl on the shoulder. "Enjoy your hot chocolate." He walked right up to Jo.

"I'll see you tomorrow night." And, before he could stop himself, he dropped a kiss on her cheek. When he stepped back, her eyes were huge. She might be surprised, but she wasn't angry. If anything, she looked pleased. Not that she was happy about it.

He winked at her, ignoring the way she frowned in irritation, the way she stood straight as if prepping for battle. He touched his hat at Jo, said good-night to Carl and slipped from the house.

It was cold and dark, a steady pelting of icy rain clicking against the sidewalk. But, even with the winter wind cutting through his thick Carhartt jacket, he wasn't too bothered. If anything, he was excited. It had been a long time since anticipation warmed him.

"Took you long enough," Eli mumbled when Hunter arrived at the high school. But he didn't let his son's tone or long-suffering sighs get to him. Instead, he turned up the radio, blasting Christmas carols the entire ride home.

Once he'd closed the door behind him, he turned to find Eli waiting. "Dad," his son began.

He put his hands on his hips. Eli had no idea how close he'd come to being publically put in his place. "Yep?"

"I owe you an apology."

That was the last thing he expected to hear. "You do?"

"Yes, sir." Eli looked at him. "I was disrespectful."

"To me?" he asked, trying not to feel impatient.

Eli's mouth pressed shut.

Hunter sighed. "Why do you think you owe me

an apology? You weren't bound and determined to make me uncomfortable tonight."

"I wasn't trying to make anyone uncomfortable tonight."

Hunter shook his head and hung up his hat and coat. "Now you should apologize."

"I just did," Eli shot back.

"No—" Hunter folded his arms across his chest. "Not for your behavior tonight. But for the lie you just told."

Hunter watched his son. Eli had a temper on him, but he'd never let it slip. It killed Hunter to see his son's hands fist, see the raw anger twisting his boy's features. That was bad. But watching his son turn, storm out of the room and slam his bedroom door shut behind him made Hunter feel as if he'd been kicked in the gut.

Chapter 7

Josie was tired, bone-tired. But watching Dara and Lola at work, being part of their comfortable chatter, made the daylong baking less of a chore. When Dara and her father had shown up early this morning looking for breakfast, Josie had offered to let Dara stay and bake while he did some holiday shopping. Lola had knocked on the door at seven, bringing in a basket of fresh biscuits and some fresh jam, and set to work alongside them. They'd been mixing, baking and decorating gingerbread, sharing stories and laughing the whole time. At the rate they were going, they just might have a complimentary cookie for everyone in Stonewall Crossing.

Dara piped an icing smile onto the gingerbread girl she was finishing, then placed a small gummy spice drop right in the middle of the bow she'd made. Josie watched the girl, noting the satisfaction on her young face. "Sure you've never done this before?" she asked.

Dara shook her head. "My mom doesn't like to bake. If she can't buy it at the store, we don't have it at our place."

Lola clicked her tongue. "Well, that's just wrong. Baking is good for the soul." She paused, winking at them both. "If not for the waistline."

They laughed.

"You're welcome to lend a hand anytime," Josie added. "Once you're old enough to hire, believe me, I'll tell Dad to hire you."

"He does too much on his own. The ol' coot," Lola agreed. "Would do him some good to hire some help."

Josie agreed. When she couldn't sleep, she'd organized her father's financials. He was making a tidy profit. He didn't need to be a one-man show. Josie loved seeing him relaxing, putting on a little weight, smiling and laughing. He needed to get out, to have a life beyond the four walls of his bakery. With Lola Worley.

"If I can convince my mom." Dara sounded a little wistful.

"She doesn't want you working?" Lola asked. Lola, Josie noted, didn't mince words when it came to conversations. "A woman should have skills."

Josie agreed. But there were women, her mother included, who still believed the best career a woman could have was marrying a rich man. Her mother's idea of a well-rounded education had included pouting, exercising and the importance of thorough grooming. Aging gracefully was a concept her mother disdained. She claimed it was an excuse for letting yourself go and getting complacent.

"I think my mom worries about me. She doesn't want me to be a housewife. She wants me to be a lawyer or doctor or something." Dara shrugged, her cheeks turning a deep red. "I like making things."

"What do you want to do?" Josie asked the girl.

"I don't really know. Do I have to? Right now?" The young girl looked between them both.

"No." Lola laughed.

"Sometimes I still don't know," Josie added.

Annabeth arrived. "Hey, guys. Sorry, Cody's play-date got started late. What did I miss?"

"Dara wants to know when she has to decide what she wants to be," Josie said.

Annabeth frowned. "Ugh. Not for years and years?"

"Good." Dara sighed. "I'm more interested in learning to drive and what my first kiss will be like."

Josie, Annabeth and Lola shared a smile.

"Sounds about right to me." Lola gave Dara a one-armed hug.

"You remember your first kiss?" Dara asked Lola.

"Of course I do." Lola nodded, moving cookies from the baking pan to the cooling rack. "It was with Theodore Boone."

"Really?" Josie glanced at the woman.

"Do tell," Annabeth said as she washed her hands before jumping into the cookie making.

Lola nodded, a look of pride on her face. "I was

a looker and the menfolk were all very flattering. Of course, Magnolia hadn't moved to town yet, so I didn't have much competition. But he was sweet on me. So was my Henry. In the end, Henry was the right pick—even if Teddy was a better kisser." She giggled. "Henry got better, in time. You have to train them right."

Josie laughed, taking note of Dara's round eyes and startled expression.

"Speaking of first kisses, I'm assuming Hunter was yours?" Lola asked Josie.

Josie nodded, staring at the dough.

"Take after his daddy?" Lola asked. "Meaning, he knows how to kiss a girl?"

Dara made a strange little noise at the back of her throat.

Annabeth giggled and Josie sighed. "Lola—"

Lola looked back and forth between the younger women. "What?" She waved a dismissive hand at Josie. "Dara should know what she's got to look forward to. It's plain to see Eli's sweet on her."

Dara squeaked this time.

"Lola." Josie couldn't help but laugh then.

"Fine, fine." The older woman went back to rolling out a new batch of dough, grinning from ear to ear.

After a few minutes of companionable silence, Dara asked, "Where's Dr. Boone taking you tonight, Miss Stephens? Not much to do around here, unless you're playing bingo."

Lola nodded. "And no offense to you, sweetie,

but you two are too young to be hanging out with my crowd tonight."

"What?" Annabeth tossed some flour at Josie. "You're going on a date?"

"Yes." Josie smiled. "I don't know where we're going or what we're doing. He just said to wear something nice."

Lola looked thoughtful. Dara and Annabeth looked excited. So why did she feel petrified?

"Nice?" Lola tapped her chin with one finger. "Hmm, sounds like he's got *something* planned."

Josie nodded. That was why she'd spent most of the night tossing and turning, wondering what Hunter had planned—what he was thinking. No answers were coming, so she'd climbed out of bed and started baking. At 3:00 a.m. She stared down at her flour-covered shirt. "I'll definitely need a shower."

Dara giggled. "Don't worry, Miss Stephens. You're one of the prettiest women I've ever met."

"Isn't she?" Annabeth smiled.

"And just as nice on the inside, too," Lola agreed. "Where it matters most." Lola looked at the young girl. "Don't you let anyone tell you different, either, Dara, you hear?"

"Yes, ma'am."

Josie nodded in silent agreement with Lola. If her father was man enough to make an honest woman out of Lola Worley, she'd finally have the mother she always wanted. Lots of advice, love and willingness to lend a hand when needed. Nothing like her flesh-and-blood, look-but-don't-touch mother.

"I wouldn't worry too much about what you wear," Lola said. "It's clear that boy's got it bad for you."

Lola's words were hardly comforting. It's not that she didn't want Hunter to have feelings for her... Wait, she didn't want that. Did she?

Dara stopped piping icing onto the cookie and said, "That's true, Miss Worley. The way he looks at you, Miss Stephens." She sighed. "Like a present on Christmas morning. It's like he wants to talk to you, you know? Really talk to you. Like he has something important to say, but he's too nervous."

Josie stared at the girl, torn. Did Hunter really look at her like that?

"He's always looked at her like that." Annabeth laughed. "He looks like that when he talks about her."

Lola arranged a fresh tray of cookies on the cooling rack. "It's the way a man should look at the woman he loves—"

"Lola," Josie cut her off. "I think... I think I'll wear a dress. Maybe?"

"He's not the only nervous one." Lola nudged Dara.

Dara glanced at Josie. "Is that normal? To feel all..." The girl shrugged. "Out of sorts, in a good way, of course. Like you can't stop thinking about them. Even when you want to stomp on their foot and never talk to them again?" Dara added with a hint of agitation.

It took a lot to keep Josie from laughing.

"Oh, most definitely," Lola agreed. "The more irate they make you, the fiercer the love is."

"Within reason, Dara," Josie offered. "Fireworks are fun, but they can be destructive."

The others looked at her again, this time without the smiles.

"How are things going with my father?" Josie asked, needing a diversion. And because she was curious.

"You and Mr. Stephens?" Dara looked shocked.

"It can happen," Lola said. "Even at my age."

Dara shook her head. "I didn't mean that, Miss Worley. I guess I didn't think Mr. Stephens was all that aware of women."

"Oh, honey, men are always aware of women." Lola started cutting out new cookies to put on the tray. "Some of them are too old to do anything about it."

Josie sincerely hoped her father did not fall into that category.

"And some men have been too burned to know how to try again." Lola was looking at her as she said that last part.

"Maybe they shouldn't. Maybe they should move on," she murmured.

"Man's heart doesn't always wander the way his eye does, Joselyn. I'd hazard to say quite a few fellas I know are far more true-blue than a lot of lady friends I have." Lola put a new tray of cookies into the oven.

"Listen to your heart," Annabeth added.

"Isn't that a song?" Josie tried to tease.

"Oh, stop it. I'm serious. Do what you can to make your heart and soul happy." Annabeth spoke with such force Josie paused. Yes, Dara was young and naive and full of hope. But Annabeth and Lola had been married, happily. Maybe she shouldn't dismiss what they had to say.

What did she want? What did she really want?

They spent the next few hours listening to music, sharing stories and laughing. They taught Dara to do the chicken dance. Lola taught them the twist. And Josie's dad joined them long enough to share chicken and dumplings for lunch.

"I'd best be heading home," Lola said, hanging her apron on the hook by the counter. "Not much time to pull myself together before the festivities tonight."

"Thank you for all your help," Josie said as she hugged the woman.

"No problem at all." Lola smiled. "You have fun tonight," she said, pulling the door shut behind her.

"I should probably head out, too." Dara hung her apron beside Lola's. She glanced at Josie. "The thing is, I really like Eli. Or I did. But now that he's acting rude, I'm not so sure."

Annabeth looked at the young girl. "Eli's been rude to you, too? I couldn't believe the way he acted at Career Night."

"Oh, no, not me." She blushed, shaking her head. "But toward you, Miss Stephens—"

Josie shrugged. There was no denying the way Eli felt about her.

"I know he's worried his dad's going to get his heart broken. Oops, sorry." She looked at Josie. "I think it's sweet that he wants to protect his dad, but not how he's going about it. I mean, can't he just talk to his dad? Can't they come to some sort of understanding?"

"Men don't talk the way women do." Annabeth sighed. "They'll work it out, eventually."

Josie felt sick to her stomach. What was she thinking? Why was she considering going out with Hunter, knowing that his son was dead set against her. She tried to smile at Dara. "Try not to be too hard on him, Dara. I know he's a good kid."

"It's natural for him to be worried. Maybe even a little jealous, too, since Hunter hasn't been interested in another woman...well, ever." Annabeth laughed. "You're uncharted territory."

Josie nodded. "I need to talk to Eli. I would never come between him and his dad. He's been lucky to have a strong family all his life. I don't want him to think I'd try to change that."

Dara's father showed up shortly afterward. Josie and Annabeth sent them on their way with a plate of Dara's cookies.

"You ready for tonight?" Annabeth asked. "Do we need to have *the* talk?"

Josie rolled her eyes. "Um, I don't think so."

"Just don't get too far into your head, Josie. Try to have fun. Try to remember that this is the guy you loved with your whole heart." She hugged Josie. "And try to remember that if you marry him you'll live here and we can hang out and have fun."

The bakery was too quiet once Annabeth left. All Josie's fears and insecurities reared up, reminding her how clearly wrong tonight was. She should get out of town earlier, put a few thousand miles between

Hunter and her heart, for all their sakes. It was the right thing to do. Her dad was getting better now that he was listening to the doctor. And Lola was around to help keep him on the road to recovery. Now she needed a way out of tonight.

The phone rang. "Pop's Bakery," she answered.

"Wear your sexy underwear." Annabeth's voice was laced with laughter. "Not your cotton granny panties."

Josie groaned. "There will be no underwear viewing tonight." She chewed on her lip. "As a matter of fact, my head is killing me—"

"No, it's not," Annabeth argued.

"Yes, it—"

"Stop it, Josie," Annabeth snapped. "You're fine."

"It's my head. I think I know when I'm getting a headache."

"Oh, please. You are chicken."

Josie sighed. "Maybe. A little."

"Well, that's just pathetic. I have to get my kicks from naughty texts, while you're passing up on the real deal."

Josie's interest was piqued. "Naughty texts? With who?"

"No one you'd know," Annabeth huffed in exasperation. "Besides, texts can't compare to actual kissing and touching. Period."

There was a pause.

"Does your head really hurt?" Annabeth asked.

Josie closed her eyes. "A little."

"Fine. Take Advil. Cancel tonight and add it to your list of regrets. Go to bed. Whatever."

"Gosh, thanks."

"You can't expect me to support your life on the sidelines, Josie, you just can't. Your *dad* is getting more action than you are."

"Um, gross." Josie winced. "I'll call you tomorrow."

"Sure, I guess," Annabeth muttered. "I mean, if there's anything to tell."

She hung up, put the cookies away and did a lightning-fast cleanup of the kitchen. She stopped to nudge her father awake before heading to the shower. A long, steamy, hot shower gave her time to consider her options. Lola and Annabeth said to listen to her heart, but Annabeth also said to listen to her libido. Unfortunately, or fortunately depending on how you looked at it, both her heart and her libido were supremely interested in spending the evening with Hunter Boone.

She could cancel tonight, book a flight and leave first thing in the morning. But then she'd be letting people down…again. And, dammit, she didn't want to be that sort of person. She didn't want to be her mother.

Okay, fine, then she was staying. She was going on the date with Hunter. And she was not going to overanalyze everything that happened.

Her closet didn't have much to offer. She'd packed for caregiving and nights in with her dad, not dates or a night on the town. She had one black dress, no frills. A clingy wrap dress that was cut low but traveled well. Her only real option.

She laid the dress out on the bed and opened her underwear drawer. Pretty silky garments or practical cotton foundation wear. That was the real question.

Chapter 8

Hunter tugged at the collar of his shirt, adjusting the collar and tie for the fifth time since he'd parked in front of Pop's Bakery. He felt like an idiot. He was too old to be getting dressed up, to feel this tongue-tied and flustered.

Eli was right. What was he thinking? A vision of his fuming, red-faced son didn't ease the knot in his throat or the twist in his gut. They'd never argued like that, ever. The two of them were thick as thieves, working through any disagreement without losing their cool. He'd raised his son to be rational, looking at a situation from all sides, putting himself in the other person's shoes and keeping an open mind. And, thank God, Eli was like him—no drama.

But when it came to Jo, Amy had planted a seed

of hate deep in his son. He hadn't realized just how deep until Jo got here, until he saw the look in his son's eyes and knew how much he blamed Jo for his and Amy's divorce.

Was he a bad father for leaving Eli angry and taking Jo on a date? Was he selfish for wanting time with her? Eli sure as hell thought so. Tonight was something Hunter had to do. If he didn't try, if he let Jo slip away, the regret would cripple him.

He pushed the truck door open, a blast of frosty wind forcing it wide. Pulling his jacket tight around him, he hurried up onto the porch, out of the wind. But then he froze, staring at the door, nervous and uncertain all over again.

He was about to knock when he heard a strange thumping followed by a highly frustrated shriek.

"Sprinkles!" He knew that sound. Jo was fit to be tied. And Hunter couldn't stop the smile that spread across his face. "Stop, dammit, I need that."

Clicking, probably Sprinkles nails on the wood floor, followed by more thumps. He knocked, but there was no answer. He waited, then eased the door open. "Hello?"

"Come on, Sprinkles, give it to me." Jo's voice was muffled. "If you're a good girl, I'll give you a treat." Sprinkles barked in answer.

He closed the door, sealing the cold out. "Jo?"

"I swear, dog." Each word was getting louder, less coaxing. "I will buy more face cream and leave it out just for you."

He chuckled, following the sound of her voice into the back of the house. "Jo?"

"That's it, Sprinkles," she cooed. "Just a little closer."

He found her then. Halfway under her bed, her fuzzy robe revealing two long, toned legs and barely covering her mighty fine rump. "Jo?" He cleared his throat.

Jo squeaked, rearing up. A distinct thud made him wince. "Damn, Jo, you okay?"

Her groan was muffled. "I see stars." She pushed herself out from under the bed, one hand coming up to hold her head.

He knelt beside her. "I didn't mean to scare you. I knocked, I promise."

"Yeah, well, I didn't hear you."

He nodded.

Her face was screwed up tight from pain. "I'm not exactly ready."

"I got that."

She opened her eyes, scowling at him. "Damn dog ran off with my stockings. Once she'd decided she was done with them, she took off with my brush."

"How'd the stockings hold up?" he asked.

She shook her head. "They'll be good for tying up Dad's tomato plants in the spring." She rubbed her temple. "Ouch. Goose egg."

He leaned forward, noting the red welt rising along her hairline. "You always did have a knack for scrapes." He tilted her head back, trying not to appreciate her bared creamy shoulder or the long curve of her graceful neck. "Let's get some ice on that."

She sighed, pointing under the bed. "*She* still has

my brush. And unless this—" she pointed at herself "—is acceptable for a night out, I need it."

"Let's get some ice." He stood and held out his hand to her. "Then we'll get the brush." He pulled her up, catching a whiff of citrus and soap. She smelled like heaven.

"I meant to be ready. I did." She reached up to cradle her head. "That dog hates me."

Hunter chuckled. "She's probably a little jealous of you."

Jo paused, disbelief plain on her face. "Jealous?"

"Sure. You're an interloper." He led her into the kitchen, putting ice into a clean kitchen towel. "It's natural for her to assert her dominance. Or try."

"I thought that meant peeing on my shoe or something." Jo took the ice pack and pressed it to her head. "Thank you for the ice."

"I didn't mean to scare you, Jo."

She smiled, waving his apology away. "I know." Her expression changed, nerves and uncertainty clouding her clear gray eyes. She fidgeted, tugging her robe down while trying to smooth her hair. Her hand landed on one of the large rollers covering her head and her eyes went round. She froze, shook her head and sighed, closing her eyes. "My mother would die. No, no, she would disown me for this." She pressed the ice to her forehead.

He laughed. "I won't tell." He paused. "But I'll see if I can get your brush for you. I don't know if the museum has a dress code or not, but I'm pretty sure hair rollers and bathrobes aren't on the short list."

She adjusted her ice pack so she could level him

with a sexy-as-hell, narrow-eyed smile. "Museum?" She was interested, he could tell.

"An Impressionist exhibition. A few Monets. Still your favorite?" Her anger gave way to surprise, then pleasure...then something else that was warm and promising. His lungs emptied, hard and fast.

He stooped, breaking the connection to search cabinets. He didn't want to get sidetracked from the night he'd planned. If he wasn't careful, it'd be all too easy to get lost in her silver-gray eyes. He kept searching until he found the dog treats. "Good thing there's a lock on this one." He pulled the bag from the cabinet and shook it. Jo, he noticed, was pulling rollers from her hair and tucking them into her robe pockets. She was awkward and nervous and all sweet, soft woman.

"Does my head look bad?" she asked, smoothing her hair before holding the ice back to her temple.

He shook his head but didn't trust himself to speak. Instead, he called, "Sprinkles. Come on, girl." He kept shaking the bag, hoping the crackle it made would be too hard for the little dog to resist. It was. The rapid *tap tap* of Sprinkles's claws announced her speedy arrival. She sat, putting her little paws up to beg. He gave Sprinkles a biscuit and graced Jo with a smug smile.

"Oh, please." Jo sighed. "Really?"

"I get this from all the girls," he teased.

Jo burst out laughing then. "I bet you do." She stood, setting the ice and towel in the sink. "I'll leave the two of you alone while I go recover my brush... and anything else she's hidden under the bed."

He watched her go. Her pockets might be bulging with rollers, but the sway of her hips was unmistakable.

Sprinkles scratched his jeans.

"That's how it is?" he asked, giving the dog another biscuit. "You don't deserve another one, picking on Jo like that."

Sprinkles whimpered, spinning around twice.

"Yeah, you're cute and you know it."

Sprinkles sat and yapped at him, ears perked forward.

"No!" Jo's cry had Hunter headed back down the hall to her room.

"What now?" he asked, leaning against her door frame.

She spun, holding her dress out to him. "Hates me." Holding up the dress, it was clear to see a series of tiny teeth marks along the little slit up the back of the dress.

"I can stitch it," he offered. "Believe me, this is nothing." He took the dress from her, inspecting the tear. "Needle and thread?" He glanced at Jo to find her staring at him, her expression thoughtful.

"Hunter, I can wear something else." She glanced around her room.

He did, too. "Uh-huh." Organization wasn't one of Jo's strong suits.

She grinned at him. "Fine." She hurried out of the bedroom, returning minutes later with what looked like a mini black suitcase. She handed it to him. "Thank you. Again."

"My pleasure." He took the dress and bag and

headed back into the living room. "I'll let you finish your hair or whatever." Because if he stayed there, in her disaster of a bedroom, he'd never want to leave.

Josie sucked in a deep breath as she climbed into the truck. "I'm sorry about tonight."

"What for?"

"Where should I start? Finding me crawling around on the floor in a robe. Having to apply first aid on my head, sewing my dress up—"

He laughed, a deep, rich sound that filled the cab. "That's not exactly the way it happened."

"Storyteller, remember?" she teased.

"Not the way your dates normally start?" he asked, still smiling. He started the truck and backed up, pulling down Main Street.

"If I had a normal dating protocol, I'd have to say no." She laughed then. "What about you? I guess playing doctor is a possibility—"

"Nope." He shrugged. "Not much opportunity, between work and Eli and all."

"No?" She didn't want to point out that she'd been here for less than two weeks and he'd found the time to cook her dinner, make a house call for her dad and take her on a date. "I can't imagine how hard it is, being a single parent." Not that she hadn't thought about being a mom. She had, a lot. But motherhood meant relationships and that, she knew, wasn't going to happen.

He shook his head. "Not really, not for me, anyway. It's more like Eli's got four fathers. And my dad and sister, Renata, make sure to spoil him now and then."

Eli was lucky to have so much love. Eli, who couldn't be happy about his father's date tonight. She sighed, not wanting to think about the rage she'd seen in the young boy's eyes, not tonight. "So, what do you do, besides work and fatherhood?"

"That's about it, Jo," he answered, amused. "A man's gotta sleep."

She sighed. "So you're a hobbyless, dateless hermit?"

He chuckled. "What about you?"

"I work, a lot. And when I'm not doing murals or teaching classes or working on a book, I'm painting. You know me..." She broke off, glancing at him. "Guess I haven't changed all that much."

He looked at her. "Not much." He turned his attention back to the road, but she saw the way his hands tightened on the steering wheel and wondered at it. "Dad mentioned a new job. Does that mean you're moving?"

She nodded. "New Mexico Art Institute offered me an artist-in-residency position. It could be a great opportunity. Guess it's time for me to think about putting down some roots."

"And New Mexico is where you want to be?" If it was, that was all the answer he needed.

"I don't know. After spending the day with Annabeth, Lola and Dara, I've learned one thing. I'm not sure what I want. Except that, if I don't make some decisions, I'll be homeless and unemployed." Her laugh sounded forced—she heard it. But she was beginning to wonder if the job, the move, the starting over, was really what she wanted.

"That's not true, Jo. You'll always have a home.

Carl would love to have you back in Stonewall Crossing. I know it's not where you imagined yourself ending up, but—"

"I don't mind it," she admitted. When she'd been lying there, wide-awake, she'd mulled over the possibility of staying there longer. Her new story idea was really shaping up. Who knew, if she stayed, maybe more ideas would come. "Stonewall Crossing, I mean."

"No?" He sounded surprised.

"Not anymore. Time and distance can put things into serious perspective. I was so…so ready to escape. Not that I had anything to escape from, but I didn't get that then. Dad was good to me, more than good. Things were stable." She dared to glance at him. "I… I was young. And stupid. And scared."

"Of?"

"Life has shown me one thing, Hunter. When things *were* good, when I was safe or happy, it wasn't going to last. If I stayed and…" She didn't finish the sentence, because she'd lost Hunter, anyway. She'd left because she was too scared to fight for him, to trust him, and her worst fears were realized. "Like I said, I was young and stupid. Somehow I thought leaving would make it less painful—since it was my choice."

"Jo." He sighed. "Your mom's version of family and love was messed up. I won't argue with that. But you had Carl. You had people who wanted you to stay." His tone was hard. "People who would have gone with you, if you'd asked."

People who would have gone with you, if you'd asked. She stared at him, stunned. Was he talking about him? Was he—

His phone started ringing. He pressed a button on the steering wheel. "Dr. Boone."

"Hunter, Archer here." The clipped voice spilled into the truck cab. "Mars is in trouble."

Hunter's head dipped, his voice tight. "Define *trouble*."

"Accelerated heart rate. Labored breathing. Hold on." There was some background noise, rustling and voices. "Pups are fine at the moment. You'd wanted me to let you know if something changed, so I am."

Even in the dim illumination, she could see Hunter's jaw lock.

"You need to go?" she asked. She didn't know who Mars was, but Hunter was worried. If Hunter needed to be with Mars, then that's where they needed to be. "Let's go."

"There's no reason for you to come in," Archer said. "I can handle this."

"Hi, Archer," Josie called. "I was just telling Hunter I wanted to come visit the hospital, you know, without Sprinkles as a patient."

"You sure?" Hunter asked, already pulling onto the shoulder of the road.

She nodded. "Absolutely."

His crooked smile warmed her heart. "All right. I'll be there in twenty minutes." And he hung up, pulling across the empty four-lane road and heading back to town. "Are you sure you don't want me to take you home?"

"Sounds like you need to get there. And I'd be up for a tour of the hospital, after you save the day in your dashing white coat, of course."

"You said it was irresistible," he reminded her, grinning broadly.

"Did I?"

He sighed, shaking his head.

"I know you can't talk about the case. Doctor-patient confidentiality and all that," she teased. "But I *am* curious."

He shook his head. "Why doesn't that surprise me?"

"Do you always get attached to your patients?"

"No." He smiled. "But every once in a while, an animal stands out. Depends on their personality, their nature. Just like people."

"That makes sense," she agreed. "Some people are way more likable than others."

He laughed. "Ain't that the truth?"

"You just said *ain't*." She giggled.

He shot her a look as he turned into the parking lot and parked in front of the large glass doors. The lights cut through the dark, casting a welcoming glow into the cold night. "Mars is a sweet thing." He got out of the truck.

Before he could come around and open the door, she hopped out. "You don't have time to be all gentlemanly right now." She hooked her arm through his and pulled him toward the door.

The thick glass doors slid open without a sound and four faces peered at them over the admissions desk.

"Dr. Boone," one of the young men said. "Dr. Boone…er, your brother is in OR 1 waiting for you."

"Dr. Boone, don your super coat and save Mars." She glanced at him. "Okay, admit it, that sounded *hilarious*."

He laughed, reaching up one hand to stroke her cheek. She froze, her heart racing and her lungs desperately seeking air while his intense blue-green eyes bore into hers.

"Good luck," she whispered.

He nodded. "Be back soon." His attention wandered to the fourth-year students at the desk and his hand fell to his side. He shot her a small smile, then disappeared behind the swinging door labeled Staff Only.

She waved at the students sitting behind the admissions desk before taking in the waiting room of the teaching hospital. Last time she was here, she'd been too caught up in her father and Sprinkles to appreciate the facility. She read over one of the framed articles hanging on the wall, baffled by the list of contributors and clinicians praising the work done at the school and the educators on staff. UET wasn't just one of the best teaching hospitals in the country but, apparently, the world. *Good for you, Hunter.* The sting of tears surprised her, but the swell of pride didn't. She'd always known Hunter was capable of anything.

Movement distracted her, drawing her attention to the massive aquarium full of brilliantly colored fish and coral. She wandered closer, watching the rich sunshine-yellow, vibrant cobalt-blue and fiery-red fish hide behind whatever cover they had.

"Would you like some coffee?" a young woman asked.

Josie turned around. "No, thank you." Her stomach grumbled, loudly. "But I'm starving. Have you guys eaten? And where can a girl order pizza around here?"

Chapter 9

Hunter stroked Mars's head. "You did good." He spoke softly, noting the dog's respirations and heart rate on her chart. Normal. They'd made the decision to go ahead with the surgery on her back tonight, since the dog would already be sedated. A few pins in three vertebrae. They'd realigned her spine and alleviated the stress off her compressed nerves. In a few days, they should know if Mars would recover use of her legs.

"She'll be fine." Archer checked Mars's IV solution. "Puppies are, too. I told you there was nothing to worry about."

Hunter glanced at his brother. Archer wasn't a fan of small-animal medicine. His passion was large animals, not someone's lapdog. If Mars had been a bull or even a mountain lion, Archer would be over-the-top excited right now. Instead, his brother was almost bored.

"Cute puppies," one of the students, Lori or Linda or something, said.

Hunter nodded. They were. Two yellow and one feisty chocolate. All healthy and, undoubtedly, hungry. "Need to get some formula mixed up." He washed his hands, mentally going over Mars's chart again.

"I can do that, Dr. Boone," Marco, one of the veterinary assistants, offered. "Tonight was awesome, totally awesome, getting to assist."

"Nothing too edge of your seat." Archer led him to the door. "Go on, Hunter, finish your date."

Hunter clapped his brother on the shoulder. "Thanks for the call and the help."

"I would say that's what brothers are for, but this is also my job." Archer tucked his glasses into his coat pocket and headed toward his office.

Hunter laughed, making his way from the operating room and through the maze of hallways and patient rooms to the front desk. When he pushed through the waiting room doors, he found Jo standing on top of a chair, measuring the wall with a yardstick. Two of his students stood nearby, watching Jo as she teetered on one foot.

"Do I want to know?" he asked, crossing to Jo. She'd twisted her hair up, two pencils sticking out of the messy bun at the nape of her neck.

"Hey." She was all smiles, for him. And he liked it. "How did it go? Is Mars okay?"

"Fine." He nodded.

"Puppies, too?"

"Puppies, too." He wanted to grab her out of that chair and hold her close. "What are you up to?"

She frowned at him. "I'm not up to anything."

"You're standing on a chair with a yardstick." He arched an eyebrow and waited.

"I had to do something while you were working."

"And that would be?" he asked, aware that both students were trying to edge their way back to the admissions desk without being noticed.

"Nothing." She held her hand out to him, rolling her eyes in exasperation. He took her hand, noticing for the first time that she was barefoot. He helped her step down from the chair, smiling down at her.

"What?" she asked.

"You're just so damn cute."

She grinned. "You're not so bad yourself, Dr. Boone." She smoothed her hands over his shoulders, her fingers skimming the collar of his white lab coat. "It's the coat."

He had trouble focusing. "Hungry?"

She shook her head. "We got pizza." She pulled him over to the admissions desk. Five boxes of pizza were spread over the counter. "They were hungry. I figured you'd be hungry, so—"

"You bought pizza." He looked at the students. "Been a quiet night?" he asked them. "No calls?"

One of the students jumped up, reading from the call log. "We did have one call about a dog that couldn't go to the bathroom."

Hunter shook his head. "Talk about an eventful night."

"So, pizza?" Jo asked. "Canadian bacon and mushroom?" Which was his all-time favorite pizza. She'd remembered.

He nodded, taking the box one of the students offered, watching Jo cross the waiting room to a set of chairs. That's when he saw the papers spread across them.

It was the mural, the note from Dr. Lee and several more pages stapled together. "The commission?"

She nodded, holding up the picture, then looking at the wall.

He sat, holding the pizza box in his lap. "You thinking about it?" He pulled a slice of pizza out, waiting, nervous.

She glanced at him, the picture, the wall, then him again. "You said it—the only guarantee in my future is uncertainty. I guess…" She swallowed, looking at the picture in her hands. "I guess I'm toying with the idea of staying. For a while, maybe."

"Good plan," he managed, taking a huge bite of pizza before his smile revealed how happy she'd just made him.

She turned to him. "It's a lovely idea. The mural, I mean."

He nodded. "You ready for that tour?" he asked, grabbing another slice and standing. "Might help you make up your mind about the mural." And staying.

She tucked all the papers back into an envelope. "Lead on doctor."

And he did. They toured the exam rooms, the

pre-op area, the post-op area, the operating rooms, the lecture halls—pretty much anything that would impress her, he showed her. The hospital was just as big a part of his life as the ranch, and her opinion mattered. And then he pulled out the big guns.

"These are Mars's puppies." He pointed to the three pups wiggling around on a heat pad wrapped in soft blankets.

"Poor little things." Jo's forehead creased. "Think they're looking for their mom?"

He smiled. "That blanket belongs to Mars. They're getting plenty of mama-scent and not having to fight to eat. Bottle-fed pups have it easy."

"Where's mom?"

"She'll be sleeping for a while. If she's all right, we'll put them with her for a while tomorrow. We'll just wait and see." He reached into the box, cradling one of the pups in his hand. "She'll do better with her babies around her." He assessed the puppy, turning it over, lifting its head, running his fingers over the small stomach and smiling when it whimpered.

"Pass inspection?" Jo asked, watching him. Her eyes seemed to make note of everything he did without revealing a thing.

He set the puppy back on the mat. "This wasn't what I had planned for tonight."

"So I shouldn't be flattered you arranged all this—" she pointed at the puppies "—for me."

He stepped closer. "Is that what you're feeling? Flattered?" Her cheeks turned a rosy red and hope bloomed in his chest. He reached up, pulling the pencils from her hair. It tumbled around her shoulders.

She held his gaze, her voice husky. "What are you up to, Dr. Boone?"

"Kissing you," he answered, cupping her face in his hands.

Her breath hitched before she stepped in toward him, tilting her head back.

He bent his head, his mouth finding hers, sealing them together. He groaned and pulled her against him. Her curves made thought impossible, but he could hear alarm bells ringing in his head. He softened his kiss, keeping it tender, gentle and teasing.

Before he lost himself to the feel of her, he stepped back and drew air deep into his lungs. "It's late," he whispered. But the sight of her made the fire in his stomach burn higher. Her eyes were still closed, her face still angled for his kiss. "Jo?"

Her eyes opened, heavy-lidded and dazed.

He pulled her back against him. One hungry look was all it would take to make him forget about going slow. His arm kept her close while his fingers traced the side of her face. "I should get you home." He needed to say it, out loud, so he'd do it.

She blinked in confusion. Her cheeks flushed a deep red as she put some space between the two of them. She took his hand in hers and nodded.

"Thanks for the ride," Dara said, climbing out of Josie's little red rental car.

"Thank you for all your hard work." Jo put the car in Park. "Dad's cookies always taste good, but I don't think they've ever looked so pretty. I know people will be really impressed at the parade, Dara."

The girl's blush was precious.

"Do you need help carrying any of this?" Josie glanced in the backseat at the bags of lights Dara had brought to decorate the float.

"I can make a couple of trips if you need to get back," Dara said.

"The bakery's closed. Between Dad and Lola, I think they've got things under control." She smiled at the girl and turned the car off. "I didn't want to be the third wheel." She was very pleased to see her father kiss Lola on the cheek this morning, in front of half of Stonewall Crossing. She figured the other half knew all about it by now. "Besides, the weather's too pretty to miss." For the first time in three days, the sun was warm and the breeze wasn't frigid. She climbed out of the car and popped the trunk, revealing more lights and some green plastic garland.

If she was completely honest with herself, she wanted to stay. This was where her story was coming from. The parade, the holiday, the float. Something about those lights in the park, all warm and brilliant, like the colors of Christmas wrap and holiday dresses, had started her off. Then the float, the kids, all stacking up to be a wonderful holiday story of small-town Texas life—what she wrote and illustrated best.

The fact that they were putting together the float at Boone Ranch was another perk.

She'd fallen asleep with the searing memory of Hunter's kiss still hot on her lips. It wasn't as if she hadn't been kissed plenty of times—she had. But this was more than a kiss. And, since she was admitting things to herself, she might as well face the fact that she was falling in love all over again. She just didn't know what to do about it.

"Hey, Josie." Fisher joined them. "Looks like you got here just in time."

"Oh?" she asked, looking up at him.

"We were about to head into town, for more of these." He reached into the trunk and pulled out the garland. "Eli, Tyler, Rogan!" he called, waving them over to her car. "You staying to help?"

"If you need it," she said, risking a glance at the boys hurrying to the trunk.

"More help is always needed," Fisher said. "Come on."

"Man, Dara, you buy the place out?" Eli was all smiles for the girl.

Dara was playing it cool. "We got what was on our list," she said, handing out bags. "Hope it's enough."

Fisher nodded. "Should be. If not, we can get Hunter to stop off on the way home to pick up anything missing."

So Hunter wasn't here to run interference between her and Eli. But that didn't matter. No interference was necessary. She could be charming. She could show Eli she wasn't really an evil homewrecker. Well, she could try. She winked at Dara, grabbed the last shopping bag of lights and her art case, and headed toward the trailer.

She worked for two hours. Every time Eli walked by she'd smile or say something funny, but he'd just nod and keep going. Dara joined in, making Eli wander by more often, but still no luck. While she was doing everything in her power to draw Eli out, Dara seemed just as determined to shut the boy down. She hoped Dara wasn't still holding his moodiness against him. She tried to observe the two of them, unobtrusively. Eli was polite, asking to help or to bring the girl a drink. Dara was equally polite, but there was no denying her disinterest. They were too young for this, weren't they?

Preteen romantic drama aside, she and Dara worked hard. They wrapped garland tightly around the four-foot wire frame that would eventually be a topiary rabbit. Once it was suitably green and fluffy looking, they started to unroll lights.

"Looks good." Hunter's voice startled her.

"Well, hello there, stranger." And just like that she was happy. "How was work?" She stood, stretching her back after being hunched over for so long. "How are the puppies?"

"Pups are getting fat, like pups do." He stepped forward, close enough to touch her if he wanted to. And, from the look on his face, he was thinking about more than touching her.

She stepped back, glancing around. She may want him to touch her, but this wasn't the place for it. Eli wasn't glowering at her...yet. "And Mars?" she asked, dropping back to her position beside the lights.

Hunter sat beside her. "She's good. Some movement today."

His nearness complicated her breathing, so she stared at the tangle of lights in her lap.

His voice was low. "You don't want me to kiss you."

She glanced his way, then back at the mess of lights. "No."

He cleared his throat before asking, "No, never again or no, not right now?"

She heard the hesitancy in his voice and met his gaze. "Not right now," she managed to whisper. She wasn't ready to make a public statement with him.

He gave her a quick grin, then asked, "Need help?"

"You should take a break, Miss Stephens," Dara said, taking the lights from her. "I got this. We get volunteer hours."

Josie smiled at Dara. "Okay." The wind kicked up, cutting through her flannel shirt and the thermal underneath. "When did it get cold?"

"Clouds rolled in." Hunter looked up at the sky. "Four years without snow or ice and now we're getting both."

"Guess it followed me from Seattle." She glanced at the sky. "If you're sure you don't need me…"

"Leaving?" he asked, standing beside her.

"No." It took a lot not to hold his hand. "I thought I'd stay awhile and draw. If that's okay?"

"Anytime, Jo. Make yourself at home."

Chapter 10

No matter what Hunter was doing, he was aware of her. She'd staked out her perfect location on a large willow rocking chair on the corner of his porch, tucked her legs beneath her and opened her sketch pad across her lap. Her presence, her grace, the fluid movement of her pencil back and forth across her sketch pad, fascinated him. Some of her hair had slipped free from her braid and lifted, dancing in the wind, but she didn't bother tucking it into place. She was lost in the world she was creating.

By the time the sun was on the horizon, he was dragging. The float was always an exercise in patience, for the kids and their parents. But in the end nothing smoothed feathers and filled everyone with pride like seeing their work come together. Now that the build was behind them, the mood grew more celebratory.

"I called Gabriel, and he's getting the grill ready," Carol Garcia, one of the moms, said. "Anyone hungry?"

Hunter smiled at the explosion of whistles and yells from the kids. A quick glance at Jo showed she was completely unaware of anything going on around her. He accepted handshakes, offered a few claps on the back, helped locate stray phones or coats, then rounded up any remaining supplies before everyone loaded into their cars and trucks. But Jo kept working.

"Dad?" Eli pulled his coat on, looking more animated than he'd been all day. A glance over his son's shoulder showed Dara climbing into the Garcias' family car. "Greg Hayes wants me to sleep over after the cookout," Eli all but begged.

Hunter looked at his son. He'd been a real handful all day, sullen one minute, smiling and funny the next. He didn't know what to do with him, but he knew keeping Eli home would result in another bout of pouting and he didn't have the energy or the patience for that right now. "Fine. But listen to his folks, remember your manners and don't be too late tomorrow."

Eli nodded, a strange look settling on his face. His son's gaze bounced back and forth between him and Jo. "Okay." His son swallowed before asking, "You gonna come to the cookout for dinner?"

Hunter shook his head. "But you have fun."

Eli's mouth tightened. "See you tomorrow." He

shot Jo another look—a look that almost made Hunter call his son back to his side for a talking-to. But he was beginning to wonder if talking to Eli was the answer. This might be a situation Eli should work through on his own.

Hunter nodded at Greg's dad as Eli climbed into the truck. With a nod back, Mr. Hayes and the boys left.

He walked around the trailer, checking wires and cords, testing the rope tie-downs and tucking extra blankets in. He stood at the edge of the porch and coughed several times, loudly. Jo stretched, arching her back and bending her arms as far back as she could. He watched her come back to reality, slowly, confusion registering as she took in the deserted lawn. "Everyone gone?" she asked. She shivered, turning her big silver-gray gaze toward him.

He nodded. "Didn't want to interrupt you."

"I totally zoned out." She tucked her pens into the small zipper case at her feet. She stood, nodding at the trailer. "That looks amazing."

"You sound like you're surprised." He took the steps two at a time, coming to stand by her on the wooden porch. He turned, surveying the trailer.

"No, not really." She nudged him in the side.

He nudged back. "You were gone today."

She glanced up at him, a slight furrow on her brow. "What do you mean?"

"When you work." He let his gaze wander over her face; the tip of her nose was red. "The world around you fades away." He knew how it was. The world seemed to fade away whenever they were alone, as they were now.

"Sometimes." Her words were husky, her gaze getting tangled up in his. "Hunter, what are we doing?"

Starting over. But all he said was, "Decorating a float." He knew exactly what she was asking, but he didn't know what she wanted to hear. His fingers tucked a curl behind her ear. "Getting ready for Christmas."

Her voice was unsteady. "Is that all?"

"Is it?"

She shook her head, cupping his face in her hands. "You're not standing here, freezing your butt off, waiting to kiss me?" He smiled, because even though they were completely alone, on several thousand acres, she'd whispered.

His eyes closed, absorbing her touch. "I'll keep waiting, Jo. Until you're ready," he said, daring to meet her gaze. In her eyes, he saw all the need and want and uncertainty that gripped him. He smoothed her hair back from her forehead. "When you're ready, I'll be here."

She leaned into his touch, but her gaze never left his.

"It's cold. Come inside? I've got some stew and corn bread, if you're hungry." He offered her his hand. She could reject him—he sort of expected her to. But he hoped. When it came to Jo, he'd always hope.

She nodded, easing the tension in his stomach. She beamed at him as he held the door open for her. She brushed against him and a whole new range of emotions took over. He watched her, the way her hands twisted in the hem of her shirt, the way her eyes zeroed in on the fire burning low in the grate.

He crossed the room, kneeling before the fire to add some logs and stoke up the flames. When he turned, she stood before him, staring down at him. He stood, aching to drag her against him. If he only knew what she was thinking. "Jo?"

She reached for him, tangling her fingers in his hair and pulling his head to hers. He caught her then, tenderly cradling her face. The sheen in her eyes surprised him, as did the way her lip trembled. "Hunter, please." Her words were husky, rough, needy.

With a growl, every last bit of resistance left him. He'd wanted to be gentle, to love her tenderly, to take time to savor every inch of her. Maybe next time. He bore them back into the wall, nuzzling her neck and ear with his nose.

She smelled like cinnamon, spice and Jo. She ignited every nerve, making his heart ache and his body throb. His lips brushed hers, lingering on her lower lips and making her gasp. He turned into her, sealing her mouth with his. God, he wanted her, he needed her. She stirred a hunger in him that shook him to the core. It was powerful, and relentless.

He nudged her lips open and breathed her in deep. He kissed her then, without restraint. Pure emotion, mingled breaths, his hands cupped her neck, holding her to him. His hand tangled in her hair, tilting her head and holding her, letting his tongue explore until they were both breathless. He ran his nose along her neck, listening to the sound of her ragged breath. She was trembling as his lips latched on to her earlobe.

"Hunter." His name, torn from her lips, set his blood boiling.

He stopped, pulling back. In that moment, he knew there was no one who would ever make him feel the way she did. It was more than her touch, the texture of her skin, her scent. It was Jo. His Jo. In his arms. Where she belonged.

Her eyes opened.

Her hands slipped beneath his shirt, surprising him. She tugged his undershirt free from his jeans, her palms cold enough to make him shiver but not shy away. And then she was kissing his neck, her hands moving over his stomach, his chest, driving him crazy. When she realized his shirt snapped, she yanked, popping it open. Her urgency fueled his— she wanted him and he wasn't going to let her down. He shrugged out of his shirt, ducking down to let her tug his undershirt over his head. She stood there, shaking her head.

"You okay?" he asked.

"It's just… It's you. Different, sure. But you, you know?" She took his hand in hers. "It's still *you*."

Words failed him. She wasn't just talking about his body. She felt it, too? She had to. She blew out a long, unsteady breath.

"I missed you, Jo." His thumb ran over her lower lip. He had to kiss her, had to touch the soft skin beneath her sweater. She was like silk, too fine for the roughened pads of his fingertips. But now that he was touching her, he couldn't stop. He trailed his fingers up her sides, then back down, needing more. "Stay?"

She nodded, taking his hand in hers.

He looked at their joined hands, then led her to his bedroom. He turned, wanting to tell her the truth. He loved her, he wanted her... But before he could say a word, she pulled her sweater off and dropped it on the floor at their feet.

Josie gasped. One minute he was staring at her, the next she was lying on her back in his big bed. He leaned over her, the hunger in his eyes inflaming her.

His fingers trailed the edge of her pale blue lace bra. He dipped his head, nuzzling her chest. He pressed soft kisses, the tip of his tongue tracing the valley between her breasts. She clasped his head to her, twisting her fingers in his hair, exhilarating in his touch.

He stood, unhooking his belt and unbuttoning his pants. She rose on her elbows, watching. He raised an eyebrow but didn't say anything. She grinned. She'd been dreaming about Hunter, about his body, about the way he made her feel. Now it was happening and she didn't want to miss a thing.

"Want to help me with my boots?" he asked.

She stood, letting him sit on the edge of the bed. She turned, tucked his foot between her legs and grabbed the heel of his boot. Then she grabbed the other. She faced him, tossing the boot over her shoulder.

His hands gripped her hips, pulling her between his legs. He buried his face between her breasts, his arms an unbreakable vise about her, holding her, protecting her, loving her. She ran her fingers along his shoulders, arching her back as his mouth nipped at the skin along her bra line.

Her hands traveled along his shoulders. She loved the feel of him, the raw strength of his body.

His fingers fumbled with the clasp of her bra while she shimmied out of her jeans and panties. It had been a long time since she'd stood naked in front of anyone, but the look on his face made her feel beautiful. She was lost to the rasp of his breath, his hands gripping her hips, pulling her against him, skin to skin. His hands were relentless, exploring each curve, stroking and teasing until she thought she would burst.

He kissed her, laying her back on the bed beneath him. At some point his boxers joined the mass of clothes spread out all over his bedroom floor.

She cupped his face, her gaze taking in his every reaction. Flared nostrils, locked jaw, his eyes radiated hunger and need barely restrained. Her fingers trailed along his cheek, his neck, tracing the corded muscle along his sides to grip his hips and arch against him. He groaned, his molten-hot gaze searing her as he slowly entered her. Such sweet torture. Breathing was a challenge. He stopped then, buried deep and breathing hard, and rested his forehead against hers, letting them both adjust to the feel of one another.

His hand smoothed the tangled curls from her face before he kissed her. When he moved, they came together, which drew her into a place of pure sensation.

Each touch, each sigh, left her wanting more. She moved with him. She'd forgotten how magic they were together. Sweet and soft, hot and hard, his body pushed her higher. She welcomed each thrust, holding on to him with all the strength she had. When her body tightened, the power of her climax forced her to cry out. His body bowed, each and every muscle contracting against her. Together, they fell over the edge. From raw and unyielding hunger to flushed, peaceful fulfillment, she was content.

He lay at her side, his hand sliding across her stomach to cup her breast. She looked at him. He smiled back. "Warm enough?" he asked gruffly.

She started giggling. "I've still got my socks on."

He sat up, glancing down. "Sexy." He flopped back down beside her.

She shook her head, stroking the side of his face.

His hand covered hers as he leaned down to kiss her.

"Jo..." His face turned serious, worrying her.

She covered his mouth. "Tonight, let's leave the past and the future on the other side of that door." She pointed at his bedroom door. "Please." She hadn't meant for this to happen. Okay, maybe that wasn't entirely true. But now that it had, she didn't know what to do about it. She loved him, she knew that. But saying those three words didn't mean things would simply fall into place. There were complications, lots of complications. She didn't believe in happy endings or forever love stories. And, even if she wanted to believe, she knew she'd mess it up.

And there was Eli.

He was frowning—she could feel it against her palm. "Tell me what's happening at the school. How are the puppies? Mars?" She moved her hand.

"Getting stronger every day." His fingers stroked along the inside of her arm. "How's your dad?"

She closed her eyes to absorb the sensation. "Getting stronger every day."

He chuckled. "He and Lola. You good with that?"

"I'm great with that." She shivered as he drew a finger from the base of her throat to her belly button. "I don't want him alone." She glanced at him. "It's nice to know, no matter where I am, they'll look out for each other."

His hand cupped her breast. "Any decision on the job?"

"Still thinking—" But his mouth on her nipple prevented her from finishing her sentence.

"When do you need to decide?" he asked, looking at her.

"Soon. The job doesn't start till May—"

"Plenty of time to consider all your options." His voice was low, his breath hot against her breast.

"I'll call soon—" she managed to whisper before her nipple was sucked deep into his mouth.

He released her. "I'm hungry."

She blinked, staring at him.

"You hungry?" he asked, smiling a little too smugly.

Food. He was teasing her? Now? Her body was already humming again, but it was a different kind of hunger.

"No?" His fingers trailed across her stomach.

"You're playing with fire, Dr. Boone." She rolled on top of him.

He laughed. "Am I?"

She nodded, aware of his every breath, twitch and reaction. He wasn't as unaffected as he was acting. "You are."

"Jo, you're my kind of fire." His hands came around her, tangling in her hair to pull her face to his.

But before he could kiss her, she pushed off his chest and sat up. "Actually, I could eat." She jumped up before he could grab her.

He sat up and threw a pillow at her. "Mean."

She stuck her tongue out at him. "You started it."

He ran a hand over his head, smiling at her.

"What?"

"You're naked." He wobbled his eyebrows at her. "And damn fine to look at. I'd have to say you're the prettiest thing I've ever seen in my life, Jo Stephens."

Her heart was thumping like crazy, but she said, "You're just hoping you'll get lucky again."

He nodded. "But it's true. Every word of it."

She crossed her arms over her chest, shifting from one sock-covered foot to the other. "I... Th-thank you," she stuttered. "I— Let's eat?" He stood up then, all glorious manliness, and it was her turn to stare.

"Here." He tossed her his undershirt.

She smiled and tugged it on. She rolled up the sleeves, hugging herself and sighing at the intoxicating scent of Hunter.

He pulled on his boxer shorts and his flannel snap-up shirt. "Stew?"

"Stew."

They warmed up two big bowls of stew and a plate of honey corn bread, carrying it back into the living room to picnic before the fireplace.

"Yummy," she said between bites.

"Cooking." He held up the bowl. "One of the many skills I hadn't planned on picking up."

"Cooking is a good skill to have."

"I didn't want Eli to grow up on frozen dinners or scrambled eggs. I used my mom's cookbook a lot, in the beginning." He took a long drink of water. "Can't touch her cooking, but we don't starve."

She grinned, imagining Hunter poring over cookbooks and meticulously following each recipe. He was a scientist, methodical and calculating. She had no doubt he'd spent hours making sure he'd done his mom's recipes proud. Unlike Josie's mother, Mags Boone was one of those women who excelled at motherhood. She had died in a car accident a year after Josie had gone to New Mexico. Josie had come back for the funeral—she'd had to. Seeing Hunter so sad, the Boone family so uncertain, had been a nightmare. So was seeing Amy with Hunter's tiny son. She'd given each of them her sincere condolences and headed back to the safety of school. But she'd often thought about Hunter and the family, written countless letters and emails she never sent. Nothing she could say would ease the ache of Mags passing.

"I bet she would've loved that you cook her food for Eli." Josie beamed at him, loving his answering smile. "What's another skill you never thought you'd learn?"

Hunter sat back against the couch, his long legs stretched out in front of him. He stared into the fire. "Well...potty training." He laughed. "I mean, I was planning on helping out. I just thought it'd be a team effort."

Josie sat her bowl on the floor at her side. "When did Amy leave?"

Hunter looked at her. "We lived under the same roof for a little over a year. Then she went back on the rodeo circuit, stopping in now and then."

"B-but Eli was a baby." She couldn't imagine leaving something so little and helpless. "You... How... Wow." She took his hand in hers. "So, you were in school with a baby, on your own."

He shook his head. "I was never on my own, Jo. My father, my brothers, Renata, hell, my aunts came down to help out whenever they could."

She nodded. "I know. It's just—"

"He never had a mother." He squeezed her hand. "You know all about that."

She scooted across the floor to snuggle against his chest. "Oh, I have a mother. She's on husband number seven. But this is the second time she's married this one, so maybe he'll be a keeper."

Hunter's laugh was low. "You like him?"

"I don't know him, really. They came up when I had a show in Montesano last year. He seemed nice enough. He's younger, of course, but he loves her." She shrugged. "I think."

"What about you?" he asked. "Learned any skills you never thought you'd learn?"

"Where do I start?" She sighed. "Changing a tire

and my oil—it's cheaper than having everything serviced. Once a mechanic finds out you're a single woman, they see dollar signs. Minor plumbing repairs and electrical repairs."

"Cooking, too?"

She smiled up at him. "Cooking for one is boring."

He frowned. "Why one?"

She swallowed. "I was almost engaged. But I just couldn't do it."

"What did he do?" His voice was gruff, angry.

"He didn't do a thing. He was a really nice guy. He still is a really nice guy."

"You're still involved?"

"If I was, this wouldn't have happened." She shot him a look. "He'd like to be, but nothing's changed."

"Then what happened?"

She sat up, reaching for her glass of water. She didn't know what to say, exactly. "It's me. I'm not wired that way. The marrying way, I mean. If I was, Wes would be a good husband. He's this sweet, supportive, funny guy who loves me. But I didn't love him that way." She swirled her water glass, staring into the fire. She didn't really want to talk about Wes... She didn't know how long they'd have time like this together. She glanced at Hunter to find him watching her.

Hunter took the glass from her. "You're too hard on yourself, Jo."

She frowned. She wasn't hard on herself—she just accepted her limitations. Not that looking at Hunter, all ruffled and manly, didn't make her wish she was another kind of woman. A true-blue veterinarian cowboy's wife type of woman...

He lowered his head, his mouth latching on to hers with a passion that startled her. His hand slipped under the edge of her shirt, gripping her hip. When his tongue traced the seam of her lips, she inched closer. Not close enough. She loved his soft groan, the hitch in his breath, as she straddled him.

"Still hungry?" she asked, nipping his bottom lip.

"Yes, ma'am," he rasped. "For dessert."

Chapter 11

Morning sunlight spilled into the bedroom, waking Josie with a start. She lay there, staring at the aged wood beams running across the ceiling. She was here, really here. And Hunter was snoring softly beside her. She grinned, turning her head on the down-filled pillow. His features were peaceful when he slept. She stared at him, torn. She wanted to stay. She wanted to run her fingers over the stubble on his chin. She wanted to wake him up and make love to him again. She wanted to talk about possibilities. And that terrified her.

Nothing had been said last night because she'd told him not to say anything. Doubt reared its ugly head.

Maybe nothing had been said because neither of them wanted to go *there.*

Yes, they were attracted to each other. They had a history and they liked each other. But a future for them couldn't be that easy. She and Hunter had a complicated relationship. Another thing her mother had warned her away from: complications. Complications led to distractions, which led to disinterest, and being left.

So words like *possibilities* and *relationships* shouldn't come into play, for both their sakes. Instead, last night was...the best mistake of her life. An amazing, magical, earth-shattering, mind-blowing mistake. She needed to end this now before she let her stupid heart convince her otherwise.

They weren't kids anymore. Other people would get hurt—like Eli. Eli, who might be home at any minute.

She lay there a second longer, memorizing everything about Hunter. She couldn't let him in. She couldn't love him. Her hand hovered over his cheek, itching to touch him.

The cold, hard truth was too big to ignore. It was too late. She did love him—she always had. The trick would be leaving without making things even more complicated than they already were. He could never know how she felt and she needed to get a grip on her out-of-control libido.

First step: getting out of his bed. She slipped from the bed, then spent a good ten minutes finding her clothes. No matter how hard she searched, one sock was missing. She dressed as quietly as possible, tugged her hair into a sloppy ponytail and eased from his bedroom.

She made it to the front door when his growl of

a question made her jump. "Where are you going?" He was all sleep-rumpled, bleary-eyed and shirtless.

"Home," she whispered, even though there was no reason to do so.

"You weren't going to say goodbye?" He frowned.

"You were asleep." As far as excuses went, she knew it was lame. From the disappointment on his face, he knew it was lame, too. "I… I didn't want to wake you up."

"You wanted me to wake up alone?" His long stride erased the space between them. His expression was confused and, maybe, a little sad. "Why are you running out on me?"

She blinked, shaking her head. "I'm not—"

"Stop, Jo." His hands clasped her upper arms. "Let's have some coffee and talk."

"Hunter," she said, "my dad—"

His hands slipped from her shoulders as he stepped back. "Admit you're scared. But don't use your dad as an excuse to avoid talking to me."

Her first instinct was to fight. The only problem with that? He was right, that's exactly what she was doing—and feeling. Which meant arguing with him was stupid. But talking to him, actually talking about feelings, would be bad. Especially now that she knew she loved him. What if he asked her how she felt? What if he loved her?

Joy and anticipation and pure, unfiltered panic pressed in on her, forcing the air from her lungs. Leaving was the best option, for both of them. She glanced at the door two steps away, the doorknob within easy reach.

"I don't want another eleven years of silence, Jo." His words were so raw, so hard, she had to look at him. Pain filled his eyes, so deep she was drowning in it. "Whatever you say can't be as bad as saying nothing."

She couldn't look away, no matter how much she wanted to. It killed her, to see him hurting. "I don't know what you want me to say."

He sighed, rubbing a hand over his face. "Why are you leaving?"

She shook her head, then shrugged. "I... I'm not good at the whole one-night-stand thing." She heard how callous her words were.

He was scowling now. "That's not what this is."

She couldn't stop the words from coming. "What is it? What is this?" She pointed back and forth between the two of them. "Hunter..." Her voice broke. *Damn it.* She didn't want this. Her heart might be a traitor, but she wasn't going to give in. She wasn't.

His hand cupped her cheek. "Would falling in love be that bad?" Why did he have to look at her like that? With tenderness and hope. Hope, which led to disappointment, disillusionment and heartbreak.

"Yes," she rasped. "It would be a mistake. A huge mistake. Like last night...all of this." She was spiraling out of control—she could hear it in her voice.

His gaze was relentless, searching and intense, while his thumb stroked along her cheekbone. She tried not to shudder, she did, but she failed. His posture changed, and he relaxed. His crooked smile appeared, and one brow arched as he leaned forward. "People make mistakes in life—it happens all the time." His hand grasped her chin, tilting her head back. "Loving you isn't one of them."

Was he saying he loved her? Now? Was the room spinning? And he was kissing her... Holding her in a way that told her he'd never let her go. How could she be so happy and so miserable at the same time?

"Stay, Jo," he murmured against her lips.

"I can't." She pressed against his chest.

"You can. If you weren't so stubborn, you'd see that."

"Always have been—" She sucked in a deep breath, hoping to shake off the all-too-tempting invitation his lips were issuing as they traveled along her neck. "Stubborn," she whispered.

His laugh was low, his breath warm on her skin. "It's hot as hell," he murmured, lightly biting her earlobe.

She gasped. If she didn't push out of his hold now, she'd be pushing him back into the bedroom. Pulling away was hard, a lot harder than she wanted to admit. She was still a little breathless when she said, "You don't play fair."

He smoothed her hair from her face. "All's fair in love and war. Can't help it if I get you all hot and bothered." He shrugged, his smile fading. "I can't make you stay, if you're set on going."

"I am." She nodded, trying to convince them both.

"Then go." His hand rested at the base of her neck, his thumb resting in the hollow of her throat. She swallowed, his touch a brand against her flesh. He grinned, his thumb stroking her neck. "I'll see you at my dad's later for dinner."

She scowled at him, then yanked the door open and stepped out onto the front porch. She ignored him, and his laughter, as she walked out. He followed her, just to poke at her, she knew. It was cold and he was wearing his boxers and not much else. She was about to point that out to him, when someone cleared their throat. A woman stood, her arm resting on the hood of a big shiny four-door pickup truck.

Not just any woman. *Amy.* Not that Amy even looked at her—her brown eyes were glued on Hunter. She stepped forward, blond hair swinging, all sass and attitude. "Are you kidding me?"

"Amy?" The look on Hunter's face told Josie he wasn't expecting his ex-wife any more than she was.

Amy laughed, a hard, angry sound. "Talk about a homecoming."

Hunter's calm was surprising. "What are you doing here?"

"Eli called and asked me to come home." She tossed her head back, her hands resting on her hips. She'd kept in shape—her skintight jeans and plunging neckline made that clear. "So, I did. It's Christmas and all. But I'm guessing you weren't expecting me. Or maybe you were. Maybe you knew I was on my way." She leveled Josie with a glare so hostile there was no mistaking her implication.

Whatever Amy was thinking, it wasn't pretty. Josie had never been on the receiving end of such unfiltered aggression. Amy might be looking for a fight, but that was the last thing she needed. Eli disliked her now, but he would really hate her if she went toe-to-toe with his mother. "I was just leaving," Josie muttered.

"I sure as hell hope Eli isn't home." Amy put her

hands on her hips. "A boy his age doesn't need to see his dad sleeping around."

"Are you serious?" Hunter's tone was hard.

"Hell, yes, I am. Where is he? Where's our son?" Josie heard Amy stress *our son*—it was impossible not to hear it. As if she needed to be reminded that Eli was their son.

"He's sleeping over at Greg's," Josie said.

Amy's nostrils flared, her eyes narrowed. "Was I talking to *you*? Did I ask *you* where my son was?" She stepped forward, fists clenched.

"Amy, that's enough," Hunter said. "This is my place—"

"Where *my* son lives," Amy argued. "I don't give a shit about who you're sleeping with. But her? I know Eli has a problem with her. You know it, too. You might not give a rat's ass about your son's feelings, but I sure as hell do."

"You really want to go there?" Hunter's voice was deceptively soft.

Amy's eyes went round, her lips thin and pinched. She didn't say a word, but it was hard for her, Josie could tell.

"I think you need to leave." Hunter crossed his arms over his chest. "Now."

Josie glanced at Hunter, torn. Amy was laying it on thick, but she wasn't entirely wrong. And they all knew it. Hunter must have guessed what she was thinking, because he frowned and shook his head. "Jo—"

"I'm going to be late," Josie said, stepping blindly around Amy and hurrying to the barn. It was one of the longest walks she'd ever made. Her heart echoed in her ears with each step, and her eyes burned from the tears choking her.

She heard Hunter call after her, but ignored it. She couldn't stop. Not with Amy primed for battle, screaming at Hunter. "What the hell is the matter with you? You bring that woman here, into Eli's home? After everything—"

Hunter's voice was too low to make out, not that she wanted to hear their conversation. Instead, she walked faster. What was she doing? What had she been thinking? What if Eli had come home last night? He would have been devastated to find her there. And his relationship with his father would have suffered for it.

She fumbled with her keys, trying to unlock her door, but dropped them instead. She knelt quickly, reaching for them, slipped on the dew-slicked grass and ended up on her knees. She sat, leaning against the car and staring up at the pale blue sky. The wind whipped her curls around her face and stung her eyes, making it okay for her to cry—a little. She sniffed, hugging her knees to her chest.

How many years had she spent avoiding complications? How many opportunities had she passed up because she didn't want pain? When she'd left Stonewall Crossing, she'd been testing Hunter. She knew that now. Was it fair? No. Had she set him up for failure? Maybe. She knew what a catch he was. Amy wasn't the only one waiting to swoop in when she wasn't around. But she'd gone, anyway. And life, in all its complete misery, had eventually moved on.

She had moved on. Sort of. Her attention followed a stray cloud across the blue sky.

She'd never stopped loving him. And that one, stupid emotion was the reason everything was falling apart. All those years of proving she wasn't her mother, only to act exactly like her. Following her heart, regardless of the consequences to everyone else.

"Jo?" Hunter's voice was soft. He stood, jeans unbuttoned and shoved into his boots, shirt flapping wide enough to reveal every gorgeous ridge and dip of his muscular chest and stomach.

She almost groaned in frustration, angrily wiping the stray tears from her cheeks. "I dropped my keys." She pushed up, turning to unlock the door.

"You locked your car? Out here?" His hand came around, taking the keys.

She wouldn't face him. Instead, she held her hand out. "Keys."

"Nope."

She clenched her fist, then opened it again. "Keys!" She waited, and waited, but he didn't say a word or give her the keys. She spun around, all restraint gone. "Give me the keys," she hissed.

He tucked the keys in his pocket. "In a minute." He grabbed her shoulders, pulling her against him. "Don't leave like this."

"Like what?" Why did he have to smell so good?

He held her so tightly she couldn't push him away. "Thinking this is wrong. Amy's wrong."

"Eli hates me."

"He doesn't hate you." He sighed. "Look at me, please."

She stared at his chest. It was hard, covered in the lightest dusting of hair, coarse beneath her fingers. She swallowed, staring at his neck instead. The strong, sun-kissed neck she'd enjoying kissing not too many hours ago.

"Amy is part of my life—she always will be. I can't say I'm happy about that, but it's the truth." He paused. "But I *want* you in my life, Jo. To stay, here, with me and Eli."

She stared up at him. "But Eli—"

"Is my son. It might take some time, but he'll come 'round. He wants me to be happy." He kissed her forehead. "And, damn, Jo, you make me happy. Always have."

She felt the tears building then, hating the weakness they showed. This was bad. He was saying everything she wanted to hear, everything she'd dreamed he'd say. But it wasn't enough.

She'd never completely gotten over the hurt her mother had caused, never forgotten how it felt to be passed over for her mom's happiness. She'd resented all the men in her mother's life and held them at arm's length because she knew they weren't there to stay. In time, she'd come to terms with the choices her mom had made, but she'd never forgotten how betrayed she'd felt. She, who was always there to love and support her mother, didn't make her mother happy. The thought of Eli feeling that way about the father he adored was too much. "I can't."

The range of emotions that crossed his face was quick, but she soaked in every spellbinding expression. "Yes, you can." His determination was clear.

"And this time, I'm not gonna let you go without a fight. You hear me?"

She shook her head, forcing the pure joy his words stirred deep down inside her. She drew in a deep breath and spoke carefully. "There's no fight. Last night was amazing, no denying that." She cleared her throat, her heart rebelling against the next words she forced out. "But this isn't where I want to be, Hunter. This isn't my life."

His hold lessened on her the slightest bit. "You keep telling yourself that, Jo. I'm happy to prove you wrong." He pressed a kiss to her forehead before he released her, leaving her unsteady on her own two feet. He unlocked the car door, held it open for her and handed her the keys when she was sitting inside. She hadn't realized how cold she was until she was out of the morning wind.

And there he stood, basically shirtless, smiling at her like that. She could see his breath on the air. He had to be freezing. "Get inside before you catch a cold," she snapped.

He laughed. "Yes, ma'am."

She shook her head, scowling at him until she was pulling down the driveway. Glancing back provided her with instantaneous relief. Amy and her big red truck weren't parked in front of the house. Not that she had any right to feel one way or the other about Amy being there. Hunter had told her the truth, as far as he was concerned. And what he'd said… All sorts of ridiculous and conflicting emotions warred inside her. Tears were streaming down her face, some happy, some not so happy.

Chapter 12

Josie made sure each loaf of sweet bread was wrapped in waxed paper, then tin foil, before packing them into the plastic travel container. "Are you ready?" she called out to her father.

"In a minute," he answered. "Still can't believe your car broke down last night. You need to let the rental car people know. Maybe you can get your money back."

"Sure, Dad. I'll do that," she said quickly, hating lying to her dad. Sprinkles, who'd been watching her from the doorway, yapped at her. "What?" she asked. Sprinkles cocked her head to one side, making a strange little growl. Of disapproval? Did the dog know she was lying? She put her hands on her hips and frowned at the dog. "Give me a break,

Sprinkles," she whispered. The dog yapped again. "I am not going to tell him I had a…sleepover at Hunter's place. And I'm not going to let something that eats my face cream make me feel guilt." She turned her back on the dog and straightened up the kitchen.

Why did staying with her father make her feel as if she needed to sneak around? He'd made no secret that he wanted her to give it another chance with Hunter. Heck, her dad would probably throw them a party. Maybe that was why she didn't say anything. In the twelve hours since her night with Hunter, she'd felt more at odds than ever.

"Everything packed up?" Her father peeked into the kitchen. "Can you feed Sprinkles for me?"

"If you'll hurry up." She shot a pointed look at the shaving cream on his face. "Lola will be here any second."

"We're picking her up," her father said, returning to the bathroom. "Awfully eager to get there, aren't we?"

She didn't answer. She *was* eager. She wanted to see Hunter and Eli. Tonight was an opportunity to pretend she was part of that family. She hung up her apron and flipped off the kitchen lights. The dog was still sitting in the doorway. "Is that what this stare-down is about? Are you hungry, Sprinkles? Sorry, I'm still not fluent in dog speak yet."

Sprinkles did her little growl-yip thing. Josie chuckled.

It took an hour to get ready. Her father had changed shirts six times and nicked himself while shaving. She'd picked out a new shirt, located a

Band-Aid and fielded several phone calls concerning the Gingerbread Festival while trying to lure the stubborn little terrier into the kitchen for dinner.

"She likes to eat in the dining room, like me," her father explained after Josie had circled the kitchen table for the fifth time.

"Really, Dad? But you're not eating in the dining room, so why can't she just be a dog and eat in the kitchen?" Josie put her hands on her hips. Sprinkles circled her, yipping loudly. "Am I supposed to set you a place at the table? Or will you have your meal on the floor?"

Her father frowned at her. "Don't get all sassy. A man gets lonely without a companion." A strange look crossed his face and he patted his shirt pocket. "Be right back." He moved, more quickly than she'd seen him move in a while, back down the hall to his room.

Josie poured Sprinkles a heaping bowl of dog food, then refilled her water bowl. "What, no thank-you?" Sprinkles eyed the food, then the water, then flopped down in her dog bed. Josie shook her head and loaded the food they were bringing into her father's small extended cab pickup truck. Her father came out, looking rather dashing.

"You look all spiffed up, Dad." She noticed the slight color on his cheeks. "So, how was bingo last night?"

"Oh, fine. Lola won, as always. I'm convinced she's got the game rigged." He locked the front door behind them.

"By using magnetized bingo balls or something?"

Josie couldn't help but tease as she climbed into the truck.

Her father joined her, staring at her. "I never thought of that one. Hmm, sounds like a lot of work—"

"Dad, I was kidding." She laughed.

"You sure we made enough?" Her father eyed the six loaves of sweet bread and tray of assorted delectable holiday treats. "There are a lot of Boones out there."

"I think we'll be fine, Dad."

"You should see Fisher eat. And Eli. Boys must have hollow legs."

They picked up Lola, and Josie moved to the back-seat, listening to them chatter about the upcoming festivities on the square and any little snippets of gossip Lola had to share, as well.

"I know she's a friend of yours, but there's a rumor that Principal Upton has herself a fella." Lola turned in her seat.

Josie shook her head. "Not that I know of. Anna-beth's been pretty up-front about being lonely." She didn't mention the sexting to Lola. She might adore the older woman, but she knew Lola Worley loved to talk. "Out of curiosity, why?"

Lola nodded. "Well, her neighbor saw flowers being delivered to her house. And she's had a baby-sitter three more times than she usually does."

Josie didn't say a word. One of those nights, Annabeth had been with her. And she'd had Career Night, too. But that was all she knew of. She sighed. Was she really going to dissect Annabeth's babysitting schedule to determine whether she was dating? No. No, she wasn't. And she wasn't going to ask her, either. If Annabeth wanted to tell her, she would.

The closer they got to Boone Ranch, the more nervous Josie felt. Once they parked, she took more time than necessary collecting the travel containers of food. Her dad and Lola were inside when she heard, "Can I help?"

Hunter pulled her against him, his hands sliding down the length of her back to her hips and back up to rest on her shoulders.

She felt so good against him. As though she was made for him.

"Hi." Her whisper was unsteady. He liked it.

He nodded, bending to kiss her.

"Hunter—"

"Hold that thought," he murmured, pressing his lips against hers. It was one of those deep, open-mouthed, soft kisses that had her clinging to his shirt and swaying into him. With a soft groan, he loosened his hold on her. As tempting as it was to load her into his truck and take her to his place, he knew better. Instead, he dropped a swift kiss on the tip of her nose, asking, "What were you saying?"

Her breathless laugh warmed him through. "I think I was going to say something about being seen or this wasn't a good idea…" She trailed off.

"That's what I thought."

"You knew I was going to say that? And you kissed me?" He watched her eyes narrow.

"Worked for me," he argued, collecting the containers from the truck. "Good thing it's cold out here or everyone in the house would know I was hungry for something other than food right now."

She stared up at him. Something about ruffling her feathers made him a little too happy. He winked. "Come on. We stay out here too long, Lola will talk."

She hurried up the steps to the porch, holding open the door for him.

"Happy holidays!" His father was all smiles, giving Jo a big hug and kiss. "You look as pretty as one of your pictures."

Hunter disagreed. Pretty didn't begin to describe how Jo looked. Her black sweater fitted her snugly, hugging her breasts and reminding him of how well they fit in his hands.

"Aren't your pictures normally animals?" Fisher picked her up in a bear hug. "Or landscapes? Don't be offended, Josie."

"Hi, Fisher." She laughed. "You really don't have to pick me up every time we see each other."

"No?" his brother asked.

"No," Hunter answered before he thought.

His brother grinned, ear to ear, as he set her down. "Looks like he can't stand a little competition, Josie," Fisher whispered, winking at her.

Hunter ignored his brother's teasing, but not the rosy hue of Josie's cheeks. If he didn't get a grip on his emotions, tonight was going to be one hell of a long night.

"Joselyn." Archer nodded at her. "Nice to see you."

"You, too, Archer." She smiled in response, her nerves showing.

Ryder winked in greeting, and she waved back.

"Hey, Josie." His sister, Renata, was all smiles.

Josie stared at Renata before pulling her into a hug. "God, you're gorgeous."

He grinned. His little sister was a little too gorgeous for his liking. Too blonde, too blue-eyed, with a figure that turned too many heads. Thank God she had a good head on her shoulders or he and his brothers would be headed for trouble.

"She's all grown up," his father agreed.

Renata laughed, hugging her back. "It has been a while since we've seen each other."

"Time goes faster the older you are." His father hooked arms with Josie. "That's why it's so important to make every minute count."

"You sound like my dad," Josie said.

"Imparting words of wisdom is a father's job." Teddy patted Josie's arm. "Come say hello, Eli. We've got guests, so pretend like you've got some manners." He winked at his grandson.

Hunter had never had to punish his son before, not really, but Eli had never treated anyone with such disrespect. He barely nodded at Jo, before shaking hands with Carl and letting Lola kiss his cheek.

"Santa's big on manners." Renata poked Eli in the side, making Eli smile reluctantly.

Dinner was a mash-up of good and bad. Hunter sat beside Josie, enjoying every accidental brush of her hand against his. When he passed the rolls or the butter, he let his fingers linger just so he could watch her cheeks turn rosy. He couldn't resist touching her. The way her breath caught in her throat when he let his hand fall from his lap to her thigh almost had him dragging her from the room. She shifted to the opposite side of her chair, her grip on her wineglass tightening. He couldn't stop grinning. He couldn't ignore the pull between them. Electric, hot, charging the air between them. Damn, but he was hard with want before they'd started eating.

Conversation ebbed and flowed, but every second he was aware of her. The way she looked at her father and Lola was so hopeful and happy. The longing on her face as she laughed at his siblings' teasing... She hadn't had a lot of family get-togethers and love in her home growing up. He knew her mom had done a number on her, muddying the waters when it came to real love and commitment. And his betrayal, with Amy, hadn't helped. But, if she'd give him another chance, he'd show her that family could be loyal, sticking together to the end, even when things were tough.

Josie stiffened, her entire body rigid.

"Jo?" he whispered, the others engrossed in one of Fisher's stories.

She looked at him, her silver-gray eyes searching his.

"You okay?" he asked.

"Fine." But he heard the tremor in her voice.

"You can write a book about that," Fisher finished. "Not sure it's fit for kids, though."

Hunter had no idea what his brother had been saying, but he smiled. "Don't think so."

Fisher shrugged.

"When are you leaving?" Eli asked.

Hunter stared at his son. So did everyone else at the table.

"I… I mean," the boy stuttered, seeing his mistake, "you're going back to Washington, right, Miss Stephens?"

Hunter was stunned. And more than a little hurt. What had he done to make his son worry so? To think Eli would be replaced by anyone in his heart? It pissed Hunter off that his son was talking to Jo like that. But there was something else going on with Eli, and he needed to find out what it was—soon.

"I'm trying to convince her to stay," her father said. "Seems to me, she can write anywhere."

"And all her stories are about Stonewall Crossing, anyway," Lola chimed in. "I've got that little stone cottage needing a tenant."

"Any news about the university job?" his father asked.

"I told them I'd get back to them in January," she admitted. "There's a chance for me to do a lovely in memoriam mural at the vet school I'd really love to do before I go."

"You're staying?" Eli's voice was tight.

"No." Josie shook her head. Pain laced Eli's words. Hunter heard it, and Jo heard it, too. There was no doubt how his son felt about Jo, about Jo being a part of their life. "Eli, I'm… I have no plans to stay." Hunter looked at her, wanting to argue. But she didn't look at him—she was too busy watching Eli. Her sadness twisted his heart. His son's rigid jaw, the way he stared at his empty plate, all but ripped Hunter's heart right out.

A heavy, awkward silence descended.

"Dessert?" Renata asked.

"I'll help clear." Jo jumped up, a smile pasted on her face. She made her way around the table, collecting plates, before disappearing into the kitchen with Renata.

A few minutes later, Renata appeared with a pie in one hand and a large platter of cookies in the other. But no Jo. He waited another five minutes before he headed for the kitchen. Jo's sleeves were pushed up, her hands submerged in a sink full of soap suds and dinner dishes. She scrubbed each dish, attacking it until Hunter knew they didn't need to be run through the dishwasher. She loaded them in anyway, her movements jerky and stiff. When all the dishes were loaded, she scrubbed down the counter and tidied up. He watched her pull in a deep, shaky breath. Was there anything he could say to her? Any way to convince her that their love was worth the trouble? Her eyes went round when she turned to find him leaning against the doorway.

"Feel better?" he asked, not moving.

She shook her head.

He almost crossed to her, almost took her in his arms. But she held herself so rigidly he was afraid he'd break her. "He's a kid, Jo."

"A kid that doesn't like me much." She smoothed her black sweater.

She was hurting. And vulnerable. "I *like* you enough for both of us." His gaze held hers, willing her to see things his way.

"Dad." Eli squeezed between his father and the door. "Grandpa Teddy wants you."

"Okay." He paused, looking at his son, then Jo. "Help Jo make the coffee. She doesn't know her way around the kitchen."

He didn't know who was angrier, Eli or Jo. But damn it, his son needed to know Jo for the woman she was, not the monster Amy had made her out to be. He gave Jo a wink, leveled a warning at his son and left.

Chapter 13

Eli glanced at her, wary, before opening the kitchen cabinets. No point in ignoring him. She could try to talk to him. Hunter obviously thought it was a good idea. "So, Eli," she began, speaking to his back. He didn't turn around or acknowledge her, but she kept going. "The float looks great. You happy with it?"

He shrugged but didn't turn around.

"You do this every year?" She plugged in the coffeepot, filling it with water. "The club, I mean."

He nodded, putting mugs on the counter.

She paused, swallowing back her sigh. Well, this was going well. "Can you point me in the direction of the coffee?"

He opened another cabinet and pulled out a large

container of coffee. He set it on the counter beside her, without looking at her, or saying a word.

"Thank you." She added several scoops of coffee, searching for some way to crack his armor. She glanced at the boy, an idea taking shape. She knew she was playing dirty, but she was getting desperate. "How long has Dara lived in Stonewall Crossing? I get the impression she's new."

He glanced at her. "She just moved here."

"I thought so." She watched the coffee brewing, trying not to react to the fact that he was talking to her. "She's still learning the town, asking lots of questions. She's been such a help at the bakery."

"She's been working at the bakery?" he asked.

Josie nodded. "I'd been talking to Miss Worley about how much work it is, with Dad's injury and all, and she volunteered. She's a solid baker, but she loves the decorating part. I think her cookies are the prettiest in the shop."

"She's artsy. Real creative." He stopped, turning one of the mugs around in his hands. "Still need help?"

Josie couldn't hide her surprise. "Really?" He must really like Dara, to offer his help to her. "S-sure." In case he didn't know, she added, "I... I'll be there, too, you know?"

"Yeah." For a split second he wasn't fuming. His blue-green eyes assessed her carefully before he frowned. He sounded a little sad, a little irritated, when he said, "But my dad won't be." He was watching her, as if he was waiting for something.

She didn't really know what to say, so she murmured, "Oh."

Renata swept into the kitchen, eyeing them both before asking, "Coffee ready? Eli, where are the trays? We can't go back and forth with everything." She paused. "Wow, Josie, did you clean up? It looks great, thanks."

"Of course," she said. "It's the least I can do after the lovely dinner. Your dad's quite the cook."

"I guess that's what single men do—learn to cook." Renata smiled. "My dad, your dad, all of my brothers. Well, not Ryder. But he's really good about visiting right at dinnertime so he never goes hungry." She put the sugar pot on the tray, then pulled out a small pitcher and some milk. "Hunter's the best cook, after my dad. Guess he's got more than himself to feed." Renata nudged her nephew, earning her a smile from Eli.

When she carried the coffee into the living room, conversation was in full swing. Hunter was sitting at one end of a long leather couch, with enough room for her to sit beside him. And as much as she wanted to sit there and sink into his side, she didn't. Instead, she perched on a small stool in front of the roaring fireplace, taking care not to look at Hunter or the inviting spot beside him.

"I don't care what the zoo official says." Archer was shaking his head. "I'm sick and tired of the excuses. Bottom line is they don't want the cheetah, even if she is rehabilitated."

"But why?" Lola asked. "I don't understand, Archer."

"Money's tight, funding is hard to come by, and she's one more mouth to feed and body to vaccinate."

"What will you do?" Josie asked, doctoring her coffee with extra sugar. "Can you keep her?"

Archer shrugged. "It's not like the preserve is flush with extra funds. But I'll figure something out."

Fisher was talking then, but Josie let her attention wander. The years had been good to the Boone family.

She studied Archer Boone. He'd always been a serious sort, even as a boy. His brothers were tall, thick and broad. But Archer was taller, lean and trim. Her gaze traveled to Fisher, sprawled in an armchair, devouring cookies. He was the thickest, a tree trunk of a man. He'd been the smallest as a boy. But, no matter how much his physique might have changed, he was still the joker she remembered. Now, Ryder... She had to bite back a smile, remembering Annabeth's undisguised lust for the youngest Boone brother. There was no doubt Ryder was probably the best looking, and he knew it. But there was also no question he was trouble.

When she finally allowed herself to look at Hunter, he cocked an eyebrow at her. She smiled, holding her mug in front of her mouth. The slight tilt of his head, the quirk of his mouth... She loved him. And it felt wonderful and warm and horribly painful. His brow furrowed before she turned away, staring into her mug to collect herself.

What was she doing, sitting here, daydreaming? Never in her wildest dreams had she thought she'd be in Stonewall Crossing having dinner with the Boones, talking animals and family, a week before Christmas.

"We should be getting on home," her father said. "It's getting late and tomorrow's going to be crazy. And we still have to get Miss Lola home."

Did her dad just wink at Lola? She glanced at Hunter, and he was smiling from ear to ear.

"Everything's ready, Carl, don't fret." Lola patted her father's hand. "Between Josie, Dara and me, we've made an army of cookies, and then some. Unless Fisher's eaten them all, that is." Lola shook her head as Fisher ate another gingerbread man in two bites.

Fisher grinned. "They're good."

"Obviously." Renata smirked. "Chamber's ready, too. Of course, everyone's a little too excited about the reporter coming from the State Tourism Department. We want Stonewall Crossing to shine as a tourist destination. And a safe place to get an exceptional education." She smiled at her brothers.

"Exciting times," Lola said.

"Nice for our little piece of heaven to get such positive attention," Teddy Boone added, sipping his coffee.

Ryder was clearly unimpressed. He shot Josie a look, then rolled his eyes. Maybe the youngest Boone wasn't as content with life as the rest of them appeared to be.

"You might be just a little bit biased, Daddy." Renata kissed her father's cheek.

"What time does everything start up tomorrow?" Josie asked, standing. "Do I need to do anything?"

"I'll come get you around three. They start lining up for the parade pretty soon after that." Hunter stood, moving to her side. "Thought maybe we could walk around the square afterward. Carolers. Hot chocolate. That sort of thing."

It would be all too easy to get lost in his blue-green eyes, to forget Eli and Amy and how terrified she was of commitment. Especially when he was looking at her like that, as if she was the only woman in the world. Not caring that they had a room full of observers, his son included.

"I— You'll be too busy, won't you?" Her voice was a little unsteady. "Taking the float apart?"

"It can wait. Times like tomorrow don't come very often." He took her hand in his. "It's important to make every minute count."

"Damn right," Teddy Boone said.

Hunter knew exactly what he was doing. No way he was going to let her leave without making it plain to everyone what his intentions were.

The look on her face almost broke his resolve to take things slow. Holding her hand was one thing— wrapping her up in a kiss that claimed her would be something else. But the surprise on her face and the pleasure that creased the corners of her eyes were tempting, very tempting.

"What do you say, Jo?" he asked, squeezing her hand.

Her nod was slow. "I'd love to."

She looked so pretty he had to fist his hand

to keep from reaching for her. "I'll help you load things up."

He ignored the expressions of everyone in the room. He knew Carl and his father were tickled pink. Fisher and Lola, too, undoubtedly. Ryder and Archer wouldn't care. Renata…well, she was worried about him. She'd told him to take things slow, to keep a rein on his heart. As if that was ever a possibility when it came to Jo.

And Eli? He looked at his son and smiled. His boy needed to know that Jo made him happy, that holding her hand meant smiling. Eli was red-faced, angry tears in his accusing eyes.

Hunter walked by, refusing to cave. He helped Josie get everything loaded into Carl's truck, waiting as everyone said their goodbyes before helping Lola into the cab and dropping a swift kiss on Jo's cheek.

"Hunter—" The worry in her voice stopped him.

"I'll talk to him, Jo." His hand cupped her cheek. "I'll see you tomorrow."

"I don't want to cause problems, Hunter. I—"

"You're not." He smiled. "I'll figure it out."

She didn't look convinced as he loaded her into her father's truck. He watched the taillights until they'd faded into the black night. He stood a little longer, letting the crickets chirp and the wind calm him before heading back into the house.

He loaded Eli into his truck ten minutes later. His son didn't say a word as they drove, but his hands were clenched in his lap, his head turned away.

Hunter let it go until they were home. He needed the time to think through what he needed to say. He went 'round and 'round, hoping for a way to avoid a fight… But that wasn't going to happen.

When Eli headed toward his room, Hunter stopped him. "We're going to talk."

Eli's face was rigid. "About?"

Hunter sighed, running a hand through his hair. "Why are you so angry with Jo?"

"Why?" Eli's voice broke. "She's the reason you and mom are divorced—"

"Eli." Hunter shook his head. "That's not true."

"You're only saying that so I'll like her."

"I want you to like her, yes, but I've never lied to you. I'm not going to start now." He paused. "Your mom and I had problems that had nothing to do with Jo."

"You've made your mind up. She's who you want, no matter what I think. She's the only thing you've ever wanted."

Hunter frowned. "Son, if you weren't the most important thing in my life, I wouldn't be here, talking to you, fighting with you. But I am. I didn't run after Jo—I stayed to raise you. I thought you knew you were my world." He'd lived every single day with his son's well-being foremost in his mind. He loved his boy. Every dirty diaper, first step, scrape or tumble, call from the principal, had kept Hunter alive and breathing.

"Because she wasn't here." Eli's voice rose.

"Damn it, Eli. Whether Jo is here or she leaves, you're always my son. You'll always be first. Always."

Eli shook his head. "You said you'd never lie to me, but you are. How can I be first, if you're *with* her?"

"There are times we're not going to agree on things. I imagine it'll happen more the older you get." He paused, searching his son's face. "You don't like Jo, I get that. I won't force the two of you together anymore. Tomorrow night, the float, that's it. But in my spare time, I will see her."

"Until she leaves you again!" Eli shouted.

Hunter's nod was tight. He couldn't guarantee she'd stay, that much was true. But he'd take any time she gave him. "Until she leaves."

"Dad." Eli shook his head, seething. "You're an idiot."

"I'll tolerate you being angry, Eli. But I will not accept your disrespect. Whether you're talking to me or Miss Stephens, you will watch your tone. You hear me?"

Eli's face crumpled, his chin quivering. "Yes, *sir.*"

"It's late." His eyes stung, hot and sharp, but Hunter stood his ground. "Go on to bed now."

Eli turned, stomped down the hall and slammed the door behind him.

He didn't know what was worse, the fact that his son was hurting so much or that he had no way to make it easier. Not seeing Jo, giving her up and going back to the way it was— He couldn't do it. He loved his son, he always would. And he loved Jo, too. He'd be damned if he couldn't figure out how to have them both.

Chapter 14

"Shit," Annabeth muttered. She sipped her coffee. "This is bad. Lola's probably got half the town talking about me dating this mystery man." She shook her head, then spoke up, "Cody, honey, try to chew with your mouth closed."

Cody nodded, his face covered in frosting and gingerbread crumbs.

"Why is it bad?" Josie asked. "It's not true."

Annabeth glanced at the small group of regulars who frequented the bakery each morning. "Maybe."

Josie laughed. "Maybe? So you're keeping secrets from me?"

"Pot, meet kettle," Annabeth said pointedly.

Josie glanced at Cody, who was smearing his frosting across the tabletop. "Maybe we should have this conversation later?"

Annabeth sat back, a huge smile on her face. "Um, definitely now." She saw Cody's creation. "Cody, sweetie, that's gorgeous, but please keep it on the plate for Mommy."

Cody nodded.

"He's quite the talker." Josie smiled.

Annabeth shrugged. "He's pretty quiet, but the counselor says it can be normal, after losing someone."

Josie looked at the little boy. He was precious. And fatherless.

"I just hope Miss Worley will stop the gossip before it gets carried away." Annabeth finished wiping up Cody's art with a mass of napkins. "Small towns like to talk. Which is fine as long as it's not about the elementary school principal, you know?"

Josie nodded, looking up as the little bell over the bakery door rang.

Amy stood there, her hair back in a ponytail. She wore a burgundy scrub top with the UET Vet logo on the left shoulder. She walked forward, her brown eyes fixing on Josie. "I'm here to pick up an order for the vet school." She pulled out a credit card and slapped it on the counter. "And I'm in a hurry."

Josie took the card, running it through the machine. "Was it called in?"

"Y-yes."

"Dad?" Josie called out. "Did we get an order from the vet school?"

Her father came out, carrying a large box. "Got it right here." His entire expression changed when he saw Amy, and his eyes widened as he looked at her shirt. "What—"

"I got it, Dad," Josie said, patting his arm. "Thanks."

"You sure you don't need help?" he asked.

"You have the sweetest daddy." Amy waved her fingertips at him. "Carl, you get cuter every time I see you."

He didn't say anything as he disappeared back into the kitchen.

"So, Amy." Annabeth shot Josie a look. "I didn't know you were back in town."

"For good, since Hunter got me a job at the vet school," Amy added.

Josie was very proud of the way she didn't react. She didn't burst into tears. Or scream in frustration. Or throw the box of pastries at Amy. Nope, she didn't even twitch. She stood there, staring at the credit card machine, praying it would hurry up.

"Well, isn't that something?" Annabeth pulled Cody into her lap.

"Guess the gossips haven't got wind of it yet. But when they do, tongues will be wagging." Amy laughed. "I love to give 'em something to talk about."

"And you were always so good at it." Annabeth smiled sweetly.

Amy ignored Annabeth, tapping her nails on the counter as she asked Josie, "What's the holdup?"

"Old machine." The machine spit out the receipt, which Josie handed over. "Just needs your signature."

Amy signed it, grabbed the box, then paused. "Want me to tell Hunter hi for you when I get to work?" Her smile was a little too self-satisfied.

"Thanks but no thanks," Josie said, keeping her tone light. She could hold it together until Amy walked out. After that, all bets were off. Relief swept over her as the other woman turned to go.

But Amy turned back suddenly, her brown eyes sweeping over Josie from head to toe. "Hunter's a big boy, so it's his own fault for making the same mistakes over again. But—" she lowered her voice "—you hurt my boy, and there will be hell to pay."

Josie stared at Amy, surprised and a little impressed that the woman had any maternal instincts. She managed a tight grin. "You have a good day."

Amy left, the little bell over the bakery door breaking the silence. And just like that, the entire bakery, all eight people, were whispering and talking among themselves.

Annabeth stood, putting Cody's empty plate and cup on the counter. "Why would he get her a job?"

Josie's heart ached. "She's Eli's mom. You know Hunter. If she needs help, he's going to take care of her. For Eli." It was one of the reasons she loved Hunter. And one more reason she should book that flight straight to New Mexico. She would always have to contend with Amy, with drama, with uncertainty. Hunter might love her, but he was loyal to his family. Eli and Amy were his family. Was there really room for her?

She'd find out tonight—she had to. There was too much to sort through, too much still left unsaid. If it couldn't work, she'd start over again. It's not as if she was tied to a place... She could go anywhere, thanks to her books.

Now she just needed to know where she was going.

"Josie?" Annabeth asked. "You okay?"

Josie nodded. "Yeah."

"You sure?"

"I think so."

The little bell rang again, and this time Lola Worley walked in.

"Is she gone?" Lola asked.

"Just missed her," Annabeth said.

Lola put her hands on her hips. "Probably for the best. I don't know what she's up to, but she had no business coming in here, stirring up trouble."

Josie shook her head. "She was picking up pastries—"

"She was stirring up trouble, mark my words," Lola affirmed. "That one lives for it. After Hunter kicked her out, she spent a good month causing fights around town, getting the men all dazed and confused by her big…" Lola waved her hands in the air. "Well, you know."

Annabeth nodded.

"Hunter kicked her out?" Josie asked.

"Teddy told me all about it. He was fit to be tied." Lola nodded. "He'd come home to find Eli in his crib, screaming and filthy. Amy was gone."

"Eli was alone?" Josie was horrified. "But—" How many times had Annabeth or her dad tried to bring up Hunter? But she'd cut them off, too caught up in herself to consider what those she'd left behind were dealing with. She hurt for Hunter. And Eli.

"He gave her a lot of chances, Josie." Annabeth nodded. "When Eli started kindergarten, he was one of those kids that was always in the office after school when it was her turn to have him. She'd forget to pick him up, or didn't want to." Annabeth looked at Lola, who nodded.

"She was real good at coming in with presents, big smiles and stories for Eli before she'd leave again." Lola moved around the counter. "That boy holds on to those memories, desperate to have a real mother, I guess."

"That's natural," Josie argued. She knew what it was like to want a mother. How many times had she made excuses for her mom? Rationalized her behavior? There were flashes of brilliance. Museum visits. Opera performances. Traveling to exotic locations… But the everyday version of her mother was something altogether different.

"Seems to me his daddy did a good enough job for two parents." Lola beamed at Cody. "Look at how big you are. I swear, you look more like your pa every time I see you, Cody."

The little boy grinned.

"You want a cookie?" Lola asked him.

"He just had one," Annabeth protested.

"One's not near enough for a growing boy." Lola winked at Cody as she handed him a huge frosting-covered sugar cookie.

Annabeth laughed. "We don't need a nap today."

Lola hugged her. "Sorry, sugar. It's the holidays, you know? Calls for extra treats and breaking the rules now and then."

Annabeth smiled. "It's fine."

Josie's father came out of the kitchen. "Did you

believe that Amy? I didn't know what to say to her. Can I ban her from the shop?"

"Absolutely not." Josie sighed. "If she is back for good, we will all be on our best behavior. For Eli."

Lola, Annabeth and her father looked at her.

"Okay?" she added, needing their cooperation.

Annabeth and her dad nodded quickly.

Lola sighed and said, "I'll try, Josie, but I sure as hell won't like it."

"Dr. Boone," a voice called over his intercom. "Your two o'clock is here."

"Have Frank get Jester's vitals and put them in an exam room. I'll be there as soon as I can."

"Yes, Dr. Boone." And the intercom went silent.

Tripod leaped onto his desk corner.

"What are you doing here?" he asked, rubbing the black cat firmly along the back of his neck. "Too many dogs in the clinic today?"

Tripod yawned, revealing a long pink tongue.

"You go on and nap, and I'll just get back to work." Hunter gave the cat a last scratch before finalizing the chart on his tablet. The pharaoh hound was going to be a daddy. It had been a long road and the poor dog had no idea what he'd been missing out on, but puppies were definitely on the way.

"Hunter?"

Hunter looked up, completely floored to find Amy in UET scrubs. His stomach dropped. "What's with the getup?" he asked.

"I got a job." She smiled. "A tech position."

He sat back in his chair. "At the hospital?"

She nodded, coming into his office. "Yes."

"This hospital?" he clarified.

"I'll be over in the large-animal clinic, mostly." She sat in one of the chairs opposite him. "Unless someone here needs me."

"And you think this is a good idea?" he asked. "Last time we talked, you were heading to Vegas, following the circuit, living the dream."

Her smile tightened a little. "And then my son called me and asked me to come home."

Now he felt as though he'd been punched in the gut. "Eli called you?"

She sat back, looking far too comfortable in the chair. "Ask him."

"Why did he call you?"

"Hunter." She laughed the laugh that usually had any man looking at her, appreciating her. It made his skin crawl. "Contrary to what you think, some people want me around. That person just happens to be the boy we made together. He's upset."

He waited.

"Josie being here." She paused, frowning. "Well, he's just torn up about it. He's worried about you. And about me."

"About you?" He shook his head. "You weren't here."

"But he knows I still love you." Her brown eyes bore into his. "He knows I hold out hope every single day that we'll reconcile."

"Just because I didn't go public with why we divorced then doesn't mean I'm going to keep covering it up. Eli's getting old enough to figure things out. To

realize you left us long before our divorce was final."
He stood, pulling on his white coat. "I don't know
what you're hoping to gain, but I can't keep protecting Eli from your mistakes. This time, I won't."

She smiled up at him, shifting in her seat. "I'm
not planning on making any mistakes."

"Amy, if you're on the clock, I suggest you get
to work. The school doesn't run without everyone
working at one hundred and ten percent. You'd be
smart to remember that."

She stuck her tongue out at him. "Always so responsible." She stood, stretching so that her chest
was impossible to miss. "Fine. I'll see you later on.
I was thinking of having Eli for a sleepover tonight."

"We'll talk later." He brushed by her, heading
straight to the clinic.

This was the last thing he needed. Eli was already
stretched too thin. Throw his mom back in the mix,
let her play her victim card and things would get bad.

"They're in exam four," Martha said once he'd
reached the admissions desk.

He nodded, opening the door to find Jester. The
dog growled, deep in his throat, a nerve-racking
sound considering Jester was a nasty-tempered mix
that tipped the scales at almost two hundred pounds.

"How's he doing?" Hunter asked Clarence Shaw,
Jester's owner.

"He walked into the door frame today." Clarence
shrugged. "I can't stand to see him this way, Doc.
You gotta fix him up."

Hunter scanned the dog's chart. "You sure?"

Clarence patted the broad head of the massive

dog. "He's my baby, Doc. I'm sure. How long until he's better?"

"Cataracts are pretty bad." Hunter kept his voice steady, soothing for Jester—and Clarence. "Especially for a dog this age. After the surgery, he'll be seeing in a few hours."

"No kidding?"

"No kidding." Hunter stood, rubbing the dog's head and neck.

"He'll like that." Clarence was smiling. "Hell, I'll like that. It's hard on a body, carryin' Jester around."

Hunter smiled. "I can imagine."

Jester lay flat, resting his head on his paws. "You'll be fine, big fella. You'll see," Hunter said.

"What's next?" Clarence asked.

It took twenty minutes to get Jester checked in to the hospital and settled in a cage.

Tripod came around the corner as Hunter closed the cage door. "I'd stay away from this one, Tripod. He can't see you." He watched the three-legged cat wind his way between his legs. "Either way, I imagine he'd rather eat you than cuddle with you."

"Dr. Boone." Mario, a tech, laughed. "I'll keep Tripod out of Jester's way."

Hunter grinned. "I'll check in on him tomorrow."

"Headed to the parade?" Mario asked. "Tell Eli good luck with the float."

"I will." He nodded his goodbyes, heading back to his office. He hung his coat on the rack and dug for his keys. With a quick glance around the room, he flipped off the light and locked the door behind him.

"Dr. Boone." Dr. Lee was in the hallway. "I was

wondering if you'd heard anything from Miss Stephens. Any interest in the mural project?"

"I'm on my way to see her now." He tugged on his jacket. "I'll see what she's thinking."

"I'd appreciate that." Dr. Lee smiled. "Enjoy your evening."

"You, too." He nodded.

"Thank you for sending Mrs. Boone to us. It seems you have a very talented family."

Hunter stopped cold. "I didn't send Amy to you, Dr. Lee. To be perfectly candid, I would not have recommended her."

"Oh, I see." Dr. Lee frowned. "I suppose we'll have to make the best of it. Enjoy your evening."

The drive from the hospital to the bakery took fifteen minutes. It took every second of that time to ease the tension from his shoulders. He wanted to enjoy tonight, enjoy being with Jo. The streets were blocked for the night's celebration, so he had to walk, which did him good. Nothing like seeing the smiling faces of the community, the kids piled in the backs of minivans or sitting in lawn chairs to set things right again.

By the time he reached Pop's Bakery, he wasn't thinking about Amy or Dr. Lee or the pile of charts he needed to review.

He pushed into the bakery, the little bell chiming. Most of the lights were off, but he heard movement in the back room.

"Jo?" he called out. Sprinkles greeted him by jumping up and down and yapping excitedly. "Good to see you, too—especially since you're not throwing up or needing a diaper."

He walked through the connecting door from the bakery to Carl's house. "Jo?"

"Hunter?" she called out, her voice thin and stressed.

He followed the sound of her voice to her bedroom.

She was sitting on the bed, bundled in her robe, tear tracks down her face. She rubbed her nose with the back of her hand and sniffed, loudly. He didn't know whether to laugh or pull her into his lap. He sat and drew her close. "What's wrong Jo?"

She shook her head, hiccuping. "N-nothing."

"Come on now. Something's wrong. You're not one to cry for nothing."

Her big eyes peered up at him. "You mean I wasn't… For all you know I c-cry at the drop of a hat."

"Okay." He wiped the tears from her cheeks. "I'd still like to know why you're crying."

"My dad—" She sniffed. "My dad proposed to Lola."

"And that's bad?" He wasn't sure how to respond.

"No. It's g-great." She sobbed.

He laughed again.

"It's not f-funny," she moaned, pressing her face against his chest.

"Sorry." He cleared his throat. "It's not funny. And it's not bad. But you're crying."

She nodded.

His hold tightened on her. "What can I do, Jo?"

He felt her breathe deep, felt her hands grip his

shirtfront. "I'm happy for him. And relieved. H-he doesn't need me to stay."

Her words clawed at his heart. "You think so?"

"I want him to be happy. And Lola is wonderful. She'll keep him young—" Her voice broke. Her hands twisted in the flannel of his shirt.

"He wants you to stay, Jo." The words rasped out.

She froze, looking up at him. Her silver-gray eyes were full of pain, bone-crushing misery. "I'm a h-horrible daughter."

He laughed then, though he tried not to. "You are not."

"I am, Hunter." She swallowed, her gaze wandering over his face. "A good daughter wouldn't be jealous."

His hand cupped her face. "Jealous?"

"I hate that I'm the way… I am." She frowned.

"What way?" He frowned, too. "I don't understand."

"I'm t-terrified."

"Of what?"

"Commitments and relationships, losing control." She sighed, sniffing. "Hurting others to get what I want. Like you. And Eli." Her gaze wandered to his mouth. "You make me remember how to feel things I've tried to forget. And it scares me."

He rubbed his nose against hers. Her words revealed so much. "Let me love you, Jo."

He felt her tremble and pulled her close. His lips were firm, parting hers and stealing her breath. She shuddered again, but he didn't let her go. He didn't care if they were late for the festivities. Right now, he was where he needed to be.

Chapter 15

Josie rested her head on Hunter's chest, listening to the thump of his racing heart. Her hand drifted back and forth across his bare chest and stomach, stroking the muscles along his side. He offered comfort and strength, surrounding her with his warmth. She closed her eyes, tempted to stay put. She didn't really want to ride on the float, anyway. But they were already late. Any later and people might come looking for them.

She sat up, running a hand over her tangle of curls. "We should go."

"Like this? Lola will have plenty to talk about."

She giggled. "Um, no. Clothes, taming this—" she pointed to her hair "—and *then* we go."

He lay there, naked and gorgeous. "You okay?"

She nodded, enjoying the view a little too much. "Sorry."

He sat up, smoothing her hair from her face. "For?"

"Crying. Being pathetic." She shrugged. "Being emotionally overwrought. It was a long day."

He nodded. "I hear ya."

She attempted to pull her robe from beneath him. Since he wouldn't give it up, she stood, bravely walking across the room to pull clothes from her closet. "Anything new at the hospital?"

"A dog. A monster of a dog." He chuckled. "Two hundred pounds of drool and muscle."

She pulled her panties up and looked at him. "Two hundred pounds?" She arched an eyebrow. "Are you telling me a fish story?"

He shook his head. "Nope. You should go like that." He nodded at her pink-and-white cotton undies.

She pulled on her red bra, clasped it in front and saw his frown. "Hunter." She laughed. "So what does this beast need you to do to fix him, Dr. Boone?"

"He can't see."

"Poor baby." She frowned. "What's the matter with him? I mean, can you fix him?"

"Yep. The hospital can handle almost anything. He's got some terrible cataracts, but he'll be fine." He pulled his pants on, giving her the most delightful glimpse of his firm rear and muscled thighs. "Speaking of the hospital…"

That doused the rising hunger. She gripped her red sweater, waiting. "Yes?"

"Dr. Lee wanted me to touch base with you about

the mural." He pulled on his undershirt, then started buttoning up his plaid flannel shirt. "You said you wanted to at dinner, but I didn't want to speak for you."

She'd thought about it a lot. Working with Hunter was a perk. Doing something for this family, honoring their son, was important. Supporting the school, also significant. She'd made up her mind to do it. But Amy changed everything. "I don't think I can work there." And since he wasn't going to bring it up, she would. "Not with Amy around." She pulled her brown corduroy pants on and looked at him. "She came by the bakery this morning—"

"I'm sure she did."

"She had an order to pick up for the hospital." She ran her fingers through her hair, distracted.

"She's not happy unless she's making everyone else unhappy." There was no mistaking his frustration. "Not the best way to start the day, I imagine." He brushed her hair from her shoulders, tilting her head back so they were eye to eye.

"She said you got her the job," Josie whispered.

His eyes narrowed, his brow furrowing deeply. When she slipped from his hold, he didn't stop her. But she noticed the way his jaw muscle ticked as she met his gaze in the mirror. "You think I got her the job?" he asked.

She picked up a clip, fiddling with the clasp. "It made sense. She's family. You help your family out—"

"I found out she was working there today." He came up behind her, slipping his arms around her waist and pulling her against his chest. He spoke clearly, leaving no room for interpretation, "I didn't help her get the job, Jo. And while it's generous of you to think I'd be that self-sacrificing, I'm not. I might help her get a job, in Houston or Amarillo. But not here, not now."

"Oh." She couldn't stop the smile from spreading across her face.

"Oh?" He laughed, spinning her around and pulling her against him. His face grew earnest and real and so damn gorgeous her heart was on the verge of bursting from her chest. His kiss was featherlight, but his words made her light-headed. "I love you, Jo. I'm doing my best not to screw things up here."

She blinked. He said it. He loved her.

"Come on." He glanced at his watch. "We're late. Any later and people *will* talk." His kiss was deep, leaving her heart and body spinning.

"Because we're late?" she asked, still processing.

He smiled, stroking his fingertips over her cheek. "You don't know what you want yet—I get that." His voice faltered. "Until you do, I'd rather keep things a little discreet." He kissed her forehead, sighing. "That way it'll be easier for Eli, your dad and me if you go. We'll still be here, you know?"

He wasn't embarrassed or ashamed—he was protecting her, protecting her father and his son. And she loved him all the more for it. She should tell him. She should say it. But a flash of Eli, of Amy's smug grin and the agony of losing Hunter silenced her.

"I need five minutes," she pleaded, pointing to the makeup.

"You don't need it." He shook his head but gave her enough time to put on some mascara, a little eye shadow and some bright red holiday-cheer lipstick.

"Ready?" He took her in, head to toe, before shaking his head. "I'm fine being late, Jo." He pulled her close, bending forward to kiss her.

She laughed, covering his lips with her fingers. "I'm ready."

He pressed a kiss to her fingers, sighing dramatically. "Fine."

She shook her head but took the hand he offered her. "How's Mars?" she asked as they put on their coats and headed out of the bakery.

"She's good, taking a few steps. Her pups are a handful, so we're not letting them nurse all the time. Their poor mama needs time to recover." He paused. "Owners offered me a pup and I'm thinking about giving one to my dad." Hunter led her around the corner.

"Wow," she said finally, looking at all the floats, the lights, the carolers, the canopies that dotted the courthouse lawn. The air hummed with excitement, warding off some of the night chill. "Was it this big when we were in high school?"

"Gets bigger every year. Good to see you, Lance." Hunter nodded at someone but kept them moving.

She called out "hellos" and "nice to see yous" as Hunter led them around another corner. Their float was waiting, hooked up to a large hunter green truck with *Boone Ranch and Rehabilitation Reserve* on the doors. The younger kids were all giggling and playing tag while the older kids were checking the garland and float decorations.

"They're here," someone called out. All the kids waved.

Hunter waved back, giving her a quick grin over his shoulder.

"They wanted to send out a search party," Fisher whispered to Hunter as they walked up. "I figured that might not be the best idea. Didn't want them to find you two in a compromising situation. Might scar them for life."

Hunter punched him in the shoulder. "Got side-tracked with—"

Fisher held up his hands. "Don't need or want to know."

Josie couldn't help but notice Eli. The boy looked so downtrodden, she wanted to hug him. But since she was probably the reason he was upset, she should keep her hugs to herself. His one long, lingering glance at Dara spoke volumes, though.

"Hey, Miss Josie." Dara was red-cheeked and excited, her green sparkly Santa hat and mittens only adding to her adorableness. "Your chair is nice and secure. I rode on it here, just to make sure."

"Thanks, Dara." Josie hugged the girl, surveying the float. It looked even better now, the fairy-light glow illuminating the hours of work the kids had put into making *34* and *Floppy Feet* come to life. "It's just amazing. You guys did a really incredible job." She spoke to Eli, too, who was circling the perimeter of the trailer to check that the garlands and lights were secure.

Eli looked at her, then Dara, shoved his hands in his pockets and mumbled, "Guess so." His attention wandered back to Dara, but the girl was making a point of ignoring him.

Josie didn't know what to say, or do. Young love could seriously suck.

"Are you Joselyn Stephens?" A man approached, his smile a little too appreciative.

She didn't recognize him. "Yes."

"Renata Boone suggested I interview you for the piece we're putting together on the best undiscovered small towns of Texas." He held his hand out. "Ray Garza, State Tourism Department."

"Nice to meet you." Josie shook his hand.

"Would you be free after the parade? We'll be set up by the stage to get some shots for the special." His smile grew. "I'll find you a cup of hot chocolate and let you show me around."

Josie glanced at Hunter, who was watching with interest. "Renata would be better suited for showing you around, Mr. Garza."

"Call me Ray." His smile might be charming, but the way he looked her up and down made her skin crawl.

"Ray." She didn't smile in return. "I'm not sure there's much I can say to sell Stonewall Crossing. It sort of speaks for itself."

"I'd like to hear a little more about what you mean by that." There it was again, that sweeping, slightly-too-lascivious-to-be-ignored appraisal of her figure. He was far too interested in her chest. "We'll meet you by the stage, with hot chocolate, after the parade, then."

Hunter took her hand in his. "You ready, Miss Celebrity?" He shot Ray Garza a look—a look that spoke volumes. She loved that look.

"I guess so." She took his hand and stepped up onto the float. "I'm happy to chat with you for a bit right after the parade, Mr. Garza."

Ray Garza shook his head. "I won't take up much time, I promise. Tonight's about spending time with family." Ray Garza nodded at Hunter, then her, and headed to the small stage where the parade judges were seated, smack-dab in the middle of the square.

"You need an escort for that interview?" Hunter asked, watching Ray Garza go.

She chuckled, leaning over the side of the trailer. "Jealous, Dr. Boone? Don't you know I prefer my men in white coats?"

Hunter looked up at her, tipping his hat back. "I recall hearing something along those lines."

If he kept smiling at her like that, she'd kiss him—no matter who was watching.

He winked at her and stepped back, helping the younger kids climb aboard. She watched his every move, the way he swung each kid high, giving them a word or smile of encouragement. He knew them all, cared about them, about this. This was his home, a place as ingrained in his blood as the color of his incredible eyes.

She'd never felt that way about a place. But something about the camaraderie and affection among this bunch made her rethink, again, the value in her solitary life.

Hunter's voice was stern as he called out, "Remember the rules." He paused, making certain all eyes were on him before he continued. "No standing up, no moving around and no horseplay. Your job is to stay safe, sit on your hay bale and wave like crazy at all the people. And don't forget to yell out 'Merry Christmas' now and then. Got it?"

A dozen hat-and-scarf-clad heads nodded. There was something poignant about their red noses, bright eyes and on-the-verge-of-bursting-with-excitement energy. The mood was contagious. Josie sat in the chair, tucking her hands under her legs. It was cold and, in their haste, she'd forgotten her gloves.

"Miss Stephens?" The little girl had red braids peeking out from under her hat and a smattering of freckles across her nose. "Are you really going to read to us? *Floppy Feet* is my favorite. I have two rabbits that look just like the ones in your book."

"You do?" Josie asked, a sudden warmth chasing away the cold. "What are their names?"

"Floppy and Jack," the little girl answered.

Josie laughed. "Those are great names." She took the book Eli thrust in her face. It was old, the paper jacket creased and worn. There was a faint ring on the back cover, where someone had probably put their iced tea or coffee cup. "Thanks, Eli." She glanced at the boy, wishing he'd give some sort of acknowledgment that she existed. She wanted to ask if this was his copy, the one Hunter and Fisher had read to him when he was little. But the words got stuck in her throat.

He looked at her then, searching her face for one long moment. He swallowed so hard she knew he was holding something back.

"Thank you," Josie repeated, feeling the all-too-familiar sting in her eyes.

"Come on, Eli." Hunter waved his son to the side of the trailer. "Your job is to keep an eye on the little ones," he said to Eli, Dara and four older teenagers who were helping corral the youngsters. Hunter shot her one more smile before climbing into the truck cab.

When the truck pulled forward, the kids squealed with glee. Josie beamed, glancing around the trailer at each little face. The teenagers were smiling, too. Even Eli. Until he saw her smiling at him.

Hunter nodded at the thumbs-up in his side mirror from Eli. Some garland had fallen loose as they cleared the last stretch of road, but everything was secure again.

"Can you go any slower?" Fisher asked as they scooted an inch forward.

"Got a hot date I don't know about?" Hunter glanced at his brother.

"No. But we might just get the kids back to their folks before midnight," his brother shot back.

"I guess a little thing like the twenty kids on the flatbed trailer we're pulling shouldn't matter?" Hunter glanced at the clock on his dashboard. "For the record, it's nine-fifteen."

Fisher snorted. "Look who's all feisty tonight."

Hunter grinned.

The parade had gone well. No one had fallen out or pitched a fit. The lights and music had stayed on. And, from what he could tell, everyone had enjoyed their turn around the square.

As he pulled the truck and trailer into the large parking lot behind the senior center, he saw the sea of parents and cars waiting for their kids. He edged forward slowly, making sure they weren't hanging out onto the street, and parked.

He was cordial to the waiting parents, smiling and shaking hands and enjoying the overall success of the evening. But inside, he felt like a teenager again. A teenager who wanted, more than anything, to get Jo, take her hand in his and savor the rest of the night together.

He caught a look at her, all red-cheeked and wild curls. She was still sitting in her chair, a little girl on her lap. The two of them were reading *Floppy Feet*, so engrossed in the story that neither seemed aware of what was happening around them.

"Kelsey," the little girl's mother finally said. "I imagine Miss Stephens is ready to get out of this cold."

"Aw, Momma." Kelsey frowned.

"I'll read the book to you tonight," her mother coerced.

Kelsey wriggled from Jo's lap, shooting Jo one big gap-toothed grin before running over to Hunter. "Thanks for letting me ride."

"Hope you had fun."

She nodded, wrapping her arms around her mother's neck.

He looked at Jo, the yearning on her face as she watched Kelsey and her mother startling him. She caught him staring and rolled her eyes. Damn, but she was beautiful.

"What can I do?" she asked, nodding at Eli, Dara and Tyler. They were already uncoiling the lights and garlands, making neat coils and stacking them aside.

"They'll get most of it. So nothing flies off on the way back to the ranch." He waved at the older teens working. "You can keep an eye on the two strays," he teased, nodding at two little boys hopping from hale bale to hay bale around the trailer's edge.

He turned to Jo. "Once they're back with their herd, I'll get you to your interview." If she left, tonight would be one of those memories that he held on to for years to come. It wasn't just the sex, though sex with Jo was truly special—it was the intimacy they shared, the connection. He'd be damned if he let her go without a fight.

"What's that look for?" she asked, her pale eyes studying him.

He shook his head, knowing this wasn't the time or place to make his case. "I'll tell you later."

"Dr. Boone, this is hardly the time or place for your wayward thoughts."

"Wayward thoughts?" He bent forward. "What did *you* think I was thinking about?"

She blushed, swallowing.

Every inch of him hardened. "You can tell me about it later." His whisper was rough.

"Dad," Eli called out. "This tire looks low."

It tore his heart out to see the smile Jo gave his son. Eli didn't smile back but, for the first time, he didn't glare at her, either. For Hunter, it was progress. Jo clearly didn't see it that way.

"Duty calls." He excused himself. Eli was right. They'd have to air up the tire before they made the drive back to the ranch. "Good catch," he said, ruffling his son's hair.

Eli groaned, but Dara's soft laugh turned Eli's frown into a grin.

Hunter glanced back and forth between his son and Dara. She'd gone back to working on the trailer while Eli stood staring at her. Hunter nudged him, gently, before heading back to Jo, the boys and their newly arrived parents.

He was shaking hands with the boys' fathers when Amy arrived. He barely managed to keep his face neutral. Last thing he needed to do was make things worse with Eli. His son was barely speaking to him as it was.

"That was adorable, ya'll," Amy cooed. "Eli, honey, I think it's the best float yet."

"Thanks, Mom," Eli murmured. Hunter watched him blush as Amy draped an arm around his shoulders. "I didn't do it on my own." Eli glanced around. He might not be as grown-up as the others, but he hated being treated like a child. Especially in public.

"I know." Amy's brown eyes paused on him for a split second before she turned to Jo. Hunter braced himself as Amy said, "You must be tickled pink to have a whole float dedicated to you, Josie." She paused. "I mean, your books."

Hunter fought to keep his reactions in check. Amy was a master at manipulation, charming and soft-spoken one minute, ripping out the jugular the next. Not that Amy would ever let that side of her show—not with her son at her side. She needed him to think the best of her. It was one of the only things that assured she'd behave in public.

Jo looked lost, her gaze bouncing between Amy, Eli and himself. "It's amazing," she finally said. "These kids are—"

"Amazing?" Amy's teasing was infused with a healthy dose of sarcasm, sarcasm neither he nor Jo missed.

Jo nodded, not taking the bait.

He held out his hand, helping Jo from the trailer. When her feet were on the ground, she pulled her hand from his, barely meeting his eyes. "I think I'll go meet with Mr. Garza now." Her voice was thin, tentative.

He nodded even though he wanted to grab her hand and keep her at his side. "I'll catch up to you in a bit," he offered, wishing he could say more. Instead, he watched her walk back to the main square, her hands stuffed deep in her coat pockets.

"Sounds like you've got plans." Amy looked at him, eyes narrowed. "So I guess I can steal our son?" She turned to Eli. "You done for the night?"

"I guess." Eli shrugged. "I was gonna hang around for a while."

Hunter didn't miss his son's quick glance at Dara. But Amy was oblivious.

"You can hang out with them anytime." Amy tucked her arm through Eli's. "How long has it been since we had a sleepover, anyway?"

"Where?" Hunter asked, leaden concern filling his belly.

"My hotel." Amy smiled. "I haven't found a real place to rent...yet. I'm staying at the Main Street Hotel. And there's two beds and cable," she added. "We can get a pizza or something, whatever you want."

Hunter watched Eli's every reaction. His son was uncertain, which Hunter understood. He had a tough choice to make. He could keep Eli from spending the night with Amy, but then he'd ensure Amy was the victim and Eli her defender.

His son looked at him, bracing for a fight.

Hunter didn't fist his hands or clench his jaw or bite out, "Your call," no matter how much he wanted to. Instead, he managed to keep it together, staying neutral and calm.

Which didn't sit well with Eli. "Thanks, Mom. If you're sure you don't have any plans. Wouldn't want to get in the way." Eli shoved his hands in his pockets, staring at the ground at his feet.

"Eli." Hunter's voice was low. "You're never in the way, ever."

Amy glared at Hunter, the look on her face a visible replay of the argument they'd had on his porch the week before.

"Yeah, sure." Eli's tone sharpened, and he outright scowled as he added, "You have fun tonight."

Hunter could tell Eli to get his butt in the truck—his every instinct told him to do just that. He could drive his son home and the two of them could have another fight over Jo and Amy. But then he'd end up with a son who hated him, an all but sainted ex-wife, no Jo and no closer to resolution on any account. And, no matter how impossible it seemed right this second, he wanted the best possible outcome for everyone.

He took a deep breath. "I don't appreciate your tone. And we've talked about this. You're never in the way." He shook his head, searching for the right words. "I understand wanting to spend time with your mom. If that's what you want to do tonight, then go ahead. But don't think you have to go or that I want you to go, all right?"

Eli's anger faltered, his blue-green eyes going wide.

"You're going on a date with someone he can't stand." Amy's words were quick, tipping the scales in resentment's favor. "Of course he doesn't want to stay. How do you expect him to feel, Hunter?"

There wasn't anything he could say to that, not without making things ten times worse. He hated that Amy put words in Eli's mouth, that she had no problem using Eli to vent her thoughts and opinions. But Eli was old enough to speak up now. How many times had his son challenged him? Until Eli set Amy straight, Hunter's hands were tied. He watched Amy leading him toward her truck. "You want to get something to eat first? Some hot chocolate or something?"

Hunter stood waiting, hoping for some sort of look or acknowledgment, some sort of softening in his son. But Eli never looked back. Hunter watched Amy's taillights disappear.

"You okay, Dr. Boone?" Dara asked.

Hunter nodded, working hard at a smile. "I'll give ya'll a hand." He set to work beside the others, getting the trailer ready for the drive back to the ranch.

Chapter 16

The phone was ringing. Josie glanced at the clock. It was three in the morning.

Who would call at this hour? Her mom? Lola?

She sat up, pulled on her robe and ran to the phone. Not that her dad would hear it, since he took his hearing aids out at night.

"Hello?" She was a little breathless and barely awake, so it came out like a croak.

"Josie? Miss Stephens?" The voice was high, strained and scared. "It's Eli. Eli Boone."

"Eli?" Josie came fully awake in seconds. An ice-cold weight ballooned in her stomach. "Is everything okay?"

"I guess…" There was a tremor in his voice. He was scared. "Didn't know who else to call."

"It's fine." She prompted, really worried now. "You can call anytime."

"Yeah…" Eli's voice broke. "Can you come get me?"

Something was very wrong. Her fingers tangled in the phone cord as she processed his words. "Where are you?" She spoke as calmly as possible.

"My mom's hotel room. Roadside Motel, next to the gas station and the bar."

"Off the highway?" she asked, knowing which place he was talking about and hoping Eli was wrong. She had a hard time believing Hunter would approve. To hear Lola talk about it, if something shady or illegal was happening, it had to have started at *that* bar. Of course, Lola was known for dramatics… Still, the bar was in the middle of the hotel parking lot where Eli was. "Where's your mom?"

"Don't know. Woke up and she was gone. She's not answering her cell phone."

"Did you call your dad—"

"I called Uncle Fisher and Uncle Ryder, but they didn't answer. Dad's working. And he'd get really mad and they'd fight and I… I just want to go home." He cleared his throat. "Will you come get me, please?"

Josie's heart was in her throat. "I'll be there in five minutes." There was no way she could refuse him.

"Thanks," he murmured, then hung up.

She tugged on her father's boots, pulled her black wool coat over her blue plaid flannel pajamas, grabbed her rental car keys and headed out the door. It was eerily quiet up and down Main Street. Most of

Stonewall Crossing was asleep, the storefronts darkened and the streets deserted. She drove on, reaching the edge of Main Street as it intersected the highway. The Roadside Motel was there, off the on-ramp, next door to a run-down bar and a twenty-four-hour truck stop. She might not have any kids, but this was not the sort of place you left a child alone.

She pulled into the parking lot, focused on the windows of the motel for any sign of Eli. She slammed on her brakes as room seven's curtains dropped and the door opened. Eli all but ran out, a duffel bag over his shoulder and his cowboy hat on his head.

He nodded at her as he climbed into the car.

"You okay?" she asked.

He nodded again.

"Did you leave your mom a note?" Josie asked. "So she doesn't get back and worry over you?"

Eli snorted then.

"She will, Eli."

"I left a note," he grumbled, hugging his duffel bag close.

"Okay, good. Want me to take you home?"

He looked at her. "Yeah."

"You're shivering," she said, turning up the heat as he snapped his seat belt into place.

"Heater in the room was broken." He shrugged, holding his hands out to the warm air.

She looked at him, fighting back a million questions. Rage wasn't an emotion she was familiar with. But right now, she was so furious with Amy she could barely see straight.

Eli looked at her.

Amy and anger could wait. She searched his face. He was so mature for his age, but she knew he had to be hurting right now. "We should call your dad," she murmured.

"He'll get all riled up." Eli frowned. "You don't understand."

And while Josie thought Hunter had every right to get upset over his son being left in some off-the-highway one-night-stand motel, she suspected Eli wouldn't want to hear that. "You'll talk to him as soon as you get home?"

He nodded.

She didn't want to be in the middle of anything. She didn't want to keep secrets from Hunter, not where Eli was concerned. "Thank you." She beamed at the boy.

He was watching her closely. "Dad said your mom wasn't the best in the world."

She answered carefully, trying to decide what she should or shouldn't say. "That's true." She added, "She loved me. I know she did the best she could by me." Josie put the car in Drive, turning them in the opposite direction. "She didn't really know what to do with me."

"What do you mean?"

She hesitated for a minute. "My mom wasn't the motherly type. She was more interested in her…hobbies." Men, marriage, weddings, that sort of thing.

"Guess my mom and your mom have a lot in common." His words were soft, but sad.

Even though she wasn't her mother's biggest fan,

it was a hard comparison to hear. "You think so?" she asked, offering Eli the chance to vent. Whatever had happened between Amy and her son, he'd needed rescuing tonight. And he'd called her to do the rescuing.

"Rodeo calls and, bam, Mom's there. *I* call?" He shook his head, anger coloring his words. "She doesn't show up when she says she will. But when she does, she's full of...of *it*." His hold on his bag tightened. "She believes what she says when she says it, but it never lasts. Like tonight, telling me and Dad we were staying in town, ordering pizza and hanging out." He sucked in a deep breath, calming a little before he went on. "Dad always tells me to be careful—to not get my hopes up. And that really bugs me, because I hate that he's right about her. If he'd just believe in her, she might change, you know?"

She knew exactly what he wanted to hear. "Nice thought, that someone can change someone else. I wish it was true."

"It might help."

"It might." She retreated a little, desperate to keep him talking. "But my experience is change is a personal choice, Eli."

"I guess... She's my mom, you know?"

"I do." And she did. She really did. She smiled at the boy again.

"Dad doesn't get it. His mom was the best."

"She was," Josie agreed, remembering Mags Boone with real affection. "She was pretty much the perfect wife and mother. She kept a neat house, always had food on hand for anyone who stopped by, and looked put together without trying." Josie laughed. "Of course, I was used to my mother, so Mags was like a real-live fairy godmother. She liked everyone—"

"She didn't like my mom," Eli interrupted.

Josie could imagine that. Mags had always been fiercely protective of her boys. Sure, Amy hadn't gotten pregnant on her own, but Mags would have found a way to believe it wasn't Hunter's fault. It was the first time Josie ever felt even the slightest twinge of sympathy for Amy. One glance at the ten-year-old boy and the sympathy was gone.

"I don't think they ever made Mom feel welcome," Eli muttered. "Maybe that's why she leaves. Maybe she comes back, thinking things will be different. Then she sees it's still the same and there's not enough here to stick around for."

She looked at Eli and ached. *You are enough.* She blinked back tears. *He* was enough. Amy had this amazing boy's love and she chose to leave. She sniffed, tears dangerously close to spilling over. If he was hers, he'd have been her world and she'd make sure he knew it.

Eli continued, "Guess I feel like I need to make up for that."

"Oh, Eli, that's a big job for one man."

He nodded. "Guess so."

"All you can do is love her," Josie said. She glanced at Eli, who was staring out the front windshield, jaw clenched and hands fisted in the straps of his duffel bag. Life could be hard. But for someone like Eli, with a family who would move heaven and earth for him, it didn't need to be. She tried again. "We have something else in common, Eli."

"What?" He glanced at her.

"Our fathers are amazing. My dad would bend over backward to help me out. He's always there, full of advice." She paused, shooting him a conspiratorial look. "Even when I don't want him to be."

Eli nodded, his short laugh a relief.

"He's the person I call when my world is falling apart. Or when I have news I have to share with someone because I'm bursting with excitement, ya know?" She glanced at him.

"Yeah." His answer was soft.

"I am sorry about tonight, Eli." She turned onto the road leading into the Boone ranch. "I wish I could make it better."

There was silence before he asked, "You do?"

She swallowed. "I do. I really do." She slowed down as a rabbit sprinted across the road and into the opposite field.

"You can drop me here," Eli said, pointing at the Lodge. "Dad's working emergency duty."

"I know you're worried about your dad being mad. But if he is mad, it's because he loves you so much." She kept the car and the heater running. "Talk to him, Eli, okay?"

"I will. I gotta sort out what I'm going to say." Eli nodded, gathering his things.

"That makes sense," she agreed.

"Thanks for the ride." He looked at her, a shadow of a smile on his face.

She watched him climb the steps of the Lodge, waiting until he was safely inside before turning around and heading back into town. Thoughts of Eli and Hunter and Amy went 'round and 'round. Should she call Hunter? She didn't know if she'd done the right thing. Eli had called and she'd responded. Maybe she'd overstepped, but surely Hunter would understand.

By the time she parked her car at the bakery, her head ached. She slumped over the steering wheel, second-guessing every minute since Eli's phone call.

The bakery lights flipped on, startling Josie. She glanced at the clock on the car dashboard. Five o'clock. Dad would be up, making coffee, letting the dog out and getting things ready for the morning. She watched as Lola and her father appeared, smiling and talking, carrying mugs of coffee. It was a glimpse of her father's future and she liked what she saw.

Now, if only she had a crystal ball to see what her future looked like.

Hunter didn't see Amy's truck in the parking lot. Where were they? He'd texted her he was on his way. He yawned, wiping the sleep from his eyes. He'd been called in to scope a Great Dane who'd managed to swallow his tennis ball on a rope. After a two-hour surgery, the ball and rope were removed from the dog's stomach and intestine. One thing he could say about his job, it was never boring. He still found real satisfaction working with animals, even when he got next to no sleep.

Once he picked up Eli, he'd go see Jo at Pop's, get some kolaches and go home for a few hours of sleep.

He knew Jo's time clock was ticking. He knew she loved New Mexico, and the job she'd been offered was right up her alley. But she needed to know that he wanted her to stay, with him, here. And he was going to make sure he said that, no misunderstandings or miscommunications.

He stepped out of his truck at the same time Amy's truck plowed into the Main Street Hotel's lot. Her vehicle bounced as she came to a complete stop, then her door flew open and she charged at him.

"What the hell is the matter with you?" she yelled.

He sighed, crossing his arms over his chest. He was too tired for her drama this morning. "Morning to you, too."

She poked his chest with her finger. "Morning? Are you shittin' me?"

"Where's Eli?"

Amy paused, took a step back. "What do you mean?"

He waited.

"She came and picked him up this morning," Amy snapped.

"Who came and picked him up?"

"Josie." She frowned. "You didn't send her to get him? She said you did. She said you called her to come get him."

He was beyond confused now. Why would Jo pick up Eli? Why would she tell Amy he'd sent her? Why would Eli go with Jo? He wasn't exactly her biggest fan. "Where is he?"

"I don't know." Her voice spiked. "She has him. Why did she take him? Why did she lie?"

Hunter watched Amy. Something wasn't adding up. For one thing, Jo wasn't the one with the track record for lying. "When did she get him?"

"Must have been around seven—"

"Where were you?" he cut in, frustration giving way to anger.

"*I* was in the shower." She shook her head. "She comes and takes our son who knows where and lies about it and you want to know where I was? Damn, Hunter, are you that blind to that woman?"

Hunter sighed. "I'll call Eli."

"Already tried," she argued. "His phone is off, I guess."

His eyes narrowed. "I will talk to him—"

"Good. Go talk to him. Now. After you find him." She shook her head, climbing into her truck. "I'm not gonna argue with you when I could be looking for my son. I've half a mind to press charges against her."

Hunter watched her peel out of the parking lot as he climbed into his truck. Even though he was pretty sure Eli was with Jo, there was no fighting the fear in his heart until he knew for sure. He picked up his phone, headed toward home and called his father. Eli was most likely there. Those two were peas in a pod.

"Figured you'd call." His father answered on the first ring.

"He there?"

"Sleeping."

Hunter rubbed a hand over his face, relief so sharp

he was almost breathless. "You couldn't call?" He tried not to snap.

"Whoa now, boy," his father soothed. "I called the hospital. You were in surgery."

Hunter sighed. "Thanks, Dad. Sorry. Amy—"

"I can imagine." He paused. "She with you?"

"No, but I should probably let her know where Eli is. Be there soon." He hung up and called Amy.

"What?" she snapped.

"He's at my dad's."

"Oh, thank God." Her voice was muffled. "Hunter found him." She was louder then, her voice unsteady. "Is he okay?"

"He's asleep. I'm on my way."

"I'm coming—"

"No." He was going to talk to his son alone.

"No?" She was crying then. "No? My son gets taken from my hotel room, disappears, and now you're not going to let me see him?" Her voice was muffled again. "No, Officer, I don't know about pressing charges yet."

Hunter groaned. "I'll call you later." Ten minutes later he was inside the Lodge, staring down at his bleary-eyed son.

Eli started with "I'm sorry."

"For what?" He sat on the bed by his son. "First thing I need to know. You okay?" When Eli started crying, Hunter pulled him into his arms and held him close. Sometimes he forgot how young Eli was. Sometimes he forgot how sweet his hair smelled, how small his frame felt against him, but he never forgot how much he loved his son.

"Yeah." His answer was muffled against Hunter's neck.

"You sure?" he asked, holding his son tighter.

"I should have called you," he said. "She…she said you wanted me to come to Granddad's, so I went with her."

He froze. "She?" He tried to pull Eli back, to look at him, but his son was clinging to him.

"Josie…" Eli cleared his throat. "She said you were working and she was going to take me home."

Jo? It didn't make sense. Jo didn't want anything to do with Amy—she'd done her best to avoid all interaction with his ex-wife. Stirring up trouble like this, out of the blue, didn't add up.

Eli was sobbing and Eli didn't cry. Even when he was a toddler, he'd rarely had tantrums. Whatever had happened, his son was torn up about it. "What's got you so worked up?"

"I didn't want you to be mad at me."

"Worried is more like it."

"And M-Mom's phone message. She was s-so worried." He sniffed. "I didn't mean to worry her like that. You can't blame her or be mad at her or not let me see her anymore. It's not her fault."

Hunter sighed, hearing Amy's words. "Eli, what happened?"

Eli sat back, frowning. "I told you."

"Nothing else? You didn't talk to Jo when she was driving you home?" In his gut he knew there was more to it. "Your mom is at the police station right now."

Eli's eyes went round. "Why?"

"She was talking about pressing charges against Jo, for taking you."

Hunter saw fear on his son's face, pure, unguarded fear. "She didn't... B-but... All Josie did was pick me up. She picked me up and brought me here. That's all."

"She took you without talking to me or your mom. That's a big deal. Some might say it's kidnapping." Hunter watched him.

"Kidnapping?" Eli was staring at him now, more tears appearing. "She brought me home. That's all."

He chose his words carefully, hoping to learn more. "Maybe. But she didn't have permission. Did she say why?"

"She said... She said..."

Hunter took his son's hand. "What did Jo say?"

Eli looked at his father, swallowing hard. "She said you sent her." He cleared his throat. "You wanted her to pick me up 'cause you were working and she was supposed to take me to Granddad's. That's all." His lower lip was wobbling. "You really think Mom will have her arrested?"

"I hope not." He frowned. "No point, since you're safe and sound. But I'm not too sure why she did it in the first place."

"She..." He cleared his throat again. "She was acting a little weird."

"Weird?"

"She smelled funny... Like Uncle Ryder does sometimes."

"You're saying she was drinking?" Hunter frowned. "Were you in danger?"

Eli opened his mouth, then closed it. "I... I didn't feel safe until I got here."

Hunter's stomach tensed. He stood up, rubbing his hand over his face. His son, who knew good and well how he felt about honesty, was telling him Jo had been drunk when she picked him up?

His Jo?

Jo wasn't a drinker. Hadn't been a drinker. Hell, they'd barely been old enough to drink when things fell apart. Was she a drinker? It might explain what had happened...

He glanced at his son, at the heartbreak on his young face. If she had been drinking, she'd put Eli at risk. Anger rolled over him. His son hadn't felt safe. He could barely choke out his words. "Anything else I need to know, Eli? You can tell me anything, you know that."

Eli nodded, staring at him for a long time. A few times, he looked as if he was going to say something, but he'd stop himself. All he added was, "I'm sorry."

"No reason for you to apologize, Eli." Hunter bent down and pressed a kiss to his son's forehead. "I'm sorry you were put in this situation." He ruffled his son's hair. "You look beat. Get some sleep."

"What are you going to do?" Eli asked, clearly still uneasy.

"I'm going to sort this out." He shot his son what he hoped was a reassuring smile and pulled the door closed behind him. He closed his eyes, trying to make sense of the past forty minutes.

"Need anything?" His father's voice was low, soothing.

Hunter straightened, pushing off the bedroom door. "Go in and sit with him awhile?"

His father nodded. "Everything okay?"

He shook his head. "No, Dad. It's not."

His father gripped his shoulder. "Well, now, it's nothing you can't fix."

"Maybe this time there's nothing left to fix, Dad." His heart had been broken before and he'd survived, barely. This time, he wasn't so sure.

Chapter 17

Josie pulled the sheet pan from the oven, eyeing the brandied fruitcake. She was exhausted. It was eleven o'clock and she hadn't heard from Hunter or Eli. Every time the phone rang, she jumped.

"You're as jumpy as a jackrabbit." Her father stood back as she turned the tray and pushed it back into the large oven.

She glared at him before returning to the bakery dining room.

"This is my favorite." Annabeth pointed to the peppermint-flavored coffee Lola was testing on the customers. "Very holiday-y."

"One more?" her son asked, pointing at the mini sweet rolls in the basket on the table.

Annabeth raised an eyebrow at him.

He smiled brightly. "One more, please?"

She put another sweet roll on his plate and cut it up for him. "Thank you for using your manners."

Josie grinned, watching the little boy gobble up the sticky goodness in two huge bites. "Someone has a good appetite."

Annabeth nodded. "Gonna eat me out of house and home before he hits puberty."

Josie's smile faded as Hunter's truck parked in front of the bakery. She smoothed her hands over her wayward ponytail and dusted off the flour from the holiday apron she wore.

The first thing she noticed was Hunter's exhaustion. His shoulders drooped, his steps were hesitant; he seemed broken. They locked eyes then, and the look of complete devastation in his pulled her around the counter to meet him. She didn't know what to say, what she could do, but she would be there for him. There was nothing she wanted more than to be there for him, now and forever.

"Did you talk to Eli?" she asked, unable to imagine how Hunter felt.

He nodded, barely looking at her.

"Is he okay?"

"Not really." His voice was sharp. "He was crying pretty hard when I got home."

She tried to take his hand, but he pulled his away, shoving it deep in his pocket. He was upset, that was all. He had every right to be upset. "Can I do anything?"

He looked at her then, raw and defeated. "Jo—"

"I feel so bad. He's so grown-up, it's easy to forget he's still so young." She shook her head.

"But he is young. And impressionable." He paused, straightening. "I can't put his safety in jeopardy." His eyes bore into hers. "I don't understand why you picked him up." His voice was accusing. "Why, Jo?"

She blinked, stunned. Something was wrong. Something was very wrong. "I was trying to help."

His brow furrowed. "Help? How the hell do you think what you did helped?"

She stepped back, glancing around the bakery. "Hunter—"

"Eleven years is a long time. People change." He swallowed, the hurt on his face cutting through her. "I never thought you'd put a child in harm's way."

"What?" She gasped.

"Amy talked to the police." Hunter lowered his voice.

She held on to the back of one of the diner chairs. She knew he'd be angry with Amy—he had every right to be. If he felt it was necessary to bring the police into it, then things must be worse than she knew. "I'm sorry it led to this."

"What did you expect to happen?" His eyes searched hers. "I don't know if she'll press charges or not. But I can't defend you."

And just like that, the floor was pulled out from under her. It was hard to breathe, let alone ask, "What...what did Eli tell you?"

"Everything. After Amy showed up, screaming about Eli missing."

"Missing? But he... Eli left a note." What was happening?

"He left a note, Jo?" Hunter ran a hand over his face. "So that makes it okay that you took him without Amy knowing?"

"I—"

"How much did you have to drink last night?" he asked, leaning forward.

"What?" she gasped. "What are you insinuating?"

"I'm not insinuating a thing. I'm asking for clarification."

She couldn't decide which was stronger, the pain in her heart or the anger rushing through her veins. She chose anger—it was easier to deal with. "What did Eli tell you?" she repeated slowly.

"God, Jo, you can't remember?" He sighed, clearly disgusted.

"Humor me," she snapped.

"You showed up, told him I'd sent you to take him back to my dad's, since I was working late." He put his hands on his hips.

"And Amy was?"

"In the shower." He took another step closer, so there was barely an inch between them. "The worst part is that he didn't feel safe, Jo. He's my son."

She stared at him, pain trumping anger. "Eli said that?"

Hunter nodded.

She sat down then, too blindsided to stay on her feet. Eli had lied to Hunter. He'd made her out to be the villain. She knew, without a shadow of a doubt, he was protecting his mother. Chances were, Amy had something to do with the story. But it didn't make it hurt any less. Eli had lied and Hunter believed it.

Hunter believed she was a drunk who'd all but kidnapped his kid. He wasn't asking her for her side of the story or asking for the truth. No, he was telling her he wouldn't defend her if she had charges pressed against her. She wanted to scream at him, to tell him the truth, to defend herself. She looked up at him, blinking back the sting of tears.

She stood, pushing the chair in at the table with careful deliberation before she stepped back. "You're a good father, Hunter. Please tell Eli I'm sorry. I never meant to cause any problems for your family."

"I don't understand…" His expression shifted, a mix of confusion and desperation.

If she told him the truth, it would be her word against Eli's. Eli already thought of her as the bad guy. She'd never thought he hated her this much, but still… This wasn't how she wanted them to end up, but she was foolish to believe anything permanent was an option for them.

"Everything okay?" her dad asked.

"Fine." She smiled. "Just saying goodbye."

"Goodbye?" Hunter asked.

"I fly out tonight," she answered quickly. "Lots to do before the move. I am sorry I won't be able to do the mural. I'll let Dr. Lee know."

"Josie—" her father started.

"Tickets are a steal Christmas Eve." She pressed a kiss to her father's forehead. "Lola's waving you over, Dad."

Hunter waited until her father was out of earshot

before asking, "You couldn't wait till after Christmas to leave?"

She shrugged. "Dad's better. That was the only reason I was here. The only thing keeping me here. Besides, I've caused enough damage, don't you think?" She wrinkled her nose, trying not to break. It wouldn't help for him to see just how devastated she really felt. She had to get out of here, she had to get out of this room away from these people, before she lost her control and her dignity.

His eyes raked over her, his expression hard and unreadable. "Good luck to you, Jo." He turned, heading from the bakery without a backward glance.

"You, too, Hunter." She choked out the words before stumbling blindly from the bakery, through the kitchen and into her father's house.

"Josie?" Annabeth was calling out.

Two sets of footsteps followed.

"I need a minute," she answered.

"Like hell you do," Annabeth appeared, followed by Lola. "You need to tell us what's going on."

"Nothing—"

"Joselyn Marie Stephens," her father barked, coming up behind Lola. "I want the truth and I want it now."

She shook her head. "It doesn't matter, Dad."

The bell over the bakery door rang. Her father and Lola exchanged a glance before he headed back into the bakery.

"You can't leave," Annabeth argued.

"Try to stop me." Josie sighed, heading toward

her bedroom. "You've got Dad taken care of, right, Lola?"

"Of course, sugar," Lola answered. "But I'm going to side with your father on this one, Josie. Annabeth and I won't tell a living soul what's going on, but we're not leaving until we know the whole story."

Fifteen minutes later, Annabeth and Lola were speechless.

Josie clicked the buy button for her eight-fifteen airline ticket back to Seattle, then pulled her suitcase out.

"You're sure about this?" Annabeth asked, eyeing the suitcase.

Josie nodded.

"You don't think he deserves the truth?" Lola asked.

Josie nodded again. "But it's Eli's truth to tell. I can't be the one to ruin everything. And to Eli, telling the truth would ruin everything." She started shoving things into her bag. "I won't come between Hunter and his son."

"Josie, damn it, this is ridiculous. What I wouldn't give to smack Eli Boone on the butt," Annabeth said with a scowl.

"I don't necessarily agree with you leaving." Lola sighed. "But I respect your decision about Eli."

"What?" Annabeth shook her head. "Why?"

"He already hates me…obviously more than I understood." Josie continued packing.

"He's a child. Children think about one thing— themselves." Lola started picking up the clothing Josie had thrown in the suitcase, folding each item neatly before stacking it back inside. "Somehow Amy has convinced that boy Josie is the reason for all the bad in his world—"

"From his parents' divorce to global warming," Annabeth interjected.

"If she comes in there, barrels blazing, and calls him out, she's only confirming his deepest fear." Lola tucked a pair of Josie's shoes into the side of the suitcase.

"Which is?" Annabeth asked.

"He'll lose his father," Josie answered.

"That's ridiculous," Annabeth countered.

"No, it's not. I understand Eli. I was Eli. I was never enough for my mother. Now I'm just like her, no roots, no commitments. His father is what matters most—he can't lose him, too... Especially not to the enemy." Josie scanned the room, finding one red sock under the edge of her bed.

Annabeth sighed, frowning deeply. "It's not fair, though. Hunter loves you. You love him. Eli—"

"Is a good boy. I want him to be happy," Josie cut her off. "I need him to be happy. Honestly, it'll make all of this drama worth it if he and his father come out stronger on the other side of this."

Annabeth snorted.

Lola clicked her tongue. "One thing, Josie, hear me out. You're nothing like your mother, honey. You try, you really do, hopping from place to place. But your heart is loyal. Why else would you still love Hunter? Why else would you still be inspired and happy in this place? If you ask me, sweetie, you're true-blue. Just like your father."

Lola's words left Josie conflicted. If only that were true. Her father was a stick-till-the-end-through-thick-and-thin type. Everything she wanted to be. But if that was true, why was she shoving everything she owned back into her battered suitcase?

Hunter flipped through the Great Dane's chart. Maximus was still pretty sedated, but his vitals were regular. He listened to the dog's abdomen with his stethoscope, noting healthy sounds of active intestinal motility and gas movement.

"Let me know if anything changes," he said to Jarvis, one of the veterinary techs who worked in the operating and recovery rooms.

"You okay, Dr. Boone?" Jarvis asked. "You look a little worse for wear."

Hunter nodded. "I feel it, too."

"Isn't Dr. Archer on tonight? For Christmas Eve and all?" Jarvis asked.

Hunter nodded. "Had a few things I wanted to clear up before I left." The truth was a little different. He wasn't up for seeing anyone. Work was a great way to distract him from the pain in his heart and the engagement ring in his desk drawer. Tonight wasn't going to be the Christmas Eve he'd planned on.

He walked along the deserted halls. Except for emergencies, the clinic was closed for the next two days. He stopped in to check on the animals in residence. Mars had left this morning, on all four paws, with her pups. But the other doctors had patients in-house, so he flipped through their files before moving on.

There was a ray of light from under the medicine closet, which was unusual. The hospital had a huge pharmacy, so the door was kept locked at all times. Only a few clinicians had a key, so he was surprised to see the door was ajar.

Amy was inside, loading her bag with bottles of pain medicine and steroids.

"Amy?"

She froze, spinning around.

"Bag." He held out his hand. "Now."

She opened and closed her mouth, then handed the bag over. "I was…"

He looked at her, waiting. "Go on."

She clamped her mouth shut.

"Nothing?" He peered into the bag, whistling softly. "How much is all this worth?"

"Hunter—"

He looked at her, not bothering to conceal his anger as he pushed the door closed behind him. "Yes?"

She glanced nervously at the closed door. "What are you doing?"

"Watching you restock these shelves," he said. "Best if no one sees you doing it." He held the bag out to her.

"You're not turning me in?" she asked.

He didn't say anything. Instead, he pointed at her bag, then the shelves.

"Sometimes you still surprise me, Hunter Boone." She smiled her charming smile before pulling a bottle out of her bag. She placed it on the shelf, then glanced back at him. "Guess it's hard to send me off to jail on Christmas Eve. Not the best present for Eli."

He wanted her gone.

"I was talking to Winnie about parenting. She thinks you're the best dad around." She kept stacking. "I told her you were definitely the hottest."

He wanted her to stop talking.

"Did you know she has the hots for you?" Amy asked.

He didn't bother responding. Today had become one of the longest days of his life. When he saw his key ring, the one he kept in his office drawer, clipped to her belt loop, he lost it.

"You done?"

She nodded.

"Bag." He held his hand out.

She frowned. "I put it all back."

He reached forward and took the bag from her. He dumped five more bottles of pills and several vials of injectable steroids onto the metal counter. "Enough."

His tone must have reached her, because she froze.

"I've spent the last ten years raising Eli to believe the best in you."

She crossed her arms under her breasts, drawing attention to her chest. "I'm not a bad person."

He looked at her, then the medicine. "I'd like to think there's good in everyone, Amy. The last few years, it's been harder to find good in you. I don't want you around our son anymore."

"I have every right—" she protested.

"You have a right to one weekend a month and alternating holidays." He held his hand up. "But this—" he pointed at the medicine "—would take that away."

She glanced at the medicine, then at him. "You're blackmailing me?"

He sighed. "If that's how you want to look at it. I'd like to think we're negotiating how we plan to move forward."

She put her hands on her hips. "What do you want?"

"I want you to leave. Send him a card on his birthday and the holidays. Call me before you call him."

"For how long?" she snapped.

"Do you understand that I have every right to call the police on you?" He stepped closer, his voice rising. "Don't you care that what you're doing is illegal? What do you think Eli would do if he found out about this?"

"He'll never have to," she yelled. "He'll have the Boone fortune to support him."

"If you need money—"

"I do. I need money." She pointed at the medicine. "Rodeo is what I love, what makes me feel alive. I can't give it up, you know? But it's expensive."

"So is spending years in jail. Might not cost you money, but it will cost you time." He shook his head. "I'll make sure you have money—"

"And I'll go." Her voice was lower. "Just don't make him hate me."

Hunter frowned. "Why would I do that?"

She shrugged. "You and Joselyn Stephens—"

He held up his hand. "I'm not talking about Jo with you." He sighed, taking his key ring off her jeans and pulling the door closed behind them. He locked it, pocketed his keys and pulled out his wallet.

"You're a good guy, Hunter." She took the five hundred dollars and tucked it into her pocket. "I know Eli will turn out just like you."

He didn't leave the hospital until she was gone. Once he rechecked all the doors were secure, he waved goodbye to Jarvis and headed home. He took the long way around town, needing the time to get his head in the game. It was Christmas Eve and his son needed cheering up.

The Lodge was aglow with white illuminated lights and a massive wreath mounted on the front of the house. Hunter climbed up the steps and went inside.

"About time you got home." Renata hugged him. "Eli's sick."

"Sick?" Hunter asked.

"I'm not sure what's wrong with him, but he doesn't want to get out of bed."

Hunter looked at his dad.

"Don't look at me," his father answered. "He fell asleep after you left, but he was fitful."

"You left this." Renata handed him his phone. "See if you can get him up for dinner. It's beef tenderloin, his favorite."

"I'll see what I can do." He did his best to relax and smile before heading into the guest room where Eli was propped up, playing his handheld game.

Eli sat up. "Hey."

Hunter sat on the edge of the bed. "What are you playing?"

"Nothing." Eli put the game down. "You okay?"

Hunter nodded.

"You don't look okay." Eli's hands fiddled with the blanket.

"I'll be okay," Hunter promised. "Long day."

"Yep," Eli agreed.

"You feeling bad?" he asked, touching his son's forehead. "No fever."

Eli shook his head. "You look sad."

Hunter looked at him. No point in pretending. "I am."

"About what happened?" Eli asked.

Hunter nodded. "I thought I knew Jo. It's hard when you think you know a person and then find out you were wrong."

"I know." Eli nodded, frowning at his game. "You're disappointed in her."

"And myself. Thought I was a better judge of character." He sighed. "Jo was real important to me, Eli. I really loved her. Next to you, she's what matters most. Losing her again, it hurts."

"You didn't love Mom?" he asked.

"You can love people differently, son. And Jo and I, we're like puzzle pieces. I thought we still fit, but I was wrong." He looked at his son.

Eli's eyes were filled with tears. "You still love her?"

"Probably always will. But it'll get easier in time." He smiled, patting his son's legs through the blanket. "What she did, well, it's unforgivable."

"Dad," Eli's voice was low. "I'm sorry."

Hunter hugged Eli. "Let's stop all this moping

around and get up for dinner. It's Christmas—time to celebrate."

Eli climbed out of bed, then grabbed Hunter's hand. "She didn't do it. I'm so sorry. I know what I did was wrong. And bad. I want to fix it."

Hunter looked at his son. "What?"

"I was scared. Mom left me in that hotel by the bar. I called Uncle Ryder and Uncle Fisher, but they didn't answer. I found Mr. Stephens in the phone book and called Josie." Eli's words ran together, his nerves making things hard to understand.

Hunter sat on the edge of the bed, his heart pounding in his ears. Amy had lied about everything, from where she was staying to Jo. It didn't surprise him that she'd lie, but Eli… He looked at his son.

"Josie came right away. The room heater was broken, so she blasted the heat in her car and told me it was all going to be okay. She said I was lucky to have you for a dad and brought me home. I told her not to call you 'cause you were working…"

Hunter shook his head. "You lied to me."

Eli was crying. "Yes, sir. And it was wrong."

"Why did you do it, Eli?"

"I was scared. M-Mom said you'd never let me see her again if you knew I'd been alone in the Roadside Motel. And she said Josie would take you away from me, that I'd be alone. Please forgive me, Dad."

His heart ached, the fear and regret on his son's face both a burden and a relief. "I forgive you. But no more lies, okay?" Hunter waited for Eli's nod before pulling him against him. "You are my son. No matter what, you're stuck with me."

"I know." His arms tightened around Hunter. "I know that. And I feel real bad for causing trouble between you and Josie. She's really…nice. I like her."

Hunter's laugh was breathy. "I do, too."

"I don't want you to lose her." Eli looked at his father.

Hunter closed his eyes. "Oh, Eli. Sometimes you can love a person and it still doesn't work out."

"I know. But not for you and Josie." Eli tugged Hunter into the living room. "You need to go talk to her. I can go, too. I'll tell her I lied. I'll tell her why I lied."

Renata and his father appeared, listening.

"It's Christmas Eve, son. I want to spend time with my family."

Eli nodded. "So go get her."

Hunter touched his son's cheek, awed by the love and support Eli was offering.

Chapter 18

Josie stared at the arrivals and departures board. The green digital letters were updated as flights came and went. She'd been sitting here for hours. She'd been boarding, in line, bag in hand, but she couldn't leave.

Now she sat, staring at the screens, trying to figure out what to do next.

Hunter believed the worst of her.

Eli didn't want her in his life.

Amy was back in Stonewall Crossing.

But her father was getting married.

Her best friend in the whole wide world was right here.

And she was finally writing and painting again.

Could she find a way to be here without Hunter? Could she coexist without feeling that jolt of awareness whenever she saw him? Or smile when she heard his name mentioned? Could she bear it if he moved on, finding love and a family?

She felt nauseous and rested her elbows on her knees. She loved him. She loved him more because he accepted his son at his word, even if it destroyed the only glimmer of happiness she'd ever really had.

If she left... She could move to New Mexico. She'd sign on as one of the Institute's resident artists and teach. She'd write and paint when she had time. So pretty much every evening. It would be a regular job, which she didn't necessarily need but would keep her occupied. The biggest perk was the location. It was the closest alternative to the Texas Hill Country and Stonewall Crossing.

She sighed and sat back, feeling an idiot all over again.

This was home. Why go someplace else like it when she could stay here with the handful of people she actually cared about?

It was almost ten o'clock. Tomorrow was Christmas morning. She could spend it with her father, watching him open the framed painting she'd done of Sprinkles. She could watch Lola open the scrapbook supplies she'd purchased. And the gift certificate to a naughty online adult store for Annabeth that was a joke—sort of.

From the corner of her eyes, she saw movement. It was pretty quiet, so she glanced over to see the new arrival.

It was Hunter.

Her breathing accelerated.

He was talking to the ticket agent, too far away to hear. The agent shook her head, no doubt apologizing. Hunter kept talking, and the agent kept shaking her head.

He was here. Was it too much to hope he was coming after her?

She watched, her hands clasped tightly in her lap, as he stepped back from the ticket agent. His hands rubbed back and forth over his face, and he let out a sigh that seemed to deflate him.

He tried again, clearly agitated now. But the ticket agent didn't budge.

Hunter glanced around, the shadows under his eyes visible from where she sat. His gaze traveled over her quickly, almost blindly, before he froze.

She couldn't move.

He strode across the airport terminal, bag in hand, staring at the tile floor, heading directly for her and the row of joined chairs she'd occupied for the past few hours.

He sat beside her, glancing at her.

She glanced at him, fighting against the smile that bubbled up inside her. "Where are you headed?" she asked.

He laughed, soft and nervous. "Seattle."

"It rains a lot." She paused. "What's in Seattle?"

"Someone I need to apologize to." He shifted in his seat, giving her his full attention.

Her cheeks felt hot. "Oh? What did you do?"

"I doubted her," he answered. "And then I let her go without a fight."

Her heart thumped like mad. "But she went. So maybe she's not worth fighting for." Her gaze met his.

"She didn't leave." He rested his elbows on his knees, his face inches from hers.

"She tried."

"What stopped her?" he asked, his gaze lingering.

"For the first time in my—her—life, she realized she had something worth fighting for." Her throat was thick with emotion. She stared at him, lost in his gaze.

"Big realization." His voice was low, husky.

She nodded, incapable of words.

"Eleven years is a long time, Jo," he murmured. "I don't want another day gone without you with me." The fear on his face was so real, so raw... And she understood it. He needed her the way she needed him.

"Okay," she agreed. "I love you, Hunter."

He smiled. "Damn, I love you, too." He took her hand in his, lifting it to his mouth so he could kiss each knuckle, then each fingertip.

"Eli?"

"Wants to talk to you." Hunter stood, pulling her up beside him. "He wanted to come, but I wouldn't let him."

She nodded. "He's okay?"

"He's more than okay. He's ready for you to be part of the family now."

"Now?" She didn't know what now meant, but she'd happily marry him this second.

"Now." His hand cupped her cheek. "You will marry me?" he asked.

"Yes, I'll marry you." She twined her arms around his neck. "I can't wait to marry you."

"Have any plans for New Year's Eve?" he asked, pressing a light kiss to the corner of her mouth. "Nothing like a new year for a fresh start and a wedding."

"And fireworks," she added, parting her lips beneath his.

"I like making fireworks with you, Jo." His mouth sealed hers, mingling their breaths and making her blissfully light-headed.

"I was talking about the fireworks set off to ring in the New Year." She shivered as his lips latched on to her ear.

"I like those, too," he whispered against her skin. "You ready to go home, Jo?"

She pulled back, staring into his eyes. "Take me home."

* * * * *

Amanda Renee was raised in the northeast and now wiggles her toes in the warm coastal Carolina sands. Her career began when she was discovered through Harlequin's So You Think You Can Write contest. When not creating stories about love and laughter, she enjoys the company of her schnoodle, Duffy, as well as camping, playing guitar and piano, photography and anything involving animals. You can visit her at amandarenee.com.

Books by Amanda Renee

Harlequin Western Romance

Saddle Ridge, Montana

The Lawman's Rebel Bride
A Snowbound Cowboy Christmas
Wrangling Cupid's Cowboy
The Bull Rider's Baby Bombshell

Harlequin American Romance

Welcome to Ramblewood

Betting on Texas
Home to the Cowboy
Blame It on the Rodeo
A Texan for Hire
Back to Texas
Mistletoe Rodeo
The Trouble with Cowgirls
A Bull Rider's Pride
Twins for Christmas

Visit the Author Profile page
at Harlequin.com for more titles.

THE LAWMAN'S
REBEL BRIDE

Amanda Renee

For Grandma Trudy.
You are forever in my heart.

Chapter 1

"Harlan Slade, you owe me a wedding!"

Belle Barnes stormed past the police department's front counter, pushed through the attached swinging door and marched over to the deputy sheriff's desk. Gasps aside, no one attempted to stop her. She'd seen the inside of the station more times than she could count. And Lord knew her history with Harlan was as well-known as it was long.

"Belle!" Harlan jumped from his chair, almost knocking it over. The incredulous stare of his piercing blue eyes almost made her turn tail and run. He gave the room a quick scan before returning his attention to her. "What are you talking about?"

"I need you to marry me...well, at least pretend

to." There was no sense in sugarcoating why she was there.

Harlan cocked his jaw, grabbed the Stetson off the top of the filing cabinet behind him and pulled it down low, covering his thick chestnut-colored hair. "Let's discuss this somewhere more private."

Private was the last thing Belle wanted. Private meant being alone with Harlan and that conjured up all sorts of memories and uncomfortableness she'd prefer to avoid. But she was desperate and she didn't have time to waste on foolish pride.

"Fine." She followed him down the back hallway, away from prying eyes. If only she could pry *her* eyes away from the view of his jean-clad backside. The county sheriff strove for friendly casual and Harlan wore it well. The sound of his boots on the worn linoleum echoed against the walls, masking the thudding of her rapid heartbeat. Harlan swung open the heavy steel door and waited for Belle to exit first. She walked past him into the parking lot. Her bare shoulder brushed against his chest, causing her skin to prickle on contact. She inhaled sharply. Big mistake. The woodsy scent of his cologne transported her back to firelit nights snuggled up beside him. A time best forgotten.

"What's this all about?" Harlan's hat shaded his features from the midmorning sun, making him more difficult to read. His tan button-down uniform shirt stretched taut across his shoulders and biceps as he folded his arms. He stood wide-legged in front of her, bringing his six-foot-one-inch height closer to her five foot four. "I'm fairly confident I'm the last person you want to marry."

That was the truth. She'd already stridden down that white-lined aisle only to watch him bolt for the church doors midceremony. There was nothing like the man of your dreams jilting you on your wedding day in front of the entire town. Belle shivered. It was close to eighty degrees in Saddle Ridge and her nerves were in overdrive. The past and the present were about to collide and she couldn't put on the brakes. Not now. Not when her grandmother needed her most.

Belle leaned against a parked police SUV for support. "My grandmother's Alzheimer's causes her to regress more each day." Saying the words aloud made the situation even more real. "She has no concept of the present, yesterday or even last week."

"Belle. I'm sorry." Harlan's deep, rich voice soothed. "I've wanted to visit Trudy in the nursing home many times but I wasn't sure I would be welcome."

"Oh, you're welcome." Belle silently prayed for strength. "She believes we're still getting married. There's no convincing her otherwise. I even tried telling her we already were, but she'll have none of it. She keeps asking for you and I'm hoping if she sees you, maybe we can tell her together that we're eloping and it will put her mind at ease. I don't know what else to do. In a week or two, she might regress further. I can't promise she won't ask for you again, but she's growing more agitated each time she does and you're not there."

Harlan reached for her. His rough thumbs grazed the top of her hands. "I'm sorry you're going through this."

Belle pulled from his grasp. "Don't do that." She didn't want to be comforted or touched…at least not by him. Her heart couldn't take it. "This isn't for me. It's for my grandmother. I don't want to be anywhere near you, but I will do whatever I must to make her last days comfortable, however many she has. And if that means pretending to marry you, then so be it. But I can't do this without your cooperation."

"I'll do it." Harlan checked his watch. "How about I meet you there at noon? Is Trudy still in the same place down the road?"

Belle nodded. The ease with which he agreed caught her off guard along with him knowing where her grandmother resided. Then again, their sleepy little town of Saddle Ridge in northwest Montana only had one nursing home, so it wasn't too far of a stretch.

"Okay." Belle tugged her keys from her bag, not wanting to be near him any longer than necessary. "I guess that's it then. I'll see you later. And—um— thank you." She hadn't wanted to make eye contact again but felt the inexplicable need to do so. The second she did, she regretted it and turned to leave.

"Belle, before you go—"

She spun to face him. "Don't you dare say *I'm sorry* one more time. I've heard eight years of sorry every time I see you, which is why I do everything in my power to avoid you." She gripped her keys tighter. She needed Harlan's help and yelling at him in the police station parking lot was a surefire way to get him to back out of their agreement. "Can we please do this without dredging up the past?"

"You're asking me to pretend to still be your fiancé on the eve of what should have been our eighth wedding anniversary. Kind of impossible, don't you think?"

Belle's heart hammered against her rib cage. "You remember?"

"August 1. Of course I remember." Harlan closed the distance between them. "You've never let me explain why I left that day."

"Left? Ha! You tore out of that church like your tuxedo was on fire. There's nothing to say. Nothing to rehash. Please."

"Okay." Harlan held up his hands. "I'll meet you at the nursing home at noon."

Belle headed to her pickup, wishing she'd worn something other than flip-flops. They didn't make for a graceful exit when you're trying to walk away quickly. Walk? Forget that! She'd rather run just like he did. If her grandmother hadn't still lived in Saddle Ridge, she would have fled this godforsaken town long ago and never come back.

She hopped up into her battered old truck and jammed the key in the ignition, praying it would start. Money was tight since she'd had to sell her grandmother's house to pay for the nursing home. She had everything budgeted and there wasn't one extra cent to dump into the thirty-two-year-old Chevy. Ol' Red was loud, but she turned over. Belle stepped on the clutch and shifted into first, easing the truck onto Main Street. She arrived at the nursing home a few minutes later. Her boss, Dr. Lydia Presley, had been gracious enough to give her the day off. Working as a large-animal veterinarian assistant meant she wasn't always needed during the day. Nights were a different story. When Lydia was on call, Belle was, too.

"Miss Belle, we didn't expect to see you back so soon." Nurse Myra greeted her as she entered her grandmother's room. "Trudy fell asleep soon after you left."

"I wanted to check in on her once more." Belle lowered herself into the chair across from her grandmother. The woman who'd always been so active and full of life lay frail and motionless. The hospital bed and large safety rails dwarfed her body. Her once round cheeks and flawless complexion were sallow and gaunt. "After this morning, I'm not sure if my being here helps or upsets her."

Trudy stirred and Myra brushed a stray lock of hair away from her face. This was one time Belle was thankful she lived in a small town. Everyone in the nursing home knew her and her grandmother. She'd heard horror stories about the poor treatment of the elderly in some facilities. While she hoped those incidents were rare, she didn't have any concerns when it came to her grandmother's care. Trudy used to be Myra's Sunday school teacher, as she had been to quite a few other nursing home employees.

Her grandmother was only sixty-five and had battled Alzheimer's for the past five years. Early onset of the disease was uncommon and only accounted for

5 to 10 percent of all cases. Belle was well schooled in life-isn't-fair. That didn't stop her from asking, "Why Trudy?" every single day. Her grandmother was the only family she had. Her mother had given birth to her at age eighteen and took off when Belle was six. Took off as in she left Belle alone in a hotel room in Texas, never to return. At least her so-called mother had possessed the good sense to scrawl Trudy's phone number on her left arm so the police had someone to call. Now she was losing the only person she'd ever loved, except for Harlan, and he'd stopped mattering to her a long time ago.

"Were you able to find Harlan?" Myra asked.

"How did you know?" Maybe the nursing home staff knew her better than she realized.

"I'd like to say it was a lucky guess, but Gail saw your truck at the police station on her way in."

Of course she did. Gail was another nurse at the home. Sweet as the day is long, but the biggest gossip Saddle Ridge ever saw.

"He said he'd stop by later."

Myra nodded, not pressing for further details. Belle was too anxious to sit around waiting for the hour of doom. She kissed her grandmother goodbye and told Myra she'd see her later. She had a few guests staying at her apartment and she needed to make sure they weren't wrecking the place.

At noon, Harlan parked his police SUV outside the nursing home. He dug into his pocket for a roll of antacids. Tearing the foil open, he popped a couple in his mouth. The three cups of coffee he'd drunk earlier were burning a hole in his chest. Steeling his nerves, he pried himself from the vehicle and made his way to the front entrance.

He removed his hat as he opened the door and looked around. Maybe it was his imagination, but the nursing home seemed too quiet as he approached the front desk.

"May I help you?" the woman behind it asked.

"Hi," he squeaked. Well, that was embarrassing. He cleared his throat and tried again. "I'm Harlan Slade and I'm here to see Gertrude Barnes. Belle Barnes is expecting me."

"Oh! You're the guy." A lightning bolt of recognition lit her face. She'd heard of him and presumably not in a favorable way. "She's waiting for you in room 219. Down the hall, last room on the right."

Pretending to be Belle's husband—even for a few minutes—was damn close to a root canal without anesthesia. Not because he hated her. He wished it were that simple. No, Harlan had been cursed with still loving her. She'd put every ounce of faith and trust in him since the day they met in first grade. And instead of marrying Belle as planned, he'd knocked up her maid of honor.

He'd run out on their wedding because he was nineteen and nowhere near ready to be tied down. Only he ended up married to Belle's best friend a few months later. Correction, former best friend. And he certainly didn't do it out of love. It had been one hundred percent obligation and it came back to bite him in the ass. Molly walked out of their lives within a year, leaving him to raise their daughter alone.

Which suited him fine. He'd rather raise his child in a happy, single-parent home than with a woman who blamed their little girl for ruining her life.

"Mind if I come in?" Harlan poked his head in the room. Belle jumped as if a mousetrap had gone off under her chair.

"Not at all." Trudy beamed from her bed. "I've been waiting for you. Come sit with me." She weakly motioned to a chair on the other side of the bed. Her appearance took him by surprise, but he tried not to show it. She'd always been a robust woman. The last time he'd seen her, she'd taken Dukie—her beloved schnauzer—for one of their mile-long hikes. The woman before him was almost unrecognizable.

"Hey, babe." He set his hat on the table next to Belle, leaned in and gave her a quick kiss on the cheek.

The steel daggers that shot from Belle's icy blue eyes were just about enough to knock him dead on the floor. Okay, so he didn't need to kiss her, but he wanted their relationship to look believable.

"Belle, what's the matter with you? Give your husband-to-be a hug. Only one more day." Trudy clapped. "I can't wait."

Belle plastered a smile across her face and rose from her chair. Even in faded jeans, flip-flops and a plain white tank top, she looked like a million bucks. He used to call her his *platinum angel*. When the sunlight hit her long blond hair just so, she had an ethereal glow about her. He caught a glimpse of it this morning.

She wrapped her arms around his neck and gave

it a squeeze. A little too much of one if you asked him. The scent of lavender vanilla filled his nostrils. Some things never changed. She still used the same shampoo.

"Make this quick," she whispered in his ear. Her warm breath against his skin sent a shiver down his spine and straight to his... Nope, he needed to focus on the job he'd come to do. She released her choke hold and entwined her fingers in his. Her death grip almost brought him to his knees. "Grammy, Harlan and I would rather get married at the courthouse instead of having a big wedding."

"Nonsense." Trudy waved her hand. "I've already paid for everything."

The comment was a harsh reminder of the money Trudy had shelled out for the first wedding that had never happened. He had tried to repay her, but she refused to take it. Telling him to keep it for the baby. And that cut him even deeper.

"It's not that, Trudy." Harlan's mind raced for an excuse. "The church is double-booked tomorrow and we can't get married there."

"What do you mean double-booked?" Trudy scowled. "I've been a member of that church since I came to this country as a child. Everyone knows tomorrow is your wedding day."

Belle stood there shaking her head. So, it wasn't the best excuse, but she hadn't offered any other suggestions either.

"You two are getting married tomorrow," Trudy shouted. She shoved the covers aside and shook the bed's safety rails. "Let me out of this contraption. I told you people I'm fine to walk. It's only a bruised hip."

Belle rushed to her grandmother's side before she took a dive over the edge. "Grammy, you have to stay in bed." She looked to Harlan for help. "She thinks she's in the hospital after that bad fall she had a few weeks before our wedding."

"Why are you talking like I'm not here?" Trudy stopped fighting against her and sat up in bed. "I fell and I *am* in the hospital." Trudy looked around the room. "I've had enough of this place. I want to go home."

Harlan moved to stand beside Belle and attempted to cover Trudy's bare legs with a sheet. The older woman had gone from zero to overdrive in a matter of seconds.

Belle reached for the call button and pressed it. "I know you do, Grammy. You will. You'll go home soon."

A nurse came in and helped ease Trudy back against the bed. She adjusted it into a reclining position and double-checked the safety rails. Another woman entered the room and stood in the corner, silently watching.

"Stop fussing over me." She swatted both women away. "Go to the church and straighten out this wedding business. You tell them I booked the date first and you're getting married there tomorrow."

"Okay, Grammy. We will." Belle removed her handbag from the back of the chair and slung it over her shoulders. "I love you. We'll go now." Belle ran from the room.

"I'll see you tomorrow, Trudy." Harlan grabbed his hat and headed down the hall in search of Belle. When he reached the front desk, the woman who'd greeted him earlier pointed to a side door. He found Belle sitting in a white rocker on the covered veranda staring toward the blue-gray mountains of the Swan Range.

Her gaze met his as he approached. "I don't know how to watch her slip away like this." Her fingers trembled in her lap as his own ached to brush away the lone tear trailing down her cheek before she averted her gaze.

He crouched in front of her and held her hands between his own. He expected her to recoil from his touch as she had earlier, but instead she turned her hands upward and gripped his. The longing to tug her into his arms and soothe her pain took him by surprise. He hadn't come within a street's width of Belle in eight years, and in a matter of a few hours her skin had seared him multiple times like a branding iron on a steer's rump.

"I'm here for you." His thumbs slid across the soft warmth of her inner wrists. "Whether you want me to be or not."

Harlan sympathized with her anguish. He'd lost his father four years ago and as terrible as that had been, he couldn't fathom having to watch his last remaining relative slowly slip away. It was only a matter of time before Belle would be alone. In many respects, she already was. He couldn't—wouldn't—allow her to face that grief on her own.

"I appreciate it and thank you for coming here." A dry sob stuck in her throat. "I guess it was a waste."

"Excuse me." The woman who had been in Trudy's room a few minutes earlier approached them. "We haven't met yet. I'm Samantha Frederick, the new director here. I hope I'm not overstepping, but I overheard your dilemma. It's not much, and nowhere near as beautiful as your church would have been, but you're welcome to get married here tomorrow. We don't have the space for a big reception, but the garden is in full bloom and you wouldn't have to do anything to it. Reverend Grady is here now and I just spoke with him. He said he'd be happy to perform the ceremony. It will allow your grandmother to be a part of your wedding."

"Oh!" Belle laughed.

Harlan stood, unable to hold back a chuckle of his own at the irony of the situation. "That's sweet of you."

"But completely unnecessary," Belle interjected.

"Well, wait a minute." Harlan tapped Belle's shoulder. "It's not a bad idea. Let's at least give it some thought."

"Please do." Samantha smiled. "My office is next to the front desk. Come see me when you've decided. We'd love to have you."

"Thank you." Harlan removed his phone from his pocket. Tomorrow was Tuesday and he didn't have any court dates planned. He reasoned Sheriff Parker would give him the day off to get married.

"Harlan, we can't do this."

"Why not?" He knew the idea sounded crazy, but

it was only temporary. "We'll stay married until—" He hated saying the words knowing they'd hurt Belle. "Until your grandmother's memories fade. What's a few months or even a year?"

"More like a few weeks at the rate she's regressing." Belle stared at her hands.

"However long, we'll get married, live our separate lives like we already do. We'll meet up here and visit her together, and then we'll have it annulled."

"How will we explain the lack of guests?"

"We can ask the employees to fill in for a few minutes. It will be fast."

Belle stared up at him. "We can't get a marriage license by tomorrow."

"There's no waiting period in Montana, but we would need to see the county clerk before she leaves today. If we sign the blood test waiver, we'll be good to go. Besides, like you said, I owe you a wedding. It's the least I can do."

"Or we can hire a fake reverend," Belle said.

"We could." Harlan crouched down in front of her again. "But knowing you the way I do—or the way I used to—I think lying to your grandmother about something this big would bother you. I saw the look on your face in there when you told her she'll go home soon. You hated lying to her. I don't think you'd go through with this if it wasn't real."

"I would go through hell to make my grandmother happy."

"There you have it. What's more hellacious than marrying me on our not-so-wedding anniversary?"

"Ha!" Belle held out her hand to him. "You've got that right."

He took her hand between both of his, causing her to shake her head. "What?"

"It's supposed to be a handshake, Harlan." She withdrew her hand and offered it again. "We're making a deal, so let's shake on it. And in case I don't say it later, thank you for doing this."

This was the second craziest thing Harlan had ever done. The first had been walking out on Belle. "Let's get hitched."

Chapter 2

Belle didn't like to wait. She hated it. Utterly despised it. Waiting meant something bad was about to happen. She'd waited for her mom to come back to the hotel room and she never had. She'd waited for Harlan in the church and he had never returned. Here she was, waiting once again on her wedding day. Granted she was there three hours early, but that was only at her grandmother's insistence. Trudy may have forgotten many things, but every last detail of Belle and Harlan's wedding remained fresh in her mind. A little too fresh. What made Belle think she could possibly go through with marrying Harlan? Any recollection of their first wedding left her stomach in knots.

"You look beautiful, Bubbe." Her grandmother

had been calling her Bubbe, short for *bubbeleh*, since
the day she picked her up in Texas. It meant *darling*
and was Trudy's little term of endearment reserved
solely for Belle. Something so simple and yet she
knew she would miss it one day soon. Trudy would
regress to a point where she no longer remembered
her. Belle's heart physically ached at the thought.
"I loved that dress on you the moment we saw it in
the store."

Dress shopping with Trudy had been her favorite
part of planning her original wedding. She'd tried on
countless gowns while her grandmother waited pa-
tiently. The instant she stepped into the simple strap-
less A-line with delicate bodice beading, she knew
it was *the dress.*

As beautiful as the gown was, Belle wanted to
tear it off and burn it. She'd attempted to once, but
her grandmother told her she would one day regret
that decision. So she packed it away and stored it in
a cold dark corner of the basement with the wedding rings. When she cleaned out Trudy's house,
she'd contemplated throwing the dress out. Thinking
someone might have better luck with it, she opted to
consign it. Six months later, the shop returned the
dress to her when it hadn't sold. It had been sitting
in a storage unit with some of her grandmother's belongings ever since. After Trudy had drilled her over
its whereabouts first thing this morning, she'd spent
an hour climbing around the storage unit until she
found the blasted thing. She had hoped it wouldn't
still fit. Unlucky for her, it did.

"I can't believe you wanted to wear a sundress today."

"Grammy, it's hot out. It was only a suggestion." Belle flashed back to the morning of her first wedding. She'd been so happy and thrilled to begin a new life with Harlan.

Today brought a fresh start in a different way—a sense of closure. And she needed that to rid herself finally of the man she loved. Well, once loved. Her heart had slammed the door on that emotion long ago.

"You're putting your hair up, right?" her grandmother asked.

"Yes." Belle stared at her reflection in the mirror. She had to pull herself together and tamp down the desire to run for the nearest exit. If only she could draw the curtain on the disastrous movie of her first wedding that kept replaying in her head. Thankfully they weren't doing this in the church again. Belle had her limits and that would have pushed them to the max. She inhaled deep, summoning the strength and courage to get through the day and make her grandmother happy. Grabbing a brush and bobby pins from her bag, she gathered her hair into a low ponytail. "I'm wearing it in a French twist."

"I loved that style the best out of all the ones Matilda showed us. Too bad she came down with a cold this morning."

Matilda had been her grandmother's hairdresser since the beginning of time. She'd been the master of the updo, but had died three years earlier.

"That's all right, I can manage." Despite her nerves about facing Harlan again wearing the same dress, with the same hairstyle, holding the same rings and set to recite the same vows, she enjoyed these quiet moments with her grandmother. She didn't know how many more they had left. As painful as reliving the past was, she wouldn't trade it in for anything in the world. She'd always thought it was impossible to turn back the hands of time, but that wasn't entirely true. Now if she could only figure out how to stop time, she'd be set.

Samantha had become an impromptu wedding planner, buzzing around the nursing home and getting all the ambulatory residents ready to attend the ceremony. She even found time to put together a lovely bridal bouquet of fresh cut flowers from the garden. A few times, Belle had to remind herself that none of it was real.

Samantha popped her head in the door. "Are you ready? Your groom is waiting."

This was the day she wished Harlan hadn't shown up.

"I'm ready," she lied. No amount of primping would make her ready either. At least she looked the part. A nurse's aide came in and helped Trudy into a wheelchair. The walk down the corridor to the garden seemed a mile long. Her stomach twisted as Myra opened the door. And that's when she saw them.

"Who invited all those people?" She glared at Myra.

"We thought you did," Myra whispered as the aide and Trudy passed them. "We'll be right there," she said to Trudy.

"I did no such thing." Belle's pulse quickened. "We wanted to keep this quiet." But they knew. They *all* knew. Probably thanks to the county clerk, Harlan's boss, most of the nurses and the residents at the facility. When you get married in a small town, everybody knows. "Close the door." Belle collapsed against the corridor wall, gasping for air. "I can't do this."

"Yes, you can." Myra removed a handkerchief from her pocket and dabbed Belle's forehead. "Far be it from me to pry, but I think I've known you long enough to understand why you're marrying the man you should have castrated years ago. You and Harlan both got caught up in the charade for Trudy's sake. Despite the insanity of it, I admire the sacrifice you're making for her."

"Now we're deceiving everyone." Belle paced the small area. "This should have been a personal moment meant for my grandmother. One we'd quietly undo later. Do you realize how many people will be furious with us when we have this annulled? There better not be presents out there."

Myra pocketed her handkerchief. "You can return them." She opened the door again and smiled. "Now hide your crazy and get out there before Trudy wonders where you are."

Belle blew out a breath along with a handful of expletives before squaring her shoulders. "Fine."

The second her foot touched the garden's stone pathway, a lone violin played Mendelssohn's "Wedding March." "What the—?" Everyone turned to face her. There weren't any chairs, so she had to walk through a throng of people before she reached Harlan, who appeared more dashing in a tuxedo this time around. Thank God she'd worn her gown. She would have looked out of place standing before him in her discount sundress.

She stood under the rose-covered arbor in front of many of their friends and neighbors. The same ones she stood in front of once before. Harlan reached for both of her hands and squeezed them tight. Fear reflected in his eyes. She'd seen that same fear eight years ago to the day. And this time she had it, too. She couldn't tell if she was close to passing out or throwing up. Either way, she wasn't sure she'd remain on her feet much longer.

"Are you okay?" Harlan asked.

"No, but let's get this over with," she whispered. Reverend Grady frowned at her comment, but she felt too ill to concern herself with his feelings.

"Dearly beloved, we are gathered here today to join this man and this woman in holy matrimony."

Holy matrimony. Holy. Matrimony. The words sounded foreign and terrifying at the same time. She braved a glance at the crowd and immediately wished she hadn't. Her grandmother looked beautiful in her purple dress. It was the same dress she'd worn to her wedding the first time. One of the nurses had taken great care in altering it to accommodate Trudy's dramatic weight loss.

"I do," Harlan said.

What?

"And do you, Belle Elizabeth Barnes, take this man to be your lawful husband…" Anything the reverend said after that sounded like the teacher's voice on the *Peanuts* cartoon. Harlan gave her hand a gentle squeeze at her cue.

"I do."

"May I please have the rings?" Reverend Grady asked.

Harlan's eyes widened as he mouthed *I forgot rings*. Belle shook her head subtly to reassure him she hadn't. Only because her grandmother wouldn't let her forget.

Trudy handed the rings to the reverend and he blessed them.

"Harlan, please slide this ring on Belle's finger and repeat after me. With this ring, I pledge my commitment."

Harlan's intense gaze met hers as the cold, hard band slid onto her finger. "With this ring, I pledge my commitment." And she knew deep in her heart he meant those words. Eight years after the fact, but she truly believed he would commit to this marriage as long as her grandmother recognized it.

"Belle, please place this ring on Harlan's finger and repeat after me. With this ring, I pledge my commitment."

Belle opened her mouth to speak, but her words were silent. She inhaled deeply and tried again. Her fingers trembled as she slid on the gold band. "With this ring, I pledge my commitment."

"By the authority vested in me by the State of Montana, witnessed by your friends and family, I have the pleasure of pronouncing you husband and wife. Harlan, you may kiss your bride."

Kiss? What kiss?

Before she had a chance to even process what was happening, Harlan drew her to him and claimed her mouth. Her breath escaped her lungs as the raw power behind the traditional gesture overtook her. And in an instant, the past eight years never happened. The last time he had kissed her like that was the night before their wedding. The man could kiss. She'd forgotten how much she missed the touch of his lips against hers. She wound her arms around his neck in response, not wanting to let go. Not wanting to *ever* let go. The thunderous applause surrounding them jarred her back to the present. She broke their kiss as abruptly as he began it.

What had they done?

Harlan hadn't meant to kiss Belle. Well, he had—just not as intensely. He hated the cliché *caught up in the moment* excuse. He'd heard it numerous times on the job and it only made him slap the cuffs on faster. But damned if he didn't understand the expression today.

"Toast, toast, toast," their wedding guests chanted. Where did they come from? And the champagne and wedding cake. He hadn't even planned on wearing a tuxedo until Samantha told him Belle looked beautiful in her wedding gown. He'd made a mad dash for the tuxedo rental place and prayed they'd have one. The fit wasn't perfect, but he was presentable.

"Belle and Harlan." His uncle Jax raised a glass in the air. "It's anyone's guess when you two got back together, but I'm glad you did. Here's to a lifetime of health and happiness."

Harlan clinked his glass against Belle's. He wasn't sure if she was in a state of shock, overheating in her dress or was about to toss her cookies on his shoes. Regardless, the deer-in-the-headlights look didn't suit her.

Belle had looked stunning as she walked down the makeshift aisle. Never in a million years did he imagine she would still have the dress and the rings. She was even more beautiful than she had been during their first wedding. They both had matured since then. If they had waited to get married instead of allowing their teenage hormones to make all their decisions, they probably would have had a chance at something real and lasting.

"What did that man mean when he said he didn't know when you two got back together?" Trudy asked.

Harlan squatted beside her wheelchair. "That's my uncle Jax. He has a lot going on at his guest ranch, so I guess he got a little confused."

"I never liked that man. Where is Ryder? Isn't he supposed to be your best man? And where are your parents?"

Trudy's questions caught Belle's attention. She set her untouched glass of champagne on the table behind them.

"Grammy, why don't we go inside?" Belle turned Trudy's wheelchair toward the door. "It's too hot out here for you in the sun."

"All right, Bubbe. I'm a little tired."

"I'll take her in," a nurse's aide said. "Enjoy your wedding and congratulations."

"Thank you." Belle faced Harlan. "I'm sorry. She doesn't remember."

Harlan shrugged. "It's okay." He made a mental note to drive out to see Ryder at the state penitentiary in Deer Lodge soon. It had been a few months, but the three-and-a-half-hour drive wasn't exactly next door. He missed his brother every day. They'd been best friends until the night Ryder killed their father. The decimation of his family had been instant. His mother had moved to California shortly afterward and he and his four brothers rarely spoke anymore except for him and Dylan. He missed the family they once were. "I understand. Did you expect this many people?"

"Absolutely not." Belle scanned the crowd. "And I can't wait to hear the gossip once we have this annulled. I'll be pitied. You'll be vilified. They'll wonder what's so wrong with me that you ditched me twice. It will be a regular Saddle Ridge free-for-all. Happy days ahead." She frowned. "They still whisper about our last wedding debacle. This was the last thing I wanted."

Harlan sighed. He'd been responsible for every ounce of gossip. She'd always been an awkward social butterfly because of the past her mother bestowed upon her, but she had been an active part of the community. She had organized parties for friends and had even been on the church's social committee alongside her grandmother. All of that ended eight years ago to the day when he left her at the altar. And then her life burst in flames once more when he married Molly. Belle had become a rebel who'd rather spend her time with animals than people. The rumors rolled off his back, but she shouldn't have to endure them. Not again.

"Then we stay married." Harlan said the words

without thinking twice. He owed her. "I'm not saying we have to stay together forever." Although he'd willingly spend the rest of his life seeking redemption. "But a few months longer than we had intended. Then we can say we gave it a shot and it didn't work. I'll take the blame."

"I want to argue with you, but I can't think of a better solution right now." Her shoulders slumped in defeat despite the smile she wore for their guests' sake. "I am grateful to you and for all of this, but I should get home. I've already been gone longer than I had anticipated."

"Is someone waiting for you?" An uneasiness swept over him. Okay, maybe there was a twinge of jealousy in there, too. But why? He had no claim to Belle, except for the fact he was legally her husband.

"Time for cake," Samantha interrupted before Belle answered him. "I realize it's not big and multitiered, but when the kitchen learned you didn't have a cake, they insisted on making one."

If that didn't amp up the guilt factor, Harlan didn't know what else would. He vowed to make an anonymous donation to the nursing home to cover all the expenses for the event. The least he could do was pay for one of his weddings to Belle.

After they cut the cake, Belle fed it to him with a bit too much enthusiasm. Her uninhibited laughter more than made up for his face full of frosting. He had missed that laugh as much as he had missed her.

His phone vibrated in his pocket. He'd set an alarm for two o'clock so he'd be home when Ivy got off the bus. Their neighbor across the street watched her after school, but he didn't want to chance her hearing what happened today from somebody else. He hadn't expected news of their wedding to become public knowledge or else he would have told Ivy last night…if he had found the words. How was he going to explain to a seven-year-old he'd pretend-married the woman he once jilted? He was about to find out.

"I'm sorry, Belle. I have to leave," Harlan whispered in her ear as their guests mingled. "I need to have a little talk with Ivy."

"I'm sure that won't be easy." Belle twisted the ring on her finger. "I shouldn't have gotten you into this mess."

"I talked you into marrying me, remember?" He covered her hands with his own. The warmth of her skin caused his heart to still. In that briefest of moments, everyone around them faded away. Their wedding should have been spectacular. They should be sharing their first dance and celebrating the rest of their lives. Instead the woman he'd never stopped loving had been forced to settle for a charade of a marriage. "It will be okay. We'll get through it…together."

She lifted her gaze to his as happiness dissolved into reality. "Sure, okay." She withdrew from his grasp and gathered up her skirt, rebuilding the wall between them. "I'll walk out with you. I want to bring my grandmother a piece of cake before I leave."

The two of them managed to sneak away and head down the hallway to Trudy's room unnoticed. She was already asleep and Belle told him to go on ahead. She wanted to stay a little while longer. He sat beside her and took her hand in his as they watched Trudy in silence. Pretend marriage or not, Harlan had meant his vows. In sickness and in health was the reason they were together again, for however long. He wouldn't leave Belle. Not with a garden full of wedding guests and not when she needed him most.

It was close to five o'clock by the time he picked up Ivy. He'd called his neighbor and filled her in on some of the details. Between her chiding tsks, he persuaded her to keep Ivy inside and away from any of her friends until he arrived home. He'd run into some of her playmates' parents at the wedding and by now they were aware Ivy's father had remarried.

"Hey, pumpkin." Harlan scooped his daughter into his arms and swung her around in a big hug. "How was school today?"

"It was good. Why are you all dressed up? Did somebody die?"

Mental note: he needed to take his daughter to more events where people wore something other than jeans and cowboy boots. "Daddy went to a wedding." He set Ivy down and grabbed her backpack. "Let's head home and I'll tell you all about it."

After he changed out of his tuxedo and made dinner, he asked his daughter to join him in the living room. "You might hear things from your friends and I want you to know the truth in case someone tells you a bunch of made-up stories." Ivy's eyes grew wide in fear.

"Relax, honey. It's nothing bad. The wedding I went to today was my own."

"You got married? Without me?" She pouted. "Daddy, why?"

"It's not a happy-ever-after wedding like in your fairy tales." Even though that's what Belle had deserved. "My friend's grandmother is sick and she doesn't remember that Belle and I had dated and broke up years ago. We got married today so her grandmother would feel better. But it isn't a real marriage."

"Is it legal?" Ivy asked. "You always tell me I have to obey the law."

"Oh, it's legal, all right." Now that the wedding was over and he was home with his daughter, the day's events seemed like a distant dream. If it hadn't been for the rented tuxedo hanging by the door, he might've doubted his own sense of reality. He'd been all for it this morning when he woke up, but he hadn't realized how much he wanted to marry Belle. Or how deeply invested he'd become in their marriage. Outside of raising his daughter and becoming a deputy sheriff, nothing else had felt more right to him.

"Is her grandma dying?"

"Yes, she is."

"Then you did the right thing." Ivy climbed onto his lap and threw her arms around him.

"Thank you, sweetheart. In a month or so, Belle and I will get what's called an annulment and the marriage will be like it never happened."

"Is Belle moving in?"

It certainly hadn't been part of their original plan, then again, neither was a very public wedding. Harlan wasn't sure he was open to Belle moving in with them, regardless of how much he owed her for the past.

"We haven't discussed it." Ivy sighed and flopped against the back of the couch. "What's wrong, sweetheart?"

"I thought you getting married would mean I'd get a mommy."

Harlan covered his mouth. As much as he hated what he did to Belle, and as much as he despised Molly for walking out on their daughter without a second thought, he'd never resent or regret their relationship. If the series of events hadn't happened, he wouldn't have his daughter. She was the best thing that ever happened to him. He wished he could give Ivy what she wanted. His relationship with Belle was only temporary and he hadn't dated since Molly left. Not that he didn't want to, he just hadn't found a woman he wanted to spend time with or introduce into his daughter's life.

"Why do you look so sad, Daddy?"

Before he could answer, his phone rang. He looked at the display. It was one of the other deputy sheriffs. "Hey, Bryan, what's up?"

"Harlan, you need to come down to the station right away."

He stood and motioned for Ivy to grab her shoes. "Why, what's going on?"

"Well, we arrested your wife. And she's not alone."

Chapter 3

"Where is she?" Harlan stormed through the front door of the station after dropping Ivy off at his brother's house. "And what did you mean she isn't alone? Who's with her?"

"It's not a who. It's a what," Bryan said.

"Again?" Harlan's shoulders slumped in relief. Marriage of convenience aside, the thought of Belle with another man tore his gut in two. "What are the charges?"

"Trespassing, breaking and entering, and theft." Bryan laughed. "You sure know how to pick 'em. Did my wedding invite get lost in the mail?"

"I'll explain that later." Harlan headed to the back of the station, swiped his access card and walked through two sets of double doors to the prisoner holding area. There she was. Wet, muddy and clutching something tucked inside her shirt.

"Hey, sweetheart. I forgot to tell you...our marriage comes with one stipulation. You can't get arrested while we're together. You've racked up three charges within two hours. That must be a record, even for you. It's time to aim for some new goals."

"Get me out of here, Harlan." Belle hurried to the bars and angled her chest toward him. "This piglet needs milk replacer and fast."

"Oh, it's a pig this time. That explains the mud. Tell me the story first."

"There's no time," Belle pleaded.

"Tough." Harlan gritted his teeth. He gripped the bars and lowered his face to hers. "You need to tell me what happened so I can attempt some damage control."

"Fine." Belle huffed. "I received a call shortly after I got home. There was an eighteen-wheeler delivering pigs to the Johnson farm way out on Back Hollow Road. This person who shall remain anonymous said they saw the pigs herded off the trailer into holding pens and the piglet tossed in after them. They said it was a life-threatening condition. I couldn't ignore the situation. I had to do something."

"So instead of calling me or another deputy sheriff, you put yourself in danger and stole it."

"It's a she and I rescued her. I couldn't wait for you or anyone else," Belle hissed. "It was too big of a risk. Especially out there. This pig isn't even a week old and she's sunburnt from being in the back of that trailer for heaven only knows how long. I don't know the last time she ate or even if she'll live. Harlan, either you get me out of here or you call Dr. Presley to come take her. I don't care what happens to me, but you have to help this poor animal."

Harlan slapped the side of his thigh, hating the position she'd put him in. Belle's fierce stare starkly contrasted the piglet's weak gaze. Rescuing animals had always been her greatest passion and he wouldn't have expected anything less of her. Unfortunately, it was bound to adversely impact his job. It had been one day and he already felt powerless around her. Between his past mistakes, a terrifying prospect of a future together—however temporary—and a muddied present, second thoughts crept into his brain. Lucky for Belle, his heart controlled the moment.

"I'm not sure I can get you out of this mess tonight." He reached through the bars and stroked the top of the piglet's tiny head. "But, I'll do what I can. Stay here."

"As if I have a choice." Belle rolled her eyes.

After promising to pay triple the price of a full-grown pig, Harlan persuaded the farm owner to drop the theft charge. She was still on the hook for the B&E and trespassing, but at least it meant he'd get her out of jail tonight.

"Where am I going to put you?" Harlan looked her up and down. "You're not getting the front of my cruiser all dirty. Oh, I know." He strode over and opened the back door. "Hop in. It's not like it's your first time."

"So you're going to treat me like a criminal?"

"Are you serious? Where are we right now? It's either this or you walk."

"You're such a charmer." She scowled as she climbed inside. "I already miss the man I married."

"Speaking of that." Harlan slid behind the wheel. "I would like to be elected sheriff one day and that means my wife can't run around getting arrested. As long as we're husband and wife, I implore you to stay out of trouble. I mean it, Belle. Not just for my sake. It's for my daughter's, too. Whatever you do now reflects on her. This isn't the little secret wedding you and I thought it would be. Everyone knows and I can't allow anything negative to affect Ivy. Do we have an understanding?"

"Yes. I'll be more careful next time."

"Oh, okay. I can see you paid close attention to that conversation." He steered the SUV onto Belle's street.

"Please don't be mad. I did the right thing."

"I'm not mad. You frustrate the hell out of me. Always have. It's like you're permanently under my skin. I made a commitment to you and I'll honor it. My daughter even asked if you'd be moving in with us." Belle's gaze met his in the mirror. "Not because she's scared of you. She was hoping you'd be her mom. Do you have any idea what that did to me?"

"I'm sorry Molly turned out to be such a jerk. I never expected that of her." Her voice softened. "I never expected a lot of the things she did. And I don't wish abandonment on anyone. Child or adult."

Message received loud and clear. First Belle's mom had abandoned her, and then he had, too. If any man ever treated Ivy that way, Harlan would probably be behind bars and Belle would be the one bailing him out.

Harlan parked beside her truck, shut the engine and opened the back door for her to exit.

"How did my truck get here?" Belle asked as they walked past her red Chevy.

"I had it towed here instead of the impound lot. Consider it and the piglet a wedding present."

"Honey, you shouldn't have." She reached up and gave him a kiss on the cheek. He wasn't sure if she meant to be sarcastic or sincere, but he wasn't about to turn her away.

Belle glanced at her front door. "What's that?"

Harlan recognized the fluorescent orange notice without even having to read it. "You've been served your walking papers."

"They can't evict me. I pay rent." Belle ignored the paper and unlocked the door.

Harlan reached above her head and tore it off. "This is from the board of health."

"Whatever. Stand back when I open the door. Sometimes Olive gets a little aggressive when I come home."

Harlan followed her in. "It says you're harboring livestock?" Before he had a chance to look up, a tiny goat hurled into him, almost taking out his shin in the process.

"I warned you." Belle stepped over a baby gate and flicked on the kitchen light.

Now he understood the livestock. "Belle, please tell me you didn't steal these animals."

"First, I'm not a thief." She set a spoon and a bowl on the counter next to a large container of instant milk replacer before disappearing into the other room and returning with a towel. "I'm a rescuer.

When people call me, I go. And second, I'm fostering these guys until I can find a home for them. It was one thing when I lived at my grandmother's house. We had room in that big yard of hers. I don't have that luxury anymore."

He had to give her this much—between the small kiddie pool of hay the goat happily lay in, the tiny black lamb standing on his hind legs in a playpen, a duck waddling around the entryway and now a piglet, the rest of the apartment was relatively clean.

"I need you to take her while I mix the formula."

Harlan joined Belle in the kitchen. She lifted her shirt up so he could take the piglet tucked between her breasts. He froze, not knowing how to handle the animal without touching her.

"Hey, don't judge. It was the safest and warmest place I could hold her."

"It's not that."

"Oh, for heaven's sake, Harlan. They're just boobs. I have a bra on."

He lifted the piglet into his arms and Belle immediately wrapped the towel around the little girl. She mixed the formula before withdrawing an oral syringe from the drawer. She tore open the package and pulled the plunger until it filled halfway with the off-white liquid.

"Here you go, sweetie." The piglet hesitated at first, then readily took the mixture. "Thank you, thank you, thank you," Belle repeated under her breath. "I don't know what I'll do with you." She nuzzled the little critter, then looked around the room. "Or any of you, but I'm glad you're safe."

"Oh, Belle." Harlan looked to the ceiling and prayed for strength. "You know exactly what you're going to do. You and your menagerie are coming back to the ranch with me."

After a shower and a change of clothes, Belle and Harlan packed up what they could from her apartment, crated the animals and drove to his ranch. She always thought you had at least thirty days to vacate once you received an eviction notice. Turned out it was only three days in certain cases—livestock being one of them. She pulled in behind him, still trying to wrap her brain around the day. This morning she was single and independent. Tonight, she was married and relying on her worst enemy to put a roof over her head. Maybe *worst* was a little harsh. He had earned significant brownie points during the past twenty-four hours. That still didn't mean she forgave him for what he'd done. She doubted that would ever be possible.

Harlan leaned in her passenger window. "Are you coming?"

"In a minute." Belle glanced up at the white farmhouse. It should have been her house. They had picked it out together and Harlan's uncle Jax had fronted them the down payment until they could afford to pay it back. She loved the house. Had envisioned exactly how she would decorate it. Only she never had the chance to spend a single night in it. Molly had had that honor.

She needed to get it together. The ranch was a much better place for her wards. The previous owner had rebuilt the stables, along with the apartment above it. At least there had been an apartment eight years ago.

"Come on, let's get them settled, and then we'll get you situated in the house."

"I don't think so, Harlan." Belle looked up at the main house again. "Where's your daughter?"

"She's staying with Dylan and my uncle Jax at the Silver Bells Ranch. I'll pick her up tomorrow."

"Is there still an apartment over the stalls?" Belle dug the tip of her boot into the hard dirt drive. "I'd rather be near the animals. Lillie needs constant care."

"Lillie?" Harlan furrowed his brows. "Ah, you named the pig already."

"I'll have to take her to work with me." Belle began unloading the truck. If she kept moving and talking, she wouldn't have a chance to change her mind. "She needs to be fed every couple of hours and that will wake up you and Ivy. So if that apartment is available, I think it's best if I stay out here. I'll pay rent until I can find another place. I don't want to upset your routine, or raise Ivy's hopes."

Harlan closed the short distance between them and gripped both of her shoulders. "Breathe, Belle, breathe."

She didn't want to look up at him and see the pity he must feel for her. "I'm breathing." She turned away and grabbed the pet carrier from the front seat and held it up. "Isn't that right, Lillie? We're both breathing."

"The apartment's yours. It's been a few weeks since I last cleaned up there, so there might be a few cobwebs. Ivy likes to use it as a playhouse."

They finished unloading both vehicles and set the animals up in two of the stalls. Olive bounced around like an overexcited child, and Samson, the two-week-old black lamb, settled right in.

"This will work out well. Olive will be able to go outside to graze and I need to introduce Samson to grass soon to activate his rumen. I prefer grazing to only giving them hay."

"Rumen?"

"It's a large fermentation vat where bacteria and other microorganisms live. Sheep and goats are ruminant animals. Like cows. They have a four-chamber stomach."

"Okay, what's with the duck?" Harlan sat on a hay bale and watched the large white bird waddle down the stable corridor, squawking at the horses as she passed. "She seems old enough to be on her own. Why do you have her?"

"Imogene can't fly, so she's a—"

"Sitting duck. I get it now." Harlan smiled. "She can't defend herself."

"Lydia—Dr. Presley—is working with me to help create a nonprofit animal rescue center for injured and abandoned animals." Belle picked up Imogene and sat next to Harlan on the hay bale. "The main goal is to foster them until they find their forever homes. Finding and affording the land is the biggest obstacle. I'm hoping I can convince one of the larger ranches to donate some acreage, but I need to file for my nonprofit first. My, um, police record doesn't help matters."

"Then why do you continue to put yourself in that situation?" Harlan asked.

"When you work for a large-animal vet, you amass an extensive network of animal hospitals, foster homes and volunteers willing to help give animals a second chance. I'm sure you experience the same thing on a human level. For each success story, there are many that never make it. When someone calls me, or Lydia, we go. We'd love to navigate through the proper channels every time. And sometimes we can. Other times it's an emergency. If Lydia gets arrested, she can lose her veterinary license. I have nothing for them to take."

Harlan reached out and petted the top of the duck's head. "Everyone has their passion."

"Yours is law enforcement. Mine's animal rescue. Sometimes that means we butt heads." Belle stood and placed Imogene inside the stall with Olive. "These two love to snuggle together at night. Care to show me upstairs?"

Harlan led Belle to the studio apartment. It was larger than the one-bedroom she'd just been evicted from. It was nicer than she remembered. Little frilly touches here and there. She wondered if they had been Molly's doing or possibly his mom's or Ivy's.

She'd never met his daughter before, only seen her from afar around town. It had surprised her when Harlan had told her Ivy wanted her to move in. It was one more reason not to stay in the main house. She didn't want to involve Ivy in their fake marriage drama any more than she already was.

"I think I'm going to turn in. It's been a long, interesting day." Belle smiled up at him, not sure what the proper protocol was for saying good-night. They may be husband and wife, but there was no way they'd ever consummate the marriage.

Harlan jammed his hands in the front pockets of his jeans, eliminating the awkward hug she wanted to avoid. "There's plenty of room in the barn behind the stables. We can pick up the rest of your things tomorrow and store them in there for the time being. If you need anything, just ask."

"Thank you. I think I've gone above and beyond my favor quota for the week."

Harlan laughed. "It's okay. I've always said your heart is in the right place. How you go about doing certain things is a little more questionable. I know you mean well. Please promise me something."

"Yeah, yeah. Stay out of trouble." Belle smiled. "I promise to try."

Harlan nodded. "That's all I ask. I'll leave you and Lillie to it. Good night, Belle."

"Good night, Harlan."

Belle watched him shut the door behind him as he left the room. He hadn't even tried to hug or kiss her. It was exactly what she wanted. Any chance of a future they had together had shattered into a million shards of glass long ago.

Belle ran to the door, threw it open and bounded down the stairs, hoping to catch him. By the time she made it to the stable entrance, he was already halfway up the porch steps. As he reached the top, he hesitated. Belle held her breath and willed him to turn around, but he continued into the house.

Chapter 4

Harlan stood at the kitchen sink and stared out the window toward the stables. Last night he'd summoned an iron will to keep from carrying Belle back to the main house and celebrating their marriage the way a man and wife should. He'd expected the band around his finger to feel heavy. It had when he'd married Molly. This time was different. Despite the circumstances, this time felt natural. And his relationship with Belle was anything but.

He filled two travel mugs with coffee and headed out the back door. His breath caught in his throat at the sight of her. He didn't know why. He'd poured her coffee knowing she was there. But seeing Belle muck the stalls confirmed yesterday hadn't been a dream. She was back in his life. And the fine line between terrified and excited blurred with each passing second.

"Good morning. How's Lillie?"

"She made it through the night and had two more feedings." Belle continued to shovel without looking up. "She's taking a nap before I bring her to work."

"I brought you coffee." Harlan set the mug on a hay bale, maintaining his distance. The closer he got to her, the faster his heart beat. "You don't have to do this." Outlaw poked his head out of the empty stall Belle had moved him into. "I don't expect you to work for me or tend to my horses."

Belle shrugged in acknowledgment. "It's the least I can do. I would have fed them but I saw two different pellets in your feed bins and I didn't know who got what. If you show me, I'll take care of them for you."

"Trying to keep me out of my own stables?" Harlan's body tensed.

"It's not that." Belle's shoulders slumped before she looked up at him. "Okay, maybe it is." She rested the shovel handle against the crook of her arm and tugged off her gloves. "Everything else aside, I feel guilty about not coming to see you when your dad died. Your family has always been wonderful to me and I should have swallowed my pride and tried."

Harlan picked up her coffee and handed it to her. "You did. I saw you at the cemetery." Her eyes widened at his admission. "At first I wasn't sure it was you off in the distance, but when Dylan noticed you, too, I had my confirmation."

"It wasn't enough." Belle averted her gaze from his once again. "How is your mom?"

"Good. She remarried and seems happy with her new life in California. I've only been out there once." Now it was his turn to feel awkward. Four years had passed since Ryder had been convicted of vehicular manslaughter. Harlan still didn't believe the circumstances surrounding his father's death, but he'd been forced to accept them after his brother pled guilty and had been sentenced to fifteen years in the state penitentiary. "I should fly out there sometime soon. I know Ivy would love to see her grandmother. Maybe over Thanksgiving."

"Please give her my best." Belle flipped open the top of the mug and took a sip. "Thank you. You even remembered how I take my coffee."

"Light and sweet." How could he forget? He used to tease her about it. *Light and sweet, just like you.* "But seriously, Belle, I don't want you to feel you owe me anything for staying here. I know we can't ignore the past, but we can try to keep it there. I appreciate the gesture."

"I will still clean the stalls because, believe it or not, busy work helps me think. The sooner I can get my rescue operation open, the more animals I'll be able to save." She plucked her phone from her back pocket and tapped the screen. "Come look at this." She sidled up to him as he entered the stall, her shoulder grazing his upper arm. "It's a nonprofit with locations in California and Tennessee called The Gentle Barn. It provides a safe haven for animals in need while educating the community about kindness and compassion. They even have a cow with a prosthetic limb. Isn't it remarkable?" Belle beamed as she continued to scroll through the photos. "My goal is to provide my rescues with whatever medical care they may require. If I can adopt them out into loving forever homes, wonderful. If not, that's okay, too. Either way, they'll never suffer again."

The sincerity in Belle's voice was another reminder why he fell in love with her so long ago. She did everything with purpose and her whole heart. The rescue was a great idea. Ivy would love it, especially since she wanted to become a veterinarian.

"Why are you looking at me like that?" Belle stepped away from him.

"I have a proposition for you." Harlan feared he'd regret what he was about to say, but even worse, he feared he'd regret it even more if he didn't. "I have more acreage here than I need. You and I chose this property because of its spectacular views of the Swan Range. I think it's only fair for you to use part of it for your rescue. No strings, no cost. We'll call it your first donation."

She opened her mouth and for a second he thought she'd balk at the idea. "Are you sure you want me this close to you and your daughter?"

"Belle, I have nothing against you. And I admit, I am concerned with you interacting with Ivy. She's an inquisitive child and as soon as I pick her up after work she'll want to meet you. Are you okay with that?"

"I don't harbor any resentment toward her." The corners of her mouth turned downward. "I resented the situation and a part of me still does. But Ivy is an innocent child who became the victim of a bad situation. I can sympathize with that. I know what it's like to have a mother walk out and never return. I'll be her friend, but I don't want her to believe you and I are a real couple because it will break her heart when I leave."

Leave? Of course she would leave eventually. But if she accepted his proposal, she would just be on the other side of the property. Granted he wouldn't see her every day, but he'd know she was there.

"Ivy's aware of your grandmother's illness. She doesn't know the specifics, but she knows enough. I'll remind her so there's no confusion. Does that mean you'll accept my offer?"

"I'd be a fool not to." She exhaled slowly. "And I might be a fool to say yes."

"I have a little over a hundred acres. You're welcome to half of it."

Belle shook her head. "Fifty acres is much more than I can handle."

"I'll deed you whatever you feel you need now, and if you want to add more later, you can. There's another entrance to the ranch on the back side of the property. Start with that parcel. The land's fairly clear and there's already an outbuilding there. I can't guarantee it's not a complete teardown. I haven't been out there in a while. But if it is, I'll help you with that, too." Harlan fought to stop rambling. "It's up to you. You need to be comfortable with it."

Her expression filled with worry. "Are you comfortable with it? Or is this an attempt to clear your conscience?"

"Belle, I'll never escape the guilt of leaving you at the altar, but that's not why I'm offering. I have one major concern. I can't have my daughter affected by your sometimes reckless choices. If you can promise to call me before doing anything rash, I would be happy to help you start your rescue."

"Then I think we have a deal." She gave him a soft, warm smile.

Belle held out her hand. This time he knew enough to shake it. The feel of her palm against his set his heart aflame. A small ball of forbidden desire burned in the pit of his stomach. He wanted to seal their arrangement with a kiss. To give her what was rightfully hers and what should have been hers all along. The land and his heart. But he couldn't. He'd had his chance. If he hadn't bolted on their wedding day, Belle never would have faced half the challenges she'd endured. And she most likely wouldn't have a police record. He'd set off a chain reaction eight years ago and it had deeply affected Belle and his daughter. He might be able to right some of his wrongs, but he'd have to live with the consequences of never knowing what could have been.

For the second day in a row, Belle couldn't believe how much her life had changed overnight. Harlan's generous land offer touched her more than she'd ever admit. At least she wouldn't admit it to him. Was that petty and childish? Maybe. But she wasn't ready to destroy the protective wall she'd built around her heart. Not only to keep him out, but to keep herself from wanting more.

Harlan was an old habit, one she craved with each passing second. She refused to give in to it. She'd worked hard to form new, less dependent relationships. None had resulted in any long-term romances, but she'd learned to value her friendships and stand on her own. And until she saw the deed transferred into her name, she couldn't afford to get her hopes up.

Who was she kidding? She silently cheered behind the steering wheel of her truck, not wanting to startle Lillie. She was over the moon thrilled. Any attachments she had to that property had faded long ago. Or so she thought. This morning had been difficult. It was the first time she woke up on what should have been hers. Not that she'd gotten much sleep, and she lived in the stables, but it was close enough. And it stung.

She drove onto Dr. Lydia Presley's ranch and parked in front of the stables. It was strictly an ambulatory practice, but Lydia used the ranch as home base. Breaking the news to her friend and employer about her arrest wouldn't be easy. Harlan hadn't been the only one warning her to stay out of trouble.

She reached over to the passenger side and unlatched the seat belt. "It was all worth it, wasn't it, Lillie?" She lifted the carrier and climbed out of the truck. "Let's go make sure you're okay."

"Good morning," Lydia greeted her from the supply room. "Is this our newest patient?" She peered in the carrier. "Wow, she is tiny. Let me take a better look at her." The piglet squealed in Lydia's deep, bronzed hands. "Shh. It's okay, baby girl. I don't like the look of this sunburn. She already has a blister forming."

"I'm estimating she's only a couple days old."

"I agree. What did you name her?" Lydia placed the piglet on the scale.

"Lillie with an *i e*. She reminds me of a pink lily-pad bloom."

"She's close to the size of one of those flowers, too. Lillie only weighs 1.2 pounds. She's severely underweight for a newborn commercial pig. Let's start a round of antibiotics and treat the burn. We'll vaccinate in three weeks and begin her boosters in four. You never told me how you acquired her." Lydia raised one perfectly arched brow. "Or will my knowing make me an accessory after the fact?"

"No, no, she's been bought and paid for." Belle gnawed on her inner cheek.

"That's good to know." Lydia smoothed a light coat of ointment on Lillie's back. "She'll need this reapplied throughout the day. As soon as it looks dry again, apply another layer. Do you even have room for her at your apartment?"

"Not quite. I got evicted last night."

"To be honest, I thought it would have happened long before now." Lydia's dense spiraled curls bounced as she shook her head. "Where are you staying?"

"With Harlan."

"Harlan? The same Harlan who left you crying at the altar?"

"I did not cry." Her mind tumbled to push that day further into the past. She had relived it enough times over the last eight years.

"Oh, honey, I was there and you not only cried, you ugly cried. When did this reunion happen?"

"Well…" Belle wrung her hands. "Technically, two days ago. But then there was our wedding yesterday and we had planned to live separately until he had to bail me out of jail."

"Say what now?" Lydia stilled.

"That's how I got Lillie. I rescued her from the Johnson farm."

"What would a Belle Barnes rescue be without a trip to the hoosegow? But that's not what concerns me. Well, it does but we'll discuss that later. What is this about you marrying Harlan? You mean you told Trudy you were getting married at city hall, right? Please tell me you didn't actually marry him."

Belle slid a stool toward Lydia. "You'll need to sit down for this one."

Twenty minutes later, Lydia was still cradling Lillie and staring at Belle in disbelief. "You could have at least invited me to the ceremony."

"It happened so fast." Belle still hadn't sorted her thoughts about the entire situation. "No one was supposed to be there, but the news of it spread. Unfortunately, it didn't reach you out here."

"That's all right. I would have tried to stop you, anyway."

"I know you would have." Despite the fifteen-year age difference, Lydia was Belle's closest friend. "I had to do this for my grandmother. You should have seen her face light up yesterday. And I'll always have that memory, long after she forgets."

Lydia reached over and squeezed her hand. "I can't imagine how difficult this is for you."

Belle fought back the tears threatening to spring

free. "Every time I walk into her room, I wonder if this will be the day she doesn't recognize me. Some days she takes longer to make the connection. And poor Harlan. She asked him where his parents and Ryder were. He handled it without missing a beat, but I'm sure it hurt just the same."

"I won't say he's the man for you, because he's not. But if he's willing to go along with this charade for Trudy's sake, then he's earned a few redemption points in my book."

"Wait until you hear what he gave me this morning."

"Oh, yuck." Lydia stood up. "Keep your sex life to yourself."

Heat rose to Belle's cheeks. "I assure you we didn't and we won't. He offered me part of the ranch for the rescue and I accepted."

"And you'll live where? With him?"

Well, that wasn't the reaction she expected. "I hadn't thought that far ahead. I guess I could live on the ranch—my side of the ranch. Maybe I'll get one of those cute vintage trailers."

All Belle's plans had factored in her still having an apartment. And she couldn't stay above the stables forever. It was too close to Harlan. Too tempting to create new memories to erase the old. But the old ones would never die. Her scars wouldn't let her forget even though her heart ached for a fresh start.

"Belle?" Lydia waved her hands. "Where did you go?"

Belle fought to regain her composure. "Nowhere. And there's plenty of time to work out my living arrangements. The point is, I can finally move forward.

Are you still willing to partner with me?" A few other people were interested in the event Lydia changed her mind, but she'd always envisioned the project with her friend by her side. "I need two signatures on the articles of association to show its creation."

"Yes."

"Okay." Lydia's terse response surprised her. "I thought you'd be more enthused than this."

"I'm concerned your arrests will kill your dream before it ever gets off the ground." Lydia gently placed the piglet in Belle's arms. "I suspect you and Harlan had this conversation last night. That man has aspirations, too. I'm no fan of his, but it sounds as if he's trying to do right by you. You need to grant him the same respect, despite what happened."

"We've already discussed it. From now on, I am on my best behavior." Belle swaddled Lillie to keep her core body temperature warm and placed her in the carrier. "Last night was an exception to the rules. The other pigs would have trampled her to death if I hadn't acted when I did. I'm surprised she survived at all."

"Do me one favor. When you begin to remember the good times you once shared with Harlan, remember the aftermath, too."

"I promise." She'd never give Harlan that power over her again.

"Okay, then." Lydia handed her one of the mobile supply bags. "Today's castration day. Let's take the world by the balls."

Chapter 5

Belle's pickup spit and sputtered the entire way to Harlan's ranch, reminding her to change the oil sooner than later. She was glad to be home—well, her temporary home. Lillie had been with her, but between the castrations and visiting her grandmother at the nursing home, she'd had to run back to the ranch throughout the day to check on Samson and Olive.

Samson had been orphaned at birth and required feedings throughout the day. Olive was born last fall and lost her ears to frostbite during the winter. She was a third of the size of a normal goat, but healthy and full of mischief. Belle hoped to find her a forever home with other goats to bond with, but until then she'd play surrogate mom. It wasn't ideal and she had to keep Olive separated from Samson for fear she'd head butt the black fleecy bundle, but at least her wards were safe.

She'd picked up a salad and looked forward to a hot shower followed by a relaxing evening. The instant she parked in front of the stables, all thoughts of relaxation ceased. Harlan stood near the doorway grooming one of his horses while Ivy sat on a hay bale, petting Imogene.

Harlan had warned her Ivy wanted to meet her. And Belle was okay with that. She couldn't help but think the seven-year-old should have been hers...not Molly's. Belle wanted kids. She had once envisioned her and Harlan having a houseful of them. Maybe she would still have the chance one day. Not with Harlan, but with another man if she ever found one worthy of her love. At this point, she didn't believe anyone was worth the risk. Except animals. They provided unconditional love.

"Hi." Only Harlan's deep voice had the power to make her body tingle with one syllable. She needed to correct that and fast. "I hope it was okay for her to visit with the duck. I forgot her name."

"Ivy can visit Imogene whenever she wants. These animals need as much love and affection as they can get." *So do I.* Belle shook the thought from her head. "Are you going to introduce us?"

"Sweetheart, this is my friend Belle." Harlan rested a hand on the small of her back, weakening her knees more than they already were. "Belle, this is my daughter, Ivy."

"It's a pleasure to meet you." Belle knelt before

the girl, freeing herself from Harlan's touch. "I see you made friends with Imogene. She loves attention."

"She's so soft. I've never petted a duck. Daddy won't even let me have a dog."

Belle side-glanced at Harlan. "Since when are you against dogs? You had a bunch of them growing up on your parents' ranch."

Ivy's eyes widened. "You did?"

"You're not helping." Harlan's lips thinned into a smile. "Between my work and her school, I don't have time to come back here during the day. We don't exactly live in the center of town."

"Tell me about it." It was one of the reasons she and Harlan had chosen the ranch. "I made that drive three times since I left this morning just to check on these guys." Belle could see the longing on Ivy's face as she petted Imogene. A child, especially an only child, needed that companionship and the chance to experience an animal's love. But she had to give Harlan some credit. At least he wasn't leaving a dog outside during the frigid Montana winters, or allowing one to run free to terrorize neighboring farms. He had made a responsible decision.

"Can I see your piglet?" Ivy asked.

"Would you like to help me get her from the truck?" The girl nodded and Belle immediately noticed the resemblance to Harlan at that age. "Okay, come with me."

"I'm sorry your grandma is sick." Ivy reached for her hand as they walked outside, instantly melting her heart. "And I'm glad my daddy married you to help make it better."

"Thank you." Belle choked down a sob. What was it about this man and his daughter that annihilated any remaining resolve she had left? She didn't dare look back at Harlan. One Slade was more than she could handle at the moment. She opened the passenger-side door and lifted out the carrier. "Do you think you can bring this inside for me while I grab my bags?"

Ivy nodded.

"Hold on tight." The girl's ponytail swayed from side to side as Belle followed her back to the stable.

"Can I help you feed her?" Ivy asked.

"We have to check with your dad first." Belle looked over her shoulder at Harlan. "Is it okay if she comes upstairs with me?"

He quickly tugged his hat down to shield his glassy eyes and nodded wordlessly. Belle's first instinct was to go to him, but she thought better of it. The man deserved his privacy. It couldn't be easy seeing another woman with his daughter on their ranch. She could only hope Molly had a good reason for leaving Ivy the way she had. She'd hoped the same for her own mother. At least Molly had the good sense to leave her daughter with a responsible adult. Someday Ivy would realize that fact alone counted for something. Belle hadn't been so lucky. She'd found no trace of her mother...alive or dead. And maybe it was for the best. The reality that she was the last surviving member of her family smacked her in the face every time she visited her grandmother. And it hurt. It really hurt.

"Don't be sad." Ivy hugged her around the waist.

"I'm okay, sweetie." Belle instinctively hugged her in return. So this was what Harlan's daughter was like. It had taken her all of two seconds to fall in love with the child. And that meant trouble. Trouble for Belle and what was left of her heart. "Let's go feed Lillie."

Ivy climbed the stairs as Belle picked up the small carrier. She glanced in Harlan's direction, but his back remained to her. She followed her pint-size assistant to the makeshift kitchenette area of the studio apartment. Ivy chatted happily to Lillie while Belle mixed up more formula. She filled an oral syringe and grabbed a towel before joining Ivy in the middle of the floor. The piglet began to push on the front of her carrier door in anticipation of her next meal. It was one more positive sign she'd make a full recovery.

"Here, let's cover your lap." Belle spread the faded blue terry-cloth towel she'd brought from her old apartment across Ivy. "She's wiggly. And you have to be careful of the sunburn on her back. Are you ready?"

Ivy's enthusiastic nod and wide toothless smile warmed her soul. This was how a child should grow up. She'd only been a year younger than Ivy when her mother abandoned her in that terrifying hotel. For years, she had wondered what she'd done wrong to make her mother leave. Sometime in her early teens she realized it hadn't been her fault. While that epiphany had been freeing, the damage had already been done. She'd learned not to trust at such an early age that she'd struggled with it her entire life. Belle wanted to shield Ivy from that pain and privately vowed to remain the child's friend and protector long after her marriage to Harlan ended.

"I can't even feel her on me," Ivy said as Lillie circled on top of the towel.

"She's extremely underweight." Belle placed the syringe in Ivy's hand. "You hold it close enough for her to reach it and I'll push the plunger so she can eat."

"Okay." Ivy cradled the piglet's backside and held the syringe in front of Lillie's mouth. "Eat it all up so you can get big and strong."

Belle laughed. "When she grows up, she will probably weigh over six hundred pounds."

"Really?" Ivy's jaw dropped. "How much do my daddy's horses weigh?"

"Almost double that."

"That's a big pig. Will she stay here with you?"

Belle winced. Ivy had already decided she was staying with them long term. Maybe she wasn't too far off. If Harlan gave her the acreage he'd promised for the rescue, then she'd be on the other side of the ranch.

"Unless I find a safe forever home for Lillie, she'll stay with me."

"Will you teach me how to take care of the animals?" Ivy asked.

"Sure, unless your daddy says otherwise."

"He won't." Ivy lifted her chin. "I already told him I want to be a veterinarian when I grow up. He promised to make it happen."

How had she been lucky enough to befriend a

child with her same passions? Maybe it wasn't such an anomaly. Both Harlan and Molly had been her best friends. It stood to reason their daughter inherited their positive traits.

"I'll do whatever I can to help you make that dream happen, too."

There it was again…her commitment to a child she'd just met. Harlan's child. And being around her meant being around him. Indefinitely. Belle never believed she'd ever warm to that idea, but somewhere between the wedding and Ivy, she'd let go of the anger. And it felt good. Maybe forgiveness wasn't as impossible as she'd once thought.

Harlan hadn't intended to take Outlaw for a ride, but after seeing Belle with his daughter, he needed to clear his head. He tightened the saddle's cinch strap and mounted the horse. Halfway down the ranch road he realized he should have asked Belle if she would mind watching Ivy. He trusted her with his child. That alone bothered him, but not like he thought it would. The two had taken to each other much quicker and smoother than he'd expected. His daughter's desperation for a mother just collided with Belle's desire for a family, and the outcome—at least from where he stood—felt right. As if Belle was finally home.

But it wasn't her home. Ivy wasn't her daughter and Harlan once again feared he would hurt the two people he loved more than anything in this world. He nudged his horse into a run once they reached open land. The animal's powerful muscles flexed under the weight of his body, giving Harlan the much-needed strength to make the best decisions for his family. And he wanted that family to include Belle even though he had no right to that desire.

Harlan walked Outlaw back to the ranch, allowing the horse to cool down. Once they reached the stables, he removed the tack and filled the trough with fresh water. When Outlaw finished drinking, Harlan hosed the animal off, then walked him on the shaded side of the stables. The sun didn't set behind the Mission Mountains until nine this time of year and it almost always produced a spectacular display. The colors were equally gorgeous when the sun rose over the Swan Range every morning. He'd never tire of the views from his ranch. He was just tired of watching them alone.

Ivy bounded down the stable stairs with Belle in tow. "I fed Lillie, Daddy!" She animatedly danced in front of him. "She's so cute. But she has a blister on her back and Belle said I can help take care of her."

Harlan smiled at Belle in acknowledgment before turning his attention to Ivy. "Go clean up for dinner. I made chili. I'll be there in a minute."

"Can Belle eat with us?" Ivy reached for both of their hands and swung them back and forth.

"Honey, Belle doesn't eat meat," Harlan said. "It wouldn't be fair for her to sit and watch us."

"I don't mind eating with you. I picked up a salad on the way home."

"Then we'd love to have you join us."

Belle laughed. "Remember when we were kids? You'd order a burger, and I'd eat all your fries."

"She sure did," Harlan said to Ivy. "I went years without ever tasting a French fry."

"I wasn't that bad." She playfully swatted at him.

"Yeah, you were." His heart warmed as they shared a smile for the first time in years. "Come over whenever you're ready. Afterward, we'll pick up the rest of your stuff from your apartment."

"Calvin—Lydia's husband—already did earlier. I hope that was okay."

"That's fine. Calvin's a good man and he, Lydia and the kids are welcome here anytime they want."

"I'll let them know. Give me twenty minutes, okay? I need to clean up."

"Sounds good." Harlan ran up the back porch steps behind Ivy. He gave the house a quick going-over before he set the table. He looked around, satisfied. It was clean and reasonably organized, at least by single-dad standards.

He scanned the living room and mentally prepared himself to welcome Belle. Last night he hadn't given it a second thought until she opted to stay in the apartment above the stables. Then the realization had dawned on him. It had to be difficult for her to come into what should have been their home after everything he'd put her through.

Once Molly had left, he redecorated the house the way he and Belle had planned. It wasn't perfect. Far from it, but it was still a work in progress. Ivy added her own frilly additions, but the place could stand a woman's touch. He wasn't sure if Belle had a change of heart because Ivy had forced the issue or if her curiosity had gotten the best of her. Now he wondered if it had been such a good idea. Not for her sake, but for his own.

A soft rap emanated from the porch screen door. He ran his palms down the front of his Wranglers and noticed he still had on his uniform shirt. He wished he'd changed out of it before she arrived.

"I'll get it." Ivy ran past him to the door. "Belle's here!" his daughter shouted at the top of her lungs.

"I can see that." Harlan joined them in the kitchen and lightly tugged Ivy's ponytail. "No need to yell, sweetheart."

"Want to see my room?" Ivy dragged Belle across the kitchen without waiting for an answer.

"Don't be rude, Ivy," Harlan warned. "Belle hasn't even put her salad down."

"I feel bad not bringing anything. Like a yummy rich dessert." She reached down and tickled his daughter, immediately lightening the mood again. "Next time, huh, kiddo?" Belle straightened. "That is if there is a next time. I don't want to intrude."

"You're not intruding. Remember what I told you last night. You're more than welcome to—" Harlan hadn't had the pleasure of talking to a woman he was attracted to around his daughter before. He was learning to be more careful with his words. "Would you like a glass of wine? I have a sparkling white and a merlot."

"The white would be wonderful, thank you."

"Your ring matches Daddy's." Ivy lifted Belle's hand and fiddled with the gold band.

"I thought—"

"In case I—"

Harlan and Belle both spoke at the same time.

"I'm sorry, go ahead," Harlan said, praying his daughter would stop putting them on the spot tonight.

Belle's cheeks flushed. "It was easier to leave it on so I don't have to remember it every time I visit my grandmother."

"Me, too," he lied. The fact she cared enough to save the rings made him want to wear it. "I figured there would be fewer questions around town since everyone seems to know we got married. Turns out it was more of a conversation starter, but I handled it."

"I hate that you're going through this because of me. I deal little with the public and most of the animals don't pay too much attention to my jewelry."

Harlan poured Belle a glass of wine and handed it to her. He opened his mouth to speak, when he realized they still had an audience. "Why don't you go sit down, Ivy?" He pulled out a chair for Belle before spooning the chili into bowls for him and his daughter. He joined them at the table and reached for both of their hands. "Thank You, Lord, for these blessings which we are about to receive. And thank You for bringing Belle, along with her fine-feathered and four-legged friends, into our lives." Ivy giggled. "Please watch over and bless us all. In Jesus's name. Amen."

"Amen." Belle gave his hand a light squeeze before releasing it. "It's nice to see things haven't changed."

Harlan longed for the physical contact as soon as she let go. As much as he'd told himself they had both moved on and couldn't be together again, having a meal together as a family made him wonder if it was possible.

Dinner had gone remarkably well. He couldn't remember the last time he'd seen his daughter laugh so much. A little too much, considering she wore a good portion of her chili. Ivy surprised him when she asked Belle to read her a story instead of him. But Belle didn't hesitate to say yes and seemed touched by the request. While they were upstairs, he wondered if Belle felt uncomfortable being in the room they had chosen for their own children. He wanted to ask her when she came back downstairs and joined him on the couch, but he didn't want to ruin an otherwise perfect evening.

"I can't thank you enough for having me. I had a wonderful time." Belle rested her hand on his forearm. "And I mean that. Your daughter is amazing. You should be very proud."

"I should be the one saying thanks. I think you won her over." A warning voice grew in his head.

Belle withdrew from him. "And that bothers you, doesn't it?"

"Yes, it does." Harlan turned sideways and draped one arm over the back of the couch so he could face her. "She gets very attached to people. She doesn't have a lot of family outside of my uncle Jax and my brothers Dylan and Wes, when Wes is even around. He's stayed away since Dad's death. Ivy doesn't remember Molly. And that's a good thing. Sad but good. She only has two cousins—my brother Garrett's kids—but once Mom moved to California he stopped coming back to town."

"She doesn't see Molly's family?"

Harlan scrubbed his hand along his jawline. "They've made no effort to see Ivy. And they know she exists because we sent them a birth announcement. I had tried to contact them after Molly left. Never heard a word. I've made peace with it. This way I don't have to worry about them disappointing my daughter. It's sad she doesn't have more family, though. I grew up with four brothers and chaos everywhere. And as crazy as my family was, I wouldn't have traded them in for anything. It kills me sometimes. I always wanted a couple of kids growing up together. Ivy will never experience that bond of having a sibling close in age."

"I know what you mean." A bittersweet hint of emotion filled her voice.

"I'm such an ass." Guilt rolled through him. "Here I am rambling on about raising another woman's child without even considering how difficult this must be for you. And I know you don't want to hear this and I don't want to ruin a nice evening, but you need to know the truth. That one night with Molly was all it ever was. One night. A drunken mistake that resulted in the most beautiful gift. But we were never together again. I never meant to hurt you. Not then and not now. Yet I keep doing it, don't I?"

"You're giving yourself too much credit." A cool detachment replaced any sentiment he sensed a moment ago. "I'll admit it was difficult coming into this house and seeing it as I had always envisioned it, but none of this hurts me. You moved on with your life and so have I."

"Everything around here is mine and Ivy's. The paint color, the furnishings. I changed it all after Molly left."

"You don't owe me an explanation." Belle rose from the couch, crossed the room to the fireplace and admired the photos of his family on the mantel. "This is your home and I respect that. Things didn't work out and, honestly, I'm exhausted from holding it against you." She faced him, her expression softened. "I'm exhausted from hating you for it. And yes, *hate* is a strong word and I felt that way for a long time. Over the past couple of days, I discovered the beauty of letting go. I didn't even realize I had done it until Ivy and I were feeding Lillie."

Harlan perched on the edge of the couch and rested his elbows on his knees. Was she saying they had a chance? "What made you change your mind?"

"It just clicked." She shrugged. "I enjoy spending time with you and Ivy. I didn't know what to expect when I walked in. Seeing the house wasn't as bad as I thought it would be." Belle held up her hands in front of her. "Before you ask me again, no, I will not move in here with you. I think that will confuse matters even more. I understand your concerns with Ivy getting too attached. Providing you keep up your word on the land deal, I don't see myself walking out of her life anytime soon. Once the rescue is open, I'll just be on the other side of the ranch and she can visit me whenever she wants."

Belle's willingness to be a part of Ivy's life erased any lingering doubts he had about offering her the acreage. "I admit, your attitude surprises me."

"Me, too. But how can I promote kindness and compassion toward animals and not give you the same courtesy?" Belle's eyes widened. "Not that I'm calling you an animal, because I'm not."

Harlan laughed. "I wondered there for a second."

Belle sat next to him again on the couch. "This is good. You and I have finally reached the point where we can laugh with one another even if it's at the other's expense. Who knows what the future holds, but I think we can be friends if you're okay with that?"

"Yes, I'm okay with that." He'd much rather take her in his arms and tell her exactly how she made him feel and that he wanted to be more than friends, but he couldn't. It wasn't worth the risk of driving her away. He'd missed her infectious laughter and being able to share things that happened in his life or even throughout the day. Especially when his father had died. That was when he had needed her most. Nobody understood him the way she always had. And even though they weren't together, he'd had a sense of calm and relief when he saw her at the cemetery. No words had been necessary. He'd felt her concern and sympathy. He refused to let her slip away from him again. If friendship was all they'd ever have, he'd take it. But he wouldn't lose her again.

"I need to give Lillie her next feeding." Belle stood. "Thank you again for having me over tonight."

Harlan led her through the kitchen and once again found himself unsure how to say good-night. He opened the door. "Could we do this again tomorrow?"

"Can we play it by ear?" Belle nibbled her lower

lip. "My schedule is all over the place between my grandmother and veterinary emergencies. It makes it a little difficult to plan anything. I would like to, though."

"I'll take that as a yes and if you get tied up, then don't give it a second thought. I understand the call of duty. I've had to drop Ivy off at my uncle's house on numerous occasions."

"It's a date, then." Belle's mouth dropped open. "I didn't mean a date. I meant—"

"I know what you meant." Harlan wished it was a date. "I wouldn't be much of a gentleman if I didn't offer to walk you back to your apartment."

She laughed. "It's only a few feet away. I can manage." Belle stepped onto the porch. "Wow, that sunset is stunning. I forgot the view from here. You're blessed to see this every day."

Harlan joined her at the porch railing. "You're living here, too. It's your view just as much as it's mine."

"I can't live above the stables forever."

"You and the animals are welcome as long as you want." Harlan already hated the thought of her leaving. "You are still planning on living here until the rescue center's built, right?"

"Construction is still a long way off. I don't think you want me around that long. Maybe I'll put a travel trailer out there once I get everything operational. It's an inexpensive, although a temporary, solution. I probably wouldn't survive the winter in one. Maybe a prefabricated home somewhere down the line. I need to focus on donations to make this happen. I can't use that money for myself. And I'm still not sure how I'll balance working for Lydia and running the rescue. But I need an income. And I'll need plenty of volunteers along with paid employees. I feel guilty taking a salary for myself. Eventually, I'll have to get over it, but there's a lot I still have to work out. I am so grateful to you for the land."

"No need to thank me." Harlan laughed, amazed at how fast and long she could talk without coming up for air. He could stand on the porch and listen to her all night.

"I know, I know. I'm rambling." She sheepishly looked away.

Harlan lifted her chin with his finger. "You're excited and rightfully so. Enjoy it."

She nodded, and in that moment he wanted nothing more than to kiss her.

"I guess I should feed my little ones."

Harlan chuckled at her timing. "Yes, you definitely should. I need to check on Ivy."

"Thanks again for tonight." Belle reached up and kissed him on the cheek before darting down the porch steps toward the stables.

The sweet gesture sent his pulse racing once again. And he loved every second. Maybe there was hope for them after all.

Chapter 6

Belle woke up giggling. The sound startled her at first until she realized it was her own laughter. She sat up in bed and giggled again. And then she laughed out loud. She was actually happy. It had been a rarity in recent years. So rare she couldn't remember the last time she had been in such a good mood.

She reached over the bed and checked on Lillie in her carrier. The tiny piglet was awake and standing at the door. It was another great sign. She opened the door and scooped her up with one hand, holding her close to her chest.

"Good morning, sweet thing." Lillie wiggled excitedly in her arms. "I can't tell you how glad I am to see you moving around on your own. I guess we both slept well."

She climbed out of bed and slipped a small collar around Lillie's neck. "Let's take you outside to go potty before breakfast." It may be August but the morning air was chilly. Belle bounced up and down to stay warm. She'd started leash training Lillie yesterday at work and so far the piglet didn't seem to mind it. "Hurry up before you freeze your tail off." After ten minutes of sniffing around, she went to the bathroom. "Good girl."

The sound of a twig snapping nearby startled them both. A puff of steam four feet off the ground appeared from the corner of the stables. Belle picked Lillie up and stuffed her in her shirt before plastering herself against the wood siding. She couldn't run, for fear whatever it was would chase after them. She held her breath as a moose and her calf appeared. The cow looked in her direction, then continued walking toward the corral and along the fence. Her calf didn't follow and Belle was afraid it would pick up her scent and come in for a closer look.

Moose were larger than most people thought, weighing between eight hundred and twelve hundred pounds. Thankfully, this female was on the small end. Belle had been up close and personal with one only once and that was when she and Lydia had rescued a bull moose caught in a barbed-wire fence a few years ago. It had been one of their most difficult rescues due to the animal's size and strength.

Lillie squirmed and Belle prayed she wouldn't squeal. The calf finally lost interest and followed her mother. When they were a safe enough distance away, Belle inched along the stable's outer wall, never taking her eyes off the moose. When she reached the corner, she peered around it to make sure there weren't any more. Once she was inside, she breathed a sigh of relief and eased Lillie out from under her shirt.

"That was enough adventure for one day, wasn't it, little girl?"

She looked toward the corridor to see if the animals had sensed any trouble. Horses were usually the most intuitive and would sometimes bang against their stalls or use the flehmen response, where they curled back their upper lip, exposed their teeth and inhaled with their nostrils closed in an attempt to identify a scent.

Assured all was quiet, she climbed the stairs and continued with her morning. After she fed Lillie, swaddled her and put her down for a nap, Belle showered and changed into her work clothes, then headed back down to the stables. She couldn't seem to get warm. The thermometer outside the door read thirty-nine degrees. "Holy crap!" No wonder she was cold. Yesterday morning had been closer to sixty.

She opened Samson's stall and picked up the black lamb. She rubbed her face against his head, relishing the feel of the soft fleece against her skin. The always jealous Olive butted her head against the neighboring stall, wanting affection of her own. Belle reached over the side and scratched her back. "Be patient. You'll get yours. There is enough love to go around." Imogene honked at her from behind Olive. "Yes, I love you, too."

The stable door slid open and Harlan appeared, silhouetted by the morning sun. There was nothing sexier than a cowboy first thing in the morning. She'd denied herself the pleasure of his piercing blue eyes and slow, easy smile yesterday morning. She wouldn't make the same mistake today. Besides, the wedding ring on her finger entitled her to that enjoyment, and she deserved to partake in at least some of it. Looking was harmless, right?

"Good morning." Harlan handed her a cup of coffee over the stall door. "Looks like I got here before you started mucking. Good. Now I won't have to argue with you about it."

Belle lowered Samson into the fluffy pile of hay and sipped her coffee. "Thank you. I needed this."

"It's a cold one."

"Well, that too, but that's not the only reason I need an extra pick-me-up. Lillie and I had a run-in with a mama moose and her calf."

"Really?" He stopped midsip. "They haven't been around the ranch in a few years. I'll buy some moose deterrent in town later. Are you two all right?"

"We're fine." Belle checked the time on her phone. "Remember back in high school when that bull moose attacked the principal's car in the middle of the day?"

"I forgot about that. Poor creature thought he'd found the love of his life." Harlan laughed. "And we had to stay inside until the police came and chased him away. Good times."

Belle almost snorted her coffee. "Yes, they were." Once again she found herself easily laughing with Harlan. A part of her wanted to warn her inner self to be careful. It would be far too easy to fall for him only to end up heartbroken. They had both agreed the marriage was temporary and it needed to stay that way. Belle finally had a chance at fulfilling her dream and she wouldn't allow her feelings for Harlan to confuse the issue. The last thing she needed or wanted was for a romantic relationship—however brief—to destroy his promise to donate his land to the rescue. The animals needed her more than she needed him.

"Hey, since I'm probably closer during the day, do you want me to swing by and feed Samson later?"

"Harlan Slade!" Belle closed the stall door and joined him in the stable corridor. "You won't stop home during the day so your daughter can have a dog, but you'll do it for my lamb?"

Harlan grimaced. "True. Ivy would never let me live it down."

"Hang your head in shame," Belle teased. "It's no secret I believe in the adopt, don't shop mentality, but I know of a litter of blue heelers, and every puppy deserves a good home."

"I can't believe you remembered."

"You talked about it for a year straight. Said once we got married you'd get one and name him Elvis." Belle wondered why Harlan hadn't gone through with his plan after marrying Molly. "Surprise! We're married."

"Who has the litter?" Harlan rubbed his jawline, causing Belle to wonder if his face was still as soft as it used to be right after he shaved.

"One of Lydia's clients. If you're interested, I'll call him. I have to stop in here during the day anyway, so I can help out with puppy training. And once I'm next door, it won't be any hardship to check in on him while you're at work." The words sounded more real each time she said them aloud. She never would have thought she'd live on the ranch they picked out together.

"You'd do that for me?"

"Not for you—for both of you. Last night when I was reading to Ivy, she told me how much she wants a dog. The companionship is good for an only child."

Harlan nodded. "Okay, yeah, make the call and let me know how much."

"Will do." Belle planned to give the puppy to Harlan and Ivy in exchange for allowing her to stay on the ranch. Once Ivy had the puppy in her hands, then she'd tell him it was a gift. He wouldn't be able to argue with her then.

She realized it was dangerous to be making so many long-term plans with the man she'd only started talking to again a few days ago, but it felt right. If she maintained an emotional distance, everything would work out fine.

"Ivy, meet Elvis. He's all yours." Belle held out a blue-and-gray-speckled puppy with tan markings to Ivy. "He's a blue heeler, also known as an Australian cattle dog."

"Really?" Ivy looked from Belle to Harlan before taking the dog. "We can keep him, Daddy?"

"Yes, sweetheart. He's ours."

"Thank you." Ivy hugged the dog close to her chest as tears streamed down her cheeks. "Thank you, so much."

The look on his daughter's face took his breath

away. She was a happy child, but not necessarily an expressive one. She'd learned to compartmentalize her feelings at an early age. At least, that's what the therapist had told him. Today was different. Just as it had been after Ivy fed Lillie for the first time. He hated to admit it, but Belle brought out the best in his daughter. Not that there was anything wrong with that, except it put his emotions on the line even more than they already were.

Harlan sat down next to Ivy on the living room floor. "Honey, if you cry, you'll get your dog all wet." But Elvis had already licked her tears dry. "He's perfect." He turned to Belle. "Thank you for getting him. How much do I owe you?" He began to pull out his wallet before Belle stilled his hand.

"You don't." She knelt beside him. "And please don't sneak the money to me by hiding it somewhere in my things. This is my gift. I need to do this."

Belle didn't have a dollar to spare, let alone the hundreds the puppy must have cost her. While he was grateful for the gift, he didn't want her going into debt because of his daughter.

"This will be hard to beat at Christmas." Harlan wondered if Belle would still be living on the ranch when the holidays rolled around. While the stables were heated, the upstairs apartment never got above sixty degrees in the winter because the sun wasn't strong enough to heat the building that time of year. He'd insist on her moving into the house once the first snow fell. The idea of spending Christmas with Belle excited him more than he thought possible. He wasn't sure who would be more delighted. Him or his daughter.

"I suggest you start talking to Santa's elves now."

"What will you ask Santa for this year?" Harlan teased.

"Peace for my grandmother." Belle scooted back to rest against the front of the couch. "In whatever form that may come. I don't even know if she'll still be around at Christmas."

"Did you see her today?" Harlan joined her, giving Ivy more room to roll around on the floor with Elvis.

"Twice. She's always good in the morning. She recognized me and still remembered our wedding. She even asked about you. When I went to see her this afternoon, she was confused and didn't know where she was. Most of the time she thinks she's in the hospital for various reasons. You saw it. Earlier this week she believed she was there for her hip. When she gets like that, it usually means another chunk of her memory is disappearing. Tomorrow she may drift further back in time. I'm scared at her rate of regression this month."

"I'll stop in and visit with her tomorrow during lunch." Harlan wrapped his arm around Belle's shoulder and pulled her close. He didn't care if it wasn't part of their arrangement or worry he might push her away. Right now they were a family—however unconventional—and she deserved comfort from a friend.

She didn't resist. Instead, she laid her head on his shoulder and they watched Ivy play. Until the puppy bounded for Belle's bare, painted toes and took a tiny nip.

"Hey, those are mine." Belle tucked her legs, shifting her body closer to Harlan's. The puppy barked and attempted to squeeze between her and the couch. "I'm not candy." Belle laughed and screeched as she tried to climb over Harlan's lap before landing in the middle of it when Elvis nipped at her behind. Harlan wrapped his arms around her tight as she scooped up the puppy, flipped him on his back across her legs and tickled his chubby belly. The house filled with laughter for the first time in eight years. And it was the best sound he'd ever heard.

Almost a week and a half had passed since their wedding day. Despite only seeing each other for an hour or two in the evenings, if they were lucky, the three of them had managed to eat dinner every night together. Belle and Harlan had developed a comfortable little routine, filling in for the other when work called them away. He and Ivy now spoke fluent baby animal. Earlier tonight, Lydia had brought Belle out on an emergency call shortly after they'd finished eating. Then one of the deputies had phoned in sick and he needed to cover half of the shift.

Harlan drove away from Dylan's house after dropping off Ivy and her puppy. He hated being on patrol. It took him all over the county and too far away from Ivy. Although, he never had to worry when she was with his brother. Dylan doted on her as if she were his own. His brother's ex-wife took off with his two stepkids after he'd partnered with their uncle Jax on the Silver Bells Ranch almost five years ago. She wanted no part of ranch life and Dylan couldn't convince her otherwise. He had loved those kids more than life itself and had been devastated after they left. During that time, Ivy became a real comfort to him.

Harlan just wished he and his brother had more to talk about than Ivy. Dylan had accused Harlan of siding with Ryder after their father's death. Considering Ryder pled guilty and the case never went to trial, there were no sides to take. But Dylan hadn't seen it that way and in some respects, he'd been right.

Having been the first to arrive on the scene that night, Harlan had a gut instinct something was off. He knew Ryder. And he knew what Ryder was like when he was drunk. And that night, Ryder hadn't been drunk enough to accidentally kill their father. But that's what he had confessed in his statement. None of that mattered anymore. It was in the past and he wanted to move forward for his and his daughter's sake. He'd give just about anything to see his family together again.

His cell phone rang. A photo of Belle in her wedding dress, courtesy of his uncle Jax, lit the screen. "Hello. Heading home?"

"Not exactly."

Harlan steered his police cruiser onto the shoulder and turned on the lights for safety. Two words in and he already didn't like the sound of Belle's voice. "What happened?"

"Do you know where the Huffington cattle ranch is?"

"Mmm-hmm. I do." Harlan's jaw pulsated. "What did you do?"

"Nothing." A muffled sound came from the phone. Harlan only made out his own name. "You said to call before I broke any laws. Lydia and I both need you. We were on an emergency call when we saw a yearling with what appeared to be a broken leg. When we got closer, Lydia realized the leg is almost severed below the carpal joint. The wound is fresh. He must have caught it on something. The animal needs to be either put down humanely or brought in for surgery. Lydia's already contacted a large-animal vet in Kalispell and they will take him. But the owner won't release him to us. We need your help. This bull is suffering."

Harlan rubbed his eye with the palm of his hand. "I'm on patrol on the other side of the county. I'll call it in and see if someone closer can get over there."

"Whoa, wait a minute." Belle's voice pitched. "If someone can get here? There's no if, Harlan. The law states failure to provide medical care to a severely injured animal comes under animal cruelty."

"Poor choice of words on my part. Yes, it is considered alleged animal cruelty. I will get someone over there and I'll try to get there, too. Promise me you won't do anything."

"Just hurry, Harlan." Belle's voice sounded defeated as she hung up the phone.

"Shit." Harlan smacked the steering wheel. He made a U-turn and drove toward the Huffington ranch before something bad happened.

"You can't keep me here against my will." Belle held her hands in the air. She had no idea if someone had a gun aimed at her, but she wasn't taking any chances. She felt like a deer in the headlights.

And that's exactly what she was. Caught in the head-lights by high-powered floodlights mounted on top of the many trucks that now surrounded her within the confines of the Huffington cattle ranch. She only hoped she'd provided enough of a diversion for Lydia and her husband to get away unnoticed. "This is kidnapping."

"You're trespassing," a voice said from the dark-ness. "The sheriff's department is on the way."

Oh, Lord. She tried to imagine how Harlan would react when he heard the news. In all fairness, she'd called him, but after four hours they had to intervene before the young bull died.

"Good, I'm glad the sheriff is coming. Then he can arrest you for animal cruelty. If you had allowed us to treat the bull, we would have been on our way." Belle's legs shook, betraying the calm demeanor she attempted to convey. "And don't even think about de-stroying that animal before they get here. I took pho-tos and video and already uploaded it to the cloud, so don't get any bright ideas about taking my phone either."

"Our herd is none of your business," another voice said.

That did it. "The hell it's not." Belle lowered her arms and stormed toward the voice. No one would bully her into kowtowing to a bunch of wannabe ren-egades. She followed the sound of the man's laugh-ter until she broke through the floodlight line and finally got a good look at his face. He stood on the bed of a pickup, all big and bad. Okay, so he did ap-pear somewhat menacing up there. "Just because this is private property doesn't mean you can do whatever you want. There are laws and you're breaking them."

"So are you." The man jumped over the side of the truck's bed and landed inches in front of her. The smell of chewing tobacco and sweat offended her nostrils.

"Personal space." Belle thrust her arms forward. "You don't intimidate me. I'm protecting that bull's well-being. You're just cruel. You won't do a damn thing because you don't want to lose the money from one head of cattle. That's pathetic. Do you even own this place or are you just the hired muscle?"

"Belle, enough!" Harlan's voice boomed. "Sheriff's department. Turn off all those floodlights and cut the engines on the trucks. Now!"

"Someone mind telling me what is going on here?" Sheriff Parker demanded.

Before Belle could answer, Harlan gripped her arm and led her away from the circle of the vehicles. "I told you to wait."

"I waited four hours." Belle pulled from his grasp. "No one came."

"I had to respond to an accident along the way. I have a job to do."

"And so do I." How dare he think his job was more important than hers? She deserved just as much respect. "You could have called and told me, but you didn't. You said someone would come out, and they didn't. I promised to call you first. I did everything you asked. It accomplished nothing."

Harlan tilted his hat back, his expression softening slightly. "Tell me what happened."

Belle explained her and Lydia's plan to take the bull when they found him standing alone in the pastures. At least the Huffington ranch raised grass-fed cattle and wasn't a jam-packed feedlot. Lydia had remained with the bull while Calvin attempted to reason with the ranch's owner. In the meantime, Belle had driven back to the ranch, borrowed Harlan's trailer and returned. That's when she spotted the ranch trucks barreling toward Lydia. Belle drove straight into the foray, giving her friends a chance to escape.

"Where is the bull now?"

"That's a good question. I warned them that nothing better happen to that animal. I have video."

"Show it to me, please."

Belle handed Harlan her phone. "Look here, the lower half of that front leg is barely attached." She looked up and saw concern and disgust in Harlan's eyes. The urgency had finally registered. "He left a blood trail before—I'm sure we can find it again, provided a wolf or a coyote hasn't gotten to him already."

"Show me where you last saw him." Harlan sent the video to his phone before handing it back to her.

Within twenty minutes, they located the injured bull. Harlan didn't say a word at the sight of the animal. He pressed a button on the side of his police radio hand mic attached to the front of his shirt. "Officer 19, I found the injured bull. He's in need of immediate medical attention. Requesting authorization to contact Dr. Lydia Presley."

"Ten-four," Sheriff Parker responded.

"Sheriff, you need to come see this."

After Lydia and Calvin returned with her truck and trailer, they loaded the bull for the short ride to the large-animal hospital in Kalispell. They promised to call her once they knew more. Belle checked her phone. She'd started the stopwatch when she first called Harlan. Almost seven hours later and the bull was getting the care it needed. Hopefully they weren't too late. It never should have gone on this long. Belle debated whether she would bother calling Harlan in the future. They had lost so much time.

"Harlan, I think you need to come up here," Bryan called him on the radio.

His jaw tensed as they walked toward Belle's pickup. There was his horse trailer hooked to the back of it. "You planned on stealing a bull with my trailer?" Harlan spun to face her. "I work for the sheriff's department! How do you think this reflects back on me when one of my vehicles is involved in a theft?"

"Your ranch was closer than Lydia's and we didn't have time."

"Yet here we are, hours later, and Lydia just left with the bull."

"I made a judgment call. You told me you probably would have done the same thing."

"After I notified the station. I should arrest you and let you spend the night in jail just on principle."

Belle didn't appreciate getting chewed out in front of half the police department and the men who had tried to intimidate her hours earlier. How could someone be compassionate and understanding one minute and a total jerk the next?

"You need to worry about arresting them, not me."

"And they will be. Maybe I'll put you in the adjoining cell." The vein on the side of his forehead twitched and Belle sensed his annoyance was real.

"It can't be worse than leaving me at the altar." Belle fumed. "Besides, I have animals to take care of at home."

"Ivy and I will take care of them. I'm sure Lydia will explain exactly what we need to do." Harlan removed the cuffs from his belt. "Belle Barnes—correction, Slade—you're under arrest for the theft of my trailer. You have the right to remain—"

"You've got to be kidding me!" The cold steel encircled her wrists. "And it's still Barnes. I didn't take your last name."

"—silent. Anything you say can and will be used against you in a court of law. You have the right to an attorney. If you cannot afford an attorney, one will be provided for you. Do you understand these rights I have just read to you?"

"Is it even legal for you to arrest your own wife?" Belle tried to squeeze her hands out of the cuffs.

"I can and I just did." Harlan led her to his police cruiser and opened the door. "Look where we are again. Watch your head."

He slammed the door and left her there for the next half hour. So much for today's happiness. Surely, he'd release her as soon as he got back. Harlan wouldn't take her to jail. Would he?

Chapter 7

"You can't leave her in there," Bryan said. "Judge Sanders will have your badge for tying up his courtroom over this. Technically, she can say the trailer was community property and she had every right to use it."

"She doesn't know that. Let her stew in there for a little while longer. Her heart was in the right place, but if she had gotten away with taking that bull and someone reported the plates on my trailer, I'd have more than one problem on my hands." Harlan watched her cell on the monitor. "She'll survive another hour."

"Harlan," Sheriff Bill Parker called to him across the station. "My office."

"Here we go." Harlan trudged down the hall.

"Have a seat." Bill closed the door behind him. "You got married when? August 1, right?"

Harlan nodded.

"And what time is it now?" The older man glanced at the clock on the wall. "Five after midnight on Friday. So, you haven't even been married for ten and a half days, give or take a few hours. Am I right?"

Harlan groaned. Their conversation was headed in the direction he'd hope to avoid. "Yes, you're correct."

"Then can you please explain why your wife has been arrested twice during that time?"

"Well, sir—"

"We all agreed to drop the trespassing charge due to the animal cruelty charges against the Huffington cattle ranch. And for the record, I know your wife's employer was a part of all of this, but I overlooked it to keep the peace in your family. And can you also explain why you arrested Belle for the theft of marital property?"

"I wanted to teach her a lesson. It's not a real arrest. I wanted her to think it was, though. I'll release her soon."

Bill placed both hands and his desk and leaned over it. "You'll release her before this goes any further than this department."

"Yes, sir. Should I do it right this second?"

Bill straightened. "Harlan, get out of my office!"

He scrambled for the door. He hadn't heard the sheriff yell at anyone since a rookie drove their cruiser into the Swan River. He grabbed Belle's personal belongings from his desk, swiped his key card and entered the holding cells. Belle sat on a bench, with a half smile plastered across her face. He'd planned on letting her out once the Huffington gang was through with booking.

"Voices carry around here at night." There was no disguising her grin. She knew he'd gotten reamed out for his prank. "Serves you right."

Harlan unlocked her door and crooked his finger at her. "Come here."

Belle remained seated, her eyes wide. "No, thanks. I'm good."

"Oh, no, you're not. I'm going home and you're coming with me."

"I need to get my truck and your trailer."

"Already taken care of. I had your truck parked in the impound lot for safekeeping overnight. You can get it tomorrow."

"Thanks a lot, Harlan. I didn't even deserve to get arrested and now I have to pay for my truck. You're a real prize of a husband." She grabbed the bag from his hands and pushed past him, waiting for him to unlock the holding area doors.

"You don't have to pay to pick up your truck to-morrow. It's just there for the night."

"Fine."

"Fine."

They stood in the hallway facing each other. "If you don't mind, I have little ones at home to feed."

"After you." Harlan swept his hand to the side. "Come on. Admit it. I got you good that time."

Belle's hand froze on the doorknob. "I'm tired of

you getting me." She faced him. "I'm tired of being a joke. Your joke."

"I thought we were past all of that."

"So did I." She turned away. "I guess your plan backfired. It gave me time to think."

"Wait." Harlan reached for her, feeling her body stiffen beneath his touch. "I'm sorry. I shouldn't have arrested you tonight." He held her face gently. "You did everything I had asked and I failed you. I should have called and given you an update when I knew I couldn't get there. I should have tried harder, and I didn't."

"Harlan." Her eyes fluttered closed. She had no idea how sensuous she sounded when she said his name.

Her moistened lips begged for him to taste them. To apologize properly and kiss them the way a man should kiss his wife. His mouth covered hers. He fought to maintain control, but the fervent need to claim her overtook him. Her lips parted, allowing entry with his tongue. Slow languid strokes in time with her own. Her fingers found his chest and splayed across it. He ached for her touch everywhere. Softly, he broke the kiss and reached behind her to open the door. He planned to make love to his wife tonight and the police station wasn't the place.

Desire coiled deep within Belle during the silent ride home. Harlan's fingers, strong and firm, entwined with hers. She needed to experience those fingers on her bare skin in the most intimate of places. Tonight she'd allow herself the pleasure of being with the man who drove her utterly mad in the most delicious ways, even though she knew she shouldn't. The chance of reliving the passion they'd once shared was impossible to refuse. To feel his love and tenderness, if only for a few hours.

When his cruiser braked alongside his house, her skin prickled in anticipation. She waited for Harlan to open the passenger door. She took his hand as she stepped out, allowing him to fold her into his embrace. His mouth devoured hers. His thumb grazed her engorged nipple over her shirt, circling and teasing. Belle felt his hardness against her, needing to feel it within her.

She pushed away from him. "Slow down, cowboy." She inhaled the night air. "I have to feed Lillie and Samson first."

Harlan kissed the side of her neck and nibbled at her ear before whispering, "I'll feed Samson. I can't wait much longer."

Belle's body tingled as his lips trailed over her skin, sending shocks straight to her core. He led her inside the stables and continued to press kisses against her neck as she prepared two bottles of formula. She handed him one to take down to Samson while she stayed in the apartment and fed Lillie. The piglet devoured her midnight snack and Belle fixed her fresh bedding before ducking into the bathroom. Between the work, tonight's rescue and jail, she needed a shower before she allowed Harlan to see her naked.

She turned on the faucet, letting the water heat as she slipped out of her clothes. Steam filled the room, engulfing her in luxurious warmth. She opened the shower door as the bathroom door eased open. Harlan, raw and naked as the day he was born, entered the room. His hands sought hers as his lips claimed her bare breasts. Her body arched against him, yearning for more. He guided her under the tepid liquid, allowing it to trickle between them. His fingers caressed her in ways she'd remembered in her dreams. Tonight they belonged to each other. She'd worry about the consequences in the morning.

Hours later, Belle awoke next to Harlan. The light of the moon cast a silvery glow around the room. She stretched. Her body still tingled from the glorious passion she'd experienced numerous times during the night with the only man she'd ever shared a bed with. She lifted the covers, soaking in his nakedness. She could get used to this. But was she able to forgive him enough to move forward together into the future?

Somewhere between jail and home every wrong between them had been righted. They had even gone one step further and consummated their marriage. She wasn't sure they qualified for an annulment after that repeated act. The sudden urge to want to stay married to Harlan unnerved her. She had Ivy to consider and the impact it would have on the child.

Belle slid out of bed and padded to the window, grabbing his shirt along the way. She adored Ivy. More than she ever thought she would. She also wanted children of her own one day. Did Harlan want more kids? She wasn't even sure how to ask that question so soon into the relationship. Then again, it had been anything but conventional so far. Why stop now?

Belle pulled the shirt tight across her chest. The room had chilled dramatically since they had arrived home. When she turned to make sure Lillie was warm enough, she noticed a faint glow at the entrance of the ranch drive. *Were those dashboard lights?* There was a flash of red and then the faint sound of an engine starting. Whoever it was must have stepped on the brakes first.

"Harlan," Belle whispered. She tiptoed across the room, uncertain why she was being quiet. "Harlan." She sat on the side of the bed and lightly shook his hand. "There's someone outside."

"What?" He wrapped his arms around her waist and pulled her next to him. "It's too early and you have too many clothes on," he murmured. "Take them off so I can make love to you again."

"Harlan, there's a—"

His fingers slipped between her thighs, causing her to cease speaking. Someone most likely got lost. By sunup they'd be gone. Why waste time worrying about a stranger? She shed his shirt and tossed it onto the floor, relishing the feel of his rigid body against hers.

"Do you want more kids?" Belle panted between strokes.

"Yes." Harlan's voice was husky with desire. "Let's practice making babies now." He rolled her onto her back and he eased himself on top of her.

"There's nothing I'd love more than raising a family with you."

Welcome back, happiness.

The alarm from his phone coming from the other side of the room woke him. He hated leaving the comfort of Belle's arms, but he had to be at work by seven. After last night, he couldn't afford to be late.

His bare feet hit the cold floorboards. He had to convince Belle to move into the main house sooner rather than later. He no longer saw any reason for her not to. It wasn't as though they weren't already married. Harlan watched Belle's sleeping form before he tore himself from the bed and turned off the alarm.

They deserved a proper honeymoon. That would be new to both of them. They hadn't had enough money for one when they planned their first wedding, and his shotgun marriage to Molly hadn't warranted one.

He stepped into his boxer briefs and tugged them on as he gazed out the window overlooking their ranch. It was a long time coming, but it was finally theirs together. Maybe they'd even add to their little brood in the near future. It was more than wishful thinking. Last night had been the culmination of years of waiting to openly love Belle the way he should have eight years ago. He'd been wrong when he told Ivy they wouldn't have a happy-ever-after. Harlan wasn't a romantic man, but damned if Belle didn't bring it out in him.

A car idling at the entrance to his ranch caught his attention. The area around the vehicle was practically engulfed in exhaust. From what he could see, it didn't look familiar either. He had a vague recollection of Belle telling him someone was outside during the night. It had to be the same person. Not many people wandered onto his ranch.

He finished dressing and tugged on his boots. Lillie stood at the door of her carrier with a blanket half draped over her back. "Good morning, little one." He rubbed her head through the wire door. "Let me wake your mommy." A week and a half with Belle and he was already talking to the animals. "Belle, honey." He stroked the side of her cheek before placing a light kiss against it. "Lillie's waiting for you."

She slowly sat up in bed and blinked away the sleep. "Good morning." She smiled. He had waited far too long to wake up to that smile. "You're already dressed?"

"It's a little after six and I have to get to work. Did you try to tell me there was someone outside earlier?"

Belle nodded. "They were sitting at the entrance. I figured they made a wrong turn or something."

"Whoever it was is still there."

"What?" The sheet slipped down around her waist, exposing her breasts. It took every ounce of his strength not to spend the next hour or two making love to her again. "That's odd."

"I'll check it out." He gave her a quick kiss. "I'm sure it's nothing."

"Be careful." Belle watched him fasten his police duty belt before climbing out of bed. She wrapped the sheet around her and looked out the window. "That's the same spot they were in last night."

"I'll make us some coffee, too. And, Belle, I didn't realize how cold it was up here in the morning during the summer. You need to stay with your husband in the house. And we need to do a whole lot more of this." He pointed to the bed. "Much, much more."

Belle's cheeks flushed at his insistence. "Let's discuss it later. You have Ivy to consider."

"Fair enough." He tipped his hat. "I'll meet you up at the house."

The muscles in his legs ached as he descended the stable's stairs. The last time he'd had that intense of a workout was in the police academy. He gave the interior of the stables a quick scan before heading outside. As he approached the waiting car, the engine cut off and a woman stepped from it.

His heart stopped beating.

Molly.

Molly! Even from the second story of the stables Belle recognized her. Had she heard that Belle and Harlan had gotten married and rushed back to town to louse it up? "Brava, Molly." Belle clapped. "Your timing is impeccable."

She wanted to run downstairs and confront her former friend. And not just for her sake, but for Ivy's, too. It had been a long time coming, but she thought better of it. The last thing she needed to do was make a scene smelling like sex. Especially considering she lived in the stables and Harlan lived in the house. Molly would never let her live that down.

She trusted Harlan. Didn't she? She had to. Granted that hadn't worked in her favor where Molly was concerned in the past, but they had both grown since then. She couldn't fathom Harlan ever forgiving Molly for walking out on Ivy.

Belle took a deep breath and jumped in the shower. She did some of her best thinking in there. Maybe Molly would be gone by the time she dressed and went downstairs. Just in case, she took extra care applying her makeup, which she normally didn't put on before work. Horses and cattle didn't care what she looked like. Her grandmother always said women wore makeup to impress other women. She had never believed that statement until right now.

After feeding her animals, she casually strolled out the back of the stables with Lillie on a leash. The car was still out front, but Harlan and Molly were nowhere in sight. She wasn't sure what she had hoped to accomplish by sneaking around…maybe overhear a conversation? But there didn't seem to be anything or anyone to spy on.

"This is silly. I'm an adult and I just spent the night in my husband's arms. I am not scared of some has-been." Belle laughed to herself. "More like Molly never was."

She waited for Lillie to finish her business outside, and did a few chores in the barn before heading to the house for that long-overdue cup of coffee. It was almost seven. Both she and Harlan needed to leave soon. She still had to pick up her truck from the impound lot.

She entered the kitchen, not expecting to see

Molly sitting at the table. Her first instinct was to claw the woman's eyes out. The second was to run and avoid the drama altogether. She had enough going on in her life and she didn't need whatever baggage Molly brought with her making it worse. Instead, she crossed the room to the coffeepot, feeling the burn of her ex-friend's stare against her back. Belle poured herself a cup and faced her.

"This is a surprise," Molly said without blinking.

You bet your sweet bippy it's a surprise. "I'm sure it is."

"How long have you two been together?" she asked.

"You mean how long have Belle and I been married?" Harlan corrected.

"Oh, well I guess you two finally got what you always wanted."

Belle scoffed. "You meant what you took from me."

"I never took Harlan from you." Molly remained impassive, still staring. "He had already left you when he and I got together. You're blaming the wrong person."

"I blame both of you." Belle closed the distance between them. "The two closest people to me stabbed me in the back. Romances come and go and if Harlan and I had broken up, that would have been one thing. But I thought of you as a sister. My grandmother treated you like a daughter. Your betrayal stunned me more than his. His hurt like hell, but yours broke every girl code out there." Belle held up her hands. "But I've moved past all of that."

"Clearly." Molly scanned her top to bottom. "I don't get it. Why did you two spend the night in the stables?"

"Because we have some orphaned animals and we're keeping a close eye on them," Harlan answered. "Not that it's any of your business."

"Molly, what do you want?"

"She wants Ivy," Harlan ground out. "And as I told her, over my dead body."

Chapter 8

Belle was still reeling over Molly's arrival when she remembered this morning's court appearance. Once again, her life had done a complete one-eighty overnight.

She ran into the courtroom one minute before nine. Her court-appointed public defender waved to her from the front row. There was one good thing about remaining in the system…they always assigned her the same attorney. Jocelyn Winters. The two had become friends over the past few years and Belle held the woman solely responsible for keeping her out of jail.

Belle took her seat beside Jocelyn and scanned the room, wondering if Harlan had decided to come. That's if he even knew about today. She hoped he stayed far away. Well, as far away as the sheriff's department next door would take him. She'd already caused enough trouble for him.

"Oh, my God. What is she doing here?"

Jocelyn followed her gaze. "That's your stepdaughter, isn't it?"

"My what?" *Stepdaughter.* "Yes." Belle hadn't thought of herself as Ivy's stepmother. She guessed by law, she was. Her and Harlan's marriage was too new and fragile to place herself in a parental role. "She shouldn't be here."

Harlan had kept Ivy out of school today for fear Molly would try to contact her or even worse…take her. He needed the chance to notify everyone involved in her life before allowing her to go back to school or visit any of her friends. Belle had a suspicion all playdates would be on Harlan's ranch for the foreseeable future. Ivy was supposed to be safely tucked away on the Silver Bells Ranch with Dylan. How on earth did she get into town?

Belle reached for her phone before she remembered they weren't allowed in court. Bryan sat in the front row behind the prosecutor. Belle stood to call his name when the judge entered the room.

"All rise for the Honorable Judge Beckett Sanders," the bailiff announced.

Crap!

"You may be seated," the judge commanded from the bench. "Who's first on today's docket?" he asked the bailiff.

"Belle Elizabeth Barnes."

The judge removed his glasses and rubbed his eyes.

"Step on up, Belle." Judge Sanders had ditched any formality when it came to her years ago. "I heard you got married. Congratulations."

"Yes, Your Honor." Belle couldn't resist smiling. Maybe court wouldn't be so bad. "I did. And thank you."

"Why are you standing before me today?"

"Honestly, I'm not sure which offense this is for, Your Honor." Belle inwardly cursed herself. When had her life become so out of control she didn't know why she was in court?

The judge laughed and put his glasses back on. "That's not reassuring. Have you seen the inside of a jail cell this past month?"

"A few times, Your Honor." Belle braved a quick glance in Bryan's direction, hoping to get his attention.

"Will the prosecutor please read the charges against our resident rebel bride?"

"Miss Barnes is here for charges from July 4 and 11. Both are petty theft charges of property not exceeding $1,500 in value. Restitution has been paid to the property owners. If convicted, these two charges will put Miss Barnes over the third theft offense limit. In addition, there is one criminal trespass charge, which is associated with the petty theft on the eleventh."

"How do you plea?"

"Not guilty, Your Honor." Belle wanted to crawl into a hole and die. She wondered how many of the charges Ivy understood. Regardless, she was sure *theft* and *trespass* were two words she was familiar with.

"Do you wish to waive your right to a trial on another day or do you wish to proceed this morning?"

"Your Honor," Jocelyn began. "Miss Barnes would like to proceed today."

"Your Honor," Belle interrupted. "May I please approach the bench? It's urgent." He waved her forward and covered the microphone with his hand. "Judge Sanders, Harlan's daughter is in the back of the courtroom. I don't know how she got here, but she's supposed to be on the Silver Bells Ranch with Dylan. Molly showed up this morning laying claim to Ivy, and Harlan fears she'll take her. Can Bryan bring her to her father? He may not even realize she's gone. But if he does, he'll be frantic."

"Deputy Bryan Jones, please approach the bench." Judge Sanders peered over his glasses.

Bryan was startled at the sound of his name. "Yes, Your Honor." He crossed the front of the courtroom.

"Miss Barnes needs to speak with you."

"Ivy's in the back of the courtroom alone," Belle whispered. "Do you know why she's here?"

"No." Bryan turned toward the little girl. "Where's Harlan?"

"I have no idea and with Molly running around I'm afraid something's wrong."

The judge leaned farther over the bench. "Deputy, how many cases do you have today?"

"Just one. Speeding ticket. Fifty-five in a twenty. I don't see the guy, though."

"Belle, are you certain you don't want to postpone your appearance?"

"What's the point? I was arrested on Tuesday for rescuing a piglet. I'll be here next month. I'd rather not have all my charges announced on one day. It's kind of humiliating."

"I'm sorry, it's what?" Judge Sanders stared at her. "I never thought I'd hear those words out of your mouth."

"I never thought my indiscretions, however honorable the reasons were, would be read in front of an impressionable seven-year-old girl."

The judge scrawled a few notes on the legal pad before redirecting his attention to them. "Deputy Jones, please take Ivy to her father and, Belle, you can return to the defendant's table."

Judge Sanders waited for Bryan and Ivy to leave the room before proceeding. "Will the prosecution please explain the nature of the charges?"

After a half hour of listening to the prosecutor read her priors, Belle wanted to throw up. Hadn't she paid attention in court before? None of it was foreign to her, yet she had a difficult time associating the person they were describing with herself. Being a rebel with a cause was one thing, but she sounded like a loose cannon. She was shocked Harlan even married her with this long of a record. He was right—her actions affected his career and Ivy's life.

If Judge Sanders convicted her on both petty theft charges today, he'd have no choice but to remand her to jail for the state-mandated thirty days. When he reduced her charges and gave her a hundred hours of community service and six months of probation instead, she felt luckier than a four-leaf clover. She made a solemn vow to herself never to see the inside of a courtroom again unless she was a witness for the prosecution. And there was that pesky last court appearance she needed to make on Lillie's behalf. But neither of those were third offenses. She'd never see the inside of a jail cell again.

How dare Molly storm back into their lives and demand to be a part of Ivy's life? He'd spent the better part of the morning calling in every favor owed to him from various law enforcement agencies around the country. He wanted a detailed report of her whereabouts and who she had been with since the day she left. People had asked if he kept tabs on her over the years and he never had. She hadn't been worth the time or effort involved. A judge had awarded him full custody and nothing else had mattered.

Sheriff Parker even made a few calls on his behalf. Molly was the definition of a *town pariah*. She hadn't a friend left in Saddle Ridge after walking out on their daughter the way she had. Speaking of his daughter, he wondered if she was still mad at him after he yelled at her this morning for taking off.

Dylan had an appointment and Harlan had to bring Ivy to work with him. After explaining his reason—Molly—the department understood. Unfortunately, Ivy hadn't. What kid wanted to go to school? His. And she was mad she was missing a science demonstration they'd been working on all week. How do you explain to your child you were protecting her from her own mother? He'd do everything in his power to prevent telling her Molly wanted to see her. Unless the court ordered it, he'd do his damnedest to keep it from happening. He refused to allow his daughter to ride the Molly Weaver roller coaster. It was a sickening ride fraught with hate and lies.

He realized hanging around the station bored her, but it was the safest place in town. Once Dylan came back, then she'd be safe on Silver Bells. But bored or not, sneaking out and into the courthouse next door because she saw Belle's truck pull into the adjoining lot had infuriated him. Truth be told, he was madder at himself for not realizing she was missing. Then he'd gone on the warpath and berated the courthouse security guard for letting her in without adult supervision. He may have gone a little overboard with his reaction, but today it had been warranted.

Ivy sat next to his desk sulking and coloring. She was confused and he didn't blame her for the attitude.

When lunchtime rolled around, he was no closer to understanding what had happened to Molly. Her record was clean. Dylan stopped by after his appointment to take Ivy back to his ranch. At least she'd have her puppy and the other animals to play with and keep her company.

He hadn't heard from Belle all morning, but he already knew she'd had a court appearance thanks to his daughter. Bryan said it hadn't gone well while he was there. Belle had been genuinely embarrassed that Ivy had heard her charges. In a way, he was glad that happened. Ivy hadn't asked him any questions, and maybe this was the kick in the rear Belle needed to straighten out her life. And considering she hadn't been paraded through the police station to a holding cell, he assumed the charges had been reduced. He wanted to spend the rest of his life with her and if last night was any indication of the future, they'd be very happy together.

Harlan had promised Belle he would stop by the nursing home and visit with Trudy at lunchtime. He should have gone sooner. It was a gorgeous day and Harlan opted to walk the few blocks. He waved hello to the nurses at the front desk as he turned down Trudy's hallway.

He froze outside her doorway, recognizing the woman's voice before he laid eyes on her.

"What the hell are you doing here?" Harlan glared at Molly, sitting beside Trudy's bed.

"I'm visiting—what does it look like?" Molly replied.

"Wasn't that nice of Molly to visit with me during her lunch hour?" Trudy patted Molly's arm. "I'll only be here for a few more days, then you can come visit me at the house."

"Molly, may I see you in the hallway please?" Harlan said between clenched teeth.

She shook her head. "What for?"

"Sit down, Harlan." Trudy pointed to the chair next to Molly.

"No, thank you, I'd rather stand. I've been sitting all day."

"Suit yourself." Trudy returned her attention to

Molly. "Molly was just telling me why she wasn't at your wedding."

The careful facade Belle and he had built was beginning to crumble. "Yes, Molly. Why couldn't you attend our wedding? Come to think of it, we haven't seen you around in quite some time."

"Molly has a new job and it takes her out of town quite a bit."

"Is that so?" Harlan folded his arms across his chest. "Doing what?"

"Oh, my God! What are you doing here?" Belle stood in the doorway. She strode across the room and grabbed Molly by the back of the shirt, yanking her to her feet.

"Belle, what's wrong with you?" Trudy attempted to sit up straight.

"I'm sorry, Grammy. Molly has to cut her visit short. She's late for a doctor's appointment and she asked me to remind her. I'll show her out, but I'll be back in just a minute. Say goodbye, Molly."

"I'll see you again soon, Trudy."

Belle tugged her out into the hall, almost banging Molly's face against the door frame.

Harlan followed them. Half out of fear Belle would kill her and half for entertainment purposes.

Belle marched up to the security guard. "Do you see this woman? Take a good look at her. In fact, take her picture. She is never to come anywhere near my grandmother again. She is a menace and a threat to my family." Belle pushed open the front door of the nursing home and shoved Molly through it. "If I have to get a restraining order against you, I will. This is your one and only warning. My grandmother does not have the faculties to defend herself against you. You are not to come near her."

Harlan stepped in between them. "Molly, if you want to talk to me, then talk to me. But don't try to go through Trudy or try to get under Belle's skin to get my attention. I'm not above throwing you in jail."

"Oh, please do." Belle glared up at him.

"My intentions were only to visit with Trudy. I didn't mean to upset anyone." Molly turned to Belle. "I stopped by your grandmother's house only to discover you had sold it and she lived here. I had no idea."

"Why would you? You abandoned your family six years ago and never looked back. You wouldn't even recognize your own daughter if she was standing here."

"You're probably right. But I would love the opportunity." Molly handed Harlan a slip of paper. "I will give you some time to think it over. I'm staying here in town and if you don't allow me some form of visitation with my child, I will have the courts intervene."

"I don't know which is sadder," Harlan said. "The fact you think you can come back to town and pick up right where you left off, or that you think you have a chance of winning any form of custody or visitation with Ivy."

"This isn't the time or the place to discuss it." Belle looked over her shoulder. A small crowd had gathered in the nursing home's atrium.

"You're right," Molly agreed. "My number and my hotel are on that slip of paper. I would like to speak with you about Ivy, alone."

"Belle's my wife. She has every right to be a part of this conversation." The last thing Harlan wanted was to meet Molly in a hotel room alone. Not because he didn't trust himself. He had no interest in anyone other than his wife. He didn't trust Molly or how Molly might use this situation against Belle. He finally had everything he'd ever wanted with the woman of his dreams and he refused to allow anyone to come between them.

"Fine, just promise me we'll talk."

"We will talk. But it will be on my terms, in a location I choose, and if I suspect anything, there won't be any second chances. You're lucky I'm giving you this one."

"Understood." Molly began to walk away, then stopped and faced Belle. "I thought if anyone would understand, you would. Didn't I do what you always wanted your mother to do? I came back. How would you feel if you found out your mother had returned for you and nobody allowed you to see her? How would you feel knowing you could have had answers to all your questions, but someone stole that chance from you?"

"That's low, even for you, Molly," Harlan said.

"Please stay away from my grandmother." Belle headed inside.

"When we talk, you better be prepared to answer a lot of questions. Starting with where the hell have you been and how could you leave and never once contact our daughter? She doesn't even remember you. She hasn't the foggiest idea what you even look like and she's never asked. She doesn't give you a second thought." Molly winced at his comment as if he'd physically struck her. "What did you expect? You're not a part of her life. After you left, I wondered how this would affect her. I learned a child's resiliency is a beautiful thing. She bounced back like you never even happened. She didn't even cry, because the house was finally peaceful. When you were there, you weren't much of a mother. So wherever you went, I hope you found the help you needed. And if you ever have more children, and maybe you already do, I hope you have enough good sense and strength to treat them better than you treated Ivy."

Harlan strode into the nursing home and straight out the back door into the garden. He had finally said everything he'd wanted to say to Molly for six years. His body shook with relief. His shoulders released the tension he swore he'd been carrying all this time. It was over. The waiting and wondering if she would ever return. She had returned and he had to prepare for the fight of his life. Not that he thought he'd have much of one. Saddle Ridge was a small town in the middle of a small county. Everyone knew everyone else, and everyone knew what Molly had done. Outside of some fantastic medical excuse, nothing would make up for her abandonment.

"Harlan." Belle rested her hand on his shoulder. He covered it with his own, turned and gathered her in his arms, holding her tightly. His heart hammered in his chest as he buried his face in her hair. She wound her arms around his waist and stroked his back. "Molly's right," she said. "You should listen to what she has to say."

Chapter 9

When Belle told Harlan he should give Molly a chance to explain, she didn't think he'd do it hours later. She was alone on the ranch for the first time at night since her arrival. It felt cold, lacking the charm and emotion without Harlan and Ivy. His daughter was still staying with Dylan and probably would for the next couple days.

Harlan had given her a key to the house and told her to make herself at home. And technically it was her home. Not just because they were married, but because she had been the one to persuade Harlan to buy the ranch years ago. She'd fallen in love with it the moment she stepped on the wide front porch. The whitewashed clapboard siding provided a neutral palette against the colorful western Montana backdrop.

This had been where she planned to raise her kids. And as wonderful as last night had been, she doubted she'd get that chance. They'd already moved too fast. She'd initially excused it because of their past, but in the cold light of day, it was just plain foolishness. Neither one of them was ready for an emotional commitment. They'd slept together and now it was out of their system. It wouldn't happen again.

Lydia called with an update on the bull they rescued. Part of the front leg had to be amputated, but they knew of an animal prosthetic company willing to donate their time and materials to construct him a new limb. He had a long recovery ahead of him, but his quality of life had already improved dramatically.

After their conversation, Belle finished mucking the stalls, showered and ate dinner. She stared at the main house from the stable's apartment window. As much as she hated what Molly did to Harlan and Ivy, she'd pack up and leave in a heartbeat if it meant Ivy could have a happy home with both of her parents. Isn't that what every child deserved?

It was what she had always dreamed of. Not only had her mother abandoned her, she never knew who her father was. For that matter, her mother probably hadn't either. She'd always fantasized who Unknown could have been. Maybe somebody famous? Maybe a multimillionaire who would give her all the money she needed to start her rescue ranch. Whoever it was, she wished them well. Ivy at least had a name, she just hadn't had the opportunity to put a face to it yet. Now she would. And whatever happened between Molly, Harlan and their daughter was out of her hands. She wouldn't interfere.

The sound of Harlan's truck interrupted her thoughts. She held her breath, waiting to hear if he came in the stables or went to the main house. When the downstairs door didn't open, she braved a look out the window. The kitchen lights flicked on, followed by the upstairs bedroom a minute later. For a moment, Belle wondered if he was alone. Although, knowing Molly, she would've cackled from the truck to the back door to make sure Belle heard her.

She pulled her computer out of the tote bag next to her bed and turned it on. She prayed Harlan's Wi-Fi wasn't password protected because she needed to find a new apartment and fast. The sound of boots coming up the stable's stairs startled her. It couldn't be Harlan; he was already inside his house. She ran to the apartment door to lock it, just as it opened, knocking her to the floor.

"Oh, my God, Belle!" Harlan reached for her. "I am so sorry. What were you doing standing on the other side of the door?"

"Me?" Belle rubbed the side of her head. "I saw you turn the lights on inside your house and I thought you were a stranger coming up the stairs. Don't you knock?"

"I guess it hadn't dawned on me to knock before entering my own stables, but you're right. I should have given you that courtesy."

"Fair enough." She allowed Harlan to help her to her feet. "So, what happened? Unless you don't want to tell me?"

Harlan guided her to the bed. "Let me see your head. Are you sure you're okay?"

"It's just a bump. I'm hardheaded, in case you haven't already noticed." Levity, no matter how weak, seemed to be in order.

"I went into the house first because I figured that's where you would be." He sat beside her. "I thought we settled that."

"And then you went to see Molly." Belle pulled away from him. The more he rubbed her head, the more it hurt. "I'm okay."

"What does seeing Molly have to do with you moving in with me?" He scooted back against the headboard.

"If you and Molly have a chance to work things out for Ivy's sake, I think you should take it." The words left an acrid taste in her mouth.

"Thank you, but I can make my own decisions." He lifted her hand and placed a light kiss in the center of her palm. "Getting back together with Molly is not an option." He smiled. It was a devastating smile. One that sent her stomach to the moon and back. "Thank you for persuading me to listen to what she had to say. I already knew most of it."

"Did she give you any details?" A part of her was curious what her former best friend had been up to since Belle's wedding day. The other part didn't care what happened to the woman. She chose the high road out of respect for Ivy.

"She admitted she hadn't been ready to raise a child back then. Pretty much the same way I wasn't ready to get married. Not that I'm trying to justify either situation." Harlan kicked off his boots and reached for Belle, urging her to sit between his legs. "She had always wanted to travel and get away from small-town life. And that's exactly what she did. She works as a travel agent out of Billings. She told me when we spent that one night together she wasn't trying to get pregnant."

He wrapped his arms in front of Belle, cocooning her against him. "At least that's something." She still had a hard time absorbing his admission that he and Molly had only had sex once. Ever. A part of her had been overjoyed; the other part had been furious he'd thrown away everything they had together for a roll in the hay.

"I think I needed to hear that, because I always wondered if she had purposely trapped me. I was partially to blame, but I don't think I was willing to admit it until recently."

"Does she want you back?" Belle squeezed her eyes shut and braced for the answer.

"No. And I wouldn't entertain the thought even if she did. She said she doesn't want to come between us. Belle, she seems genuinely happy that you and I found our way back to one another. She had assumed we had been married for years, not days. I didn't explain our situation because it's none of her business. Knowing her, she would turn our quickie marriage against me. She would like to speak with you and apologize."

Belle tensed. Molly and Harlan had a lot to work through. She and Molly did not. "Sounds like she's making amends as part of a twelve-step program."

"The same thought ran through my mind. But isn't the first step always admitting you have a problem? She never abused alcohol or drugs when we were together. She just wasn't emotionally ready to be a parent. Now she claims she is. She's twenty-seven, appears stable—at least on paper—and would like the chance to know her daughter."

"Will you allow Ivy to see her?"

He blew out a slow breath before answering. "I thought about what you said earlier…how you would have appreciated the same opportunity. I don't think I could live with myself if I didn't give Ivy the chance to decide on her own. She may not be ready to make that decision, and Molly will have to accept whatever the outcome. I won't force Ivy into this."

"Are you still worried about her running off with Ivy?" It had been her grandmother's biggest fear when Belle first came to Saddle Ridge. She remembered Trudy's stern warnings to never go with her mother under any circumstances. The situation hadn't presented itself and over time, the memories of her mother slowly faded.

"I'm more afraid if I take too long, she'll take it upon herself to meet Ivy, and that's what I want to avoid. My daughter is already confused. I don't think I can keep it from her any longer. It's too late tonight. I'll talk to her first thing tomorrow morning. I think this will be the hardest conversation of my life. In the meantime, will you please move into the house with us?"

Belle shook her head. "I can't."

"Why?" Harlan swept the hair off her shoulder and shifted his body to see her expression.

She withdrew from his arms and turned around to face him. "Your daughter will experience the biggest shock of her young life tomorrow. I don't think now is the time to introduce another change into her safe zone." She reached for his hands and held them between her own. "Your house and everything it represents is home. She has you and Elvis and that's all she needs right now." Harlan opened his mouth to protest, but she pressed a finger to his lips to silence his words. "I'm added confusion. I don't want Ivy to feel she must choose between me or her mother. You have some big adjustments coming on the horizon. Take this time for you and your daughter."

"What are you saying?" The pain was evident in his eyes. "Are we breaking up?"

"We're married." She smiled, however bittersweet. "We can't break up without a divorce." Belle attempted to laugh, but her heart ached too much and it terrified her. "I think it's best if I stay out here. We're moving way too fast. That doesn't mean we can't still spend time together, because I do want that." She ran the backs of her fingers down the side of his face and cupped his chin. "I want us to both be sure we're making the right decision."

Harlan gently eased her down onto the bed, his touch light as he skimmed his fingertips over her hips through the thin cotton fabric of her boxer shorts. "I've already made my decision. I made it the day I married you." His lips grazed hers. "I may have screwed up our relationship the first time, but I would never break my wedding vows."

His hand moved under her shirt, searing a path across her abdomen. A shiver of arousal shot through her. A tiny moan caught in her throat as he lifted her shirt and his lips found her bare breasts.

"No, no, no." Belle scooted out from under him. "Sex clouds things."

Harlan sat on the edge of the bed, slack jawed. "Please tell me you're kidding."

Belle groaned. "I'm not." Saying no to a night of passion was proving harder than she thought. Especially when every inch of her body yearned for him. But it twisted her emotions. Despite what he said about Molly, she wasn't ready to chance him walking out a second time. Wisdom comes from experience, and she wouldn't make the same mistake twice.

The following morning, Harlan paced the length of his living room. Dylan was due to arrive with Ivy any minute and he still hadn't figured out how to tell his daughter her mother wanted to meet her.

To make matters worse, he was still nursing his wounds from Belle's rejection last night. As much as he hated to admit it, she was right. They were moving too fast and her moving in would probably be too much for Ivy to handle on top of Molly. It gave him one more reason not to like his ex-wife.

No sooner had Dylan pulled up outside than Harlan heard his daughter's laughter permeate the air. "Daddy, I'm home." She barreled through the screen door, Elvis clutched tight to her chest.

He lowered himself onto the kitchen chair, wrapping his arms around her and her little charge. "And how are you two this morning?"

"We're good. Elvis is learning to do potty outside."

"Only after Elvis did many potties inside." His eldest brother, Dylan, stood in the doorway.

"I didn't even think about that when I sent him over there with her." Harlan cringed. "Did he ruin any of your hardwood floors? Whatever damage he did, let me know so I can pay for it."

"Nah. We had it covered."

"Yeah, Daddy." Ivy beamed up at him. "We had it covered with lots of newspapers all over the house."

Dylan nodded behind her. "Will you two be okay? Do you need anything?"

"I think we're good. And thank you again for watching her."

"Anytime, little brother. Ivy's a treat any day." Dylan slapped him on the shoulder. "Call me later."

"Is Belle here?" Ivy placed Elvis on the floor and ran into the living room, the puppy hot on her heels.

"No, honey. She's not." Harlan followed her into the living room and joined her on the large area rug. "She had to go to work."

"How come you're not at work and why won't you let me go to school?"

"Because today's Saturday and you and I both have the day off." Harlan swallowed down the bile threatening to creep up his throat. "Daddy needs to talk to you about something. Or rather someone."

"Who?" She slowly stroked Elvis's back. The puppy's eyes were heavy with sleep. They had probably played nonstop ever since he dropped them off at Dylan's on Thursday night.

"Your mommy." There, he said it. He hadn't had to share Ivy with anyone for six years and the thought of doing so now terrified him. Ivy had only ever spent time with his family, and in recent years, that had been narrowed down to Dylan and his uncle Jax. "Would you like to meet your mommy?"

Ivy shrugged and curled up on the floor, wrapping her arms around Elvis. Harlan brushed the hair out of her face.

"Are you tired or don't you want to talk about Mommy?"

"I don't know." Fear laced her tiny voice.

"I'm not asking you to go live with your mommy." This wasn't fair. A child shouldn't be afraid of their parents. Yet the thought of meeting her mother reduced his daughter to a shell of who she'd been minutes earlier. He hated Molly for instilling that fear. "I just wondered if you wanted to spend some time with her. It could be for however long or short you want it to be. If you only want to see her for a minute, you can. If you want to spend an hour with her, you can do that, too. I will be there with you the entire time so you won't have to worry about being left alone with her."

"I want Belle to be my mommy."

While the idea alone made him smile, he didn't want Ivy to get her hopes up. Which was exactly why Belle hadn't wanted to move into the house. She understood his daughter's needs more than he did, and that didn't sit well with him. He'd allowed their relationship to distract him from what was most important. Ivy. "That's not going to happen right now."

"Is Mommy going to move in with us?" She traced the pattern of the area rug with her index finger, and Harlan wondered what other thoughts were running through her head.

"Absolutely not." It didn't matter how wonderful of a bond Ivy may form with Molly in the future; the woman would never live in his house again. "Our house is for you, me and Elvis. This house is yours as much as it is mine. We've always made decisions together and we will continue to do that."

"Where has Mommy been?"

And there was the question he'd dreaded the most. He didn't have an answer. Molly didn't have one either. Except she needed time to grow up.

"Sometimes when people have babies, they are not emotionally ready to take care of them. Do you understand what I mean by *emotionally*?"

Ivy shook her head.

"Let's use Elvis as an example. Say we got him when you were in preschool instead of second grade. Do you remember preschool?"

Ivy nodded. Harlan guessed a nod was better than no response at all.

"Can you imagine if you'd had Elvis then? You weren't a big girl like you are now. Elvis would have been sad because you would have forgotten about him and wouldn't have known how to care for him. That's kind of what happened with your mommy. She wasn't ready to take care of you, but instead of ignoring you and making you feel bad every day, she left until she felt she was ready to give you the attention you deserve. Just like you give Elvis the attention he deserves. Does that make any sense?"

Harlan rolled his eyes at his own analogy, praying she made the connection.

"Mommy's a big girl now?"

"I certainly hope so," Harlan muttered.

"Do I have to see her?"

"You don't have to do anything you don't want to do. Ever. Except for going to school and doing your homework."

"But you won't let me." Her big blue eyes were glassy with tears. Hurting his daughter had been the last thing he wanted.

"On Monday you will go back to school and everything will be normal again."

"I don't understand why I couldn't before."

"Because your daddy had to take care of some things with Mommy and while he did that I needed you to stay with Dylan. Now that everything is settled, you can go back to school."

He hated lying to his daughter. Visitation was far from settled. But he had to swallow his own fears and allow his daughter to live a normal, healthy life until he could straighten things out with Molly.

"Can I sleep on it?" Ivy asked.

Harlan covered his mouth to keep from laughing out loud. Every time Ivy had asked him if they could get a dog, he told her he had to sleep on it. At least she was paying attention.

"You can take all the time you need." Harlan lay down beside her and pulled her close to him. "Daddy's in no rush."

* * *

"We have plenty of room for you to stay here if it's getting too uncomfortable on the ranch," Lydia said as she examined Lillie's sunburn on Saturday afternoon.

"Thank you, I appreciate it. I wish I had a place on the other side of the ranch already. It would make life a lot easier. Then there'd be some distance without there being too much of one. If that makes any sense." It was awkward and uncomfortable living so close to Harlan, knowing Molly was trying to re-establish a relationship with her daughter. It would have been different if she'd helped raise Ivy for the last six years. "Molly and I are both new to her. I don't want to confuse her, but I'm not sure I'm entirely ready to walk away either. I should have never moved in there."

"Your fears about Harlan and Molly reconnecting and Ivy's best interest aside, how are you doing?"

Her heart was equally as strong as it was fragile. Her mind ran in overdrive until it made her dizzy, and the butterflies in her belly hadn't stopped fluttering since the day she and Harlan had exchanged vows.

"It's ironic. Yesterday morning, I sat in the courtroom horrified by my own police record. It's like I finally got it. I won't stop doing what I do, but I understand more of what you and Harlan have been trying to tell me. I wanted to share that revelation with Harlan and see if I could truly forgive him. Until I completely do that, we don't have a chance. And then Molly entered the picture. It's hard to forgive and forget with that reminder staring me in the face."

"You can't—not even for a single second—believe Harlan stopped loving you because Molly sashayed into town?"

"Who said anything about love?"

"It's written all over both of your faces. Calvin and I saw it in the dark in the middle of a cattle ranch. It's obvious. Keep telling yourself otherwise and you're the only one you're lying to."

"Our timing is off." Belle scratched under Lillie's chin. She was surprised the piglet had allowed Lydia to examine her this long without a single protest. "He has his hands full with Ivy and I have mine full with Trudy. I need to spend more time at the nursing home. I haven't been there as much this past week. She won't be around for much longer, at least not in a lucid capacity. I love being with Harlan and Ivy, but it's taking away from the time I normally spend with my grandmother."

"Your grandmother would want you to have fun and enjoy yourself." She handed Lillie to Belle. "Her back looks better. Your grandmother's the one who wanted you to marry Harlan. You did this for her."

"Only because she didn't know better."

"Because I love you dearly, I'm calling bull on that." Lydia tugged off her examination gloves and tossed them in the trash bin. "You were looking for a good enough excuse to talk to Harlan and don't you tell me otherwise. I've spent enough time around you to notice when you're pining for a man. We are in contact with some of the hottest single cowboys in the state and no matter how many times you've been asked out, you either go on one date or you turn them down altogether. You compare them all to Harlan whether you realize it or not."

Belle hated that there was some truth to that statement. She'd spent the last eight years comparing every man she met to the man who broke her heart. She thought it was to protect herself from getting hurt again. Now she realized it was the opposite. No man could permeate the shield she'd built around her heart, except Harlan. Only he held the key. The problem was, she'd changed the locks long ago.

Chapter 10

"Please don't go." Harlan stood in the middle of the stable the next morning. "My daughter and I need you here. Not at Lydia's." Belle had already begun packing what little there was of her belongings and planned to move what she could into her friend's spare bedroom tomorrow morning. "You won't have any privacy over there. If you want to stay in the apartment above the stables, that's fine. I'll get a couple of space heaters to warm up the place. But you can't leave. Besides, Ivy's in love with Imogene and it would break her heart if she left."

Belle gave the man credit. He knew how to play the kid card to perfection. "Ivy can have Imogene. I think she'd be very happy staying here on your ranch, as long as you keep her safe."

"We will, thank you." Harlan removed his hat and took a step toward her. "And what about you? Wouldn't you be happy staying here on the ranch? I promise to keep you safe."

The man made her knees weak with a simple turn of phrase. She tilted her head back and groaned. He closed the remaining space between them and kissed the tender spot at the base of her throat.

"That's not playing fair." Belle allowed him to trail a few more kisses along her collarbone before she broke from his grasp. "Don't you want time alone with your daughter to sort the Molly situation out? I'm always around when Ivy's home. Either she's out in the stables with me or we're all in the house together."

"I won't lie. I've thought about that, too, but you bring out a joy and happiness in Ivy I haven't seen before."

"That's only because I gave her a puppy."

"Don't belittle that connection, Belle. Please." Harlan took her hands in his. "You've had a very positive effect on her and I'd like it to continue, regardless of where you and I stand. You'll be here once the rescue center opens and I feel more comfortable with her getting to know you with me around. It shows her I'm okay with your relationship. She doesn't have another woman to confide in or talk to about female things. The woman who watches her after school is great, but she's not the warm and fuzzy type like you."

Belle laughed and returned to spreading fresh hay around Samson's stall. She'd never heard herself described as warm and fuzzy before. She kind of liked it. But the fact remained—Molly had returned and that was the bond he needed to foster.

"She has her mother now."

"Ivy hasn't agreed to meet Molly yet and I'm not forcing the issue either. Even if that all goes well, she won't be around 24/7. That's a definite. But you will be. Here or the other side of the ranch, you'll be on the property."

"Okay, okay." Belle stepped into the corridor and closed the stall door. "I'll stay."

"Great." Harlan's arm slid around her waist as he whirled her against his chest. His mouth claimed hers the way no other man could as his fingers splayed in her hair, drawing her even closer as he deepened their kiss. "I'll change your mind about me, however long it takes." His breath was warm against her lips. "Now I need you to do me a favor," he murmured.

"Yes." Belle barely recognized the sound of her own voice.

Harlan pulled away abruptly. "Will you watch Ivy? We're out of milk and I need to run to the store. She's in the house watching cartoons. I'm sure she'd love it if you joined her."

"Oh, I get it now." She playfully swatted him. "You just want a free babysitter."

"Be careful, you're assaulting a police officer. Don't make me handcuff you." He ran to his cruiser and hopped in before she attacked him again. He cracked the window an inch. "Bye, honey. I'll be back in a few."

She watched him drive away before heading

into the house. "How are you doing, kiddo?" Belle plopped beside Ivy and Elvis on the couch while *Phineas and Ferb* played on the wide screen. She didn't watch much television but she recognized the cartoon as one of Lydia's boys' favorites. She didn't even own a TV, probably because her grandmother had never been big on it. Except for *Wheel of Fortune*. Trudy loved that show.

"I'm okay. I have a mommy now." Ivy's voice was just barely audible.

Belle reached for the remote and turned down the sound. "Do you want to talk about it?"

Ivy shifted Elvis onto her lap and wrapped her arms around him. "Does that mean you have to go away?"

"Only if you and your daddy want me to." Belle hated the sadness etched across the little girl's face.

Ivy shook her head. "Daddy says she wants to see me. What if she still doesn't like me?"

Belle swallowed hard, trying her best not to cry. "Honey, she didn't leave because she didn't like you. She left because she was confused." *Among other things.* "Maybe she has something good to tell you. She came a long way to see you, so that counts for something, right?"

Belle couldn't believe she was defending Molly in any capacity. It was none of her business and Harlan would probably kill her, but Belle had firsthand experience of what it was like to be the abandoned kid. Many of her fears and questions would probably be answered in one meeting.

"Maybe. I'll sleep on it some more." Ivy returned

her attention to the television, effectively ending their conversation.

A few minutes later, Belle's phone rang. The number was unfamiliar but she answered it anyway. "Hello."

"It's Molly—please don't hang up."

You've got to be kidding me. The sound of Molly's voice reverberating in her ear made her ill. Belle's left eye started to twitch. "How did you get my number?" She stood from the couch and walked out onto the porch.

"I took a chance you still had the same one." Her voice didn't sound as confident over the phone as it had in person.

Lucky me.

"I wondered if we could meet later and talk."

"I have plans today." *Not really.* "And my schedule is pretty tight during the week between work and my grandmother. In case I wasn't clear before, allow me to reiterate. I don't want you anywhere near the nursing home. You and Harlan may have come to some sort of an understanding, but that doesn't change anything between you and me."

"Would you be able to meet me for breakfast before work tomorrow?"

Belle rolled her shoulders. "We are not sitting down to a meal together. There might be a slim chance of that happening in the future, but not tomorrow or even next month."

"Okay, I get it. I won't bother you again."

Crap! Belle hated the sound of dejection. Either Molly was really good or Belle was really weak.

"Coffee. We can meet for one cup of coffee. To go. We'll walk to the park and back."

"Thank you. Seven o'clock?"

"Six. I work on ranches all day. We get up before the roosters."

"Six it is. I noticed that little coffee shop is still in town. Meet there?"

"Sure. See you tomorrow."

Belle disconnected the call and sat on the porch steps. She drew her knees to her chest and waited for Harlan's return. Ivy's laughter carried through the screen door. As long as she was laughing Belle didn't need to go inside and babysit. Her nerves were too on edge and she was afraid Ivy would pick up on her tension.

Harlan drove up a few minutes later and joined her on the top step. "Are you all right?"

"I just finished making a coffee date with your ex."

"No, you didn't." Harlan smiled.

She exhaled deeply, and all humor drained from his face. "You did?"

"She wanted to meet today, but I told her no. I need to spend some time at the nursing home. Then she asked if I would meet her for breakfast tomorrow. I compromised with coffee."

"Should I send a deputy over for police protection?"

"Molly may be many things, but she's not physically aggressive. I'll be okay."

"I meant to protect her." Harlan jumped up and ran in the house.

"Oh, very funny!" she called after him, relishing the sound of his laughter. Ivy and Harlan had similar laughs. His was deeper, of course, but they both threw their heads back when they found something humorous and laughed with their entire bodies.

He brought her out a mug of coffee a few minutes later. "Penny for your thoughts?"

"Thank you." She sipped the hot brew. "I'm just taking it all in. I never noticed some of the peaks in the mountains." The sun had been up for a couple of hours and cast highlights and shadows over the Swan Range. "We grew up with them always being the backdrop of our daily lives, and their beauty was the major reason why I chose this house, but I don't think I've ever sat and looked at them. The last time I hiked them was probably junior high. I remember the views of the Swan Valley and Saddle Ridge were breathtaking, but I haven't done it again. I'm always going. Never stopping to appreciate what's around me."

"Wow. You're right. Ivy's seven and I haven't taken her on any hikes or trail rides. Dylan has her on the back of a horse all the time and occasionally she'll ask to ride here in the corrals. I ride this ranch all the time. She's never with me, though. We need to change that." He stood and held out his hand to her. "What are you doing today?"

"I plan to spend the afternoon with my grandmother." She reveled in the feel of his palm against hers. "I'm free the rest of the day."

Harlan released her and leaned into the kitchen.

"Ivy, go put on your riding clothes. We're taking the horses out into the valley this morning."

The sound of her bare feet smacking the floor-boards as she ran up the stairs echoed all the way outside.

"No arguments from her, are there?" Belle laughed. "You mentioned earlier that she hadn't agreed to meet Molly. What happened?"

"Well, we had our talk. She didn't react with any enthusiasm. In fact, she didn't react to much at all. I asked her if she wanted to see her mother and she told me she had to sleep on it."

Belle knew she shouldn't laugh, but she couldn't help herself. "That's too funny. I wonder where she got that from?"

"She's a regular chip off the old block."

"I remember when your dad used to say that."

Growing up, most of her friends had two parents and had been unable to relate to her only having a grandmother for family. As she got older, more people in her life lost their parents to death or divorce. She'd always felt a disconnect when she was around Harlan's massive family, despite their enormous generosity toward her. Now Harlan and Ivy both experienced that loss and emptiness. She'd never had it to miss. It must be much worse for them.

"Do you want me to saddle the horses?" she asked, not wanting to interrupt his thoughts.

"I'm right behind you." He tugged his hat down lower. "We'll take Outlaw, Dillinger and Clyde."

Belle smiled at his choice of names. She'd seen them etched on wooden plaques in front of the stalls, but hadn't had a chance to acknowledge them before. "I'm sensing a definite theme with you."

"I love my outlaws," he whispered in her ear as he strode past her.

Her mile-wide smile betrayed any composure she fought to control. *Did he just tell me he loved me?* He stopped at the tack room entrance and held the door for her, winking as she passed under his arm. *Oh, my God! I think he just did.*

The back of a horse was Harlan's second home. He'd wanted to be one of two things when he was growing up: the sheriff or a horse trainer. He still had a while to go before he made sheriff, but he had trained every one of the five horses in his stables.

Ivy rode between the two of them along the Swan River. His neighbor's ranch bordered the water and he had told Harlan he could ride their trails anytime. He'd had all this magnificent beauty at his fingertips and his daughter had been inside watching television every weekend. From this day forward, he vowed to plan something outdoorsy for them to do as a family at least one day a week.

"Daddy, is that snow?" Ivy pointed halfway up one of the mountains.

Harlan smiled. "No, baby, that's not snow. Snow doesn't move."

Belle reined her horse to a stop and followed their gaze. "They're mountain goats. That's a whole bunch of them for us to be able to see them like this."

"Remember our class trip to Glacier National Park?" Harlan asked.

"When the mountain goats were running alongside our red Jammer buses on Going-to-the-Sun Road? I kept thinking they'd run in front of us, but they didn't."

"That's the only bus we were allowed to stand up in and not get yelled at."

"You're not allowed to stand in the bus, Daddy. It's against the rules."

"You can in these, sweetie. They're vintage buses from the 1930s with a roll-back top, kind of like Uncle Jax's convertible. When you stop at various points throughout the park, you can stand up and take photos out of the roof." Harlan shook his head and looked at Belle. "Why am I explaining this to her when I can make reservations and take her there? We're only a little over an hour away."

"She's never been to Glacier National Park? It's practically in your backyard."

Harlan didn't have a response. He was ashamed to admit the idea never entered his mind. Here he had prided himself on being such an amazing single dad, at least by his standards, and he'd neglected to do anything meaningful with his daughter. Instead, he had relied on his older brother to do it for him.

"There are going to be quite a few changes around here."

Belle nudged Dillinger toward him. "I didn't mean to imply you were a bad father."

"You didn't." Harlan reached for her hand. "I'm glad you said something, though. I've missed out on too much of her life and she's been right in front of me the entire time."

They spent the rest of the morning exploring along the river before heading home for lunch. A million ideas ran through his head. Belle probably wouldn't be able to join them for some of their outings because of her schedule, but they'd make it work. Molly kept creeping into his thoughts. If she insisted on forcing the visitation issue, she'd probably have to come along on some of their trips. She lived almost seven hours away in Billings, but had told Harlan she'd consider relocating if things went well with Ivy. Selfishly he hoped they wouldn't. For Ivy's sake, he prayed they would. As much as he despised what Molly had done to them, he didn't want his daughter to grow up wondering what if. He'd already watched one child live through that nightmare, and Belle was only beginning to come into her own.

"I should head out." Belle finished loading his dishwasher with their lunch plates then dried her hands. "I'm not sure when I'll be back tonight. I may stay for the dinner service." She gave Ivy a kiss on the forehead before they stepped onto the porch. "Thank you for a wonderful morning."

Harlan slid his fingers into the belt loops of her jeans and tugged her to him. "Have I convinced you to stay permanently yet?" He widened his stance so he could look into her eyes. "You've always been a part of this ranch, you just haven't realized it."

"You're not playing fair again." She'd had another taste of family life today and it excited her down to her toes. It's what she had always wanted. "I need to get to the nursing home." She leaned in as her lips grazed his, softly at first as the anticipation thickened the air in her lungs. Her fingers brushed the nape of his neck and she felt the hair rise at her touch. Her mouth moved over his, unapologetically firm as her tongue sought his. It was the first kiss she'd initiated since they'd married. And she liked it. Maybe a real relationship with Harlan wouldn't be so bad. "I'll see you later."

"Talk about not fair," Harlan called after her.

Belle practically skipped to the stables. She fed and checked on the animals before heading into town. She uncovered a new sense of wonderment when it came to Harlan. She'd always been drawn to the man, and even fascinated by him from afar. Unbeknownst to him, or anyone else for that matter, she'd been there the day he graduated from the police academy. She'd worn a brunette wig and borrowed a dress of her grandmother's so no one would recognize her. And the day he'd been promoted to deputy sheriff, she'd watched the courthouse steps ceremony from the window of the stationery store across the street. The need to be a part of the monumental moments in his life had always confounded her. She'd have sworn on her life to anyone who'd listen that she'd gotten over him the day he left her in the church. But she'd lied to everyone, including herself.

The nursing home parking lot was full, forcing her to park next door. Sundays were their busiest days. It looked like it was someone's birthday judging by all the balloons when she walked in. She solemnly wondered if her grandmother's birthday in November would be her last.

Think happy thoughts. It was sometimes hard to do in a nursing home.

"Hi, Grammy." Belle stepped into the room and gave her grandmother a kiss on the cheek. "You look good today."

"Thank you, dearie." Trudy's eyes seemed to stare right past her. "Have you seen my granddaughter out there?"

"Y-your granddaughter?" Belle's throat squeezed shut as her heart ceased beating for a second or two. "What's her name?"

"Belle." Her grandmother attempted to lean forward and get a better view of the hallway. "I hear noise out there. Could you check for me? She has blond hair and blue eyes, much like yours, only she's ten years old."

Belle nodded, unable to speak. She pointed to the doorway indicating she'd go check. Out in the hallway, she covered her mouth with both hands and slid down the wall to the floor. It was too soon. It was much too soon. She couldn't lose her yet. *Please, Lord, not yet.*

Myra joined her on the floor and handed her a pack of tissues. "Dry your eyes, honey." She wrapped an arm around Belle's shoulder and gave it a firm squeeze. "She's been in and out all morning. We think it's because of all the commotion going on today. Three residents are celebrating birthdays and there have been a lot of kids running up and down the hallway." Myra stood and lifted Belle by the arm. "Let's get you up before someone or something runs you over. I know you're opposed to us moving her to the Alzheimer's wing and we won't until you give us the authorization, but it's much quieter in that section. The environment is more stable and that has a big impact on their demeanor."

"She hates the quiet." Belle wiped her eyes. "She always had the classic country channel on the radio playing at home. I feel like I'm stuffing her away in a closet if I move her there."

"You're not," Myra reassured. "You're providing her with the best possible care you can. And we can play the radio for her. We can start that today."

"I don't know why I hadn't thought of the music before." Belle wiped her eyes.

"Because this is a stressful situation," Myra said.

"I'm okay now. Thank you."

"Give what I said some thought and feel free to ask us any questions you might have. We're here for you."

Belle nodded in acknowledgment and walked back into the room. "I couldn't find her out there."

"Find who?" Trudy asked. "Belle, bubbe. Why do you look like you've been crying?"

Belle started to laugh out of relief. "It's just allergies, Grammy. Now that I'm living on the ranch with Harlan, I'm around a lot more hay."

"That Harlan is a good man. Don't let him slip away."

"I won't, Grammy." Belle pulled a chair alongside the bed. "What have you been up to today? Have you gotten out of your room?"

A toddler duck-waddled down the hallway with his mother close behind him. "Slow down, Trevor."

"Oh, sure. I was in the garden waiting for my granddaughter earlier, but she never showed."

She sighed. "I'm sure she'll be here soon." Belle hoped the visitors thinned out sooner rather than later. There was so much she wanted to tell her about Harlan and the ranch. She'd have to skip the Ivy parts, but she had already thought of a little white lie she could tell to explain her presence in their lives. "Why don't you tell me about her." Belle played along while she waited for her grandmother to come back around.

"My little bubbeleh. Wild as she is sweet. She gets that from her mother. The wild, not the sweet. I don't know where we went wrong with Cindy. She'd always been a shy little thing until she grew the boobies."

Belle sucked in her lips to keep from laughing. She'd never heard her grandmother talk much about her mother before. While the memory of her mom's face had blurred over time, she did remember how *blessed* Cindy had been in the cleavage department.

"Those boobies got her in more trouble. Especially when she started dating that man who had been far too old for her. What twenty-seven-year-old goes out with a high school senior? When her father and I found out she told him she was eighteen, we put a stop to it. By that point it was too late."

Wait a minute. Belle perched on the edge of her chair. "What do you mean it was too late?"

"Cindy got herself pregnant with that man's baby. Her father got so upset he had a heart attack and died that very night."

Belle was afraid to breathe. She'd never known that's when her grandfather had died. The heart attack hadn't been a secret, but the circumstances surrounding it must have been. And all these years she'd been told her mother had been young and reckless and didn't know who Belle's father was. Her mind raced in a million directions. *Okay, deep breath.* She needed to sort fact from fiction. Trudy had Alzheimer's disease so she may not even be talking about her mother. There might be a different Cindy. Maybe she mixed up the names. *Names. She needed more names.*

"What happened to the man when Cindy got pregnant?"

"Turns out he wasn't so bad after all. Probably would have done her a world of good if she'd married him. He became a successful attorney and now Beckett's a judge."

The room began to suffocate her. She needed to get air. Desperately. *Judge Sanders?* How many judges were named Beckett? She stood, grabbing on to the bed rail for support. "I'll be right out—" The room tilted as darkness washed over her. The last thing she remembered before she hit the floor was her grandmother yelling for help.

Chapter 11

"Belle." Harlan patted her hand. "Belle, it's Harlan. Can you hear me?"

Her eyes felt heavy and her head ached something awful. She lifted her free hand, but something was attached to her fingertip. "What the heck?" She tried to shake the plastic contraption off when she noticed the wires coming out of her hospital gown. *Hospital gown?* "Where am I?"

"You're in the hospital. You fainted at the nursing home and they couldn't wake you up. Trudy said your head bounced off that floor like a basketball."

"I passed out?" Belle squeezed her eyes shut and tried to remember what had happened. Her grandmother hadn't recognized her. No, that wasn't it. She had recognized her after a while.

A nurse came in and interrupted her thoughts. "You're awake. How are you feeling?"

"My head hurts." Her tongue stuck to the roof of her mouth. "May I have some water?"

"I'll get it." Harlan poured her a cup from a mauve pitcher while the nurse checked the machines she seemingly had been connected to during her unconsciousness. Belle looked up at the IV bag hanging from the stand next to the bed and followed the drip line into her arm. She frantically grabbed at it. "What is this?" A wave of nausea slammed into her and dragged her under. "I feel sick."

"Shh." Harlan stuck a straw in the cup and handed it to her. "They're just fluids. You're dehydrated and you have a concussion."

"The doctor will be in to check on you shortly," the nurse said before walking out of the room.

"You gave me quite a scare." Harlan raked his hand through his thick chestnut hair. "Do you remember anything?"

Belle sipped her water. Flashes of memories from throughout the day churned in her brain. "I remember Grammy telling me my grandfather had a heart attack and died the night my mom told them she was pregnant."

"Whoa. That's heavy." He squeezed her hand. "Myra told me Trudy didn't recognize you today."

Belle tried to shake her head, but the pain was too intense. "She didn't. I guess the noise in there was too much for her to process. She thought I was ten and kept looking for me. She realized who I was for a little while, but then it was gone. Myra said that sometimes happened in loud situations."

"Do you remember feeling sick?"

"No." Belle closed her eyes against the brightness of the room. "We were talking about my mom. And boobies. I remember boobies."

Harlan bowed his head as his shoulders bounced up and down.

"Stop laughing at me." Belle tried to swat him but ended up clunking him in the head with her finger pulse oximeter. "Oh, I'm sorry."

"Are you trying to injure me so I'll join you in that bed?"

"Oh, my God!" Belle tried to sit up. Her mind almost short-circuited. Bed. Sex. Babies. Beckett. Sanders. "Judge Sanders is my father."

"What?" Harlan jumped up. "Are you serious?"

"And how's our patient this afternoon?" The doctor entered the room. "I'm Dr. Kim, the neurologist on staff. Are you experiencing any nausea?"

"I almost threw up a minute ago." Belle didn't take her eyes of Harlan. "My head really hurts."

The doctor withdrew a flashlight from his pocket and shined it in her eyes. "Will you follow the light for me?"

The light was bright, too bright. "When can I go home?"

"Not until at least tomorrow. Your pupils are even, so that's a good sign. Are you experiencing any blurry vision?"

"No."

"Your scan results were normal. We'll reevaluate you in a couple hours. Depending on how you feel, we may run another scan. You took quite a fall and you have a good-size knot on the side of your head. Your nausea concerns me, so we're going to keep you here overnight. I'll be back to check on you later. If you feel any worse than you do now, let us know right away."

"Thank you." He left the room and Harlan returned to her side.

"Are you sure she said Judge Sanders?"

"Granted my memory's a little fuzzy right now, but she said the man was ten years older than my mom and he thought she was eighteen. Then something about my grandparents telling him the truth. I guess she was already pregnant when the relationship ended. Grammy said she shouldn't have come between them because Beckett went on to become a judge." She shrugged. "Who else could it be?"

"Okay. But you were born in Texas."

"My mom was a runaway. I don't know if she left or if Grammy threw her out after my grandfather's heart attack. She blames my mom for his death. I never knew how or why she was in Texas. I assumed she ran away first and got pregnant down there. Apparently not. It makes sense, when you think about it. All the crap I've been arrested for, and I've always got off easy."

"Yeah, you have," Harlan agreed. "I've always said you had a guardian angel. I guess you just had a guardian."

"I need you to find him and get him to come see me." Belle reached for Harlan. "Tonight."

"Don't you want to wait until we get you home? I don't know anything about his personal life or where he lives."

"If you plan to be sheriff one day, you can figure out his address or phone number. I've waited twenty-seven years to meet my father. Soon he'll be my only living relative. I have questions. Lots of them, and they can't wait." She glanced around the room. "Where's Ivy?"

"With Dylan."

"I want her to spend the night with you, not him. I won't let you spend the night here, worrying about me, when that child needs you now more than ever. I'm in good hands. So please, find Judge Sanders. Tell him it's urgent but don't tell him the truth. Let him think I'm in trouble again. I'm willing to bet he'll come to my rescue."

"Are you sure you'll be okay here alone after this news?"

"I've been alone for a long time." Belle smoothed the front of her gown. "I can handle it."

"Okay." He kissed her on the mouth before turning to leave. "I'll call you later."

Belle attempted a smile but didn't have the strength to see it through. She had a father. One who'd been nearby all along. What was it with parents abandoning their kids around here?

Harlan called Lydia on the way to Dylan's and told her about Belle's fall and her decision to stay on the ranch. He omitted the fainting episode and the father revelation. Then he called the nursing home to check on Trudy and update them on Belle's condition. By the time they arrived back at the ranch Belle's animals were long overdue on their feedings. Ivy fed them their bottles while Harlan treated Lillie's sunburn. Imogene and Olive ate and curled up together in their stall, but he couldn't in good conscience leave behind the piglet and the lamb.

Together, he and Ivy filled a small kiddie pool with fresh hay and dragged it across the yard and into the house. In hindsight, they should have filled it after they brought it inside. It just fit in the front mudroom. Nobody ever used that door anyway.

After the addition of a few baby gates and checking in with Belle again, he finally had a chance to sit down and try to locate Judge Sanders. He still didn't believe it. And he wasn't so sure Belle should either. There was only one way to find out and that was to ask the man. Five phone calls later, he had the county clerk's phone number. She must know how to reach the judge at home. Harlan looked at his watch. It was half past eight. Still early enough to call.

The phone rang twice before she answered. "Hi, this is Deputy Sheriff Harlan Slade. It's imperative I reach Judge Sanders tonight. Would you happen to have a number for him or could you contact him for me?"

"I can call him and relay the information. May I ask what this is regarding?"

"It's an urgent matter regarding Belle Barnes."

Within minutes, an incoming call came in from an unknown number. "Harlan Slade," he answered.

"Harlan, it's Beckett Sanders. I received a call

about Miss Barnes. Or should I call her Mrs. Slade."
The man chuckled.

How about calling her daughter?

"She's still going by Barnes." At least that's how
he registered her at the hospital today. "Belle had an
accident earlier at the nursing home. She requests to
see you right away."

"Is she okay?"

"She has a concussion. She said to tell you the
matter is extremely urgent."

"Is she in county?"

"Hospital, not jail." Harlan felt the need to clarify
that statement. They were talking about Belle after
all. He gave the judge the room number and then
phoned Belle with an update. He wished he could
be there with her when she found out the truth, but
she had been right. He belonged with Ivy tonight.

Harlan walked in the living room and found his
daughter watching cartoons and Elvis, Samson and
Lillie curled up sound asleep beside her.

"Ivy, how did they get out of their pen?"

"I took them out. Elvis was lonely."

Of course he was. He mentally tabulated how
much it would cost to get animal poop out of the area
rug, because sooner or later, one of the three would
spring a leak. Then he remembered the extra shower
curtain liner he had in the upstairs bathroom. A few
minutes later, the crisis had been averted. If they
stayed on the plastic, everyone would remain happy.

"Daddy?"

"Yes, sweetheart?"

"When can I see my mommy?"

A flaming ball of barbed wire hitting him at warp speed would've been preferable over the gnawing ache churning in the pit of his stomach. "Have you slept on it?"

"Yes."

"And you're sure."

"Yes."

"Can you give me more than one-word answers and tell me how you're feeling?"

"I thought about how sad I would be if I never met you." She flopped against him on the couch. "I don't want to be sad for not knowing Mommy."

That was more deductive reasoning then he'd given her credit for. "I can call her and set up something for this week."

"Can I meet her now?"

"Ivy, it's almost time for bed." She didn't argue. She just stared up at him with those big blue eyes and he was putty in her hands. "Okay, you win. I'll call her and see if she wants to come over tonight. I can't make any promises." He should at least let Molly know Belle wouldn't make their coffee date tomorrow morning.

Harlan was an idiot for doubting Molly would rush straight over. He greeted her on the porch first and warned her that the visit would be brief. "I mean it, Molly. A half hour at the most. She needs to get to bed."

The last time the three of them were in the same house together, it was the day she walked out on them. Molly followed him through the house and into the living room.

"You'll have to ignore the temporary animal play area. I brought the menagerie in while Belle is in the hospital."

Harlan watched Molly's eyes as she took in her surroundings. Instead of zeroing in on Ivy, she noticed everything else about the room, floor to ceiling.

"You changed the place."

Harlan nodded from the doorway. He hadn't allowed her past the kitchen the other day. Her voice was quieter tonight, almost as if she didn't want to attract Ivy's attention.

"Barnyard animals are okay in the house?"

"I took the necessary precautions." Harlan sighed. Belle had been a better mother to his daughter. Molly had been in the house for five minutes and she still hadn't focused on Ivy. "Maybe this was a mistake," Harlan said under his breath.

"Why?" she shot back in a whisper.

"Because that's your daughter. The one you haven't seen in six years, yet you're worried about paint colors and a piglet."

Ivy turned around and stared at Molly. Harlan willed the woman to say something, but she remained silent.

"Ivy, sweetheart." He sat on the floor and pulled her into his lap. "This is Molly. She's your mommy, but you can call her Molly if you want." Molly's narrowed stare didn't faze him. "Remember what I told you the other day? You only do or say what you're comfortable with. Do you want to talk to her?"

Ivy nodded and they both looked up at Molly, who remained on the other side of the room.

"Molly, this won't work unless you're an active participant."

She entered the room and sat on the edge of the couch, as far away as possible. Okay, she wasn't going to come to them and Harlan had promised not to force Ivy. Now what? Harlan eased Ivy onto her feet and he joined Molly on the couch, leaving plenty of room on either side of him for Ivy if she decided to come closer. Instead she sat crossed-legged on the floor in front of them. Elvis crawled into her lap and she proceeded to scratch him behind his ears, never breaking eye contact with Molly.

"My daddy said you wanted to meet me."

"I do. I—I did," Molly stammered. "I can't believe how much you've grown. You're a big girl."

"Do you know my birthday?" Ivy asked.

Harlan had wondered the same thing over the years, considering she had never bothered to send a card.

"May 7."

"How come you never came to see me before?"

"I have seen you before." Molly leaned forward and rested her elbows on her knees. "I lived here with you for the first year of your life. You were just too young to remember."

"You lived in the house with Daddy?" Ivy asked.

Molly side-glanced at him in annoyance. Harlan hadn't seen the need to tell Ivy anything about Molly when she so eagerly renounced custody.

"I did, when your daddy and I were married."

"Like Belle and Daddy are married?"

Molly nodded. "Exactly."

Harlan coughed. The two marriages were more different than a mare and a doorknob.

"Did you live in the stables, too?" Ivy asked.

"I'm sorry. Did I what? Live in the stables? No, I lived in this house with your father."

"Ivy." Harlan shook his head. There was a piece of information Molly didn't need to know.

Molly shifted on the couch. "What does she mean…live in the stables? You and Belle came out of there the other morning. Are you all living in there?"

"Only Belle does," Ivy answered. "Daddy says they only had a pretend wedding because Belle's grandma is sick."

Molly started to laugh. "Oh, that's rich. So what was that the other day? A little booty call?"

"Molly!" Harlan warned. "First, don't disparage my wife, and yes, Molly, she is my legal wife in every sense of the word. And second, don't use that language around my daughter."

"Our daughter," she corrected. "I'm sure she doesn't know what I meant."

"And I'm sure she repeats things she hears even when she shouldn't." Harlan shot Ivy a warning glare.

"Belle reads me bedtime stories." Ivy scooted closer.

"Speaking of bedtime, you need to get ready for yours. But we need to take these three for a walk first. Do you remember where we put all their leashes?" Harlan hadn't been able to find a collar for Samson, so he borrowed an extra one from Elvis.

He had noticed Belle never left their collars on like he left on Elvis's and figured she had her reasons.

Ivy returned a few seconds later with all three leashes and two collars. The animals firmly secured, he picked up Samson and Lillie while Ivy walked Elvis to the door on his leash. He stopped halfway onto the porch and called into the living room. "Come on, Molly. That means you, too."

He wasn't about to leave her alone in his house, not even for a second. And their half hour was almost over. Molly trudged to the door. "I thought we'd talk some more."

"Nope." Harlan waited for her to exit before closing the screen door behind them. "Some other time. This was a start."

"Would you like me to read you a bedtime story?" Molly squatted down beside Ivy. "I'd love to see your room."

Now she'd pushed him too far.

"No, thank you," Ivy said, shutting her down before he even had a chance.

Good girl.

Chapter 12

Belle understood why she didn't own a television. She'd scanned the channels with the remote at least a dozen times and nothing captured her interest. It was almost nine thirty and she began to doubt Judge Sanders would show tonight.

A bouquet of flowers appeared in the doorway, causing her to smile. "Harlan, you shouldn't have. I told you to stay home with Ivy."

The man lowered the flowers, uncovering his face. *Judge Sanders.*

"Those are beautiful. Thank you, Dad."

He almost dropped the vase on the roll-away table at the foot of her bed.

"I'm sorry. Too soon?" Belle asked. He paled, almost matching the color of his platinum hair. And for the first time in her life, she wondered whose side of the family her coloring came from. "You do know what I'm referring to, don't you?"

"If you're talking about my relationship with your mother, then yes. But, I'm sorry. I'm not your father. I fear you don't have all the facts."

"I have more facts than you think I do." The more she ran over the story in her head, the less far-fetched it became. "The timeline fits. After my mother told my grandparents she was pregnant, my grandfather had a heart attack and died. I've already double-checked the date of his death and it is eight months before I was born, which adds credibility to the story. I'm still trying to figure out if my mom ran away from the guilt she carried over my grandfather's death or if my grandmother threw her out."

"I don't understand."

"Grammy fades in and out of decades courtesy of her damned disease, and today she told me she held my mom responsible for her husband's death." Belle steeled her nerves in preparation for the validity of her paternity claim. The mystery surrounding her father had been such a strong part of her life, she wondered if she'd miss it once it was gone. "How much time passed between when my grandparents told you my mom's real age and my grandfather's death?"

Beckett settled in the chair next to the bed before responding. "It was the same day."

Grammy had left that part out. Evidently, she had left out and hidden quite a bit of information. "Did my mom tell you she was pregnant that day?"

"No. I found out she'd had a child after she had

abandoned you in Texas." He stared down at his hands in his lap. "By the time you came back to town, I was thirty-three and married. My wife was aware of my past with your mother." His eyes met hers. "I had every intention of pursuing a paternity test, until your grandmother told me the circumstances surrounding Cindy's pregnancy. Let's just say it painted your mom in a rather risqué light and she feared a custody case would follow you around in such a small town. You were having such a hard time of it already. I asked for a private paternity test instead and she refused. My wife and I were more than willing to help support you. We were unable to have children of our own and you would have been welcome in our home. But your grandmother's adamancy led me to strongly believe I wasn't your father. I never had any proof you were mine."

"Well, we can get proof now. We're in a hospital and I want a paternity test. Tonight. You're a county judge. You can make it happen. This small town has been talking about me since I was six years old. Let them talk. I have a thick skin. After twenty-seven years, don't we both deserve the truth?"

"Okay."

"Okay? You mean it's that simple? I don't have to fight you for it?"

"Of course not." Beckett stood and reached for her hand, giving it a gentle squeeze. "I want to know just as much as you do. Let me go track down a nurse and when I get back you can explain how you wound up in the hospital."

Belle watched him leave, and for a moment, she

feared he wouldn't return. It wasn't as if he could hide from her. She'd be in front of him again in a few weeks for Lillie's case. Or would she? That was a terrifying thought. If Judge Sanders really was her father, another judge would have to hear her case. Possibly a sterner judge who might try to make an example out of her.

Until she had definitive proof Beckett was her father, she had to ignore the millions of questions running through her head. She stood on the fine line between elation and apprehension. The possibility alone had already contorted her sensibilities. How much more would the truth change?

Harlan dropped Ivy off at school on his way to the hospital. Ivy had wanted to see Belle, but she'd already missed enough school. He'd talked to her last night after Judge Sanders had left and she'd sounded down that they had to wait until morning for the paternity-test results.

She'd asked him to bring her a change of clothes from the ranch. She was determined to escape the confines of the hospital today. She'd said it gave her a new appreciation for what her grandmother experienced daily.

He'd originally gone up to her apartment to retrieve what she'd asked for, but the more he'd looked around, the more aggravated he'd become. He refused to have another *you stay in your space and I'll stay in mine* argument when she came home from the hospital. He'd looked up concussions last night and one of the mandatory treatments was plenty of rest.

He'd been a complete jerk for allowing her to stay up there as long as she had. Even Molly had recognized it wasn't right, despite Belle's protests. Starting today, she was living in the main house. If she felt more comfortable staying in her own room, she was welcome to use the guest bedroom. Either way, her days of living above the horses were officially over.

Harlan hated hospitals. Being a deputy sheriff meant seeing the inside of them more than most people. And it was never for a good reason. The scent of the wildflower bouquet he carried helped mask the astringent smell of the hallway. It had been a long time since he'd bought her flowers. He hoped they were still her favorite.

"Good morning, beautiful." Harlan entered her room, surprised to see Judge Sanders and a woman standing next to Belle's bed.

"Good morning." Despite her surroundings, Belle appeared much better than she had yesterday.

"These are for you." He handed her the bouquet, then looked around for a place to put them.

"Thank you." She lowered her head to sniff the blooms. "I can't believe you remembered." She inhaled deeply. "Harlan, you already know Judge Sanders."

"Please, call me Beckett." The man held out his hand to Harlan and they shook. "This is my wife, Becky."

Harlan was taken slightly aback. Beckett and Becky? You couldn't have planned that even if you tried. "It's a pleasure to meet you, ma'am."

"You, too. I hear you have quite a political future ahead of you. I'd like to talk to you about that sometime."

"I do?" Harlan looked at Belle, who shrugged. "You would?"

"My wife has managed more than a few successful political campaigns. You've come up in conversation during various events. I can see you easily running for and winning the sheriff's seat in the near future."

"Wow, thank you. That's my goal." Harlan reached for Belle's hand. "Any word on your test results?"

"I have them right here," a lab technician said from the doorway. "Would you like me to read them?"

"Yes, please." Belle squeezed Harlan's hand tighter.

"Beckett Sanders, you are Belle Barnes's father."

Belle buried her face in her hands and sobbed. Harlan wrapped his arms around her and rocked her gently. "Shh. It's all over now. You finally have your answers." Her body shook and Harlan feared she'd set off an alarm on one of the monitors attached to her. He looked across the bed to Beckett sobbing in his wife's arms.

"I can't believe it. I should have insisted on this test when you were six years old. I am so sorry you had to wait this long. We've lost so much time."

Belle lifted her head. "Can I call you Dad?"

"Of course you can. You can call me anything you'd like." Beckett gave her a hug as Harlan stepped away from the bed.

Becky gestured toward the doorway and they both slipped into the hall unnoticed. "I thought they could use a little privacy. Can I buy you a cup of coffee?" she asked.

"Only if you let me do the buying," Harlan said.

"You have a deal. I heard you have a daughter of your own."

"Ivy. She's seven, in a remarkably similar situation as Belle."

"How so?" Becky asked as they stepped into the elevator.

Over the next half hour and two cups of ultra-strong coffee, he explained his situation with Molly to Becky. The woman was easy to talk to. He'd never had that type of relationship with his mom. His dad had always been his go-to guy, and he'd missed him even more than normal during the past week.

"Beckett feels an enormous amount of guilt for Belle's—how shall I phrase it—police record I guess is the best choice. It will always hang over him. Had he been a father to her, would she have made the same choices?"

"I can answer that." Harlan nodded. "She would have. Who raised her wouldn't have affected her passion. Then again, maybe not." He sagged against the back of the cafeteria chair. "Maybe she would have become an animal rights attorney instead. Either way, she'd be involved in animal rights. Her first instinct is to protect the weak. Animals, the elderly, children. She's a protector."

"It's sweet the way you talk about her. She's a lucky woman. And your daughter's lucky to have a father willing to accept her mother back into her life."

"More like tolerate. Molly and Ivy didn't take well to each other last night. The first time Ivy met Belle, she was all over her. And Belle loves every second of it. But she's afraid Ivy will feel she needs to choose either her or Molly. I want to tell her it's okay to have two moms but I'm having a hard time accepting Molly as her mother. Belle yes, Molly not so much."

"You need to get over that," Becky said matter-of-factly. "You're allowing your feelings toward Molly to taint your daughter. Kids pick up on the tension. If she senses you are uncomfortable, she'll follow your lead. That's why a lot of supervised visitation is overseen by a neutral party. It gives the child a chance to develop their own thoughts and feelings about the person."

Harlan hadn't considered his terseness toward Molly might have influenced Ivy last night. She would have been better off with his uncle Jax supervising. That man had never met another human or animal he didn't like.

"You've given me a lot to think about. Thank you for listening."

"Hey, don't mention it." She patted his hand. "We're family now."

"I guess we are." He tapped his cup on the table and smiled. "What do you say? Think we've given them enough time?"

"They're going to need a lifetime." Becky rose and slung her purse over her shoulder. "We're the ones that will need to adjust to sharing them with other people."

And that meant sharing Ivy with Molly. He would do it to spare her the pain Belle suffered her entire life. He'd do anything for the people he loved.

All Belle wanted to do was take a long hot shower, check on her babies and sleep for the rest of the day. Harlan parked the truck almost on top of the fence behind the house.

"You wait right there." He hopped out and ran to the passenger-side door before she had a chance to touch the door handle. "Give me your hand."

"Harlan." She smacked it away. "Stop it before you drive me insane."

"The doctor said you needed plenty of rest."

He held her elbow as if she were an elderly woman crossing the street. Arguing didn't work, so she allowed him to continue his smothering. "You can help me up to my apartment, and then I'll be fine. You need to get to work anyway."

"I moved you into the house this morning."

"You did what?" Belle forced a tight smile. "I mean, that was nice of you, but you didn't have to do that. I really need the peace and quiet, and the stables are peaceful and quiet."

"It's too cold, too damp, you just got out of the hospital and it doesn't even have a proper kitchen. You can't even fix anything to eat unless it fits in that Barbie-size refrigerator up there. And before you protest some more, I set you up in the guest room. I figured you'd still want your own space."

He was setting her up in the exact situation he

told her she wouldn't like if she stayed at Lydia's. That made sense.

"You're not happy, are you?" He frowned.

"I feel icky and tired. Once I get past that, we will be good to go. I'll do that while you're at work, because you are going to work."

Once they were inside and she'd gotten over the initial shock of Samson and Lillie residing in Harlan's mudroom, she sank deep into the claw-foot tub, allowing the water to engulf her in a cocoon of warmth. She heard Harlan's truck drive away and exhaled the deepest breath she felt like she'd held since her grandmother mentioned Judge Sanders. Correction. Her father.

"Father." Belle wrinkled her nose. It sounded too formal.

"Dad." It was short, sweet and to the point. It had possibilities.

"Daddy." Too Ivy. She laughed.

"Pa." She cringed. "Papa. That sounds like a steam engine."

"Pop." She pursed her lips. Bubble Wrap pops; people don't.

The only one that sounded good to her was Dad.

"Dad." She tested the word again. How did little kids make this decision? That was stressful. Belle never had the opportunity to use the word. Harlan's father had been a part of her life since she moved to Saddle Ridge, and she had called him Mr. Slade.

Discovering her father was a bigger relief than most people could fathom. When you don't know who one or both of your parents are, your mind be-

gins to play tricks on you. When you meet someone who resembles you in some way, you wonder
if you're related. When you're dating, or considering going out with the cute guy across the room,
you wonder if he could be your brother or maybe a
cousin. A million what-ifs follow you around every
day, wherever you go. It's exhausting. You don't even
realize you're doing it, until you find yourself nursing your drink alone at the end of a bar.

One test result wiped those fears out of her life
for good. She may not have any siblings, but she had
cousins, aunts, uncles and grandparents. Why the
secrecy? Belle had asked her grandmother numerous times about her father when she was younger.
Trudy had always claimed not to know. It wasn't
like Beckett had some nefarious past. The community respected him. Maybe Trudy thought his family
would replace her, even though nobody could. She
should have had more faith in Belle. At least she'd
unearthed some of the answers that had plagued her
all her life. Now she'd never have to worry about
being alone again.

Belle stepped out of the tub when the water had
cooled and wrapped herself in a giant bath sheet.
"Score one for Harlan." The man had impeccable
taste in towels.

She rummaged through her clothes and found
nothing comfortable enough. She didn't own much
and what she did was on the tighter side. Harlan's
bedroom door stood open across the hall. She padded
into the room and looked around. Steel-gray walls,
white trim, minimal furniture. The palette was neu-

tral and could lean a little more gender neutral with the right accents.

"Let's see what you have that's comfortable to wear." She eased open the closet and stepped inside. A pair of police academy sweatpants and a T-shirt sat on the top shelf. She reached for them and gave them a quick sniff test. They were clean. She slipped out of her towel and hung it on the doorknob. The cotton of the shirt against her bare skin instantly soothed her. She pulled on the pants and tied them at the waist. They were oversize and ridiculously comfy.

Her body begged for sleep. Suddenly the other bedroom seemed a million miles away. She tugged at the comforter and crawled under the covers. Harlan's raw scent engulfed her.

Now, this was home.

Chapter 13

"Happy two-week anniversary, sweetheart," Harlan whispered in her ear.

"Mmm." Belle stretched languidly beneath the toasty warm covers. "Am I in your bed?" Her mind tried to retrace her steps. The last thing she remembered was taking a bath. "Have I been asleep since I got home from the hospital?"

"Well, you did get up a few times to use the bathroom," Harlan said. "But other than that, yes, you have been sleeping. It was exactly what the doctor ordered."

"I have to get up. What time is it?" She squinted to read the clock on Harlan's side of the bed. "Did you sleep here with me? Harlan, what if Ivy came in?"

"Relax. I slept in the other room." Harlan stood

and pulled a uniform shirt from his closet. "Lydia knows you won't be at work for the next few days, the animals have already been fed, the stalls have been mucked, Ivy's almost ready to get on the school bus and I'm heading into work."

"I could get used to this."

"I hope you do." He attempted to kiss her, before she turned away.

"Yuck." Belle covered her mouth with the sheet. "I have morning breath. If I slept for that long, I probably have more than morning breath."

Harlan grinned down at her. "You look good wearing my clothes," he said as he fastened his uniform shirt cuffs.

"Sorry. I raided your closet. I didn't have anything comfortable."

"No need to apologize. I'm glad me and my things make you feel that way. I was pleasantly surprised to find you asleep in my bed."

"That was comfortable, too." Belle rolled onto her side and hugged his pillow. "And it smells like you."

Harlan laughed. "Some people are offended by that smell." He sat on the edge of the bed. "You might want to stay upstairs for a little while longer, though."

"Why?"

"Because Molly is downstairs eating breakfast with Ivy."

"Oh. When did that happen?" Belle sat up and leaned against the headboard. Surprisingly her head didn't hurt.

"After speaking with Becky yesterday while you

and your father got to know each other better, I realized I had been projecting my anger toward Molly onto Ivy. She was defending me in her own little way. I need to give her a chance to form her own opinions about Molly without any interference. That's why they are downstairs and I'm here waking you up. It gives them some time alone without them being completely unsupervised."

"That's a good idea."

"Molly will only be in town for another week. She has a life and job to return to. She hasn't decided if she wants to move back here or stay in Billings. She and Ivy will need many more visits before she makes any of those decisions."

"Have you given any thought to visitation?"

"No." Harlan rose from the bed, effectively ending that line of questioning. "I wanted to run something by you, but I don't want you to feel obligated."

Belle slid back down the bed and pulled the covers over her head. "Do I even want to know?"

"Since you couldn't make your coffee date with Molly yesterday, I wondered if you wanted her to stay after Ivy and I left. It would give you two a chance to talk. If not, I will push her out the door when I leave."

Belle groaned. Molly wasn't her ideal way to start the day, but they had to have a conversation at some point. She flung aside the covers.

"When are you leaving?"

"Twenty minutes."

"Okay, that gives me enough time to shower."

Belle grabbed a change of clothes from the guest

room and dragged herself into the bathroom. She already felt tired and she hadn't even done anything yet. She wasn't sure if it was from oversleeping or her concussion. Either way, she didn't like having to choose Molly over bed.

She made it downstairs with a few minutes to spare. "Good morning, sweet pea." Belle pressed a kiss to the top of Ivy's head. "Good morning, Molly." Belle grinned as politely as she could before coffee. She poured a cup and sat down next to Ivy. "Your daddy told me you've become an amazing rescue-animal caretaker. I appreciate all of your help."

"Would you like me to fix you something to eat before I leave?" Harlan asked.

"No, thank you. I'll make something later." At least she'd kept her promise not to dine with Molly. If anyone had told her they'd be sitting across the table from one another during this century, she'd have pushed them into Flathead Lake.

"So, Molly." Either the milk was sour or the other woman's name left a bad taste in her mouth. "We didn't get a chance to talk yesterday. Do you want to stick around for a little bit after they leave?"

"Sure." Molly's face brightened. "I'd like that."

"I don't want to go to school." Ivy rested her head against Belle's arm. "I want to stay home and take care of you."

"Sweetie, I'm okay." Belle wrapped her arm around Ivy's small shoulders and gave her a light squeeze. "They wouldn't have released me if I wasn't." Belle glanced up and saw Molly watching them longingly. She wished she didn't understand what she was feeling, but she did. It was the same look Belle used to get when she watched other kids with their parents. Being an outsider sucked and despite the bad blood between then, Molly's pain bothered her.

"Come on, pumpkin." Harlan reached for Ivy's hand. "It's time to go."

"Bye, Belle." Ivy gave her a hug. "Take care of Elvis for me today."

"I will, sweetheart."

"Bye, Molly," Ivy said, keeping the table between her and her mother. "Come on, Dad. You're slow."

"I'll see you later." Harlan bent over and gave Belle a full kiss on the mouth. "Mmm. Minty."

Heat rose to Belle's cheeks before she realized Molly had been studying her. *Awkward.*

"How are you feeling?" Molly sounded genuine enough, but Belle wondered if Molly secretly wished she'd disappear.

"Better, thank you."

"What happened? Harlan said you fell at the nursing home."

Belle snickered. "Let me tell you something about those nursing home floors. They're hard. Like bust-your-head-open hard. Now I understand why there are so many broken hips in those places. It knocked me out cold. According to Harlan, Grammy said my head bounced like a basketball." Belle grabbed the coffeepot from the counter and topped both her and Molly's mugs. She snatched a doughnut on the way back to the table. As long as it didn't involve an eating utensil, it didn't count as a meal in her book. "I didn't fall. I fainted."

Belle hadn't officially decided how much of the story she would tell Molly, but given her situation with Ivy, she thought it might help.

"Are you sick?" Molly whispered and reached across the table for her hands.

Belle stared down at the all-too-personal contact. "I'm not sick."

"Whew." Molly sat back. "That's good."

Belle saw genuine concern in her former friend's eyes. "Grammy has her lucid and not-so-lucid moments. Yesterday afternoon, she had regressed back to when I was ten years old. She asked me if I had seen me in the hallway. It was a very surreal moment. I had to talk about myself in third person. I don't know who she thought I was—one of the nurses, perhaps—but she started talking about my mom and my grandfather."

"Your grandfather died before you were born, right?"

"Right. Turns out Grammy knew who my father was all along, and the revelation of my mom's pregnancy is what gave my grandfather a heart attack and killed him."

"No." Molly pulled her chair closer to the table. "You asked her repeatedly if she knew."

"Well, now I know. When she told me, the news literally knocked me off my feet. And that's how I got my concussion."

"I can't believe it." Molly's hand flew to her cheek. "What are you going to do now? Track him down?"

"There's no tracking him down."

"Oh, don't tell me he's dead."

"Nope, Dad is alive and well. He only lives a few miles away."

"Had you heard of him before?"

Belled nodded. She didn't know how much Molly knew about her police record and even though it was available to the public, Belle preferred the less-is-best approach.

"He's an acquaintance."

"That was one of your worst fears."

"We confirmed his paternity yesterday when I was in the hospital, but we haven't discussed when or how we'll tell people we're related. We're in the getting-to-know-you stage and it's awkward, yet comforting in the same respect. Do you understand what I'm trying to say?"

"It's not very different from me and Ivy."

"Exactly. I can relate to your situation from Ivy's point of view. She's very cautious and she tends to mull over various scenarios in her head before she acts. And I think that's what she's doing with you, based on what Harlan told me. I'm a jump first, then worry if there's water in the pool type of person. Ivy wants to know how much water's in the pool, the type of water and the temperature before she jumps. She's very thorough."

"She definitely gets that from Harlan," Molly said. "My rarely think mentality has gotten me in more trouble."

"Do you have any other kids?" Belle asked.

Molly smiled. "I had my tubes tied the day Ivy

was born. I didn't see children in my future back then."

"What's changed?"

"Therapy, for one. I didn't bond with Ivy when she was born. There was something missing and when I look back on it now, I should have sought help. I may have had a touch of postpartum depression. I didn't talk to anyone about it until last year. I just ran and kept moving. I've traveled to every continent and more countries than I can count. I love my job with the travel agency, but despite what Harlan or anyone else thinks, I didn't forget about my daughter. I did her a favor because I would have made her life miserable if I had stayed."

"I had wondered if that was why you left."

"I wasn't happy when I got pregnant. I was jealous of you. You were getting what you wanted. A family with Harlan. It was an obtainable goal for you. All you two had to do was walk down the aisle. Who knew Harlan would get cold feet? When I ran into him at the bar that night, I didn't have some master plan to destroy your life. We drank too much, we shared our fears and we made a bad decision. And I'm sure in the back of my mind I was thinking that by sleeping with Harlan I'd destroy your dream forever. Honestly, I didn't even remember it had happened. My only proof was Ivy."

"Is that supposed to make me feel better?" She'd heard both sides, but a betrayal was just that...a betrayal, and no lame excuse changed it. It still bothered her, but her heart no longer ached over it. She'd forgiven Harlan. Molly not so much. Not yet. "Why did you marry him, then? You didn't love him."

"I didn't love myself either. I was scared and alone. Raising a child was terrifying enough. Raising a child alone multiplied that fear exponentially. I'm sorry my actions hurt you. You were the one person who was always kind to me. I was the outcast kid."

"I wasn't exactly Miss Popular."

"But Harlan was," they both said in unison.

"Yeah, he was, wasn't he?" Belle hadn't considered Harlan popular back then. He played football and rode on the high school rodeo circuit, but he'd always been her boy friend and that had naturally progressed into him being her actual boyfriend.

"People notice you when you're with Harlan. You're married to him now. Tell me you didn't see a shift in how people treat you."

If Molly's theory was true, she cringed to think how people would treat her once they learned Judge Sanders was her father. "I think it's negligible now versus back then. We were nineteen."

"I see the way Ivy looks at you. She's already attached."

"If anything, she may be a little starstruck or mesmerized because I'm new in her father's life and I come with baby animals. But I adore her and I'll do anything to protect her from—"

"Go ahead, you can say it. You want to protect her from me."

"I want you to be the mother she deserves. I don't want her to go through the hell I went through."

"You're one of the reasons I came back. I didn't want her to turn into you."

Belle pushed her chair from the table. "Are you kidding me?"

Molly buried her face in her hands. "That came out all wrong." Molly wiped her eyes. "I meant I didn't want her to suffer and wonder the way you had. That's why I'm here. And for the record, I'm sorry Alzheimer's is robbing you of your grandmother. That must make finding your father all the more bittersweet."

Belle stared into her coffee mug. She wanted to hate the woman across the table from her, but Molly had stepped back into her life and seemingly understood what she was going through without Belle having to explain it.

"My outlook on life is very different now. I didn't see my grandmother at all yesterday because I was in the hospital. She saw me faint and called for help. She didn't recognize me when it happened, so while she may have that memory stored, it's not associated with me. I must see her today. It's like *Wheel of Fortune*. Every time I walk in there, I'm spinning the wheel to see which year we'll land on. I would love to ask her why she kept my father from me. He even confronted her because he wanted to provide for me, but she refused. What was she protecting me from? I will never know. But I've learned life is too short to worry about it. Take every opportunity you have to spend time with Ivy. Give her a chance to get to know you. Do you feel I am in the way of your progress with her?"

"It's difficult watching you bond with her," Molly admitted. "But you're fulfilling the role I couldn't. When I came here, I hadn't counted on competing for my daughter's attention. I thought I was entitled to it. You're sitting here telling me about your father and you two seem to have hit it off because you're related. It's an instant bond. Ivy's still not bonding with me. It was similar to the way she reacted to me as a baby. She didn't look me in the eyes or want me to hug her. It didn't help no one was around to show me how to be a mother. My parents provided for me while I was growing up but they never showed any affection. It wasn't as if I could ask them for help. I should have taken the parenting classes at the hospital, but I didn't. Harlan brought me home from the hospital and went to work, leaving me alone to feed, change and take care of a newborn baby."

"I can't imagine how difficult that must have been."

"When Ivy had colic, that's when I realized I couldn't be her mother. She cried all the time. She needed love and affection and nothing I did made it better. And this ranch is so isolated. I get the appeal, but when you're a young clueless mom, you need other moms around."

Belle had a newfound respect for Molly's decision to walk away. You hear horrifying stories on the news about parents trying to kill their children. If more of them walked away and left them with a responsible caretaker, maybe there wouldn't be so many stories.

She also realized for the first time that Harlan hadn't been completely blameless.

"How would you like to do me a favor?"

"Um, sure."

"I'm not allowed to drive for a few days. Could you drop me off at the nursing home?"

"Do you need me to wait around?"

"No. Harlan can give me a ride home later. I'll meet you outside in a minute."

"Belle," Molly said from the porch door. "For what it's worth, I admire the little family you and Harlan have created. I'm glad Ivy has two people who know how to care for her."

Belle set their mugs in the sink and ran water in them. "Thank you, Molly. That's one of the best compliments I've ever received."

Chapter 14

It was Saturday morning and Harlan couldn't believe how calm and peaceful their week had been. Belle's concussion had kept her on the ranch and out of trouble. She had spent her days between the nursing home and speaking with people in various county offices trying to gather the paperwork for her nonprofit rescue center. Harlan was surprised by how many forms she had to fill out and how many hoops she would need to jump through before she would be able to open her doors. Beckett had even taken an interest in the project and helped Belle understand all the legalities. Her plans, while simple, allowed the operation to grow with provisions for future satellite locations. He gave her a lot of credit. When she wasn't working to rehabilitate the animals, she was trying to find ways to save them.

Harlan flipped a pancake in the air to Ivy's enthusiastic applause. Belle had her head buried in her laptop and Molly was still trying to find a connection with their daughter. Ivy had shown some effort, but she had become more bonded with Belle. Molly was leaving on Monday, but Harlan reassured her that she could return anytime and continue to grow her relationship with Ivy. Their family—however unconventional—had begun to function smoothly. There was only one problem. He and Belle were in a perpetual state of limbo. The last time they had really kissed had been almost a week ago. They had become roommates instead of the married couple he wanted them to be. He'd hoped there would have been some improvement by now, but she kept him at arm's length. The tension had dissipated but it wasn't enough. Not for him.

After breakfast, Harlan asked Belle to take a walk with him while Molly spent some time alone with Ivy.

"This is a nice surprise." Belle entwined her fingers in his and rested her head on his shoulder as they strolled down the ranch drive. "We never have any time alone together."

Harlan looked skyward and shook his head. "Are you saying you want to be alone with me?"

Belle stopped walking and faced him. "I'm saying I want to see where this goes. I've spent the last week around you and Molly. I can see there's no love lost between the two of you. I trust you're not going to ditch me because of her again. I was going to ask you out on a date once she went back to Billings.

But since we're alone, now's good." Belle cupped his face and drew her down to him. "I want to be with you, in every way."

Harlan gathered her to him and pressed his mouth to hers, feeling the fervent heat of her desire. The love in his heart surged through every ounce of his being. Belle Barnes wanted to be his wife and he had to show her how much she meant to him. He broke their kiss and gazed deep in her eyes. "I need you more than I've ever needed anyone. And I need you now."

Harlan didn't wait for her to reply. He laced his fingers in hers and began running toward the stables. Once inside and away from prying eyes, he lifted Belle into his arms as her legs wrapped around his waist. She grabbed his face and kissed him, harder, deeper than before.

"Make love to your wife," she whispered against his mouth.

Harlan groaned, climbing the stairs faster than he thought possible. He set her on the bed and smiled. Belle was meant to be savored, and he planned on enjoying every inch of her.

Molly's raucous coughing downstairs woke them from their postcoital slumber. Harlan heard voices coming from the outside stable and checked his watch. *Crap!* They'd forgotten Becky and Beckett were coming over to discuss the possible location of various rescue center buildings.

Harlan quickly dressed and peered down the stable stairs.

"Will you hurry up already!" Molly whispered loudly. "I told them you went out for a ride. Get yourself together and I'll get them to meet you on the other side of the ranch."

A half hour later, they'd paced off numerous sites. They were just waiting on Belle's licenses to come through before he transferred the land to her name. The one drawback to the other side of the ranch was the close proximity to other residences. Belle didn't want her rescue to lower their property values or impact their lives in any way. That meant changing her plans and running the rescue center deeper into the property instead of across the front as she had originally planned.

There was still a lot of work to be done before she opened her doors, but the happiness and contentment on her face made him want to support Belle in any way possible. The animals weren't the only ones who deserved a forever home on the ranch.

They had just sat down to dinner when a black SUV pulled down the ranch drive.

"I wonder who that is." Harlan excused himself from the table and stepped onto the porch. A man climbed out and called to him from the gate.

"Do you have a little girl, around seven or eight years old with brown hair?"

"May I ask what this is about?"

"Yeah, I find it real funny how you're supposed to uphold the law, yet your daughter stole from me."

Harlan felt the hair on the back of his neck rise as he descended the stairs and met the man at the gate. "You better have more than words to back up that statement."

"Harlan, is everything okay?" Belle and Beckett waited on the porch.

He held up his hand and faced the man again. "What are you claiming my daughter took from you?"

"My wife saw her steal our rabbit from the hutch in the backyard."

"We have animals but we don't have rabbits," Harlan said.

"She had to put it somewhere."

"When did your wife see this happen?"

"Two hours ago. She has been waiting for me to come home so I could discuss it with you." Harlan didn't like that timeline. Two hours ago they were on the other side of the ranch, very close to one of the neighbor's houses.

"Do you mind waiting here while I talk to my daughter?"

The man nodded and leaned against his SUV.

Harlan bounded up the stairs and into the house. Ivy's frightened stare answered his question before he even questioned her.

"What is going on?" Belle asked.

Ivy slowly pushed her chair away from the table and inched closer to Molly.

"That man out there says two hours ago his wife watched Ivy steal their rabbit out of the hutch in their backyard."

"She wouldn't do that, Harlan." Molly stood, blocking Ivy from his view.

"Molly, with all due respect, I need to talk to my daughter."

"Our daughter."

Belle squeezed past them and ran upstairs. The creaking of the floorboards overhead and the sound of doors being opened and closed announced her presence in every room.

"Ivy, will you please return to your seat."

Ivy slinked back onto her chair and averted her eyes.

"Ivy, where did you put the bunny?" Harlan asked.

Molly threw her hands in the air, clearly exasperated with his choice of words.

"Ivy."

Belle returned downstairs, out of breath, shaking her head. She tapped Molly on the shoulder. "Excuse me, let me sit there for a second."

Molly huffed and stood next to Beckett and Becky.

"Ivy, sweetheart." Belle held Ivy's hands in hers. "Did you find a hurt bunny?"

Ivy lifted her gaze and met Belle's.

"Did you put it someplace safe where it wouldn't get hurt again?"

Ivy slowly nodded.

Molly gasped, and Harlan uttered a muffled expletive.

"Okay, it's okay." Belle reassured his daughter. She had more patience than he did at the moment. "Will you show me where the bunny is so I can help make it better?"

Ivy stood and led Belle to the porch door. "Is it in the stables?"

Ivy nodded.

"Okay, let's go check on the bunny." Belle turned to face him. "Harlan, can you and my dad pacify that man while I examine this rabbit?"

"Hey! Where are you going?" the man yelled after Belle and Ivy.

"Hey! Don't yell at my wife and kid." Harlan's temper flared. "Don't you forget for one second that I'm a deputy sheriff. And this man here is a county judge. So zip it until we can sort this out."

"There's nothing to sort out," the man spat.

"My daughter indicated the rabbit was sick or injured." Harlan ground his back teeth.

"That rabbit's fine. And it's not sick or injured. It's fat because my son feeds it too many cookies. Your daughter stole my kid's pet."

Belle emerged from the stables, carrying the rabbit. She met the man at the gate and handed it to him. "I sincerely apologize. She thought because the bunny was in the hutch in the middle of the yard that someone left it there and forgot about it."

He placed the rabbit in the front seat and closed the door without getting in. "This isn't an injured cow in the middle of a cattle ranch."

"How did you—?" Belle scoffed. "You were there that night."

"Yeah, I guess the apple doesn't fall far from the tree. Like mother, like daughter. You're both thieves. No wonder you never go to jail. You got the law in your back pocket."

Harlan's body hardened as he clenched his fists. "Get off my land before I arrest you." Harlan closed the distance between them. "How dare you come onto my ranch and yell at my wife. She has apologized."

"I take it back." Anger lit her eyes as she took a step forward. "A rabbit hutch sitting out in the open like that is bait for wolves, coyotes, bear and other predatory animals."

The man's face reddened. "There you go sticking your nose where it doesn't belong again. Someone needs to teach you a lesson."

"That does it." Harlan spun the man around and slammed him face forward onto the hood of the SUV. No one was going to threaten his family and get away with it. He twisted the man's arm behind his back and held him down. "Belle, go get the handcuffs hanging by the back door."

"You should be handcuffing your wife. She's the thief."

Harlan tightened his grip. Belle ran to him and handed him the cuffs. "You have the right to remain silent," he began as he cuffed and frisked the man before sitting him on the ground. He sent Belle back inside for his badge and keys before tossing the man in the back of his cruiser. Becky offered to drive the bunny and the man's SUV to his wife and Beckett said he'd inform her of her husband's unfortunate overnight incarceration before he met up with Harlan at the station. Nothing like having a judge as your star witness.

Truth be told, Harlan was grateful for the distraction. He needed to cool down before he saw Belle again. He had warned her repeatedly that her actions could affect him or his daughter. Now his daughter was mimicking her. People knew who Belle was because of her record. He didn't want Ivy to suffer the same fate. The situation tonight had been bad enough. Belle made it worse when she verbally attacked the man about his rabbit hutch. Now he had to worry about this guy and his friends coming onto his ranch to teach his wife and kid a lesson. He slammed the steering wheel.

By the time he and Beckett arrived home a few hours later, Molly and Belle were engaged in an ear-splitting screaming match. This did not go on in his house. Molly didn't know how to fight at normal octaves. He always said her goal was to shatter glass.

Harlan bounded up the back stairs and flung open the screen door so hard he knocked it off its hinges. "Enough! We don't fight like this here. And definitely not in front of my daughter. Where is Ivy?"

"She's upstairs with Becky," Belle said.

"Okay, good. Molly, get out. Belle, don't say another word. I can't deal with either one of you tonight. The two of you are like teenagers again."

"Why didn't you tell me she had a police record a mile long?"

"Because it's none of your business," Belle answered.

"You're living with my daughter. It makes it my business." Molly spun around to face Harlan. "Do you know what our daughter said after you left? She couldn't understand why you were so mad since Belle got arrested all the time and nothing bad happened to her. She even said you had to arrest her last week."

"Oh, dear." Beckett sighed.

"Was that man right? Is that what's going on around here? Belle runs amok stealing animals all in the name of compassion, you arrest her and then her father lets her off? You guys have a great thing going on here. Does the county know about this? What about family services? I think they need to know."

"Whoa, there." Beckett held up his hands. "There's no need to get nasty. You don't have all the facts."

"My daughter told me she sat in a courtroom and listened while Belle was on trial."

"I had her removed from the courtroom as soon as Belle brought her presence to my attention."

"Why was she there?" Molly demanded.

"Because she was spending the day with me at work," Harlan said.

"How did she get into the courthouse?"

"She walked in." Harlan huffed. "I don't appreciate being schooled on parenting by a woman who didn't give a damn for six years."

"I guess you let her run around the courthouse the same way you let her run into a neighbor's yard and steal rabbits. I can't allow Ivy to remain in this environment."

"What are you saying?" Harlan didn't like Molly's implication.

"I will call family services in the morning and then I'll petition the court for full custody of Ivy. I walked away from my daughter to protect her from the bad environment I had created around her. Now

Belle is creating the bad environment and you two are enabling her. It's over."

Harlan stormed onto the back porch before he did or said something he would regret. No one would take his daughter from him. He'd sacrifice the world to keep her safe and by his side.

"Are you ever going to come back in the house?" Belle had never seen Harlan so angry or distant. Not even when he had arrested her. He had been sitting on the back porch steps for over three hours after everyone else had left and Ivy had gone to bed. "I think we should talk about what happened."

"You're right. We should."

That was a start. "Would you like me to put on a pot of coffee?"

"What I have to say won't take that long." Harlan rubbed his palms against the front of his jeans as he stood. "I don't want Ivy to hear us, so can you close the door and come out here, please?"

Belle eased the door shut. She hadn't broken any promises—in fact, she had done everything she could to move forward with her rescue. She was proud of the ground she'd covered and the accomplishments she'd made. She didn't need any more lectures.

"I'm going to have to ask you to leave."

Belle heard the words but they didn't register. She shook her head, trying to break free from the giant cobweb clouding her brain. "You don't mean that."

"I do mean it and I need a divorce sooner than

later. I think we're well past an annulment at this point."

The cool tone to his voice froze her heart midbeat.

"Why are you doing this? You asked me to move in and I told you no repeatedly. And then you moved me in while I was in the hospital, much to my chagrin I might add. But I went along with it. And just when I finally say yes you want out?"

"I don't have a choice. On paper, you are a terrible influence on my child. I had to arrest a man on my own property because my daughter was emulating you. And instead of just returning the rabbit and calling it a day, you elevated this situation to the point where this man said you needed to be taught a lesson. A threat against you is a threat against my daughter. Molly was witness to all of it. And to top it off, she can call Beckett as her witness. All of this happened in front of the most credible witness out there. Your dad may have helped you in court before, but he can't save you from this one. He's not going to lie under oath for you. I love you, but we're done."

"Don't you dare tell me that you love me for the first time and then follow it with a *we're done*." Belle's body trembled. "You're like Lucy with the football. You kept taunting and teasing until you got me where you wanted, and then once I'm finally happy, working hard to create a legal business, you're throwing me out? I told you I was moving into Lydia's a week ago and you stopped me. You practically begged me to stay."

"I have full custody of my daughter and at the very best, now they will probably grant me joint.

I stand to lose full custody of my daughter. My. Daughter. She might be ripped from the only place she's ever lived, because of your recklessness. And it doesn't matter if you've changed. Your actions have severe consequences and all of us are going to pay for it. Depending on how far Molly takes this, your dad can be removed from the bench. I will probably never make sheriff. But worst of all, Ivy might be thrown in foster care until they can sort this out. You're unbelievable, Belle."

A sob caught in her throat. She never wanted to hurt Ivy. She'd never wanted to disrupt their lives. She had fought, repeatedly. But she had failed, and now there was nothing left.

"I'll be out by the morning."

"I'm sorry, Belle." Harlan's cold, unaffected stare met hers. "I need you to leave tonight."

"It's almost midnight."

"You need to go. The animals can stay until tomorrow, but I can't have you under my roof in case family services shows up. I need every trace of you gone."

His words hit her harder than any fists ever could.

"No." Belle slowly shook her head from side to side. "I am not coming back here tomorrow. I'll take everything—animals included—tonight. Please pack up the belongings you moved into the house without my permission and leave them on the porch. I need to make a few phone calls. Oh, and don't worry, I won't contest the divorce."

Belle headed toward the stables to call Lydia in private. She'd known moving in with him was a bad idea. The whole situation was bad from the beginning. She should have followed her gut instinct.

She despised herself as much as she despised Harlan. She could have been stronger and remained steadfast. He was right. She'd destroyed all of them and if anything happened to Ivy it was because of her.

She removed her phone from her pocket and dialed Lydia. It was so late and she was bound to wake the kids. She had nowhere else to turn. Under the circumstances, she didn't think Beckett and Becky would welcome her with open arms.

"Belle?" Lydia's sleepy voice answered. "Do you know what time it is?"

"Lydia, I need your help. I'm in trouble."

"Aw hell, Belle."

Chapter 15

Almost two and a half weeks had passed since Harlan had thrown Belle off the ranch and she had moved in with Lydia and her family. His attorney had sent over a joint divorce petition for her to sign along with the title transfer for fifty acres of land. She tore the land transfer in half and tossed it in the trash. Hell would freeze over before she accepted anything from Harlan ever again.

Multiple yellow sign-here flags sticking out from between the petition's pages beckoned mockingly to her. She flipped to the first one and saw Harlan's signature. It shouldn't have surprised her, yet it did in a most hurtful way. How could she have allowed him to break her heart twice?

She wiped at her eyes and jammed the document

back in the envelope. She'd have it notarized on her way into town before dropping it back off at the attorney's. The sooner their divorce was official, the better.

First, she needed to finish making her rounds on Lydia's ranch. When her friend refused the rent she offered, Belle said she would work the ranch in exchange for room and board. Lydia agreed and every morning Belle spent three hours feeding and cleaning up after two barns and one stable full of animals. The woman had taken in more rescues than she had room.

Belle had left Imogene behind for Ivy. Harlan had told her they wanted to adopt the duck. It was the least she could do after uprooting all their lives. Molly hadn't made good on any of her threats. She had returned to Billings until she could find a new position in or around Saddle Ridge and had agreed not to seek custody if Harlan agreed to keep Belle away from Ivy.

Lillie and Samson continued to thrive and were old enough to stay in Lydia's barn along with the other baby animals. And Olive was finally paired with another frostbitten, earless goat. The two had become inseparable. Belle vowed to find each of the animals in their care forever homes, but she knew most of them would end up permanent residents in the rescue center. While it was a satisfactory solution, the animals didn't receive as much one-on-one love and affection as they would in a smaller environment.

Belle longed for the day when work meant stepping out her back door—when her rescues would have the freedom to roam under her watchful eye. That dream had been so close she could have touched it. Having to start over again sucked, but Lydia recently had the opportunity to buy some acreage adjacent to her own ranch. She was just waiting to see if the owner accepted the offer. While it wasn't Belle's ideal vision for the rescue, it would work with some modifications to her business plan. Lydia's support and devotion to the cause gave her hope for the future.

In four days, she would move into her new apartment. Beckett had called to check in on her a few times since that fateful night, but their relationship hadn't been the same. He still maintained contact with Harlan and had tried repeatedly to get them to talk to one another. Even if she wanted to talk to Harlan, Molly had threatened an all-out custody war if he spoke to Belle. She couldn't ask him to take that risk. Their short relationship wasn't worth it.

After Belle had finished her chores she headed into town. The nursing home was her first stop, followed by the feed and grain. Belle had approved her grandmother's move into the quieter Alzheimer's wing. She was still regressing but it seemed to have slowed down somewhat.

The memory train always seemed to stop on major events in Belle's life, not some random moment in time. She wished she had known during each of those moments just how much they would come to mean to her grandmother. It still amazed Belle the level of detail Trudy could recall about one particular event, yet an entire decade had vanished from her mind. Yesterday they had been transported back to Belle's sixteenth birthday. At least that was a time before she had started dating Harlan seriously. Trudy no longer asked for him, but the nurses had told her he stopped in every day at noon and ate lunch with her.

"Good morning," Belle said as she walked past the main desk and headed toward the Alzheimer's wing.

"Excuse me, Mrs. Slade."

Belle froze. "It's Barnes," she said before turning around.

Samantha Frederick smiled meekly. "I'm so sorry about you and—" Belle's brows rose at the almost mention of Harlan's name. "Anyway, I just wanted to warn you. Trudy hasn't had a good morning. She flipped her tray, threw her juice box and doesn't want anyone in her room. We cleaned the food off the floor, but we are waiting until she settles down a little more before we change her gown. We'd rather not use any restraints. They cause injuries."

Belle sighed. "She gets extremely agitated when she has a urinary tract infection. Can you test to make sure she doesn't have another one?"

"Yes, we can." Samantha removed her phone and tapped a note into it with a stylus. "We will probably have to sedate her later this morning, and that's when we'll test her."

Belle hated the idea of her grandmother wearing adult diapers and someone changing her like an infant. She understood it was necessary, but it was demeaning just the same. She never wanted to reach the point where she couldn't take care of herself.

"She hasn't eaten today and at her body weight, it's important that she does. She has one of those complete meal drinks in there, but let me give you a few other flavors to try in hopes she'll drink one or two of them."

Belle followed Samantha to the drink station. "What are her favorite flavors?"

"Definitely chocolate. She was born in Switzerland, so she is a certified chocoholic. No chance you have wine flavor in there?"

"Wine?" Samantha's face contorted. "I'm afraid not."

"Okay, that was a joke," Belle said. "When I was growing up, my grandmother always had an open chocolate bar and a glass of red wine sitting on the top shelf of the refrigerator. Throughout the day, she would break off a piece of chocolate and take a sip of wine. At the end of the day, the chocolate was gone and the glass was empty. She didn't go a day without either one." The memory made Belle smile. "Every time I open a refrigerator, I expect to see that."

Samantha squeezed her hand. "These are the memories you should always hold on to. Share these stories often to keep them fresh in your mind."

The sting of tears threatened to destroy her composure. "I will. I'll take a chocolate and a strawberry."

Belle stood outside the entrance of Trudy's room and listened carefully before she turned the corner. She'd already been beaned by a full bottle of meal replacer during an earlier visit. She scanned the hallway floor and the wall across from her door. No food or dents. It was a good sign. Belle peered around the corner.

"Grammy?" she called. "It's me, Belle." Her grandmother sat upright in her recliner with the table tray locked in place across her lap. It was like a high chair for adults. It allowed her to sit up and watch television, eat or craft on the table, while preventing her from falling or trying to stand up. And it had wheels so the staff could move her around the facility and grounds without worrying about getting her in and out of a wheelchair.

Belle didn't see the bottle of meal replacer Samantha said was in the room. She grabbed a straw from the box in one of the upper cabinets and unwrapped it.

"How would you like a chocolate drink today?" Belle shook the bottle. Her grandmother looked angry. Belle twisted off the cap and dropped the straw into the drink. "Here you go, Grammy."

Trudy slapped her hand away as Belle offered her the drink. "Who are you?" she demanded.

"I'm Belle. I'm your granddaughter."

"You're not my granddaughter. My Belle is a little bitty thing. You're too old." Trudy grabbed Belle's wrist. "Who are you and why are you in my room?"

Belle decided to try another approach. "Mom, it's me, Cindy. I came back to see you."

"No, you're not. Cindy's gone."

"Where did Cindy go?" Belle asked. It had been twenty-one years and she still wondered how her mother dropped off the face of the earth. Beckett believed she had her name changed. That way no one could follow her.

"Get out of here." Trudy knocked the open bottle of meal replacer on the floor. "Get out. Security. Security!" Trudy wailed.

"It's okay, Trudy. I'm leaving." Belle held up her hands and backed toward the door. "See, I'm leaving."

Samantha Frederick ran down the hallway. "Are you okay?"

"Oh, yeah." Belle nodded. "I'm just emotionally bruised. I guess this is when you recall the good times."

"Exactly."

"She knocked her drink all over the floor. Please warn whoever goes in there next that it will be slippery. I'm going to head out."

Belle didn't wait for Samantha to respond. She found the nearest exit and flew through the door. She didn't want to cry. So she ran, fast and hard. Until her lungs felt like they would explode. She started walking to cool down and then stopped when she realized she was almost in front of the sheriff's office. She could see Harlan's cruiser from where she stood. And he could probably see her from his desk. Right now, she just wanted to go home. If only she had one to go to. Living with Harlan and Ivy felt like home. It was warm and inviting. She belonged there. She believed it in the depths of her heart. Yet she could never return. She was banned from the people she loved the most. They had all rejected her and she'd never felt more alone.

Belle swiped the tears from her face and walked back to her truck. She'd done enough feeling sorry for herself today. She needed to stay busy and keep from thinking about what she'd lost. She wished a vet call would come in. Something, anything to distract her. *Community service.* She had a couple hundred hours she still needed to fulfill from her various sentences. That would keep her busy. Just as long as it kept her busy and away from Harlan.

Harlan watched Belle from the second floor of the courthouse. Something was seriously wrong for her to sprint. It was a defense mechanism he had taught her in high school when she felt the world was closing in on her. She paced the street below and for a moment, he thought she would head into the sheriff's office. She disappeared somewhere below him, which he assumed meant she was in the building.

He wanted to go to her and soothe away her pain. He could see her truck in the nursing home parking lot. Trudy must be having a bad morning.

Harlan regretted the words he said to her the night he kicked her out. Another thing he never should have done. He'd taken something broken and pulverized it into the ground. He had let Molly control the situation, just as he always had. In the end, she'd done nothing she said she would do. He should have called her bluff. Molly couldn't handle conversing with her daughter for an hour, let alone be a full-time parent to Ivy. They still hadn't formed a connection and whenever Molly left, Ivy relaxed. His kid was very intuitive and Molly was loud. He wouldn't doubt

Ivy had overheard some of her mother's threats. And it was all over things that had happened in the past. Belle had kept her word to him. And he had broken his vow when he told her to leave.

It was done. It was over. Maybe one day he could apologize. Harlan needed to get back to work before he drove himself crazy. He opened the stairwell door and descended the stairs. He had barely heard the faint sound of a door opening either above or below him. It wasn't until the scent of her perfume hit that he knew they were alone together in the stairwell.

"Belle?" He called her name.

No footsteps, no breathing, no sound at all. Yet he knew she was there. He peered over the center rail, hoping to catch a glimpse of her hand or a flutter of clothing. He looked up and down and nothing.

"I still love you."

He hoped that would generate a response. She probably considered it an insult after the way he said it the last time. He heard the door below him open and then close. He supposed it was fitting. He had opened the door to her heart, only to slam it closed again.

Harlan couldn't sleep. He had spent the last two hours arguing with Molly over the phone. He felt the inexplicable need to set up some form of a visitation schedule they could agree upon and adhere to. Molly wanted to come and go as she pleased. Harlan refused to uproot his daughter whenever Molly came to town on a whim. She seemed to like the idea of being a parent and talked a great game, but when it came down to actually doing the work, she didn't want any part of it.

She had also clued him in on just how much of an ass he had been when they were married. They'd both known going in that it wasn't for love, but he hadn't realized how cruel and cold he had been by leaving her completely alone every day. He had been pining over Belle and up to his ears in regret. He'd fixated on his own issues and ignored Molly. He never tried to be her friend, let alone her partner in raising a child. Looking back, he couldn't blame her for leaving him. Leaving their daughter was a different story.

Harlan had just drifted off when his phone started ringing. He answered it, half in a daze.

"Harlan Slade, this call is regarding Gertrude Barnes. Are you her grandson-in-law?"

He swung his legs out of bed and grabbed his jeans off the chair.

"Yes, I am."

"Mr. Slade, we are trying to get in touch with your wife."

"She's not here. Can I help you?" He cradled the phone against his shoulder as he zipped his fly.

"Gertrude had an episode and fell. The ambulance is en route to the hospital. Can you locate your wife and let her know the situation?"

"Yes, either my wife or I will be there. Thank you for calling me."

Harlan hung up, quickly dialed Dylan and asked him to come stay with Ivy. He tried both Belle's and Lydia's numbers but they went straight to voice mail.

And he didn't have Calvin's. He called Beckett next, but he hadn't heard from her either.

Harlan prayed Belle wasn't off somewhere getting in trouble. He'd stopped in to see Trudy at lunchtime and they had filled him in on what had happened earlier with Belle. He knew she was hurting and when Belle hurt, she had a strong desire to save the world. Her pain lessened when she took away someone else's pain. And she would go to whatever lengths possible to fulfill that desire.

He met Dylan in the ranch drive. "No time to explain. If you hear from Belle, tell her to get to the hospital right away."

Harlan's gut instinct took him back to the cattle ranch. Especially after the run-in she'd had with one of their employees on his ranch a few weeks ago. There was no sign of her truck. He continued to drive out toward Lydia and Calvin's, scanning every dive bar parking lot along the way. Barhopping wasn't normally her thing, but given her current mood, he'd rather err on the side of caution.

Belle's truck wasn't parked in front of Lydia's house. Various work trucks were lined up along the fence and he couldn't be sure if Lydia was home or not. It was a little past one in the morning. He had no choice but to ring the Presleys' front doorbell.

Calvin answered the door angrier than a grizzly awoken during hibernation.

"This better be good, Harlan."

"Is Belle here?"

"Oh, geez. You two are like lovesick teenagers. You need to stay married and work your problems out." Calvin scratched his rump and leaned outside. "Do you see her truck out there?"

"No."

"Well then, there you have it."

He started to close the door until Harlan jammed his boot in it. "It's about Trudy. I need to find Belle."

"Oh, that's unfortunate. Is she okay?"

"No, no she's not. Is Lydia home?"

"She was." He scratched his chest. "And then she wasn't. Wait. Hold on. When she gets night calls, she leaves the address in the kitchen in case we need her."

Harlan bounced up and down on the Presleys' front stoop. Fear and anxiety coursed through his veins.

"Here it is." Calvin handed him a piece of paper.

"Thank you." Harlan ran back to his cruiser and punched in the address. It was all the way on the other side of the county. He turned on his police lights when he pulled onto the highway.

Twenty minutes later he drove onto the ranch. Belle's and Lydia's trucks were parked side by side in front of a large stable. He tried the main doors, but they were locked. He ran around to the side and found one that was open.

"Sheriff's department," he called out as he walked through the door. He didn't want to take anyone by surprise.

"May I help you?" A woman approached him.

"Ma'am, I'm looking for Belle Barnes. That's her red truck out there. I believe she's here on a veterinary emergency. It's very urgent that I speak with her."

"Right away. Follow me." The woman jogged down the corridor. "We have a mare foaling twins. The first was fine. The second one is breech."

The woman led him to a large stall. A mare lay on her side, breathing heavily, while Lydia was up to her armpit in the horse's backside.

"I almost have her turned around," Lydia said. "Get a mask and a resuscitation bag ready."

Belle dug through a large duffel, removed two towels and shook them out. Then she unpackaged a mask and resuscitation bag and connected them together. For a brief moment their eyes met before she looked away.

"I have her head!" Lydia cried. "Harlan, get in here. Belle, get behind me."

Belle dropped to the stall floor and wrapped her arms around Lydia's waist.

"Pull!" Lydia ordered. "We have to get her out now."

The foal slid onto the hay-covered floor. Belle scrambled to her knees and cleared the amniotic sac away from the newborn's mouth and nostrils. "Breathe," she whispered under her breath. "Breathe."

"Roll her onto her right side," Lydia instructed. Belle, and Harlan quickly repositioned the foal while Lydia listened for a heartbeat with her stethoscope. "I'm not getting anything."

Belle reached behind her and grabbed the towels, tossing one to Harlan. She wiped any remaining amnion and hay from the animal's mouth then began vigorously drying the foal. "Do what I'm doing," she said to Harlan. "We need to stimulate breathing."

"We're going to need that resuscitation mask."

Belle reached out and stilled Harlan's hands. She placed the mask over the foal's nose while Lydia extended the animal's neck and applied pressure along the left side. Harlan assumed it was to prevent air from entering the gastrointestinal tract. Belle squeezed the bag with both hands. Each compression expanded the foal's chest. They continued the squeeze and release cycle for a good thirty seconds before Lydia looked up at him.

"Harlan. Grab the oxygen tank. I left it on the outside of the stall." He retrieved it and knelt beside Lydia as Belle continued to squeeze and release the bag.

"Okay, stop squeezing," Lydia said. She withdrew a sealed pack from her medical bag, tore it open with her teeth and removed an oxygen line. Quickly, she connected one end to the tank and the other to the resuscitation bag. She adjusted the regulator on the tank, allowing the oxygen to flow. Within seconds, the foal began to breathe on its own. Lydia attached a nasal tube on to the oxygen line and placed the tube inside the foal's nose.

"Harlan, I'll need you to hold this lightly in place. Remind me around the ten-minute mark. We need to check on the mare and the other foal."

An hour later, they stood and watched two healthy foals as they tried to nurse from a very tired mama.

"That was amazing." Harlan hadn't had the opportunity to see Belle at work before. Sure, he'd been there for a few of her arrests, but this—this was different. He'd thought he understood what she did for a living, but he hadn't imagined this. She was saving lives. He'd never seen her more focused and determined in the twenty-one years he'd known her. He'd completely misjudged her. "And you two do this all the time."

"Tonight was a rarity." Lydia wiped her forehead with the back of her hand. "A very successful rarity."

"Not that we didn't appreciate the help, but why are you here?" Belle asked.

Harlan gripped her by the shoulders and turned her toward him. "The nursing home called. Trudy had a bad episode. She fell and the ambulance was there to take her to the hospital. They asked me to locate you."

"Oh, my God." Belle glanced down her body. "I'm covered in—oh, my God! Lydia, I have to go."

"Wash off first." Lydia motioned down the hallway. "One of you call me with an update later."

Harlan waited outside for Belle. He'd managed to clean up outside with a hose.

"Crap! I have my truck." Belle looked from his cruiser to her truck and back again. "I guess I'll follow you."

"Belle, get in. We'll worry about your truck later." He pulled onto the highway and turned his lights on again. "Why don't you give them a call? Maybe they can tell you something over the phone."

"Okay." Belle stared at her phone. "I don't have the number."

And Harlan didn't think she was capable of looking it up right now either. Between the euphoria from delivering the foals and the anxiety over her grandmother, Belle's hands hadn't stopped trembling since they got in the cruiser. He shifted in his seat and tugged his phone from his pocket. He unlocked it and handed it to her.

"It's in my contacts under *hospital*."

Belle tapped at the screen then held it to her ear. "Hi, I am looking for a status update on a patient. Gertrude Barnes. Yes. I'm her granddaughter and her next of kin. Correct. Okay. We're on the way there. Thank you." Belle handed the phone back to him. "They don't know anything yet."

"Okay, we'll be there in twenty."

"Harlan, what if this is it?"

He reached for her hand and entwined his fingers in hers. "Then I will remain by your side for however long you need me. I'll never let you go again."

Chapter 16

"I wish they would tell us something soon." Belle sat in the hospital waiting area between Harlan and her father. A month ago she would have bet a million dollars that this scenario was impossible. Yet here she was, blessed enough to have two men who obviously cared enough about her to be willing to sit this close after she'd rolled around in horse manure and amniotic fluid. That was love.

Belle pulled her hair into a makeshift ponytail. "I need a shower. I need a change of clothes."

"You need to move back in with me."

She threw her head back and laughed. "You need to get your head examined."

"You two need to talk." Beckett rose from his seat. "And you both need a shower. You stink."

"You're high if you think I would ever move back in with you." Belle snorted. "I heard what you said in the stairwell at the courthouse. And I believe you love me. And I… I… I love you, too. But you and me, we don't work well together. It's like we live in a baggage claim and it just keeps piling on until we explode."

Belle had dreamed of hearing Harlan say *I love you* again. And when the words echoed throughout the stairwell, she'd had to cover her mouth to keep from saying the words in return. She wanted to love him freely, with all her heart. But he deserved to live and love without worrying what would happen next.

"I was horrible to you that night. I let Molly get under my skin when I knew her threats would involve too much of a commitment from her. She can't even schedule a day in advance to see Ivy."

"Why would I want to get involved in that again?" Even though it was all she thought about. "It's too much drama. I have enough drama in my life, never mind the fact that you dumped me twice. I appreciate you visiting my grandmother in the nursing home and sitting here with me. I even love the fact that you made a valiant effort to find me tonight. I love that about you. But everything else aside, Molly can play the *Belle's Past* card whenever she wants. And then you're on edge and Ivy's at risk again."

"The next time I'll call her bluff because I want to be there for you every day for the rest of our lives." Harlan lowered down on one knee and took both of her hands in his. "I want to be there the day you realize your dream. I want to be there when you hold our child for the first time. I want to be there when you come home, smelling like—" Harlan raised her hands "—this after saving a life. I want to be there and comfort you after you lose the ones you couldn't save. I want to be the man you want to come home to. The man you want to grow old with."

"Harlan." Belle wanted the same things, along with permanence and stability. She had tasted it, however brief, and it still coursed within her. But she would never put him or anyone she loved at risk ever again. "I'm so sorry. But I can't. I just can't."

Harlan released her hands and sat back on his heels. "I'll wait. For however long it takes. I'll wait."

"Miss Barnes?" A doctor approached them. "I'm Dr. Rhodes. Your grandmother has a severe kidney infection. The nursing home had mentioned she's had urinary tract infections in the past. Both urinary and kidney infection in the elderly and Alzheimer's patients are much more pronounced than what we would experience. It throws their entire system off balance. Then they don't eat, they don't drink, they become dehydrated, and your grandmother is extremely dehydrated. Her potassium is at rock bottom. She will probably be here for a week so we can level her out, and then I think you'll begin to see a significant improvement."

"What about her fall?"

The doctor shook his head, then held a finger under his nose. Belle was mortified. "Nothing's broken. But because her levels are so low across the board, it has affected everything from her reasoning to her balance. UTIs alone can exacerbate dementia symptoms."

"Within a week she went from remembering my wedding to not remembering me at all." Those images still played in her head every time she closed her eyes.

"Some of that I'm sure is Alzheimer's and some of it is the infection." The man's eyes began to water.

"Wow. Thank you so much. So, she's going to be fine?" Belle wanted to shake his hand but thought better of it.

Dr. Rhodes took a step back. "Her prognosis right now looks good."

"Thank you again. And I'm sorry I smell so bad. I just delivered twin foals."

"You look remarkably well after that." He smiled at his own joke and then quickly turned to leave. "Go get some rest," he called over his shoulder.

Belle exhaled and looked up at Harlan. "I don't know what I would have done without you by my side tonight." He had taken care of her and had given her what she needed. She'd always striven to be self-sufficient. To never have to rely on anyone. That was the true measure of success. Well, it had been until recently. He had shown her that help didn't mean she was weak. It meant she was brave enough to accept it. And she was brave enough to let go.

The sound of someone pounding on Lydia and Calvin's front door woke Belle from a deep sleep. She reached for her phone and checked the time. It was two in the afternoon. Lydia had given her the day off since she had arrived home somewhere around sunrise.

The pounding wouldn't stop. Lydia and Calvin were at work and the boys were at school. "Someone needs to be smacked."

Belle trudged through the house. She hadn't even reached the living room when she saw Molly's face pressed against the glass. "Go away!" Belle shouted.

Molly was the last person she wanted or needed to deal with. "You're making a big mistake. Open the door."

Belle stomped through the living room and swung the door open. "If you threaten me one more time, just once more, you'll be the one making the big mistake. Now get out of here."

Molly pushed past her. "Don't be so dramatic. I mean you're making a big mistake about Harlan."

She didn't want to talk about Harlan. Telling him no earlier had been one of the hardest things she had ever done. She wanted desperately to believe in him...to believe in them. It was what made signing the divorce petition more difficult. But, doing so freed Harlan and he was better off without her.

"How did you get here anyway?" Belle asked. "Isn't Billings like six hours away?"

"I took a plane after Harlan called and ripped me a new one."

"You probably deserved it."

"I did. I've done some research on you."

"That must have been an interesting read." Belle braced herself for an onslaught of new insults.

"I hadn't realized how many commendations you had received from various animal organizations.

Many of which applauded your willingness to go above and beyond to save a life, even when it meant putting yourself in harm's way."

"It's all in a day's work." Belle hated when people gave her awards. The spotlight was superficial and took away from the message to not be cruel in the first place.

"You're a large-animal vet tech. Animal rescue isn't in your job description. You do things I'd pee my pants worrying about. So instead of judging, I should have congratulated you on all you have achieved for your cause. The only cause I've ever had is me, myself and I."

"You can change that, you know." Belle had always given Molly more credit than she gave herself. "You need to swallow the fear."

"I already have, starting with no longer worrying about you being a part of Ivy's life. Harlan says she's miserable without you around. She needs you in her life. And I want you to be a part of it."

Belle had wanted to ask him about her while they waited in the hospital for news about Trudy, but the words stuck in her throat. She had become more attached to Ivy than she had thought possible.

"I want to know my daughter. To do that, I have to make time for Ivy. The only way to accomplish that is to move here. So here I am. I have quit my job and I will take whatever comes available until I can find something at another travel agency. If you know of any apartments, I'd appreciate you letting me know. I'll be at the same hotel I was staying at before."

Belle must have missed a memo somewhere. When

had Molly grown up? "I'm glad you're doing this for Ivy. She craves stability just as much as we do."

"Which brings me to you and Harlan. You guys were happy before I camped out in the driveway. And you should be happy. And I shouldn't be jealous of that happiness. I'll find my prince one day. But you have already found yours. And he's waiting for you to come home."

To say Harlan was shocked when Molly called and told him she'd spoken to Belle on his behalf was an understatement. He'd waited four days for Belle to call before he picked up the phone and asked her to come over for dinner. When she agreed, he almost pinched himself.

He and Ivy spent the afternoon preparing a three-bean vegetarian chili and Provençal summer vegetables. They had taken a few wrong turns, but by the time Belle pulled down the ranch drive, they'd gotten it right.

Before Belle reached the porch steps, Ivy ran upstairs. When she didn't immediately return, he realized she was giving him time alone with Belle.

He opened the door before she had a chance to knock. "Hi." She was stunning in a red sundress and strappy sandals. Outside of their wedding, it was rare seeing her in anything other than shorts or jeans. She cleaned up well. She'd twisted her hair up in a casual style that begged for him to release it. But he behaved instead. "You look amazing."

"Thank you. So do you."

Harlan's idea of dress casual was his best pair

of Wranglers, a white button-down dress shirt and his black boots. He'd opted to forgo the hat and felt naked and vulnerable without it. But that was all right. A large dose of vulnerability was in order.

He held the screen door open for her as she entered the kitchen. "Something smells wonderful. Did you order out?"

Harlan laughed, not sure quite how to take that. "No, Ivy and I cooked for you. We scoured a couple hundred vegetarian recipes online before we found two we could handle. She helped me shop and prep, and she set the table all by herself. Including the flowers. Those are from her."

"How sweet." Belle glanced around the room. "Where is she?"

"Upstairs." Harlan poured two glasses of Riesling and handed one to her. "She ran up when she saw you pull in. My best guess is she's giving us time to talk. And we do need to talk, Belle."

"Yes, we do," Belle said. "This is a delightful surprise."

"I read that the wine paired well with dinner."

"You really did do your homework."

Harlan nodded. "I felt I owed you that and so much more. I was so busy judging you, playing the good cop, I didn't see what was right in front of me. And I'm sorry about the other night in the hospital. It wasn't fair of me to declare my love for you in the middle of a crisis. Our relationship was the last thing on your mind and rightfully so."

"Well, that and the fact I stunk." Belle wrinkled her nose. "I wasn't exactly feeling my best."

"How about now? How are you feeling?"

"Much more human, thank you. I owe you an apology myself." Belle set her glass on the table. "I've made some really bad choices and some really difficult ones. Sometimes there's a fine line between the two. I'm sorry I put you in the position where your daughter was threatened. I'll spend the rest of my life regretting it."

Harlan set his own glass down and led her to the living room. "Speaking of the rest of your life, there's something I want to show you."

"You have a fire going?" Belle asked. "It's really warm out today."

Harlan removed an envelope from the mantel and handed it to Belle. "This is for you."

She opened the envelope and peeked inside. "The land contract?"

"Pull it out, there's more in there." Harlan moved closer to her.

All humor slid from her face. "Our divorce petition? Really? What are you telling me?"

Harlan took the paperwork from her and held up the land contract. "This is my wedding present to you. I want you to have that land. And before you say no, I heard Lydia made an offer on another property and that's fine. Either way, I want you to own half of this ranch." Harlan waved the divorce petition in his other hand. "There's a major benefit to having a judge as a father-in-law. He was able to intercept these before they were filed." Harlan tossed them into the fire. "Belle Barnes. I refuse to end this marriage. I want you back home, where you belong."

"Slade."

"What?"

"It's Slade. I am your wife, right?"

In two strides, he closed the distance between them. He cupped her chin and placed a soft kiss upon her lips. "I love you, Belle Slade."

"I love you, too. And I already love the wonderful life we are going to share together."

The sound of bare feet smacking the stairs grew louder until it stopped behind Harlan. Tiny hands pushed between them as Ivy wrapped her arms around Belle's waist. "Daddy, Belle's home."

"That she is." Harlan thought his heart would burst at the sight of his daughter and Belle together again. "I'm sure we'll make a lot of mistakes over the years, but I promise to always love you and work through whatever problems come our way. As long as the three of us have each other, we'll never want for anything."

"The four of us." Belle smiled.

Harlan laughed. "How could I have possibly forgotten about Elvis?"

"Oh, well in that case, you better make that the five of us." Belle reached for his hand and placed it on her lower abdomen.

Harlan sank to his knees and kissed her belly. Belle was carrying his child. *Their child.*

"Daddy, why are you crying?"

Belle held out her hand to Ivy. "Because your daddy just found out you're going to be a big sister."

* * * * *